DAVID DICKINSON was born in Dublin. He graduated from Cambridge with a first-class honours degree in classics and joined the BBC. After a spell in radio he transferred to television and went on to become editor of *Newsnight* and *Panorama*. In 1995 he was series editor of *Monarchy*, a three-part examination of its current state and future prospects. David lives in London.

Praise for The Lord Francis Powerscourt series

'A cracking yarn, beguilingly real from start to finish ... you have to pinch yourself to remind you that it is fiction – or is it?'

Peter Snow

'A kind of locked bedroom mystery ... Dickinson's view of the royals is edgy and shaped by our times.'

The Poisoned Pen

'Fine prose, high society and complex plot recommend this series.'

Library Journal

Titles in the series
(listed in order)

DEATH
ON THE
NEVSKII PROSPEKT

DAVID DICKINSON

ROBINSON
London

Constable & Robinson Ltd
3 The Lanchesters
162 Fulham Palace Road
London W6 9ER
www.constablerobinson.com

First published in the UK by Constable, an imprint
of Constable & Robinson Ltd, 2007
This paperback edition published by Robinson, an imprint
of Constable & Robinson Ltd, 2008

A copy of the British Library Cataloguing in
Publication Data is available from the British Library.

ISBN: 978-1-84529-360-4 (hbk)
ISBN: 978-1-84529-671-1

Printed and bound in the EU
1 3 5 7 9 10 8 6 4 2

For Alan and Heather

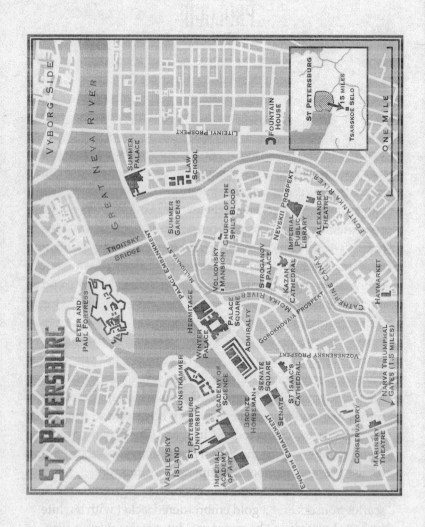

ST PETERSBURG

VYBORG SIDE

GREAT NEVA RIVER

PETER AND PAUL FORTRESS

TROITSKY BRIDGE

PALACE EMBANKMENT

SUMMER PALACE

SUMMER GARDENS

LAW SCHOOL

CHURCH OF THE SPLIT BLOOD

MILLIONNAYA ST

VOLKONSKY MANSION

STROGANOV PALACE

NEVSKII PROSPEKT

IMPERIAL PUBLIC LIBRARY

ALEXANDER THEATRE

FONTANKA RIVER

MOIKA RIVER

KAZAN CATHEDRAL

CATHERINE CANAL

LITEINYI PROSPEKT

FOUNTAIN HOUSE

HERMITAGE

WINTER PALACE

PALACE SQUARE

ADMIRALTY

GOROKHOVAIA PROSPEKT

HAYMARKET

KUNSTKAMMER

VASILEVSKY ISLAND

ST PETERSBURG UNIVERSITY

ACADEMY OF SCIENCE

BRONZE HORSEMAN

SENATE SQUARE

SENATE

ST ISAAC'S CATHEDRAL

VOZNESENSKY PROSPEKT

IMPERIAL ACADEMY OF ART

ENGLISH EMBANKMENT

NARVA TRIUMPHAL GATES (1.5 MILES)

CONSERVATORY

MARINSKY THEATRE

ST PETERSBURG

15 MILES

TSARSKOE SELO

ONE MILE

PROLOGUE

Alexander Palace, Tsarskoe Selo, August 1902

Any minute now, she knew, the proper contractions would start. It was not, after all, the first time she had given birth. Even this evening, when her family knew what was happening, she could hear the excited sounds of her four daughters as they gossiped outside in the corridors. This time it would be different. This time she would give birth to a son. Had not Philippe, her mystic Frenchman from Lyons, promised her this while he hypnotized her soul and stroked her face with those long slender fingers of his? This time, the gunners at the Fortress of Peter and Paul, over fifteen miles away on the other side of St Petersburg, would have to sound out a three-hundred-round salute for a boy rather than one hundred rounds for a girl. This time the people of St Petersburg would have to clap and cheer rather than mock and sneer as they had done so often in the past. The woman looked into her tiny private chapel with its single icon of the Virgin Mary. Mary would be with her on this journey too. Philippe had promised.

Outside the door stood an enormous Negro dressed in scarlet trousers and a gold embroidered jacket with a white turban. Lurking in the passages downstairs were police-men on duty against the arrival of an assassin, regarded as almost as likely as the arrival of a son. Sentries marched continually up and down around the perimeter of the palace. More soldiers were guarding the grounds and searching every visitor who came to call. Around the high fence of the imperial park bearded Cossack horsemen in scarlet tunics and black caps galloped in ceaseless patrol, twenty-four hours a day. Theirs was a watch that would last till eternity. For this was Tsarskoe Selo, the Tsar's Village in English, some fifteen miles from St Petersburg. It was at this time the principal residence of the Tsar of All the Russias and his wife Alexandra and their family. Alexandra was the expectant mother, anxious to bring forth an heir to her husband's throne. The threat of terror was so great that the imperial family could feel safe only here. They were too exposed in the vast expanses of their main residence the Winter Palace in the heart of their capital, St Petersburg. Two Tsars had been assassinated the previous century. Nicholas the Second, the latest target, had watched his grandfather bleed to death in the Winter Palace after a terrorist bomb ripped open his stomach and scattered bloody fragments of his body around Palace Square. Government ministers, provincial governors, Ministers of the Interior were regularly blown up by terrorist bombs. Russia did not lead the countries of Europe in many things, except for her size. But she was the terrorist capital of the world, her young people almost queuing up to die in assassination attempts, the reign of terror imposed by the secret police, the Okhrana, the despair of liberals in Moscow and St Petersburg.

Black, Alexandra thought bitterly, black was the colour she had brought to her new home from Coburg in Germany all those years ago. Black, the colour of ravens, black the colour of crows, black the colour of death. She remembered one of the courtiers at home reminding her to

2

pack her mourning clothes when she set off to join her fiancé in the Crimea where his father Tsar Alexander was dying. Nicky, or Nicholas the Second, to give him his formal title, had wept not just for his dying father but for himself, unprepared, unfit and unwilling to sit on the throne of the Romanovs. Even then, even before she was married, Alexandra had known that a major part of her role would be to support him, to try and give him the strength he needed to rule his vast empire that covered one sixth of the world's surface. As she watched him give way to his mother, to his uncles, sometimes, it seemed to her, to the last person who talked to him, Alexandra often felt that she would have done the job much better herself. Black, she remembered again, she had worn the black of mourning when she was inducted into the Russian Orthodox Church as family members arrived in droves from all over Europe to pay tribute to the dead Alexander the Third. Black on that long, slow train journey from the Crimea to St Petersburg, and the sad stops in the major cities on the way for the populace to pay their last respects to the dead Tsar and stare at the woman from Germany who had come to marry his son.

She remembered the worst week of her life which should have been the best, the week of her coronation in Moscow. Hundreds if not thousands of people had been crushed to death in a stampede at Khodynka Field outside Moscow, a crowd that had gathered to receive traditional coronation presents from the Tsar and panicked when told there would not be enough to go round. In the stampede towards the front to grab things before the supply ran out, people had fallen into ditches, or simply tripped and been trampled to death. Even now, she could still see the miserable carts they had used to take the bodies away, the corpses covered by rough tarpaulins or sections of dirty blankets.

Cart after cart had lined up to take the dead away for burial, their relations weeping into the summer air, the stench of death inescapable. That night she and Nicky, against her instincts, had gone to a ball at the French Ambassador's and been condemned as heartless by almost the entire nation. The uncles had pointed out how much money had been spent on the ball with thousands of flowers imported by special trains from the Riviera. They had pointed out how insulted the French would be. The cleverest uncle – the competition was hardly of Olympic standard – said they had to attend or the French bankers would cut off the loans that were the mainstay of the Russian economy. After that, she knew, they stopped calling her the English whore because Queen Victoria was her grandmother. Now they called her the German bitch instead. And every time she produced another daughter they called her the useless German bitch.

Philippe from Lyons would change all that, Philippe Vachot who had brought so much hope into her life. She and Nicholas had met him at the home of two Montenegrin princesses who were interested in the occult, in seances and spiritualism. Philippe was a hypnotist who was sometimes possessed of spirits and talked to them in voices of the dead come back from the other side. The room for these ceremonies was quite small, two walls lined with icons of Christ and the Madonna, pairs of sad eyes sucking you into their embrace. The Montenegrins had hundreds of candles on the walls. Sometimes they had singers in the next room so that ghostly Vespers floated through the walls. The singers were all peasants from the Montenegrins' estate in the country and were said to live in a hut at the bottom of the garden. Alexandra had misty memories of what Philippe said to her when she was coming out of hypnosis or appearing as one of her long-lost Coburg

4

relations about whom he was prodigiously well informed. First he told her she would have a son, that there would spring forth a rod from the stem of Jesse. Then he told her she was pregnant. Now she was here on her bed, waiting for the most joyous moment of her life. Philippe had told her not to tell any of the normal imperial doctors what was happening. Let God's work be a surprise to the unbelieving men of science, he had told her. Let them not pollute your body with their examinations or your system with their medicines of modernity. Rather let God work his will and his changes in the temple of your womb. But things seldom remain secret in a royal palace. Even as the Empress lay wreathed in her dreams of glory, the official doctors were pacing up and down in the corridors of the palace downstairs.

Outside it was raining heavily, great drops splattering on to the lakes and soaking the cloaks and the fur caps of the Cossacks on their endless patrol outside the walls. Upstairs was quiet now. The four daughters had gone to sleep. She could hear the faint steps of the guards as they patrolled the hallway on the lower floor. Suddenly Alix began to bleed, as she had not bled for months. There was no child. As one of the Montenegrin sisters put it, a tiny ovule came out. Then her abdomen deflated, the pains stopped. The palace doctors confirmed that she was not pregnant. She was suffering from an amnesia-related condition and should rest in bed, they told her. As they left her room she began to weep as though she had never wept before and would never be able to stop. On and on into the terrible future, a future where she had thought there was hope but now there was only despair, her tears would flow. She might be able to staunch them for her children but it would not be for long. This was the worst day of her life, in a life that had so many contenders for the position. She was humiliated. Alexandra had no doubt that word of what had happened would reach St Petersburg in a day or two, and how society would laugh at her. They had never taken to her, those aristocratic women of the capital, and she had never taken to them. Now the story of her troubles would shoot round the salons and she would be laughed to scorn. And inside the palace, she knew, there would be a campaign against Philippe, orchestrated by the doctors, amplified by the courtiers, prosecuted by the uncles. She hoped her husband would hold firm. But you could never tell. She prayed through her tears, she prayed to the icon of the Madonna in her tiny private chapel: Mother of God, hear my prayer, Mother of God hear my prayer. Don't let them take Philippe away. Please don't let them take him away from me. He's my only hope.

Wells, England, Spring 1903

Lord Francis Powerscourt was lying on the ground at the junction of the nave and the transept of Wells Cathedral, staring upwards. He was inspecting one of the most dramatic features of any cathedral in Britain, the famous scissor arches that curved and swung and swept upwards towards the roof.

'My goodness me, Lord Powerscourt,' said the Dean, inspecting his prostrate visitor. 'I know you asked me if you could lie on the floor, but I didn't think you meant it. Are you all right down there?'

'Perfectly happy, Dean, thank you very much. I thought I could get a better idea of what things must have looked like when your tower began to lean and crack open back in thirteen hundred and something or other.'

'Thirteen hundred and thirty-eight,' said the Dean with a faint note of irritation in his voice. He liked people to do their homework properly. 'Anyway, I think you'll find the cracks were more apparent higher up than they were at ground level.'

'I'm sure you're right, Dean,' said Powerscourt, rising nimbly to his feet. 'I have to go and have a tutorial from your librarian in a quarter of an hour. He's promised to tell me all about the cracks and your clever master mason William Joy who invented the arches and saved the building. The great curves, I'm told, transfer weight from the west, where the foundations sank under the tower's weight, to the east where they remained firm. I'm going to write it all down in my little black book.'

And Powerscourt patted one of his pockets which gave out a dull thud of reassurance. The Dean sighed as he looked around his kingdom of space and light.

'I envy you, you know, Lord Powerscourt. You come here and you work hard and then you move on to another cathedral for your book. We're left here with all the problems of the damp and the lack of money and the lack of interest. I sometimes wish I'd stayed where I was as Vicar of St George's in Bristol.'

Powerscourt looked closely at the Dean. 'I think you're wrong there, Dean,' he said quietly. 'Your problems may be formidable, the lack of money difficult, but you are charged with the upkeep in fabric and liturgy and service of one of the most beautiful buildings in England. It is I, and many others, who envy you, you know.'

The Dean patted Powerscourt on the shoulder in a gesture that might have been a sign of friendship or a truncated blessing. He moved off towards the Chapter House.

Lord Francis Powerscourt had not intended to become a historian of cathedrals. He was just under six feet tall, clean-shaven, his head crowned with a set of unruly black

7

curls, his eyes blue, inspecting the world with irony and detachment.

For many years Powerscourt had worked in Army Intelligence in India. When he left the military he and his great friend and companion in arms Johnny Fitzgerald had embarked on a successful career as investigators, solving murders and mysteries right across Britain. The year before, in 1902, he had been shot and very badly wounded at the end of a murder case involving one of London's Inns of Court. For days he had been on the brink of death, his wife Lady Lucy and a team of doctors and nurses in constant vigil by his side. Several months after the accident, when he was well enough to travel and to climb a few hills, she took him away to a hotel in Positano in Italy to convalesce. Powerscourt loved Positano, hanging on to its cliff above the blue water, the streets often replaced by stairs as you climbed towards the top, the foundations of the houses horizontal rather than vertical, or so the natives said, and the legends of pirates and abductions of Black Madonnas that peopled its turbulent history. And then, on the fifth morning, in a scene Powerscourt later referred to as The Ambush, Lucy sat him down on the balcony of their sitting room that looked out over the sea and took both of his hands in hers. Powerscourt had replayed the scene in his mind virtually every day since.

'Francis, my love, I cannot tell you how happy we all are to see you getting better. I want to ask you something today. It is important, it's very important to me.'

She paused and Powerscourt could see that she must have been rehearsing this speech in her mind for days if not weeks. 'I don't expect an answer today, Francis. I don't expect an answer tomorrow. Only when you're ready.'

Powerscourt thought she was delaying the heart of her message. Only when he looked into the steadfast courage in Lucy's blue eyes did he know that she was trying to spare him. He thought he knew what she was going to say. He had been expecting it for some time.

'Francis, I want you to give up detection, investigations, murders, mysteries, all of it. You know I have never tried to stop you in the past, I have never asked you and Johnny to abandon a case because it was dangerous. But that last case with the bullet wound in the chest nearly killed you. You were unconscious for days. You didn't see the agony for our children, for Thomas and Olivia as they thought their Papa might be dead. Children don't want that at the age of nine or seven. The twins would have had to grow up without a father at all. You're a very good father, Francis, no mother and no child could ask for better. But surely the greatest gift a father can give his children is to stay alive for them, to be there as they grow up, to help and bless them on their way into the world. Dead fathers may be heroes, they may even be martyrs, but they don't help their children with their homework or teach them how to play tennis or read them bedtime stories. Children need fathers built into the brickwork of their lives, into the patterns of their days and the weeks of the passing years. They don't want that contact to be with some stone monument in a cemetery with rotting flowers lying at the side of the grave.'

Lady Lucy paused, her hands still locked into her husband's, her eyes watching his face. 'Think of the number of times you have nearly lost your life, my love. When you were investigating the death of Prince Eddy, the Prince of Wales's son, Johnny Fitzgerald was nearly killed because your enemies thought he was you as he was wearing your green cloak. When you looked into the death of Christopher Montague the art critic, you and I were nearly killed in Corsica with mad people pursuing us down a mountain road and firing guns at us. In that cathedral case they tried to kill you by dropping a whole heap of masonry on top of you from high up in the building. A few months ago you nearly breathed your last on the first floor of the Wallace Collection in Manchester Square. It can't go on, Francis. Please don't be cross with me, my love, I've nearly finished. I don't know if you remember the day you came back from the dead, when Johnny Fitzgerald was reading Tennyson's "Ulysses" and little Christopher smiled his first smile at you. We were all hand in hand then, by the side of your bed, you and me and Thomas and Olivia and Christopher and Juliet, all joined in a circle of love. I want you to remember those faces, to think of them on that day, as you make your decision. I know it won't be easy, I know how much satisfaction you take from another mystery solved, from the knowledge that other people will now live because the murderer has been caught. I just want you to think of your children's faces and the love in their eyes and the relief in their hearts when their father came back to them. Please don't let them go through that again. And remember, Francis, you know it's because we all love you so much.'

Lady Lucy removed her hands at the end. Suddenly, overcome by the strain and her memories of the days when death seemed so close in Manchester Square, she started to cry. Powerscourt held her in his arms and said nothing at all. He had known it was coming, this request. He hadn't known how difficult he would find it to give her an answer. For three days he stared at the dark blue waters of the Mediterranean and took little walks along the coast as his strength returned. He was being asked to give up his career. If he had stayed in the army, he told himself, he would have been exposed to much more danger than he was as an investigator. Was it unmanly to give up his own interests for those of his wife and children? He wondered what his male contemporaries would have said about that. He tried to make a comparison, to draw up a balance sheet between Lady Lucy and his children's happiness and the dangers of an undiscovered murderer roaming the streets of London, and he knew he couldn't do it.

He watched Lady Lucy a lot in those three days. He saw the joy in her face when she looked at him when she thought he wasn't noticing. She's so happy I'm alive, he said to himself. He saw the grace of her movements as she walked into a room or crossed a street and he knew he was as much in love with her as he had been the day they were married. When he told her he was giving up detection she ran into his arms and buried her face in his shoulder. 'Francis, I promise I won't mention it again unless you do,' she told him. 'Now let's go and have a very expensive dinner and an early night.'

For a long time afterwards Powerscourt was to wonder if she chose her moment when he was still quite weak. Would he have given the same answer if he had been at full strength? For he found life growing more difficult as they returned from Positano and back into their London routine. Only Powerscourt had no routine now. Buying more newspapers in the morning, taking longer and longer walks in the afternoon, was no compensation for the lack of purpose in his life. He didn't think you could enter your occupation in some survey or census as Father. It wouldn't do. He began to grow listless. He found it harder and harder to get out of bed in the morning. He drank too much in the evening. Lady Lucy and Johnny Fitzgerald held an emergency meeting with Powerscourt's brother-in-law William Burke, a great financier in the City of London. It was Johnny who came up with a possible answer.

'Look here, Lady Lucy, William, I've got an idea. Remember what happened to me first of all. I used to be a bit wild, drinking too much when I wasn't working with Francis on a case. Now I've got my first bird book coming out soon and they want another two after that. I'm not saying that Francis should start watching the lesser peewit or the great praticole or any of that stuff, but he's so clever he could write books about lots of things. Maybe he could describe some of his greatest cases – but I suppose they'd be too delicate for that.'

Johnny paused and took a sip of his glass of William Burke's finest Chablis. 'I know,' he said, leaning forward in his excitement. 'How about this? Do you remember during our art case there was that character who was arrested for Christopher Montague's murder and we had to get him off? Buckley, that's the man's name, Horace Aloysius Buckley. He was going round the country attending Evensong in every cathedral in England when Francis and the police caught up with him in Durham, I think, no, it was Lincoln. Anyway, after he was acquitted there was a party in that barrister Charles Augustus Pugh's chambers, and I asked this Buckley person if there wasn't a book about the cathedrals for the general reader, thinking that he could have stopped home if there was and not spent all that money on the train fares. He said there wasn't. So there we are. Francis becomes an author. Francis writes histories of cathedrals. He'd like that. He dedicates one of the books to Mr Buckley, maybe. Bloody cathedrals are like bloody birds, they're everywhere, England, France, Germany, Italy, there's enough to keep him going for years.'

So here was Powerscourt, many months after his trip to Positano, travelling nearly six hundred years back in time to learn about the scissor arches that saved Wells Cathedral.

He had grown to love the strange vocabulary of cathedrals, the ambulatories and clerestories, the chantry chapels and the Angel Choirs, the sacristies and the triforia, the transepts and the cloisters, the choir stalls and the fonts, the Chapter Houses and the stained glass windows, the recent memorials to the dead in the Boer Wars, the tattered flags that had once led soldiers into battle and death. He was still astonished at the sheer size of them, how twelfth- or thirteenth-century men could have built these massive monuments to their God. He had talked to contemporary masons and carpenters and architects about their perspective on the buildings. He had tried to discover what the citizens of the cathedral cities thought of them when they were built, but no records survived. He had talked to the present-day citizens, the shopkeepers, the tradesmen, the lawyers, the publicans, the Deans and Chapters, about what the cathedral meant to them now in the first years of the twentieth century. For the citizens, he discovered, the cathedral was like a remote grandparent with eternal life, part of the fabric of their lives and their families' lives as far back as their memories extended and the city records survived. The cathedral, in Gloucester or Hereford, in Salisbury or Norwich, brought honour to the city and growing numbers of visitors to inspect its glories. But nowhere was it seen as a beacon of faith, a monument to man's quest for the eternal or the spiritual. Cathedrals were friendly, cathedrals were beautiful, cathedrals were awesome feats of construction, but they were not the light that shineth in darkness. Even the Deans, like the Dean of Wells, the men responsible for the running of these vast buildings and the scheduling of their daily services, approached their task, Powerscourt felt, in the manner of men organizing the Post Office mail delivery system or planning the transportation of an army across a continent. The cathedral, in Canterbury or Worcester or Exeter, must have seemed to its people at one early point to tower above

13

society, to float next to heaven far above the mundane concerns of the city. Once it was a miracle. Now it was just another cog in the wheel, like the town hall or the public library.

Sarov, Russia, July 1903

The film of dust, thicker than the smoke from a cigarette, less dense than a cloud, rose some twenty feet above the road and a long way out on either side. The roads were dusty in the summer of 1903 and not designed to carry so many pilgrims. These travellers had come from all over Russia, mystics from Siberia, Holy Fools from the Crimea, mountain people from the Caucasus, peasants in their rough clothes from the very heart of Russia. The sick had come as well as the healthy, amputees brandishing their crutches as they limped along, desperate mothers holding pale and diseased children in their arms, or pushing them in home-made handcarts, children who looked as if they might never reach their destination. The pilgrims carried icons of St Serafim or the Virgin, many of them muttering prayers to themselves or their paintings every step of the way. Some carried baskets of food, others had resolved to fast until they saw the relics of the saint installed in glory in the new cathedral. The mad and deranged had come, sometimes shrieking out their private visions at the side of the road, sometimes screaming in pain as the Cossack horsemen or the police beat them into silence. And at the heart of this progression of pilgrims, travelling in their imperial troikas, Nicholas and Alexandra, Emperor and Empress of All the Russias, were bent on the same journey of pilgrimage to the same destination as their subjects. Word of their journey had spread through the villages they passed. Crowds would come out to stare and shout oaths of loyalty to their Emperor, never before seen in these remote parts and never seen since.

Sarov was the goal, Sarov, home to one of the most famous holy men in Russia whose remains were to be removed from his grave in the convent cemetery and transferred to a new cathedral that was to be consecrated in his name. Serafim was the name of the holy man. He had already been declared a saint on the orders of the Tsar. Everyone, even the babies in the handcarts, knew the story of St Serafim. Many of the pilgrims had shouted out the best known of his prayers to encourage themselves on the road. He had gone as a monk to live alone in a cottage in the forest to be close to nature and closer to his God. For many years he lived the simple life there, alone with his prayers and his Creator. Then three robbers came to his hut one day and demanded money. When Serafim told them he had no money, they beat him senseless and left him for dead. Serafim returned to the monastery near Sarov and refused to let the robbers be punished. Now began his late career as mystic and healer. People believed he could make the blind see and the deaf hear and cure any number of ailments that oppressed the peasants. The numbers of the sick he had cured ran into thousands. That was why the people of Russia marched in such numbers to the consecration of his cathedral.

All of the pilgrims had their own special reason for their journey: a child to be healed, a parent brought back to health, a husband or wife restored to sight or to sanity. But one woman had a very special cause very close to her heart. In spite of the humiliation of her false pregnancy, in spite of the fact that the Foreign Service had reported that Philippe Vachot was a butcher from Lyons who had been arrested for fraud in France, the Empress Alexandra still believed in him. She persuaded Nicholas to have the offending civil servant who had imparted the news of Vachot's disgrace in his native land stripped of his position and sent to Siberia. She still believed. The candles and the incense still burned in the Montenegrins' apartment, the icons still shimmered on the walls as the mystic work went on. In some ways Alexandra was a practical woman. She bought most of the furniture for her palace from that Mecca of the English middle class, Maples department store in London's Tottenham Court Road. But she seemed to need spiritualism the way other people in St Petersburg needed love affairs or yachts or fine horses. And she carried two messages from Philippe along the dusty roads to Sarov. Among his many powers the saint was said to be able to cure the barren, to give the infertile children. Surely a man who could do that could make her bring forth a son? She was to pray to the saint for a son and she was to bathe in the holy waters of the spring that bore his name. The second message was more cryptic and Alexandra was not sure of its meaning. Philippe had told the imperial couple that he had been sent on a mission and that his mission was almost over. But after his death, he assured them, another man would take over his spirit and his work, a greater man than he, a true holy man who would bring great glory to Russia.

The first couple of days were spent consecrating the cathedral. The Metropolitan of St Petersburg, an enormous man well over six feet six inches tall, led the prayers. Some of the pilgrims went to the services, standing patiently while the choir and the priests worked their way through the special liturgy for the consecration of a cathedral, crossing themselves with the three-fingered cross of the Russian Orthodox, kissing the icons. But most of them waited. They had not travelled these enormous distances for the blessing of a new church. They were waiting for the

16

moment when the bones of the saint would be moved in their new coffin and installed in front of the chancel. Then the proper business of the pilgrimage could begin. Meanwhile they slept in the fields. The police reported that they were one of the best behaved crowds they had ever seen. Drunkenness, that curse of all Russian gatherings from two to twenty thousand people, had not appeared. The pilgrims rapidly emptied the shops of Sarov of all available food and waited, uncomplaining, for fresh supplies to arrive.

Shortly after ten o'clock on the fourth day the most dramatic part of the service began. Under the great golden dome the choir and the priests sang one of the opening sections of Matins.

Choir:	**Lord, have mercy.**
Deacon:	**For the peace from on high and for the salvation of our souls, let us pray to the Lord.**
Choir:	**Lord, have mercy.**
Deacon:	**For the peace of the whole world, for the stability of the holy Churches of God, and for the union of all, let us pray to the Lord.**
Choir:	**Lord, have mercy.**
Deacon:	**For this holy house, and for those who enter it with faith, reverence and the fear of God, let us pray to the Lord.**
Choir:	**Lord, have mercy.**

Outside, the Tsar, his uncle Grand Duke Serge and various members of the imperial family carried the gold coffin with the relics of St Serafim on their shoulders right round the exterior of the cathedral. The peasants who had been leaning against the walls or making pathetic encampments with their few belongings parted before the coffin like the waters of the Red Sea. Then the coffin was carried round the inside of the building before being placed in front of the chancel.

Slowly at first, then in a trickle, then in a steady stream, came the pilgrims. They limped, they shuffled, they came with their crutches, some of them crawled, one or two ran to kiss the coffin of the dead saint. They knew, these faithful – had not their own priests lectured them about this before they set off on their pilgrimage? – that they were not to expect God's grace to make itself manifest immediately. It might be days or weeks or even years before the Holy Spirit revealed itself. There was so much hope in the building, irrational hope, unreasonable hope that illnesses, which must of themselves be the work of God, could be halted or reversed by one of his saints. The choir sang on. The Metropolitan Antony blessed the pilgrims in the chancel. Gradually the atmosphere became very tense, as if the entire congregation and those denied entry standing outside were all desperate for a miracle. Some of the pilgrims were praying for one. The anthems and responses of the choir grew ever more hypnotic. Then there was a sign. A madman was brought up, his arms waving wildly, his eyes staring intently at some private reality of his own, two friends or relations guiding him forwards. As he kissed the coffin and received the blessing of the Metropolitan, a peace seemed to descend on him. His limbs returned to normal. His eyes stopped the staring of the deranged and looked about him intelligently. Whether it was the work of the saint or the atmosphere or a fluke did not matter to the congregation. 'He is healed!' 'Thank the Lord!' 'St Serafim be praised!' rang round the cathedral until the Metropolitan himself had to look sternly down the nave for the noise to stop. Later on a dumb child seemed to be cured. After four hours the pilgrims were convinced that their journey was worthwhile, that God and his saint had indeed come to Sarov to cast his blessings on his people and work miracles on their afflictions.

Late in the evening of the last day of the ceremonies Nicholas and Alexandra and some of their party went very quietly to bathe in St Serafim's pool. A group of Cossacks were on duty, facing outwards, in case of assassins. Staff had brought towels and dry clothes. The cathedral was outlined faintly against a crescent moon. A pair of owls could be heard hooting in the distance. The waters in the pool were very cold. As Alix slipped in and lowered herself until she was almost completely covered, she prayed to St Serafim. She prayed that he would take pity on a poor sinner whose dearest wishes had been denied. She prayed that he would take heed of her husband, a good man denied the one thing he most needed, a son and heir. She prayed that St Serafim would take heed of his own country, that he would ensure that Russia was not left to lawlessness and crime and anarchy and depravity because there was no proper heir to the throne of the Romanovs. This time, shivering slightly now in the evening chill, she knew her prayers would be answered. She knew now that she would have a son. In the end Philippe had not failed her.

St Petersburg, October 1904

Ever since she had read *Anna Karenina* two years before, Natasha Bobrinsky thought of Tolstoy's heroine every time she was in a railway station. This particular engine driver seemed intent on raising so much steam that any putative suicides would have been completely invisible. She peered, fascinated, at those enormous wheels and wondered what it would be like to be crushed to death beneath them. She shuddered slightly, for Natasha had no intention of dying just yet. The Bobrinskys had come to St Petersburg with Peter the Great and had been rewarded for their loyalty and devotion to his new capital with grants of thousands of acres. Successive Bobrinskys, in their turn, had served their Tsars and been rewarded with yet more grants of land. Natasha's father had once tried to show her on a map where the family estates were, many of them thousands and thousands of miles away. In the end her parents too had moved thousands of miles away for most of the year, not to the badlands of Siberia, but to the sunnier climes of Paris and the French Riviera. Natasha wasn't particularly interested in her father's estates. Surely girls of eighteen couldn't be expected to be interested in places that far away from civilization, which stopped, as everyone who was anyone in St Petersburg knew, at the end of the Nevskii Prospekt.

Even Natasha's four elder brothers, who had teased and tormented their only sister from earliest times, would have said she was pretty. She was taller than average, without being liable to stand out in a crowd, slim, with very dark eyes and thick brown hair. For her trip to the station Natasha was clad from head to foot in fur and reminded more than one of the passengers on the platform of Tolstoy's eponymous heroine. She had come to see a young man off on a journey of adventure. Natasha had known Mikhail Shaporov since she was a child. Just when she thought their friendship might turn into something different, something altogether more exciting, he had to leave Russia to go and live in the fogs of London. And where was he? she thought, looking up at the clock and seeing that the train would leave in nine minutes' time. If you were a Shaporov, she reflected with a smile, you probably wouldn't mind missing a train. You could probably buy yourself another one on the spot. For the Shaporovs had not been content with the great estates they had received on government service. They had branched out into banking and insurance and all kinds of other things to do with money that Natasha didn't understand. People said they were now much richer than the Romanovs.

Then she saw him, running at full speed towards her, his eyes filled with happiness.

'Natasha!' he panted. 'I'm at the other end of the train! This way!'

With that he grabbed her hand and pulled her at break-neck speed down the platform, dodging a considerable amount of luggage and annoying a great many other travellers who had to get out of their way.

'Here we are,' he said, still out of breath. 'This compartment is mine.'

Natasha saw that he had a sleeping compartment and a well-furnished living room at his disposal. Shaporovs didn't travel third class.

'Do you think you'll have enough room in there, Mikhail? You don't think you should have ordered a dining suite and a chef for yourself as well?'

The young man laughed. 'I didn't book it, Natasha. I'd have been perfectly happy with first class. My father booked it for me.'

Natasha still remembered the first time she had met Mikhail's father at a children's party. He had given rides on his back to every single small guest, some of them up the marble staircase accompanied by wolf noises. Now the man was booking luxury train suites for his children.

'You've been to London a lot, haven't you?' asked Natasha, anxious perhaps lest her young man, or one who might become her young man, be going to an alien world.

'I have been there a lot. They sent me to school there, you may remember, for two years before I went to Oxford. London's splendid. It's not as beautiful as St Petersburg and the English are more reserved than we are, but it's a fine city. And,' he went on, noticing that Natasha was looking sad all of a sudden, 'my father says I can come home after three months if I do well.'

Natasha wondered where he might be sent then, New York, or Siberia perhaps. Maybe she should find herself a more stationary sort of young man.

'I haven't told you,' she said, 'I've been offered a job as a lady-in-waiting.'

'Waiting for whom or for what?' said Mikhail gravely.

'The Empress and her children out at Tsarskoe Selo,' said Natasha proudly. 'They want to have a sensible young girl to talk to the daughters and so forth. The only thing they checked about me was whether I was fluent in French or not. I am, as you know. So I got the position.'

Mikhail looked at her carefully. Sensible? Would he have called Natasha sensible? It wasn't the first word that would have come to mind. Beautiful, certainly. Attractive, yes. Desirable, undoubtedly. Maybe Natasha was sensible too. It seemed such a mundane, a prosaic adjective to describe such a gorgeous creature.

'Congratulations, Natasha! What an honour to be picked for that post!'

'I may not like it, Mikhail,' she said. 'My mother says they're all mad out at the Alexander Palace and my father says to keep an eye out for the bombs and the terrorists.'

'Not sure it's bombs you need to keep an eye out for. Beware faith healers, ouija boards, necromancers, fakes and phoneys of the spiritual world. One of these fiends convinced the Empress she was pregnant a couple of years back.'

There was a sudden burst of whistles from the front of the train. Natasha thought she saw something like a flag waving. Mikhail hopped on to the step at the door of his compartment. He thought he would still be able to kiss her from there if the opportunity presented itself.

'You be careful in London, Mikhail Shaporov,' said Natasha firmly. 'There are all kinds of bounty hunters and wicked people over there. I read about them in a book by Henry James.'

'Not females, surely, Natasha? Not members of your own sex, trying to trap a man for his money? Impossible, surely.' The young man laughed.

The train began to move very slowly. The engine was giving out great gasps as if it were in labour. The white-grey smoke billowed back down the platform. Natasha began walking alongside Mikhail's carriage. Very suddenly he reached down and pulled her up on to the same step. He kissed her firmly and then returned her to the platform.

'Take care, Natasha,' he said, 'take great care out there in your palace.'

Natasha's head was spinning. Why did this have to happen now when he was going away? Was that the kiss of a friend or a lover? Lover, she thought, every memory on her lips said lover. She was nearly running now.

'Take care in your wicked city, Mikhail! Come back safely! Will you write to me?'

There was an enormous roar, almost an explosion, as the train gathered speed and began to move clear of the station.

'Of course I'll write,' Natasha thought she heard him say. The train was disappearing now. Natasha made her way home slowly. She was not going to tell anybody about the kiss. It would be a secret between them. Natasha rather liked secrets. And London? Well, she remembered a governess in her youth who had tried in vain to teach them about distances. London, she thought, was only about two thousand, one hundred and fifty miles away. Not really that far when you considered how far it was to Siberia.

PART ONE

THE WINTER PALACE

The Intelligentsia only talk about what is significant, they talk philosophy, but meanwhile in front
of their eyes the workers eat disgusting food,
sleep without pillows, thirty or forty to a room,
everywhere fleas, damp, stench, immorality...

Trofimov, Act Two,
The Cherry Orchard, Anton Chekhov

1

Lord Francis Powerscourt looked carefully at the number at the top of the page. One hundred and twenty-three did indeed follow on from one hundred and twenty-two. Earlier on in his perusal of this work he had discovered page two hundred and four coming directly after page twenty-three and page eighteen coming immediately after page ninety-one. His eye moved on down the first couple of paragraphs. There may be a place called Salusbury somewhere, he said to himself, there probably is, but it doesn't have a cathedral and this one should be spelt Salisbury. Sissors should be scissors. Sacistry should be sacristy.

Powerscourt himself was the author of this forthcoming volume. These were the proofs of the first in a three-part series on the cathedrals of England. He had completed all his research, travelling to every cathedral in the country, often with Lady Lucy as his companion. Powerscourt remembered Johnny Fitzgerald telling him, very shyly, of the extraordinary pride he felt in becoming a published author, of seeing a physical book with your own name on the cover. Powerscourt now felt the same and his elder children were growing incredibly excited, demanding regular bulletins on the book's progress and asking when they could go and see it on display at Hatchard's in Piccadilly.

Page one hundred and seventy-one, Wrocester did not have a cathedral, Worcester did. People did not reseive the sacriment, they received the sacrament. Powerscourt thought he might finish these proofs before lunch when there was an apologetic knock at the door and the sound of a slight cough on the far side. Rhys, the Powerscourt butler, another veteran from Indian Army days, always coughed before entering a room.

'Excuse me, my lord, forgive me for interrupting you, but there is a gentleman down below who wishes to speak to you. He says his business is most urgent, my lord.'

Powerscourt glanced down at the name on the card. Sir Jeremiah Reddaway, Permanent Under Secretary, HM Foreign Office. Did he know this Reddaway? Had he had dealings with him in his earlier life as an investigator? Was he, much more likely, one of Lady Lucy's relations? But, in that case, why not ask for his wife?

'Is he in the hall now, Rhys, the Reddaway fellow?'

'He is, my lord.'

'Show him into the drawing room and say I will join him shortly. And ask him if he would like some coffee.'

As he tidied up his proofs, Powerscourt wondered if his past had come back to haunt him, if some fragment of an earlier case had resurfaced and needed tidying up. Maybe it would blow up instead, the past returning to explode in the face of the present. Sir Jeremiah, Powerscourt saw as they shook hands in the middle of the drawing room, was extraordinarily tall and equally extraordinarily thin. Sir Jeremiah leant forward when he walked as if some bureau-cratic truth or disobedient memorandum had escaped his clutches and he was pursuing it down a recalcitrant

Foreign Office corridor. He had a long thin nose and a small tight mouth. There was a very slight air of menace about him this morning, as if he might despatch a destroyer or a squadron of horse against you if you crossed his path.

'Lord Powerscourt,' he began, sitting beside the fireplace and stretching out those long legs till they almost reached the far side, 'please forgive me for calling at such short notice and without warning. I am here on the instructions of the Foreign Secretary and the Prime Minister.'

Powerscourt bowed slightly. The previous Prime Minister Lord Salisbury he had known quite well. The current one he did not know at all.

'I have come, Lord Powerscourt, on a most delicate and most urgent mission.'

'Forgive me, Sir Jeremiah, I do not know if you are fully acquainted with my current position. As of over two years ago I have given up investigations. I attend to no more murder inquiries in society or anywhere else. My detecting days are over.' Powerscourt smiled at the man from the Foreign Office. 'I write books now, Sir Jeremiah, books about cathedrals.'

Sir Jeremiah did not give up easily. 'I look forward to reading your work as soon as it is published. But we are talking here of a matter of the utmost importance. In the Prime Minister's words it is crucial to the well-being of the nation and the Empire. It is our wish that you should take one final bow on the world stage, Lord Powerscourt, in the service of your country.'

'I do not think you have understood me,' said Powerscourt. 'I do not do investigations any more. I am a retired investigator. I am a Chelsea Pensioner of an investigator, or, if you prefer a parliamentary to a military analogy, I have taken the Chiltern Hundreds and resigned from the House. I do not mean to be rude but I don't intend to change my mind for you or the Foreign Secretary or even the Prime Minister.' With that Powerscourt smiled politely at his visitor.

Sir Jeremiah remembered the advice from a Foreign Office official who had seen Powerscourt in action during his time as Head of Military Intelligence in the Boer War. 'You've got to tempt him, Sir Jeremiah. I know you can't tell him much until he agrees to take on the job, but make it sound as dangerous and difficult as you can. That might pull him in. The man likes a challenge.'

'Lord Powerscourt, please, permit me to give the briefest outline of our difficulties. Surely you will give your country the right to enlighten you?'

Sir Jeremiah was rubbing the tips of his fingers together as he spoke. Powerscourt suddenly saw what he must be like in Foreign Office meetings. Polite. Polished. Lethal. He was not going to fall out of step in this gavotte of *la politesse* as if his drawing room had been magically transported back to the court of the Sun King in the vast and draughty salons of Versailles.

'Of course, Sir Jeremiah, you must carry out your instructions.' Powerscourt saw that Sir Jeremiah did not like being referred to as a bearer of instructions, as if he were a messenger boy or a deliverer of telegrams. A brief frown shot across his long thin face before the customary bureaucratic mask reappeared. 'But, as you say, the briefest of outlines, for my mind is already made up.'

Sir Jeremiah pulled another card from his department's investigations into Powerscourt's past. Somebody remembered sitting next to somebody at a dinner party at Powerscourt's sister's house, and the second somebody recalled Powerscourt speaking very eloquently about the glory and the grandeur of St Petersburg which he had just visited in the company of Lady Lucy.

'Do you know St Petersburg, Lord Powerscourt?' Sir Jeremiah was now purring slightly. Looking at his incredibly long legs Powerscourt thought he looked like one of those Spy cartoons that appeared in *Vanity Fair*. Perhaps he had already appeared there. Perhaps he should ask him. Perhaps not.

'I do,' said Powerscourt, in the most neutral tone he could think of. He was not going to give Beanpole, as he was sure his children would describe the man from King Charles Street, any hint of advantage.

'Did you care for the city? Did you find the architecture and so on agreeable?'

Here was an opening, surely. Powerscourt slipped through it like a rugby three-quarter making a break for the try line.

'Forgive me, Sir Jeremiah,' he said, 'I thought you came here to discuss a matter crucial to the well-being of the nation and the Empire, not to debate the architectural merits of northern Russian cities as if we were compiling a guidebook or an updated edition of Baedeker.'

The sally made no impact whatever. Sir Jeremiah seemed to be carrying steel armour many inches thick as if he were some sort of human battleship.

'As I said, Lord Powerscourt, St Petersburg is at the heart of our difficulties. Four or five days ago a man was found dead early in the morning by one of the bridges on the Nevskii Prospekt. He had been murdered. That man was a distinguished member of the Foreign Office, in Russia on a secret mission. We need to know who killed him. We need to know why they killed him. We need desperately to know if he was killed by a hostile power and how much he may have told them, under torture perhaps, who knows, before he died. That is the essence of this task. Will you do it, Lord Powerscourt?'

There was not a fraction of a second of hesitation. 'No, I will not,' said Powerscourt.

'I cannot take that answer as definitive, Lord Powerscourt.' Sir Jeremiah, Powerscourt thought, was now moving into the 'let's persuade the Minister to change his mind routine', a technique honed and perfected by the Foreign Office over many governments and many ministers and many centuries.

'I would remind you, Lord Powerscourt, of the shifting sands of contemporary European politics. For many decades Europe was at peace after the Congress of Vienna. There were occasional interruptions, the Crimea, the Franco-Prussian War, Russo-Turkish and so on. But now we are in uncharted waters. Germany wants an empire and recognition of her power for her unstable Emperor. France is frightened of Germany and seeks alliances against her. A new naval arms race threatens the peace of the high seas. The Great Powers are fighting over the division of Africa like rabid dogs over a corpse. The Russian Empire itself is racked with unrest, its politicians decimated by assassinations, its Tsar weak and indecisive, liberals and revolutionaries of every shape and size conspiring for democratic change. The death on the Nevskii Prospekt is surely a part of this mosaic, this cauldron of uncertainty and doubt that has spread over Europe like dark clouds massing before a tempest.'

Powerscourt could barely restrain himself from smiling happily at the mixed metaphors pouring from the Foreign Office mandarin.

'This is the task your country asks of you, Lord Powerscourt. Go to St Petersburg. Solve the mystery of the murdered man. Find out who killed him and come back to London. I need not tell you that your services would be exceedingly well rewarded. Will you do it? Will you answer your country's call?'

Powerscourt was furious. 'No, Sir Jeremiah, I will not. And how dare you come into my house and try to bribe me to work in the service of my country! I have served Queen Victoria for many years as an officer in her army. I have served her in dangerous places, more dangerous even than the corridors of the Foreign Office. I have risked my life in battle while you and your colleagues compose memoranda on future policy and fill the passing hours with meetings about the changing map of Africa or the tribal troubles on the North West Frontier. If I wanted to serve my King and carry out this mission I would never have asked for money. You demean yourself and your office by offering it, you demean me by making me listen to it. I have said No to your offer twice already. Now I say it again.'

Powerscourt rang the bell for Rhys. 'And now, Sir Jeremiah, if you will forgive me, I have work to do. Rhys will show you out. Thank you for considering me for this task. The answer will always be No.'

Two hours later there was an emergency meeting in the Powerscourt drawing room. Johnny Fitzgerald had been summoned from sorting out his notes on the birds of East Anglia. Lady Lucy had returned from a shopping mission with the twins to Sloane Square. Powerscourt had spent most of those two hours pacing up and down his drawing room in a state of total uncontrolled fury.

'Well, Francis,' said Johnny Fitzgerald, opening a bottle of Pomerol, 'I hear the Senate has come to the farm to recall Cincinnatus to the service of Rome. Maybe you could ask for dictatorial powers?'

Powerscourt laughed. 'I don't think you could refer to the Permanent Under Secretary at the Foreign Office as the

Senate, Johnny. Not even a consul. Maybe an aedile. Weren't they some sort of minor official?'

'God knows,' said Johnny cheerfully. 'I only got as far as consuls. What did the fellow have to say?'

'Beanpole,' said Powerscourt, 'was eight feet tall and less than eight inches wide. He looked as though he had been ironed. Some British diplomat has been found dead on the Nevskii Prospekt in St Petersburg. He was on a secret mission. Beanpole and his friends, Foreign Secretary and Prime Minister, want to know who killed him and if he spilled any secrets before he died. I said No, of course.'

Powerscourt looked at Lady Lucy as he spoke, as if seeking her approval. She smiled. 'Well done, Francis,' she said. 'I'm very proud of you.'

'Sounds bloody dangerous to me, Francis,' said Johnny Fitzgerald, taking a second sip of his Bordeaux. 'They enjoy blowing people up, those Russians, rather like other people enjoy playing football.'

Johnny Fitzgerald was fascinated by Powerscourt's reaction to this offer of a dangerous but important investigation. It was exactly the sort of challenge his friend enjoyed. And Johnny suspected his friend was ambivalent about the whole business of retiring from investigations. He was almost certain that Lady Lucy had finessed Francis into renunciation before he was fully recovered from his injuries. Of course he understood her position and her fears for the children without a father. But he and Powerscourt had led such intertwined lives, fellow army officers, fellow investigators, now fellow authors. Johnny Fitzgerald could not see his friend being pushed in his wheelchair along the Promenade des Anglais on the Mediterranean sea front in his old age without having carried out one more major investigation. Powerscourt's Last Case. Johnny had often thought about that. Maybe even

Powerscourt's Last Stand. Was this Corpse on the Nevskii Prospekt that final mission?

Lady Lucy too was perturbed. She sensed – no, if she was honest with herself, she knew that her husband would love to carry out this investigation. He had turned it down because of her and the promise she had exacted from him in Positano. She wondered if she should release him from his vows.

And Powerscourt? To be fair, even he would have said that he didn't know what he really felt about the offer. Flattered, yes. To be sought out more than two years after he had stopped investigating was no mean tribute to his powers. Part of him felt, as Ulysses said in Tennyson's poem that brought him back from the dead, that he did not like rusting unburnished, not to shine in use. But he had given Lucy his word on that hotel balcony in Positano. He could not go back on it now.

'There's only one thing I'm sure of,' he said, pouring himself a glass of wine and smiling at his wife and his friend. 'Beanpole is the advance guard, the voltigeurs, the skirmishers in Napoleon's army, if you like. He may have failed. But he won't be the last. They'll come back. And next time they'll bring the cavalry. Maybe the heavy artillery.'

Powerscourt would have been surprised to learn that Sir Jeremiah Reddaway was not unduly upset by his reception in Markham Square. For he had not expected success at the very first attempt. He felt now like a general in charge of some mighty siege operation. The siege train has been battering the walls for weeks. An infantry attempt to break through has failed. The general will simply have to continue his bombardment and plan his next attack. The main reason Reddaway had opened the assault himself was that he wanted to have a look at Powerscourt in person, to get a feel of the man. Now he had no doubt that Powerscourt was the right choice for the task ahead, if only he could be persuaded to take it on. Sir Jeremiah merely widened his net in the quest for the key or the trigger that would change Powerscourt's mind. Powerscourt's old tutor in Cambridge was contacted. Charles Augustus Pugh, a barrister who had been closely and critically involved in one of Powerscourt's cases, reported that he had been approached by some person from the Foreign Office wearing the most vulgar shirt Pugh had ever seen. 'Fellow tried to pump me for information about you, Francis, so I sent him packing. I couldn't have looked at that shirt for another second in any case,' his note to Powerscourt said. Even Johnny Fitzgerald told the Powerscourts that some chap he had known years before had tried to get him drunk at an expensive restaurant in South Kensington. His contact also worked for the Foreign Office and, Johnny announced happily, had to be carried senseless from the table by two waiters while he, Johnny, walked home unaided and pinned the rather large bill on to the man's suit as he lay stretched across the pavement. As a final touch, Johnny said, he bumped into two policemen at the end of the street and reported that a drunk was lying on the pavement further down and obstructing the King's Highway.

Two days after the meeting with Sir Jeremiah a rather nervous Lady Lucy spoke to her husband after breakfast. Powerscourt was feeling cheerful that morning. The day before he had delivered the proofs to his publisher and he was looking forward to resuming work on his second cathedral volume.

'Francis,' Lady Lucy began, 'I've just had a note. It's from one of my relations.'

'What of it, my love?' said Powerscourt. 'You must get one of those a couple of times a day, if not more.'

'Well, this one's from a cousin of mine, not a first cousin, a second cousin, I think. Anyway, he wants to come and see you at eleven o'clock this morning.'

'Never mind, Lucy. All kinds of people come and see me, even now.' Powerscourt regretted those last two words as soon as he said them. He saw the look of pain cross Lucy's face. 'Didn't mean that last bit, so sorry, my love. I suppose I have to meet this person if he's a relation. What is his business?'

Lady Lucy looked sadly at her husband. 'He's a politician, Francis, member for some constituency in Sussex, I believe.'

'Name?'

'Edmund Fitzroy.'

'You're keeping something back from me, Lucy, I can tell from the look on your face.'

'He was in the army, Household Cavalry or one of those. Now he's a junior minister in the government, Francis.' Even before she finished the sentence Powerscourt knew what was coming. 'In the Foreign Office.'

'Is he, by God?' said Powerscourt. 'Never mind, Lucy.' He smiled at her. 'I'll just have to see him off like that other fellow.'

Edmund Fitzroy was a plump young man in his middle thirties with sandy hair and dark brown eyes. He looked older than his age, always a useful asset for a politician. Powerscourt thought when they met in the drawing room that he would go down well with old ladies. Fitzroy had one main objective from Sir Jeremiah. He was to find out why Powerscourt had given up detection. Once he knew that, Reddaway felt, he might be closer to success.

'You would think,' Powerscourt said to Lady Lucy and Johnny Fitzgerald later that day, 'that even a politician would try to be polite to his host in his host's own drawing room.' But it was not to be. Fitzroy was rude from the beginning and grew progressively ruder as the conversation continued.

'I've heard from Sir Jeremiah Reddaway about your disgraceful attitude over this Russian business, Powerscourt, and I think you should be ashamed of yourself,' was his opening gambit.

'Really?' said Powerscourt, resolutely avoiding all eye contact with the man.

'You're a disgrace, Powerscourt,' Fitzroy went on, 'refusing to serve your country when we ask you. Just remember the oaths you swore when you accepted Her Majesty's commission all those years ago. Now you seem to think they mean nothing, nothing at all. I too have sworn the same oaths and regard myself as bound by them today as I was twelve years ago. You seem to have decided that patriotism is something you can put on and off like a coat on a rainy day. Others may have to endure much in the service of their country while you indulge your conscience or your reluctance for the fray in the luxury of your drawing room.'

'I think you'll discover,' said Powerscourt, in the most patronizing tone he could muster, 'if you take the trouble to find out about these things, forgive me for sounding arrogant, that my service to this country is considerably more distinguished than yours, which consisted, as far as I know, of remarkable courage shown on the parade ground at Aldershot, and bravery under fire while in charge of Royal Salutes at Windsor Castle.' Lady Lucy had passed on this last piece of information just as Fitzroy was ringing the doorbell.

'That's not the point, Powerscourt, and you know it.' Fitzroy had attended too many political meetings to be deterred, even by such a direct hit. 'I am still prepared to serve my country. You are not.'

'I served my country for many years in a variety of dangerous situations. This, thank God, is still a free country. A man may retire from the military with full honours without being bullied by politicians who never saw a shot fired in anger.'

'You've lost your nerve, Powerscourt, and you know it. Why did you stop investigating, for God's sake? Was one bullet in the chest enough to put you off? Did you just run away?'

'It was my decision, and none of your damned business, Fitzroy,' said Powerscourt, struggling to keep his temper. He could see perfectly clearly what the man was trying to do. He hoped to taunt Powerscourt with suggestions of cowardice so he would announce he was not afraid and volunteer to take on the Russian commission to prove it.

'But why, man, why? For years you were one of the best investigators in Britain, then you just throw in the towel. Why? Did Lucy make you retire?'

'It was my decision and I have no intention of telling you anything about it.'

Something about the look on Powerscourt's face when he mentioned Lady Lucy made Fitzroy think that she may have had something to do with it. But he had another line of attack to press.

'That's another thing, Powerscourt, the family. Not your Irish lot, but your wife's family, the Hamiltons. They've been in the army for hundreds of years. Military service, military loyalty is in their blood. They're not going to be pleased when they hear that an addition to the family has let the nation down.'

'Are you going to hand over the four feathers in person, or are you going to get Sir Jeremiah to do it for you in a special ceremony at the Foreign Office?' asked Powerscourt, anxious now to be rid of this incredibly offensive person.

'The family will remember, Powerscourt. They don't take this sort of thing lying down, I can tell you.'

'Right,' said Powerscourt, taking three rapid strides to pull the bell and call for Rhys the butler. 'I have had enough of this discussion. Rhys will show you out. I regard your behaviour here in my house this morning as beneath contempt. It is a disgrace to the good name of the military and unworthy of a gentleman. Don't ever try to come back here. You will be refused entry. Now I suggest you take yourself and your disgusting manners back to the gutter where you belong. Good morning.'

With that Powerscourt left his drawing room and went to the upper floors in search of a twin or two to calm him down.

'Bloody man, bloody man,' Powerscourt said later to Lady Lucy. 'He practically accused me of being a coward. I tell you what though, Lucy. He is never to be admitted to this house again. And will you please tell your relations that if he is invited to any social function, wedding, funeral, christening, death of the first-born, ritual character assassination, afternoon tea, we shall not be attending.'

The following morning Powerscourt had gone to look up some information in the London Library in St James's Square. Just after eleven o'clock a very grand carriage drew up outside the Powerscourt house in Markham Square. Lord Rosebery, former Foreign Secretary and former Prime Minister, was ushered respectfully into the drawing room. Lady Lucy was not sure her hair was what it should have been, nor was she certain of her dress, but Rosebery, apart from his public functions, was a very old friend of her family's in Scotland. As a boy he had attended her christening, as a man he had attended both her weddings, he was one of the three people allowed to call her Lucy. Because of his great position as a former Foreign Secretary and Prime Minister she had never been able to call him anything other than Lord Rosebery.

'Please forgive me, Lucy,' Rosebery began, 'for calling on you out of the blue like this. I will be perfectly honest with you, my dear. I am here at the special request of the Prime Minister and the Foreign Office about this Russian business. I feel I am better placed talking to you than I would be talking to Francis. That Foreign Office fellow thinks I can change Francis's mind. I am not so sure. Only you, I believe, can do that.'

Lady Lucy remembered that Rosebery, whatever his weaknesses as Prime Minister, was a famous orator. Even in conversation, she felt, you could imagine him on some lofty platform haranguing the faithful by the thousands. This fastidious aristocrat, she remembered, was the man who had attended a Democratic Party Convention in New York with its cheering and its fireworks and its torch-lit processions and its pre-planned spontaneous demonstrations of enthusiasm for particular candidates, and had brought some of those techniques back to Britain when he organized Gladstone's Midlothian Campaign.

'I want to put a theory to you, Lucy. It's only a theory, you understand.' Rosebery smiled and Lady Lucy suddenly felt afraid. 'After Francis was shot you went abroad a couple of years ago, just the two of you, to Italy, if my memory serves me. My theory is that on that holiday, or shortly after you returned, you persuaded Francis to give up investigating. You did it for perfectly understandable

41

reasons, of course, four children, two of them tiny, a long history of danger and attempts on his life of one sort of another. I have known Francis for a very long time. I remember when he began investigating even while he was still in the army with a terrible murder case in Simla. I know how he thought of it as a form of public service, making sure the world was rid of some wicked murderers who might kill again. I do not think he would ever have volunteered to give it up of his own accord. It would be like asking W.G. Grace to abandon cricket or Mr Wells to stop writing his stories. Only you could have done it, Lucy. Am I right?'

Feeling guilty and defiant at the same time, Lady Lucy nodded her head. Rosebery held up his hand as if to forbid her from speaking.

'Please let me continue, Lucy. So. That skeletal person from the Foreign Office thinks I am now going to persuade you to change your mind. I am not going to do anything of the sort. But I would just like you to think of certain things, if I may.'

And then, to the immense satisfaction of Lady Lucy, he rose from his chair and began pacing up and down her drawing room in exactly the same manner as her husband. Maybe all men, she reflected, have a built-in urge to walk an imaginary quarterdeck like Nelson in pursuit of some elusive French fleet or Spanish galleon, laden with treasure and the spoils of war.

'I should like you to think about courage, Lucy. Not just courage in battle by land or sea, though there are some awesome examples of that in our recent history. The courage of those with mortal illnesses and of those looking after them. The courage to go on living and caring for children after the death of a husband or wife. The courage to carry on when overwhelmed by melancholy or despair.

And then think of what happens, not if courage is taken away, but if the opportunity to display courage is taken away. I spoke a moment ago of W.G. Grace being asked to give up cricket. Let us perhaps think of Mr Gladstone or Lord Salisbury being asked to give up politics in their time. That, in a way, is what Francis has had to do in giving up investigating. He has had to show as much courage in renouncing it as you have shown in asking him to do so. But think of what it must have cost him. That fool of a junior minister virtually accused him of being a coward the other day. Francis is not just being denied the opportunity to show what he can do, he is being denied the opportunity to display his courage once again. I do not know what effect that will have. Some men could rise above it. With others it could eat away at their very souls.'

Rosebery stopped pacing suddenly to peer into Markham Square. Then he returned to his quarterdeck.

'I want you to think about patriotism, Lucy, about the love of country. Maybe I should say the chance to serve one's country, to show how much you care by offering to lay down your life for her. In the Funeral Speech in Book Two of Thucydides' *The Peloponnesian War*, Pericles tells his fellow citizens to fix their eyes on the glory that is Athens and to fall in love with her. Then they can show their true courage on the battlefield or at the oars of their triremes. Francis has shown a very great deal of that courage during his life. Now he is being denied the opportunity to display it once again. When your first husband went off to rescue General Gordon at Khartoum, Lucy, you did not ask him to stay at home in case he was killed. When Francis went off to the Boer War you did not plead with him to change his mind. You went to the railway station and waved him off, even though you must have known he might never come back.

'And finally, Lucy, I want you to think about peace and about your children. When I was Foreign Secretary all those years ago, it looked as if the long peace would go on for ever. War, a European war, seemed inconceivable. Now I am not so sure. The diplomats scurry round from capital to capital thinking up alliances, leagues, defensive groupings, pacts of co-operation if attacked by a third party. The shipyards of the major powers are racing against time and each other to produce deadlier and deadlier vessels, laden with the most lethal armaments man can invent. I recently bought a book of photographs from the American Civil War, Lucy, the most recent example of prolonged industrialized warfare. The injuries are horrendous, limbs ripped off, intestines blown away, heads cut off at the neck, bodies literally split in two. In the years after the conflict there were more cripples in Alabama than able-bodied men. And what has this to do with St Petersburg? Simply this, Lucy, simply this. I do not know the nature of the dead man's mission but I believe the Prime Minister when he says it could make peace more likely. Peace means there will be no war. I met your Robert, your lovely son from your first marriage, at a dinner at his Oxford college a couple of weeks ago. It happens to be my college too. I do not want to think of that young man in uniform risking his life on some wretched battlefield in France. I do not like to think of all those young men at his college marching off to war. Nor do I like to think of my godson Master Thomas Powerscourt in the same position. Maybe they would all come back safely. Maybe nobody would. Peace means the young men can stay alive. War means many of them will die. If the St Petersburg project brings peace a little closer, we have to think of it very seriously indeed.'

With that, Rosebery finished his pacing up and down. He bowed slightly to Lady Lucy as if he were a European rather than an Englishman and resumed his position seated opposite her.

'I shall think of what you said, Lord Rosebery, of course I shall. I shall think of it very seriously.' Lady Lucy was grave in her reply. 'You have, for most of the time, used male arguments against me. Only at the end did you find a tone that might appeal to a wife and mother. You see, Lord Rosebery, you can see, you can almost touch, all those treaties and pacts, great long documents drawn up by one country's lawyers and criticized by another's. These are real to you in a way they are not to me. I see two-year-old twins without a father, fated never to see Francis again. I see myself – when he was nearly dead in that house in Manchester Square I saw this all the time – at his funeral, holding the hands of Thomas and Olivia, both of them crying till you would think their hearts must break, knowing that when the coffin slides into the earth that is the last they will ever see of their father in this world. Forgive me, Lord Rosebery, I rather wish you hadn't come. I'm really upset now.'

With Lady Lucy on the verge of tears, Lord Rosebery took his leave very quietly. As he walked back to the Foreign Office he wondered what lever, if any, would make Lady Lucy change her mind.

Lady Lucy seriously wondered about setting off on the long march up the family drawing room that was so popular with the males. But she stood instead, leaning against the fireplace and wishing Francis was home. She wondered about what Lord Rosebery had said. Was she really taking away Francis's manhood? Was she denying him the chance to show his courage? Did men have to do that all the time? Surely he had displayed enough courage

45

to last many a lifetime. Was she trying to undermine him, to deny him the chance to show the world what he could do? No, she was only trying to keep him alive. Surely any wife would want that for her husband?

Had Lady Lucy gone to the tall window and looked out into the street she would have seen a cab draw up with two people inside. One seemed to be a very tall man who opened the door for his companion from the inside as if he did not want to be seen, the other a striking lady in her late thirties dressed entirely in black, right down to the fashionable black gloves she folded away as she advanced to the Powerscourt front door.

'Mrs Martin to see you, Lady Powerscourt.' Rhys the butler announced their guest with his usual cough.

Lady Lucy held out her hand. 'How do you do, Mrs Martin,' she said formally, 'I don't think we have met before.'

'No, we have not.' Mrs Martin sounded rather nervous as if her mission, whatever it was, seemed more formidable in reality than it had appeared before.

'To what do I owe the pleasure?' Lady Lucy was growing suspicious about her visitor, so correct in her mourning clothes. 'Perhaps you'd like to sit down.'

'Thank you,' said Mrs Martin, taking up her position in Powerscourt's favourite armchair by the side of the fireplace. 'I think I had better explain myself, Lady Powerscourt. You must forgive me for coming in like this. I think you know of my husband, my late husband. Roderick Martin was the man found dead on the Nevskii Prospekt in St Petersburg. That is the death the Foreign Office wished your husband to investigate.'

Lady Lucy turned pale. Her suspicions had been right. Death had come all the way from Russia's capital to her drawing room in Markham Square. But what did this spectre in black want of her?

'I am so sorry,' Lady Lucy managed to say. 'It must be terrible for you.'

'What I find particularly upsetting, Lady Powerscourt, is that I know so little of the circumstances. I know my husband went to Russia to carry out some sort of work for the Foreign Office. I cannot find out what that work was. They simply refuse to tell me. I do not know why Roderick died. I do not think the Foreign Office know that either. I cannot get them to recover the body and return it to us for a proper English burial. He could have been dumped out to sea for all I know. We have no children, Lady Powerscourt, but Roderick's parents are still alive. They find the not knowing even more difficult than I do. They are on the verge of tears or breaking down almost every minute of the day. Roderick's father said that his heart would break if he could not bury his only son.'

Mrs Martin paused. Still Lady Lucy did not know what was coming.

'I'm not quite sure how I can help,' said Lady Lucy, suspecting that almost anything she said to this newly bereaved woman would be wrong.

'I'm surprised you can't see it, Lady Powerscourt,' Mrs Martin replied, staring coldly at her hostess. 'I told you, it's the not knowing that's the most difficult thing. Even after the drink and the sleeping draughts, that's what keeps his old parents awake every night. It eats you up, like some parasite that chews out your insides. You see, Lady Powerscourt, the Foreign Office told us they were going to send a special man to find out the truth about what happened to Roderick. They said he was the best man in the country for this sort of work. We all felt better for a day or two after that. We thought we were going to find out the truth. Maybe this miracle worker could even come back with the body as well and my husband could be laid to rest in his graveyard. But it didn't happen. The special man isn't going. He's not going to find out what really happened. You know as well as I do who that special man is and you know as well as I do who the special woman is who's stopping him. One of those Foreign Office people told me that if it was up to your husband, he'd take the commission and go to St Petersburg tomorrow. You're the one who's stopping him. You're the one bringing misery to all that's left of my family. You're the one who's torturing those two old people who'll never see their only son again.'

'You don't understand, Mrs Martin.' Lady Lucy was close to tears. 'Francis, my husband, has nearly been killed so often in these investigations. It happens almost every time. Last time he was at death's door with the twins only a few weeks old. Imagine their growing up without a father.'

'I'm terribly sorry, Lady Powerscourt,' Mrs Martin spoke very slowly now, 'but it's you who don't understand. You think you have rights that nobody else has, rights to hold on to your husband because he was nearly killed once or twice. Think what would happen if everybody behaved as selfishly as you. Wellington's army and his commanders would never have driven the French out of Spain or won their great victory at Waterloo if their wives hadn't let them go. We would now be living in some French department with a French prefect enforcing French laws in the French language from a French town hall with a French tricolour flying from the top and statues of Napoleon in every town square. What would happen to the Royal Navy if the wives refused to let their men go back to sea, whining about the fact that they might get killed in some naval engagement? There can't be one set of rules for you and another set of rules for everybody else. We owe certain duties to society as society owes certain duties to us. But the duties have to be the same for everybody. Your rules are entirely selfish. They would lead to a feeble rather than a Great Britain. They would lead to a nation where every man could opt for cowardice rather than courage. We wouldn't have an empire. I doubt we would have our liberty. I think you pretend your rules show the mark of courage when they show the opposite. You're turning your husband into a coward, or that's what everybody will think.'

Mrs Martin began to cry slowly. 'I'm sorry,' she blurted out between her tears, 'I shouldn't have said that very last bit. I think I'd better go now.'

A watcher in Markham Square would have seen Mrs Martin climb back into the carriage she had come in at the other end of the Square. A very tall, very slim gentleman opened the door for her. He waited for her to speak. Sir Jeremiah Reddaway was most curious to learn if his latest emissary to the Powerscourt household had been more successful than the last.

Lady Lucy stared blankly at the wall with the book-shelves. She knew that Francis had already decided where to put the first of his cathedral volumes when it was published. She wondered how much pain she had caused him since the return from Positano. She wondered if he would be happier now. She wondered if she had loved him too much, trying to wrap him in a cocoon of love that would keep out the rest of the world. She hoped not. She didn't think you could love a man like Francis too much. She wondered what he would say when she told him he was released from his promise and was now free to go to St Petersburg if that was what he wanted to do. She went and sat in the chair by the window that looked out over Markham Square and waited for Francis to come home.

2

Lord Francis Powerscourt had been told by the Foreign Office that they would provide an interpreter who would travel with him from London. It was, Powerscourt reflected bitterly as he stared down the platform at Victoria station, just about all they had been able to tell him. Sir Jeremiah had, of course, known all the details of Roderick Martin's early life and career. Educated at Westminster School and New College Oxford, a brilliant linguist, fluent in French, German and Russian and able to cope in Italian, he had entered the Foreign Service with a formidable reputation. Over time he developed a judgement of men and events that was as sharp as his ability at languages. As well as his education in diplomacy, Roderick Martin was trained in the more mundane matters like codes and the use of telegraph machines. He had served in all the great capitals of Europe and by the time of his mission to St Petersburg at the age of thirty-eight, his contemporaries were already speculating about when and where he would take up his first posting as Ambassador. But of the journey to Russia they knew nothing, except that his body had been found early in the morning on the Nevskii Prospekt. Word had come from the Prime Minister that they were to send a man, their best man if possible, to St Petersburg. The Prime

Minister himself would brief him. He was to report only to the Prime Minister on his return. That was all. Martin's wife, Martin's parents knew no more than his employers. He had stepped into his compartment on this very train, Powerscourt said to himself, he had gone to the Russian capital and he had been killed. That was all anybody seemed to know about him. Maybe the Embassy there would be able to tell him more but they hadn't been able to tell the Foreign Office very much at all. Even Sir Jeremiah Reddaway, as proper and punctilious as a man in his position should be, had heard the rumours. Martin was having an affair with some diplomat's wife and had been killed by hired thugs. He had merely run across a bunch of drunken peasants or workers in the wrong part of town and been murdered for his wallet. The beauty of these theories, as Powerscourt saw clearly, was that they disconnected the murder from the mission. Powerscourt believed the opposite was the case. Maybe, Sir Jeremiah had said hopefully, those long legs stretched out in front of his own Foreign Office fire, the mission had to do with the Russian sinking of a British fishing boat and the deaths of two sailors as their navy sailed halfway round the world to fight the Japanese. Maybe they wanted a diplomatic alliance against the Germans. Powerscourt found it hard to believe any of the rumours.

And where was his interpreter? There were only a few minutes to go before departure. Powerscourt had a very clear picture in his mind of the Russian Interpreter as he referred to him. He would be middle-aged, portly, wear thick glasses and fuss a lot about his business. He would look rather like a bank manager going to seed. He would have little conversation outside the business of interpreting and would prove dull company on his journey. He turned to the door of his compartment where a good-looking young man was preparing to stow his case on the luggage rack.

'I'm afraid that seat is reserved,' said Powerscourt.

'I know it is,' said the young man. 'It's reserved for me.'

'For you?' said Powerscourt, astonished. 'That can't be, I'm afraid. It's reserved for my Russian interpreter.'

'I know,' said the young man with a smile, 'I am your Russian interpreter. You are Lord Francis Powerscourt. I am Mikhail Shaporov, sent by your Foreign Office to assist you. If you don't want my services, just let me know.'

Now it was Powerscourt's turn to smile. 'Forgive me, please. Delighted to meet you. And my apologies for the confusion. To be perfectly honest, I was expecting somebody older. I had, in fact, decided that my interpreter was going to be middle-aged and look like a bank manager going to seed.'

The young man laughed. Powerscourt saw that he was just under six feet tall with a broad forehead and a Roman nose. His cheekbones were high and he had very fair hair and soft brown eyes. Powerscourt thought he could do considerable damage to the young ladies.

'Perhaps I should tell you a little about myself, Lord Powerscourt, to reassure you that the young can be as good at interpreting as the middle-aged. My parents – well, I suppose you'd have to call them aristocrats –live in an enormous palace or indeed palaces in St Petersburg. My father has branched out into banking and other sorts of financial business. I have been working in his offices here in London to learn all about it. I lived the first sixteen years of my life in St Petersburg and then I was sent to school in England and then to Oxford, to Trinity College, if you know it. So you see, Lord Powerscourt, I know both societies. I have done quite a lot of translating for my father. I think it must have been he, or your Ambassador in Russia, who recommended me for this kind of work. I have often done it before. I rather enjoy it.'

'I'm delighted to hear you know St Petersburg,' said Powerscourt. 'I'm sure that will be a great advantage in our mission.'

'Can you tell me something about that?' said the young man doubtfully. 'All I learned from the Foreign Office was that it was very secret and I had to set out for the station as fast as possible.'

Very slowly the great train drew out of the station and began its journey towards the hop fields of Kent. A number of friends and relations were left waving disconsolately on the platform. Powerscourt wondered how much he could tell young Shaporov and decided that nothing he knew was a secret worth preserving. So he told him everything.

'That's all rather exciting,' said the young man, 'except for the fact that this poor man is dead. And nobody, you say, knows what he was doing in St Petersburg?'

'Only the Prime Minister, as far as I can tell. Have you any idea at all what could bring about such a level of secrecy as far as Russia is concerned?'

'Scandal?' said Mikhail Shaporov happily. 'Blackmail? Secrets of state? Diplomatic treaties that have to be kept hidden for a decade? It'll be very disappointing, Lord Powerscourt, if we just find that he hadn't settled his debts at the casino or was carrying on with another man's wife. Though,' he went on rather sadly, 'if people were killed for adultery in St Petersburg, the population would drop very quickly.' Powerscourt wondered if there was some personal pain hidden behind the sadness.

'The thing is,' the young man went on, 'you did say that this poor dead diplomat was a very important sort of fellow, a top dog in the Foreign Office collection, so the chances are that it has to do with great secrets. I do hope we can find out.'

Shaporov peered out of the window. 'Forgive me, Lord Powerscourt, but your England always seems quite small to me. Some years ago my parents took us all on the Trans-Siberian Railway just after it opened, thousands and thousands of miles of track. I thought it was splendid. My younger brother, mind you, he got claustrophobia after being kept in the train carriages for days and days. He hardly ever goes in a train now if he can help it.'

Powerscourt wondered if the young Mikhail's contacts in St Petersburg might be useful to him. The young man yawned.

'Will you excuse me, Lord Powerscourt? I did not have very much sleep last night and then I had to prepare for our journey. Would you mind if I went next door and had a nap?'

When he had the compartment to himself again, Powerscourt began thinking about Lucy. He had found her, on his return from the London Library, sitting on the chair by the window in Markham Square, looking out very sadly into the weak late afternoon sun. He thought she had been waiting for him. Close up, she looked more miserable still. He thought she had been crying.

'Lucy, my love,' he strode across the room to her, 'whatever is the matter?'

She burst into tears and fell into his arms.

'Don't worry, Lucy. It can't be that important. We still have each other. We still love each other.'

After a couple of minutes she composed herself. She took his hands in hers as she had those years before on the balcony in Positano.

'Francis,' she said, 'I release you from your promise not to take on any more investigations. You are free to go to

54

St Petersburg as far as I am concerned. I hope I have not made you too unhappy in the meantime. It was my first husband, you see, who went away on the nation's business and got killed. I couldn't bear to have it happen again, I really couldn't. But I've got to let you go. I see that now. I hope you don't think I'm some sort of jailer, Francis. Please forgive me for the whole thing.'

Powerscourt kissed the top of her head and held her very tight. 'Might I ask, Lucy, what brought about this change of mind? Have you had a revelation? Has somebody been to talk to you?'

She smiled. 'I had a visit from Mrs Martin, the wife of the dead man in St Petersburg. His parents are still alive. It's driving them all mad, not knowing what happened to Mr Martin, you see. And when the Foreign Office told them they were sending a top investigator to find out the truth, they cheered up, they thought they were going to find out what had been going on. Then they were even more despondent when they learnt the investigator wasn't going. She said it wasn't fair that I could keep you safe at home while he went off to die. She said Britain would have lost every war it ever fought if the wives stopped their men going off to defend the country. She made me feel rather selfish, actually, Francis.'

'Did you tell her you had changed your mind, Lucy?'

'No, I didn't. I hadn't, you see, changed my mind, not then. That came later while I was sitting by the window waiting for you to come home.'

Powerscourt handled his wife very delicately in the two days that followed her change of mind before his departure. He could only guess at how much it must have cost her. He could not imagine how she would worry while he was away. Whatever else he did, he must try to find the answers as quickly as possible. He took her out to her favourite restaurant. He promised to take her to Paris when he returned. Above all, he told himself constantly, he must not crow, he must not boast, he must not sing for joy as he walked about the house. For Lord Francis Powerscourt would never have told his wife. He would and did tell Johnny Fitzgerald. He was so happy to be back in harness, as he put it to himself, with a difficult case and a romantic location. The curious thing about his elation was that Lady Lucy saw it too. After twelve years of marriage she could sense her husband's mood without him having to speak a word. And, although she would not have told her husband this, she was happy because he was happy.

Mikhail Shaporov slept all the way across the Channel. He slept through France. Powerscourt began to wonder if he was going to sleep all the way to Russia when he finally appeared just outside Cologne. They had crossed the Rhine, the first of Europe's great rivers the train would traverse on its long trek across a continent. It began snowing just before Hamburg. The fields and the farmhouses disappeared in a soft carpet, the sharp edges of the buildings in the cities disappeared in a white blanket. Mikhail dragged Powerscourt to an open window, admitting freezing wind and torrents of snow, to see the spray shooting up and curving gracefully backwards as the great dark engine pounded forward through the white snow. They were shedding passengers now faster than the replacements were coming on board. Considerable numbers got off at Hannover. More got off for the architectural glories of Potsdam, more still for the pomp and swagger of Berlin. There were only a few hardy souls left for the long haul to Warsaw and the final route through to the Baltic glories of Riga and Tallinn. At last, after three days' travelling, at half past six in the evening, they arrived in St Petersburg. Mikhail had arranged transport for himself to his palace and for Powerscourt to the British Embassy. They arranged to meet at the Embassy at nine o'clock the following morning. Powerscourt had made a number of appointments by telegraph before leaving London.

'Leave your bags here, the porter will take them up.' The voice was languid but powerful, its owner a beautifully dressed diplomat of some thirty-five years called Rupert de Chassiron, Chief Secretary to the Embassy. He radiated an effortless charm. From time to time a hand would be despatched on an upward mission to check the status of his hair, which was beginning to let him down by going thin on top. De Chassiron sported a very expensive-looking monocle which gave him, as intended, an air of great distinction. 'His Nibs, that's the Ambassador to you and me, is off at some charity function with that frightful wife of his. I'm to take you to the feeding station.'

Powerscourt resisted the temptation to ask for further details of the frightful wife. He remembered from his time in South Africa that embassies could become very claustrophobic, always prone to feud and faction. They were walking past the Alexander Monument, surrounded by the great buildings of the Admiralty and the Hermitage and the Winter Palace, powerful and menacing in the dark.

'Been here before, Powerscourt? Seen all the stuff?'

'I came here some years ago with my wife. We saw quite a lot of stuff then.' So much stuff, he remembered suddenly, that after four days Lucy could hardly walk and had to spend the next day being ferried round the city in a water taxi.

'Here we are,' said the diplomat, 'they know me here. Booked a private room. Don't have to eat the Russian food if you don't want to. Place is called Nadezhda. Means hope. Always needed in these parts, hope, in as large a helping as you can lay your hands on.'

A nervous young Tatar waiter showed them to their room. There were no windows and the most remarkable feature was the wallpaper. It was dark red with patterns that Powerscourt could only refer to mentally as vigorous. If you were feeling kind you would have said there were loops and twirls and hoops and arches and circles of every size imaginable. If you were feeling unkind you would have said the designer was a madman. If you were visually sensitive you might well have felt sick. Powerscourt felt he knew now why this was one of the private rooms.

'Tatar pattern, Powerscourt,' said de Chassiron cheerfully. 'Local traditions not confused down there with six hundred years of design history from Renaissance buildings to Aubusson tapestries. You want a twirl, you give it a twirl. Not exactly restful, would you say?' he remarked as a waiter brought him some wine to taste.

'Excellent, he said, 'the local rich are very partial to French wine, thank God. This Chablis is first rate.'

As they started on their first course, blinis, Russian pancakes, with caviar, de Chassiron began to talk about Martin.

'Let me tell you, Powerscourt,' the diplomat paused briefly to swallow a particularly large mouthful, 'all I know about Martin. Won't take long.' He took a copious draught of his wine. 'Came here on a Tuesday. Wouldn't tell a soul what he was here for, why he had come, what he hoped to achieve. Wouldn't tell the Ambassador anything, much to His Nibs' fury. Went off somewhere, God knows where, didn't tell a soul where he was going, on Wednesday morning. Next seen dead early on

Thursday morning as you know. Not clear if he died Wednesday night or Thursday morning. Not clear if he died where he was found or somewhere else. That's it. The last unknown hours of Roderick Martin.'

Powerscourt helped himself to a few more blinis. 'They're really very good, these blinis,' he said. 'I can tell you one thing, you know one more fact than I do. Apart from the bit with the Ambassador, that's all I know too. I don't know any more than you do. All attempts to get the Prime Minister to talk have failed.'

De Chassiron wiped his mouth carefully. Powerscourt thought he might be rather vain about his appearance. As his wild boar and the diplomat's fish arrived, Powerscourt asked for a diplomatic overview of where Russia now stood, its main political and foreign attitudes that might, somewhere, contain a clue to the life and death of senior British diplomat Roderick Martin.

De Chassiron smiled. 'Be happy to oblige, Powerscourt, nothing diplomats like doing better than spinning their private theories about history and current trends. But where to start? I tell you where I'll start. St Petersburg is a very deceitful place. You look at these incredible buildings all about the centre of the city designed by Quarenghi and Rastrelli and these European architects in their sort of heavy international baroque, and you think you're in Europe, in another Milan or Rome or Munich. It's deceptive in exactly the same way that America is deceptive, except that in New York or Washington it's the common language that makes you think you share a common culture and common values. You don't. Here it's the architecture that makes you think you're just in another part of Europe. For the Doge's Palace in Venice read the Winter Palace. For the Uffizi in Florence read the Hermitage. It's not true. Even here, in a city designed to turn his fellow countrymen into good Europeans, Peter the Great never quite succeeded. And if they're not truly European in this place, think of the rest of the Russians, most of whom are peasants who have never even seen a city and wouldn't know a baroque one from a city built, or more likely destroyed, by Genghis Khan.'

Powerscourt's mind wandered off briefly to contemplate a city built or razed to the ground by Genghis Khan. Birmingham, he decided, maybe Wolverhampton.

'There's another thing about these buildings, Powerscourt.' De Chassiron paused to spear a large mouthful of his fish. 'I don't know what a democratic building would look like, maybe it would have to look classical like that damned Congress in Washington, but these buildings here, they're autocratic, they're to be lived in by one lot of autocrats and handed over to another lot of autocrats. Those great palaces outside the city, Peterhof and Gatchina and Tsarskoe Selo, they've all got a shadow over them and the shadow is that of Versailles and the Sun King. These Romanovs are the last serious autocrats in Europe, if not the world. Our King has the powers of a lowly parish clerk, heavily watched by a suspicious parish council, compared to them. And consider this.' He held up the passage of a particularly large slice of his fish and waved his fork at Powerscourt. 'What sort of representative bodies, councils, assemblies, parliaments do you think the Tsar has to help him in his work of administering this vast empire? Two? Three? House of Commons? House of Lords? Not one, not even a House of Lords. I've always suspected that Kings of England were very happy to have all their aristocrats penned up in a House of Lords. They could plot against each other rather than plot against the King. Very satis- factory all round. But here, these aristocrats may not be fully European but they know the political power exercised by their counterparts elsewhere. If you were an English lord or a duke, your power might not be as ostentatious as it once was but it's still pretty real and there's probably more of it than people imagine. If you're a Prussian Junker you have enormous power. Here you have nothing, whether you're a peasant, a worker or an aristocrat.'

'So what do the people who would be in the Lords or Commons, or the Congress in Washington, do here? Where do their political energies go?'

'That's a very good question, Powerscourt. I wish I knew the answer.' De Chassiron screwed his monocle in for another brief inspection of the wine list. 'Some of them campaign for reform and so on. Some may even join one or two of the more extreme left wing sects that spring up all the time. They gamble. Quite often they gamble huge fortunes away. They fornicate with other people's wives. Then they fornicate with yet other people's wives. There's a great deal of that going on. The wives must get worn out. The cynics say that Tolstoy wasn't writing fiction when he described the affair between Anna Karenina and Count Vronsky. Some of them drink. That's usually in addition to, rather than a replacement for, the fornication with the wives of others and the reckless gambling. Sometimes they retire to their estates in the country. Lots of these people own properties the size of a small English county, for Christ's sake. Not many last out though in the rural idyll. Prolonged exposure to the theft and violence of the peasantry sends them back to the cities. There's a story, probably apocryphal, about one aristocrat who retired to the country to read all of Dostoevsky and improve his soul. After three novels he blew his brains out. People said it was Petersburg's Raskolnikov in *Crime and Punishment* who pushed him over the edge.'

Powerscourt found it hard to see how any of these varied activities could lead to the death of an English diplomat. 'What about the violence?' he said. 'What about all these assassination attempts? Could they have anything to do with Martin's death?'

'The French Ambassador, Powerscourt, the wisest foreigner in the city, says this is a society at war with itself. There could easily, in his view, be a civil war or a revolution here. Nothing is stable. The Tsar is both symbol and cause of so many problems. Symbol because he stands for nearly three hundred years of autocratic rule, and the autocratic principle will not permit him to share power with any council or elected assembly. He is a terrible administrator but if any minister he appoints manages to do the job properly he is fired because he puts the Tsar in a bad light. Then you get more toadies and the trouble starts all over again. He and his family are more or less prisoners in that palace of theirs out in the country. The security people won't let them go anywhere else in case they're blown up. In Tsarskoe Selo, at least, they're safe because they're guarded by thousands of soldiers and police twenty-four hours a day. It's gilded, their cage, it's very gilded, but it's still a cage.'

A surly-looking waiter had removed their plates. De Chassiron had ordered another bottle of Chablis and was contemplating the menu. 'I can recommend the cranberry mousse, Powerscourt,' he said finally, placing the order before his guest had a chance to reply.

'Then there's this bloody war,' he continued, staring intently at the demented wallpaper. 'They're going to lose it and there'll be the most enormous fuss. Imagine Mother Russia being defeated by the Japanese, little better than savages in the view of most of Russian society, small inferior yellow savages at that. It'll be a terrible blow to the imperial prestige when they lose to the little yellow chaps with their ridiculous moustaches. They say the Tsar was one of the most eager campaigners for war.'

'Do you think that could have had anything to do with Martin's mission?' asked Powerscourt, rather enjoying his crash course in Russian politics. 'Could they have been asking for help with the war? A naval alliance or something like that?'

'It's possible,' said de Chassiron, 'but why all the bloody secrecy? It's not as if His Nibs is going to take a sled down the Nevskii Prospekt and shout the news aloud to all comers. I wonder, I haven't told anybody else this, and it's only a theory, but I wonder if it didn't have to do with security. Once the Okhrana are involved everything gets much more complicated and much more secretive than it need be.'

'The Okhrana are the secret police?' Powerscourt was hesitant.

'Indeed,' said de Chassiron, settling the bill. 'They've almost certainly noted your arrival and will check your movements all the time you are here. They are the most suspicious, the most paranoid organization in the world. And they will, almost certainly, follow us all the way back to the Embassy.'

Next day Mikhail Shaporov presented himself at a quarter to nine in the morning at the British Embassy. He was wearing a grey suit with a pale blue shirt and looked as though he might have been a young lawyer dressing in a conservative fashion to avoid prejudicing the judge by his tender years.

Powerscourt waved a piece of paper at him. 'I'm told this is a report from the Nevskii police station informing the Ambassador that they have found a British national in their possession. I should say a dead British national.'

Mikhail read it quickly. 'That is correct, Lord Powerscourt. And we have an appointment to see the policeman who wrote it at nine fifteen? Come, it is not far. I presume that nobody has succeeded in extracting the body from this police station? Indeed, it is probably no longer there. It may be in one of the morgues. I have the addresses of the two most likely in these parts.'

'That was very intelligent of you, Mikhail,' said Powerscourt. 'I am impressed.'

'I'm afraid it's not me you have to thank for it, Lord Powerscourt,' said Mikhail with a smile, 'it's my father. He's lived here almost all of his life. He may have bribed many policemen in his time, I do not know.'

The police station was a nondescript three-storey building behind the Fontanka Canal. A collection of drunks, sleeping, comatose or dead, were sprawled across the hallway inside the front door. Their beards were long and unkempt, their hair was matted, their clothes were filthy. A powerful smell of dirt and damp and human waste rose strongly from them. Powerscourt noticed that the young man paid them absolutely no attention. This was the background of his life, a sight he had seen so often he hardly noticed it. Perhaps it was the background to the lives of all the citizens of this city, lost souls given up to vodka to escape the pain of their daily lives, drink-sodden refugees from the tensions of everyday existence in St Petersburg who sprawled across the floors of its police stations until they were granted the temporary consolation of a cell.

Powerscourt saw that Mikhail had opened a conversation with the fat policeman behind the desk.

'He's new here,' he said to Powerscourt, 'he's gone to make inquiries. That could mean a couple of minutes or a couple of days. They don't care how they treat people at all, the local police. Not like in London.'

Just then a door at the far end of the hall opened and two burly policemen emerged. They began dragging the drunks through the doorway into some unknown territory behind.

'Cells?' said Powerscourt.

'Maybe,' said Mikhail, 'maybe they're just throwing them back on to the streets now it's daylight. This lot may have been brought in during the night to stop them freezing to death. Even here they don't like corpses lying about in the streets first thing in the morning. Doesn't look too good in the shadow of the Winter Palace if winter's victims are stretched out in front of it, dead from the winter cold. Bad for business. Might upset a passing Grand Duchess.'

The fat policeman had returned. Once more Mikhail engaged him in conversation. After a couple of minutes he gestured to Powerscourt. 'I'm getting nowhere, Lord Powerscourt. I think you need to let him have it. Sent by Foreign Secretary and Prime Minister, all that sort of stuff, big guns, heavy artillery.'

'I am afraid, Constable,' Powerscourt began, 'that I find your position very unsatisfactory.' He heard Mikhail's translation coming out just behind his own. 'I am here as a representative of the British Foreign Office and the British Prime Minister. I wish to speak to the police inspector named here,' Mikhail waved the document at the police-man as he spoke, 'who reported the death of a British diplomat to the British Ambassador some days ago. It is imperative that I speak to him.'

Mikhail translated, his emphases more vigorous in Russian than Powerscourt's had been in English. Powerscourt wondered if the man knew where Great Britain was. Did he know where Kazakhstan was? Or Georgia?

There was another burst of Russian. 'We have no knowledge of this inspector here,' said Mikhail. 'My superiors instruct me to tell you that this must be a mistake.'

'No,' said Powerscourt, 'it is you who are mistaken. This inspector made a report to the British Embassy itself. We are not mistaken. I demand to see the senior policeman here.'

Powerscourt noticed that the gap between his words in English and Mikhail's in Russian was getting shorter. Maybe when he's back in practice he really will be simultaneous, he thought. Powerscourt regarded this as a truly wondrous feat, akin to those of people who could unlock the hidden theorems of mathematics.

Very reluctantly the fat policeman retired to the inner quarters in search of a senior officer. Mikhail was looking at the paper once more. 'It couldn't be clearer, Lord Powerscourt. The inspector is reporting the police discovery of the dead Martin at one thirty in the morning of Thursday December the 23rd. It's as clear as a bell.'

Suddenly Powerscourt had a terrible thought. They hadn't dumped Martin in the hall along with the drunks, had they? Left him there for hours until rigor mortis had set in? That was not a comforting thought to take back to London and the home of the widow Martin and the parents Martin. They might never sleep again.

There was a shout from the desk. The fat policeman had been replaced by an even fatter one with a red beard and a disagreeable air of menace about him.

'Stuff and nonsense,' Mikhail began translating. 'How dare you come in here and waste police time. There is no officer here of that name. There never has been. Forging official documents is a serious offence in our country. The penalties can be up to ten years' imprisonment. Now, I suggest you get out of here and don't come back.'

With that he banged his fist on the table and pointed to the door. Powerscourt was not very impressed.

'Thank you for your suggestions, Inspector. We have an appointment with the Interior Ministry. We shall certainly raise with them our treatment at your hands. We also have an appointment at the Foreign Ministry where the displeasure and dismay of my government will be conveyed in the strongest possible terms. All we wish at this juncture is the chance to speak with your inspector who wrote this report, complete with your very own stamp on it.' With that, in a sudden burst of inspiration, Powerscourt picked up the stamp on the desk, moistened it in the pad beside it and made another mark on the other side of their document. It was identical to the mark already there.

'See?' Powerscourt went on. 'This stamp is the same as the one already on the report. Surely even you can see that proves it is genuine.'

The signs were pretty bad. 'May have to beat the retreat rather sharpish, Lord Powerscourt,' Mikhail was whispering, pulling Powerscourt back from the desk. 'This character is going to lose his temper, he's going to go up like Krakatoa.'

Mikhail told Powerscourt afterwards that he thought the inspector was going to have a heart attack. The veins in his neck stood out. His face grew redder and redder. His breathing became very heavy.

'Just get this into your heads,' he shouted. 'There is no policeman here of that name. There is no policeman in St Petersburg of that name. There was no body of an Englishman found on the Nevskii Prospekt. I do not know who has been feeding you with forgeries. I suggest you take them home. And now, get out of my police station before I lock you in the cells and throw away the key.' With that he left his desk and began advancing towards them with his great fist raised.

'It's all right, Inspector, we were just leaving.' Mikhail was translating as fast as he was walking backwards. 'Don't trouble yourself with us any more. Perhaps you need to sit down. Have a little rest. A glass of water might be helpful. Maybe you ought to see your doctor. You know you mustn't overdo it.'

Mikhail shouted his version of the last two sentences through the door as they hurried into the street. 'Well, Lord Powerscourt,' he said, 'here's a pretty pickle and me on my first morning in the job. Before we had the details of a dead man but no body. Now we don't even have the details of the corpse if we believe the red-faced policeman. What do you think we should do?'

'I know precisely what we should do,' said Powerscourt, patting the young man affectionately on the shoulder. 'Take me to your morgues.'

The road was narrow, skirting a canal. On the far side a factory was pouring great streams of smoke into the air. Young men hurried past them carrying great bundles of wood in their arms. There was a faint smell of bread baking far away.

'Do you have a lot of money on you, Lord Powerscourt?' Mikhail Shaporov sounded faintly embarrassed at having to mention money.

'I do, Mikhail,' he said cheerfully. 'Rupert de Chassiron gave me a great deal at the Embassy. I assume you are going to pay out one or two bribes.'

'I am,' the young man laughed. 'Tell me, Lord Powerscourt, you are an experienced investigator and I am a mere novice translator, do you think we will find Mr Martin's body?'

'I would be very surprised if we do,' said Powerscourt sadly. 'We have to check these morgues, of course we do, but I should be amazed if we find him there. It's interesting that we don't know how he died. Shot? Stabbed? Strangled? Maybe the truth would be too compromising, so they conceal it from us. If Martin has been murdered his killers could cut a hole in the ice and drop him down it. He might never turn up anywhere at all, just be lost at sea. If the corpse did appear on the coast of Finland or down near Riga it would be unrecognizable by then. I think he, or somebody described as him, was brought into the police station and our form filled in. That was just to tell us he was dead. Now we are meant to have got the message and keep quiet. We can't make much of a fuss after all if we don't have a body.'

Mikhail Shaporov was bringing them through a side gate into the gardens of a large, rather ugly building with lines of people waiting outside. 'This is the hospital, St Simon's. The morgue is down there at the bottom of the garden. I'm going to bribe one of the porters to get the key. Do you want to come with me or will you wait here?'

'I think I'll wait here,' Powerscourt replied. 'A stranger from Europe might put the prices up.' As he idled along the path another thought struck him about Martin, the note and the police station. Martin might never have been to the police station at all. Maybe the police inspector really didn't exist. Maybe the note handed in to the Embassy actually was a forgery, the stamp stolen from the police station, or even put on the paper by one of the police who had been ordered to kill him. So the red-headed policeman could have been right after all.

Mikhail Shaporov was waving cheerfully at him with a large rusty key in his hand. 'God knows what this is going to be like,' he said. 'My education up till now hasn't run to morgues or mortuaries. I told the porters that an old college friend had gone missing after a drinking session and might have got killed or frozen to death.'

There was a harsh squeak as the key turned in the lock. Shaporov put his hand on the right-hand wall and turned on a feeble light. 'They don't bother with refrigeration in the winter,' he whispered, 'they let nature work for them.'

The dead of St Petersburg were piled up in rows and rows that looked like bookcases with very wide shelves, seven or eight storeys high. Some had been placed in crude hospital shrouds by the nurses. Some, dead on arrival, Powerscourt presumed, had been left in the rags they had on as they passed away. One or two had obviously been wounded, strangely coloured gashes running down their faces. They were a terrifying collection, Powerscourt thought. If they were among the first to rise from the dead on the last day the rest of the citizens would quake in terror as these zombies from the morgue marched out from their wooden resting place. There was an unpleasant smell, of things or people going bad. Mikhail Shaporov was working his way methodically round the room, sometimes checking on the labels attached to each person. He ignored the women and the old and the very young altogether. Powerscourt heard him muttering to himself as he carried out this last inspection of these dead souls.

'No joy here,' he said finally. 'It's possible they brought him here to die but they certainly didn't leave him in the bloody morgue.'

The second morgue could not have been more different. It was attached to a modern hospital near St Petersburg University on Vasilevsky Island opposite Senate Square and the Admiralty.

'The only reason we're here is that it is further away than the other place from where we think he was found, but anybody who knew the city and its facilities would see to it that he ended up here rather than that other hell-hole. This whole hospital was designed by Germans so it's going to be very efficient. It's funny, Lord Powerscourt, one minute we like foreigners to come in and design things for us – the whole of early St Petersburg was designed by foreigners after all – and then another decade on they're not to be allowed in because they're decadent, or don't understand Russia or haven't got any soul.'

There was no need to bribe anyone here. A grave young man took them down and waited while Mikhail Shaporov carried out his melancholy duties once more. Here the dead were not piled so high and they had their own private space, locked away inside large green compartments that looked like a giant's filing cabinet. Name tags were pinned neatly to the handles as if they were the title of a file or a folder. Powerscourt wondered if these dead were happier here or if they might prefer the more tempestuous atmosphere of St Simon's. The young man engaged Powerscourt in conversation in halting French. Powerscourt thought he told him that if the bodies were not claimed for burial inside a couple of months, the hospital buried them in a cemetery inland. Another terrible thought struck Powerscourt, so upsetting that he had to interrupt Mikhail and bring him over to act as translator.

'What would happen to the dead body of a foreigner that was brought in here? Would he be kept long?'

'Possibly, if nobody came to claim him, he could be here for a while,' the young man said.

'And what criteria do the doctors use in picking out the corpses they are going to use for dissecting, for teaching the medical students?'

Mikhail looked perturbed as he translated this.

'You need not fear,' said the young man. 'They only use the people from the poorhouses for this. Foreigners, I think

71

not. The students and the doctors might not trust foreign bodies.'

Even so Powerscourt could not get the thought out of his mind. Bits of Roderick Martin being cut up and examined by a crowd of students. His inner organs, his heart and his liver and his spleen, all taken out like a sixteenth-century disembowelment and prodded and poked by a lot of twenty-year-old Russians. It was a relief when Mikhail came over and shook his head.

'He is not here.' They thanked the grave young man and Mikhail suddenly seized Powerscourt by the arm. 'Do you have any plans for lunch, Lord Powerscourt? You do not? Let me take you to a little place not far from here called Onegin's. It doesn't look very exciting but they serve the best cabbage soup in the city. Onegin's is famous for it.'

Ten minutes later they were seated at a trestle table in what looked like an army refectory. Powerscourt half expected some Russian sergeant major to emerge from the door at the top and issue his orders to the diners. Warriors of every description lined the walls, portraits of fierce-looking little Cossacks next to imperial admirals who stared out at their fleets with haughty disdain. There were veterans of the Napoleonic Wars here, Kutuzov the seasoned general who had fought Napoleon at Borodino the only one Powerscourt recognized. On the wall above the doorway was hung a collection of ancient musketry, some of which looked older than the city itself.

'They say, Lord Powerscourt,' Mikhail Shaporov looked very much at home here, ordering their cabbage soup and black bread with great anticipation, 'that when the next European war comes the army will be so short of weapons that they will impound all that old stuff above the door and cart it off to the battlefields.'

Powerscourt smiled. 'Is there a military academy round here? Does that account for all the portraits and things?'

'Oddly enough,' said Mikhail as two enormous bowls of cabbage soup were put in front of them, 'it's the university students who frequent this place. The prices are low, the food is plentiful – if it's enough for a peasant's main meal of the day it's enough for a philosophy student's lunch. I should leave that soup to cool down for a moment, if I were you. They send it out hot enough to burn your tongue off.'

'You were not tempted, Mikhail, to be a student here, in your own native city?' said Powerscourt blowing desultorily at his bowl.

'My father was very keen that I should go to Oxford, I don't know why,' the young man replied, 'but my elder brother was here. I can't tell you how different it is being a student in England and Oxford, Lord Powerscourt.'

'Really?' said Powerscourt, trying the first exploratory mouthful of his soup.

'It's much more serious here,' Mikhail Shaporov replied, stirring his soup slowly with his spoon. 'It's nearly an occupation in itself. In Oxford the height of fame and fashion is probably to climb to the top of Magdalen Tower or the Sheldonian or drink your college cellars dry. Here the height of fame and fashion would be to blow up a government minister or start a revolution. I don't think undergraduates in England ever take philosophy seriously. Here you find people whose student lives are consumed by it. Some of them become so wrapped up in it that they turn into perpetual students, staying on at the university in their quest for the answer to everything until they are in their thirties.'

Powerscourt was now seriously engrossed in his soup. It was thick, far thicker than any vegetable soup he had ever eaten in London. He thought he detected carrot and potato and garlic and maybe tomato and maybe lemon juice and possibly sour cream, as well as the eponymous cabbage. It was remarkably filling, giving the impression that the consumer was not in a barrack-style restaurant near the university but out in the great expanse of the Russian countryside, flat fields reaching to the distant horizon, an occasional tree providing a modicum of shade, a lone peasant pulling a handcart along a dusty road, a sense of space stretching out till eternity, cabbage soup that tasted of the earth of Mother Russia herself.

'People always think,' said Mikhail Shaporov, 'that they must have a battalion of grannies in the kitchen here, imported from the nearby countryside perhaps, who have inherited this recipe from their grannies and so on, a direct line of grannyhood going back to the foundation of the city itself, hunched over their ancient saucepans, chopping and tasting and stirring and checking their soup all day long.'

'Not so?' said Powerscourt.

'There's only two of them who make it, Lord Powerscourt. They're in their early twenties and learnt the recipe from their mother. They're the proprietor's daughters.'

'A man could do worse than marry a woman for her soup, perhaps. What do you say, Mikhail?'

'Indeed. And there are rumours that these two have been working on a surprise for Easter time. People say they've developed an entirely new borscht.'

'Cabbage soup on Monday, Wednesday and Friday, borscht on Tuesday, Thursday and Saturday. You would live like a king.'

'What I am about to ask you has nothing to do with soup or marriage, Lord Powerscourt, but with our plans today after the interview in the Interior Ministry this afternoon. Do you think you will need my services after that, after I have taken you back to the Embassy, of course? It's just that I have made a provisional arrangement to meet somebody for an hour or so at six o'clock. Don't get me wrong, please. If you need me I'll translate for you all day and all night.'

Powerscourt wondered at the mental process by which his young friend had gone from soup and marriage to discussion of his plans for an evening rendezvous.

'Forgive me for asking you, Mikhail, but would I be right in thinking you are going to meet a young lady?'

'You are quite right, Lord Powerscourt.' Mikhail went slightly pink as he replied. 'It is a young lady and could I make a further suggestion? This has only just come to me, and you may think it absurd.'

'I'm sure I won't think it is absurd, once I know what it is,' said Powerscourt.

'My friend is called Natasha. She comes from a very grand family here in Petersburg. Just now she is working as a lady-in-waiting to the Empress and her daughters at the Tsar's country palace in Tsarskoe Selo. Do you think it might help if I told her about your mission and our work in pursuit of the vanished Martin? I haven't seen or spoken to her since I went to London. Her letters to me were very stilted and stiff as if she felt somebody was reading them, I think. But it has always been said that the best-informed people in St Petersburg are the servants who wait at the Tsar's table and his coachmen and suchlike people. She might hear something to our advantage.'

Powerscourt scraped the bottom of his bowl to extract the very last drop of cabbage soup. 'Let me put it like this, Mikhail. Do you think it would be dangerous for her if she were known to be close to the British Embassy?'

'Dangerous, possibly. I don't think she'd end up dead on the Nevskii Prospekt but I think she'd be out of a job pretty quickly.'

'I think you must decide, Mikhail,' said Powerscourt, looking serious all of a sudden. 'I think it would be unwise to involve Natasha in the decision, however level-headed she is. There's nothing more attractive to some women than a whiff of danger. I think I would insist that she only listens. She never asks any questions. She doesn't poke her nose into areas that don't concern her. Some women, mind you, would find even that limited prospectus hard to stick to.'

'I will think about it before our meeting,' said Mikhail Shaporov, trotting off to pay the bill. 'I insist on paying for lunch, Lord Powerscourt. When we Russians introduce distinguished visitors to our national cuisine, it is only fitting that we should pay. I insist, I really do.'

As they made their way across the river to their next meeting Shaporov told Powerscourt some of what he knew of the Interior Ministry. Most of his information, he said generously, came once again from his father, some of it from his friends who had had dealings with it, some of it simply absorbed from the air and the streets of his city. Mikhail gave his English visitor the Russian bureaucracy in numbers. Eight hundred and sixty-nine, the number of paragraphs in Volume One of the Code of Laws that defined the rules and conduct of the Imperial Civil Service. Fourteen, the number of different Civil Service ranks, each with its own uniform and title. The top two ranks of civil servants were to be addressed as Your High Excellency. Those in ranks three and four to be addressed as Your Excellency. The less fortunate in ranks nine to fourteen had to make do with Your Honour. White trousers changing to black, red ribbons changing to blue, even adding a stripe here and there could mark momentous turning points in the orderly progression of the bureaucrat's life. He could be promoted by one rank every three years from ranks fourteen to eight and one every four years in ranks eight to five. Promotion – and Mikhail

76

emphasized how typical it was, this interface between the autocracy and the bureaucracy that would only make it less likely that either could function effectively – promotion to the last four ranks was at the discretion of the Tsar and carried a hereditary title. With great care not to displease, taking as few decisions as possible in case they gave offence, a man might reach the top of the tree by the age of sixty. This carefully modulated bureaucracy, Mikhail said, was strangling Russia, strangling it in a slow bureaucratic bear hug.

They could see several of these bureaucrats now, coming down the steps of the Interior Ministry building, some of them carrying briefcases.

'They're not going home already, Mikhail, are they? It's just before three o'clock, for God's sake.'

'You don't want to overdo it, if you're a bureaucrat, Lord Powerscourt. It's a very hard life in the Interior Ministry. Some of these fellows may have had to attend a couple of meetings in the morning. Think how exhausting that must have been for them.'

Powerscourt had been inside a number of ministries in London where the splendour was reserved for the quarters of the minister and his most senior officials. The rest had been furnished with due regard to the exigencies of the public purse and the dangers of newspapers launching crusades about governments wasting taxpayers' money on luxurious surroundings for civil servants. But nothing, he thought, could prepare you for the drabness of the interior of the Russian Interior Ministry. The floors were covered in something grey that might once have been the Russian equivalent of linoleum. The walls were painted with a dark colour that looked as if it might have been originally intended for a battleship. A long hopeless corridor stretched out for a couple of hundred yards behind the reception desk, manned by a small man with only one arm.

'Mr Bazhenov, Room 467, fourth floor. Lift over there. Enter your names in this book before you go up.'

Every public building you went into in St Petersburg, Powerscourt was to discover, took down your name and address as if they proposed to establish a regular correspondence. He wondered briefly about instituting a similar system in Markham Square.

The lift was gloomy and stank of sweat and urine. Mikhail Shaporov pressed the bell for the fourth floor.

'Do you think the more important chaps live higher up, Mikhail?' said Powerscourt. 'Only ranks eight and above allowed on floor three?'

'God knows,' said Mikhail, sounding more cheerful than the surroundings warranted. 'Do you know, Lord Powerscourt, I have lived in this city most of my life and this is the first time I have ever been inside a government building. It's a revelation.'

It seemed that Room 467 must be at the outermost limit of the fourth-floor corridor where the room numbers started illogically at 379 opposite the lift. Clerks carrying files sauntered past them on their way to unknown bureaucratic destinations. Their feet sounded loud on the grey floor covering that might once have been linoleum. One or two doors were open and Powerscourt and Mikhail had brief visions of rooms filled with desks like classrooms for the grown-up and sad-faced men seated at them reading files or making entries in great ledgers. Through the dirty windows on their right they could see a small courtyard below where figures seemed to march round and round as if on some everlasting ministerial treadmill. They passed a conference room with a fine table and velvet-covered chairs round it, waiting for another meeting. Powerscourt thought he saw a thick layer of dust on the mahogany surface as if the last meeting had taken place some time ago, the committee dissolved perhaps, the junior minister moved on. Maybe only ghosts had their being in there now, coming out only at night – God, what must this building be like in the dark – taking ghostly notes of ghostly meetings and recording them in ghostly files.

Now they had reached Room 467. The name plate announced the presence of Vasily Bazhenov, Third Assistant Deputy Under Secretary, Administrative Division, Ministry of the Interior. Powerscourt wondered what pain and humiliation had to be gone through to win these undistinguished spurs. He noted that the name plate looked very old as if Bazhenov had been in post for many years. Perhaps promotion had passed him by. Perhaps the jump from Third Assistant Deputy Under Secretary to Second Assistant Deputy Under Secretary was too much for him. Perhaps Vasily Bazhenov would be old and crabbed and waiting for retirement.

But the voice that answered Shaporov's knock and bade them enter was cheerful. So was the bureaucrat. He spoke quite slowly as if to give Mikhail plenty of time to translate. Powerscourt and his friend were seated on one side of a circular table in chairs that did not have velvet upholstery but were perfectly respectable nonetheless. Bazhenov had a number of files in front of him. He was about forty years of age with a wild shock of black hair that looked as if it repelled all attempts to control it. His eyes were grey, his nose small and his long black beard seemed to be acting in sympathy with his hair. Powerscourt wondered if he had a wife who wrestled with his appearance before she despatched him every morning on his bureaucratic Via Dolorosa. The man could have been taken for some wild Siberian preacher rather than a Third Assistant Deputy Under Secretary in the Administrative Division.

'You are interested in a Roderick Martin, I believe,' he said to Powerscourt.

'That is correct, Mr Under Secretary,' said Powerscourt, remembering Rosebery's advice to promote all army officers, civil servants and policemen. 'We were given to understand that you might have some details about him here.'

Bazhenov sighed deeply. 'In one sense, I have to disappoint you, Lord Powerscourt. I – we – cannot help you with this Martin. Under normal circumstances, there would be all kinds of information about such a man. The time and date of his arrival and departure. The record of where he was staying. If he was an important person holding important meetings with important government officials, there would be a record, as there will be of this meeting.'

The Third Assistant Deputy Under Secretary smiled. There had been almost a note of irony, Powerscourt thought, of mocking as the bureaucrat detailed his lists of information, though it was hard to tell in another language. Information, after all, was the currency he dealt in, wrested from the reluctant population to be stored in the unforgiving files of the Interior Ministry.

Bazhenov opened his hands wide. 'But we have no records for the year 1905. No place of entry. No place of residence. I wish I could help you, gentlemen, but I cannot.'

The man's lying, Powerscourt thought to himself. Surely he knows Martin came here and was killed here last December. He remembered the fat inspector with the red beard shouting at them in the police station where his investigations in St Petersburg had begun. Perhaps they're all liars. But he could see little point in an argument. Better to hear what the man might have to say.

80

'You are being as helpful as anybody could be, Mr Under Secretary,' said Powerscourt at his most emollient, 'but I would ask you to consider things from my government's perspective. Mr Martin, a distinguished member of his ministry in London as you are of yours here in St Petersburg,' Bazhenov half rose to his feet and bowed to Powerscourt at this point, 'comes here last December and holds, we believe, a series of meetings, possibly with the Foreign Ministry, we are not sure. On the evening of the same day he is murdered. The death is reported by a policeman in the police station nearest to the British Embassy. It is even committed to paper.' That, Powerscourt felt, should have maximum appeal to the bureaucrat. The spoken word, it was nothing, worthless as air. Pieces of paper, records, minutes, memoranda, these were his life's blood. 'Now the police deny all knowledge. They say the piece of paper must be a forgery.' Truly, Powerscourt said to himself, forgery would be the sin against the Holy Ghost of bureaucratic machines everywhere. It could cast doubt on everything it touched. It, or the suspicion of it, could spread through the files like the Black Death. 'They say Mr Martin cannot have come to St Petersburg. But he left London on a special mission to the Russian capital. He has not returned. We have no reason to believe he is alive. We believe he is dead. You gentlemen say he never came here at all. Who or what are we to believe?'

Then Bazhenov produced one of the classic bureaucratic ploys, a Sicilian defence amidst the paperwork. 'I wish I could help you, Lord Powerscourt. Leave it with me for a day or two. Perhaps some information has been mislaid. Perhaps one of the other organizations of the state will be able to help.'

Powerscourt was to learn later that other organizations of the state meant the secret police, the Okhrana, or other

81

even shadowier organizations devoted to the safety of state and Tsar. 'That is most kind of you, Mr Under Secretary. We are very grateful. Permit me to ask one question before we take our leave. You said at the beginning that you had no information concerning Mr Martin for the year 1905. That implied, maybe I misunderstood you, that you might have information about other months.'

Bazhenov laughed and slapped an ample thigh. 'I said to my second assistant this morning, Lord Powerscourt, that they are clever people, these English. They will surely ask the right question to unlock this information.' Powerscourt wondered how many assistants the man had. Three? Five? Seven? Perhaps he could ask the next time they came. 'No information for the year 1905 is indeed what I said. But consider our Mr Roderick Martin or, perhaps, your Mr Roderick Martin. He lives at a place called Tibenham Grange in Kent in your England. He is married. He works for your Foreign Office. Is this Mr Martin also your Mr Martin?'

'He is,' said Powerscourt sensing suddenly that some bombshell was about to arrive that would blow his investigation wide open.

'Why, then, we have only one Mr Martin between the two of us, not a multiplicity of them, not a flock or a gaggle or a parliament of Martins. We do not believe he came here in 1905, but we know he came on three other occasions in 1904, three times in 1903 and twice in 1902. We could find out if he came also in previous years by the time of our next meeting. You could say, Lord Powerscourt, that Mr Roderick Martin of His Majesty's Foreign Office was a regular visitor to our city.'

3

Lord Francis Powerscourt was trying as hard as he could not to show his astonishment. The knowledge that Roderick Martin had been a regular visitor to St Petersburg could change everything in his investigation. He noticed that Mikhail Shaporov looked completely unconcerned as if he'd known this information all along.

'That is most interesting, Mr Under Secretary,' he began. 'Might I ask if you have the dates of these visits to hand? The place or places where he stayed? The length of his visit? My government would be at your service, sir, if this information could be passed on.'

'It can be, Lord Powerscourt. It shall be. Let no one say that the servants of the Tsar are unwilling to co-operate with the King of England and the Emperor of India.' Vasily Bazhenov was expansive now, his black hair rolling down his forehead. 'It should be fairly easy to extract the information you require. I propose, gentlemen, that we meet again at the same time early next week. I shall send word to the Embassy. I hope by then to have all the information you need. I shall spend the intervening hours working for the Government of His Majesty King Edward the Seventh. A very good day to you, gentlemen.'

Powerscourt and Mikhail Shaporov did not speak on their long march down the bureaucratic corridor from Room 467. They did not speak in the foul-smelling lift. They acknowledged the greeting of the man with one arm who noted the time of their departure. Only when they were outside the grip of the Interior Ministry, walking beside the Fontanka Canal on their way back to the British Embassy, did Mikhail Shaporov break the silence.

'That's a bit of a bombshell, isn't it, Lord Powerscourt. Have you any idea what it means?'

Powerscourt laughed. 'At this moment, I have absolutely no idea.' It was now, Mikhail told Natasha afterwards, that he first realized what a lot of experience Powerscourt had, and what a devious mind. 'It could mean that he had a mistress in the city. It could mean that he had an illegitimate child or children here in St Petersburg that he came to visit. He didn't have any back in England after all. Maybe he was being blackmailed by a St Petersburg blackmailer and he had to come and hand over the payments in person. Maybe he was a secret diplomatic conduit between the British Government and the Tsar. Maybe he was a double agent of the Okhrana, come to Mother Russia for the confession of sins and the resumption of vows of fidelity to an alien power. Maybe he was all of those, though I have to say I think that's unlikely. But I tell you this, Mikhail. Whichever one of those he was, or some other kind of person, we're bloody well going to find out.'

Mikhail Shaporov and Natasha Bobrinsky were sitting in the Old Library in one of the Shaporov palaces on Millionnaya Ulitsa, Millionaires' Row, not far from the Hermitage and the Winter Palace. They had exchanged chaste, rather middle-aged kisses at the railway station and were now respectably seated on opposite sides of a small table, drinking tea. Natasha thought Mikhail looked very grown up and sophisticated after his time in London. He thought she was more enchanting than ever.

'What brings you back to St Petersburg so soon?' she began. 'I was very pleased to get your note, Mikhail, but I didn't expect to see you for months. How long are you going to be here for?'

The young man smiled. 'I don't know how long I'm going to be here for. It's rather a fantastic story, how I came to be here.'

'Do tell.' The girl was leaning closer to him. 'I adore fantastic stories.'

'I'm here as an interpreter for an English investigator called Lord Francis Powerscourt who has been sent by the British Foreign Office to find out about a man called Martin.'

'Why,' said Natasha quickly, 'do they need to send the two of you all the way here from London? Why don't they just ask Mr Martin what they want to know?'

'That would be a bit difficult, Natasha.' Mikhail was resisting the temptation to smile. 'You see, Mr Martin can't say anything very much any more. Mr Martin is dead. To be more precise, Mr Martin was murdered. They found his body on the Nevskii Prospekt.'

'Did they indeed?' said the girl, reluctant to display too much excitement in the face of death. 'But why you, Mikhail? How did you come to be selected? Have you made a habit of consorting with Sherlock Holmes and his friend Dr Watson in the fogs of Baker Street?'

'Alas, no,' said the young man, 'the answer is much more prosaic. My father has some dealings with this British Foreign Office. It was all organized through him. No doubt he will expect some favour in return some day.

Maybe they thought he might be able to help here. Come to think of it, that would have been rather clever of them.'

'And how is your translating, Mikhail? Do you go round talking to very important and exciting people?'

'I wouldn't quite put it like that,' he replied. 'So far we've been to a police station, a couple of morgues, a little restaurant that served cabbage soup – he liked that, by the way, my Lord Powerscourt, he said it reminded him of Ireland – and a Third Assistant Deputy Under Secretary in the Administrative Division of the Interior Ministry. That was so exciting we're going back again early next week.'

'And what's he like, this Lord Powerscourt? Is he frightfully handsome and clever? Would he be a suitable catch for me, Mikhail?'

'I think you need a younger man than Lord Powerscourt, Natasha,' said Mikhail in his most worldly voice. 'Young but with considerable experience of the world, lived abroad, well read, well spoken, that sort of thing. I could say more about him but I'll save it for later if I may. Lord Powerscourt is in his forties, married with four children, lives in Chelsea, a fashionable part of London and has exquisite manners. Beneath it all I think he cares very much for the poor dead Mr Martin and the bereaved Mrs Martin. And one last thing, he's extremely clever, though he doesn't show it. I only realized that earlier this afternoon.'

Mikhail remembered his conversation with Powerscourt and telling Natasha about Martin and asking her to keep her ears open.

'So does anybody know yet why this poor man was killed?' Natasha was rather thrilled that her young man – well, he was nearly her young man, a couple of kisses at railway stations were only an inadequate hors d'oeuvre in her view – should be engaged on such a mission.

'That's just the point, Natasha,' said Mikhail Shaporov, wondering what word would best describe her dark eyes, now glittering with excitement. 'At first the police told the British Embassy he was dead. Now they're denying all knowledge of him. They're saying he wasn't here this time, but that he came here earlier last year and the year before and the year before that. It's all very confusing.'

'How very difficult for everybody,' said Natasha, frowning slightly. 'And what was he meant to be doing here, the late Mr Martin who isn't in the morgues or the Interior Ministry?'

'That's another secret. Only the British Prime Minister knows the nature of his mission to St Petersburg. The Secretary at the British Embassy, the man who knows where all the bodies are buried according to Lord Powerscourt, he doesn't know. The British Ambassador has no idea. Neither Lord Powerscourt nor I know either. We're all in the dark.'

'It's all very exciting,' said Natasha. 'I wish I could do something to help.'

Mikhail rose suddenly from his chair and walked rapidly up and down the room. Ancient leather-bound volumes marched along the walls in order of date of publication and country of origin and watched his passing. The Old Library in this Shaporov palace was filled with European history and literature in the languages the books were written in. The New Library was for Russian works. Mikhail had reached Dante in a particularly elegant binding from a Venetian publishing house when he turned to face Natasha once more.

'Don't go walking up and down like that, Mikhail,' she pleaded. 'It makes me think you don't care for me. I much preferred it when you were on the other side of this table.'

The young man laughed. 'Sorry about that, Natasha,' he said, returning to his seat. 'I was just wondering if I ought to tell you something or not.'

'What sort of something?' she said, her eyes bright with the fun of it all. 'Are you teasing me?'

'No, I'm not teasing you,' he said. 'It really is quite serious. Lord Powerscourt and I think there is a chance, only a slight chance, that Mr Martin's mission may be connected to the Tsar in some way. Something to do with foreign policy in some form or other. The Tsar's meant to be in charge of all that sort of thing.'

'But something so secret that even the British Ambassador doesn't know about it?'

'Something so secret even the British Foreign Secretary doesn't know about it, Natasha.'

'But where do I come into it?' said the girl. 'You said you were wondering whether to tell me something or not. What is the something, Mikhail?'

'It's this. We want you to help us. We want you to listen very carefully to any conversations involving politics and see if Mr Martin's name comes up. But don't for heaven's sake ask any questions of anybody. If you do you may end up underneath the ice on the Neva. Just listen.'

Natasha was struck dumb. Twice she opened her mouth to speak but no words came forth. 'That is the most exciting and most grown-up thing anybody has ever asked me to do,' she said finally. 'Do you want me to go back straight away and start listening?'

'No, no,' said Mikhail Shaporov, 'you've only just left the bloody palace and you don't have to be back for another hour and a half. Anyway, it's your turn to talk now, Natasha. I want to know what life is like at Tsarskoe Selo. Are they going to make you a Grand Duchess soon?'

'I tell you what the best thing about joining your boys' club of secret agents and investigators is,' she said, 'for those of us locked up at Tsarskoe Selo at any rate. It'll be a little something to alleviate the boredom of the days.'

'It can't be boring, surely. We're talking about the Tsar of All the Russias here, for heaven's sake. He must be one of the most powerful men on earth. I fail to see how it can be tedious.'

'You wouldn't say the Tsar was one of the most powerful men on earth if you saw him up close. You'd think he might be the stationmaster or somebody of middling importance in the bank. He doesn't look very impressive.'

'I don't understand, Natasha – what makes it so boring?'

'That's easy to see when you first arrive and then gradually you are sucked into it. It's like living in a museum where the waxworks are actually alive. It's the court ceremonial that does it. There's this very old Finn called Count something or other and he can remember all the approved ways of doing things going back to Peter the Great. Meals at the same time, breakfast at half past seven for the family except Madam Alix, lunch at twelve, tea at four where the biscuits, somebody told me, are the same as they were in the days of Catherine the Great. Supper at the same time, readings from novels by the Tsar at the same time in the evening. Soldiers, policemen, enormous footmen, some of them black, some of them brown, everywhere. Tsarskoe Selo has a military force around it about the same size as the army of a small country like Denmark. Look out of any of the windows and you'll see the back of a guardsman or a policeman. After a while, Mikhail, you grow rather tired of all these backs in uniform. Any visitor to the place has their name entered in a book. Anybody leaving it, the same. I can't imagine why anybody would want to live there when they could be in that fabulous Winter Palace right in the middle of town. Why did Catherine build it if she didn't intend her successors to live in it in the winter?'

'Security, Natasha, you must see that,' said Mikhail, 'they feel safe down there. Any would-be assassins can be intercepted before they reach the front door. That's not so easy in the middle of Petersburg.'

'I think it might be jolly exciting if an assassin got past the front door,' said Natasha, treacherously. 'What do you think they carry their bombs round in? Do they just have them under their coats? Isn't there a danger that they will blow themselves up?'

'I think you should be serious about these assassins, Natasha,' said Mikhail Shaporov. 'You never know where they may strike next. But tell me, what are the daughters like, the ones you have to deal with?'

'The Grand Duchesses?' The girl stopped for a moment and a smile crossed her lips. 'They're sweet, Mikhail, really sweet. They're very strictly brought up, they have to make their own beds, they have to behave at meal times, they have English governesses, even English furniture for heaven's sake. The elder two get less pocket money than I did when I was half their age.'

'And what do they talk to you about? Or is it what do you talk to them about?'

'I can see you haven't read the Court Ceremonial Circular recently, Mikhail,' said Natasha sternly, 'really, I'm surprised at you. I can only talk to them if they talk to me. It is forbidden to talk to a member of the imperial family unless they have first addressed you.'

'So, Natasha,' replied Mikhail, holding his ground, 'what do they talk to you about?'

'This is where it becomes so sad. This is where their upbringing really handicaps them. Think of it. They've hardly ever been to a restaurant. They hardly ever go to the big shops on the Nevskii Prospekt. They go on holiday in the royal train to the Crimea, guarded by dozens and dozens of policemen on the way, or they go cruising in the royal yacht on the Baltic surrounded by dozens and dozens of seamen, handpicked for loyalty and devotion to the Tsar. They have no more idea of the lives of ordinary Russians than they do of the man in the moon. I'm not a typical Russian, as you know, but they have no idea how even people like us are brought up. They think ordinary Russians are all like the peasants who wait beside the train lines to wave at the family as they pass by. Their parents are convinced that the peasants love the royal family, it's just the decadent snobs in St Petersburg who don't measure up. The favourite thing with all four girls is for me to describe a shop with all the different things, particularly clothes, that are on sale. They would listen to that for hours at a time. The next favourite is to describe the menu in a fashionable restaurant. After that we can always fill an hour or two with them asking me to describe my wardrobe in enormous detail.'

'You make them sound like deprived children. It can't be as bad as that, surely?'

'Well, I think it is. There's no doubt their parents love them all dearly, but they can't see they're stifling the life out of them. And there's another thing, Mikhail.' The girl lowered her voice and looked about the library very carefully, as if an Okhrana agent might be hiding behind the Voltaire or the Rousseau. 'That little boy. There's something not quite right with him. I don't know what it is, I don't think they know what it is, but I'm sure it's serious, very serious.'

'What do you mean, something not quite right with him? Is he not crawling yet or whatever babies are expected to do?'

'It's not that, Mikhail. Two or three times now it's happened. He falls ill, don't ask me how. Madam Alix puts on an even longer face than usual, Tsar looks like all the bank loans are going to go wrong at once, doctors arrive from Petersburg by the trainload. Literally. Once we had seven medical professors in the Alexander Palace in one day. Fairly soon I'm going to get to the bottom of it all.'

'So is that what breaks up the boredom? Earnest society doctors coming to inspect the Tsarevich? What do his sisters say about it all? Do they know what's going on?'

'I think they have been sworn to silence, or a cutting off of the biscuit ration at tea-time. They don't say a word. There is one other thing that's happened recently though I don't know if it means anything at all. Two of the eggs have disappeared, two of the most beautiful ones.'

'Eggs? Disappeared? What eggs? Whose eggs? Royal eggs? Special Romanov eggs from special Romanov hens? ' The royal household at Tsarskoe Selo was beginning to sound to the novice Mikhail like a cross between a penal institution and a dairy farm. Even he, never a fully convinced monarchist, wasn't sure he would approve of such prosaic developments.

'Sorry, Mikhail. I should have explained it better,' said Natasha with a laugh. 'The person who makes the eggs is Mr Fabergé, the jeweller. Every Easter he is commissioned by the Tsar to make two new eggs, one for his mother and one for his wife. One of these eggs is called the Trans-Siberian Railway egg and it was made in 1900 to commemorate the opening of the Trans-Siberian Railway. The outside of the egg is made of green translucent emerald gold and has all the stations of the railway marked on it in silver. When you open it up there's a tiny little train about a foot long which actually goes when you wind it up with its clockwork key. It's got a dining car, smoking and non-smoking cars. I think it's even got a chapel carriage at the back.'

'Have you seen it go, this train, Natasha?'

'No, I haven't, but the girls have. They said it was sensational. The other one is not so dramatic but pretty special all the same. It was called the Danish Royal Palaces egg and when you opened this little chap up you got eight portraits of eight different Danish castles that the Tsar's mother or some royal Danish person must have lived in when she was growing up. I did see that one opened up and it was just beautiful.'

'So where have they gone?'

'I don't know,' she said, glancing anxiously at the clock above the door. 'One week ago they were all locked up in their own glass cabinet along with the other eggs and the next minute they'd gone. Nobody seems very bothered about it. Perhaps they haven't noticed. I must go now, Mikhail, or I will get into trouble and be locked up with all the other assassins when I get back. Will you see me to the station?'

'Of course I will,' said Mikhail. 'Any chance next time of meeting at Tsarskoe Selo? Any chance I could bring my new friend Lord Powerscourt?'

Lord Francis Powerscourt was not overjoyed at his reception back at the British Embassy. For de Chassiron, he felt sure, he brought a sense of excitement and even danger that served to add spice to a life that might easily have degenerated into foppish boredom. De Chassiron would always be glad of somebody new to talk to, some fresh recipient for his sarcasm and his cleverness. De Chassiron was not the problem. The Ambassador was. De Chassiron had given Powerscourt a fairly brutal run-down over breakfast that morning. 'Done a turn in Washington, His Nibs has, not top man but number two. Only embassy he's ever served in where he could speak the language as well as the natives, and even that was doubtful. Been Ambassador in Paris, weak on diplomatic and business French. Been

Ambassador in Germany where he offended the Kaiser and half the government by forgetting to salute in the right place at some ludicrous parade invented by the equally ludicrous Kaiser. Now he's here in St Petersburg, aiming to stay for a couple of years at most. Then he can return to London to take over from the etiolated Sir Jeremiah Reddaway as Permanent Secretary to the Foreign Office. He's already Sir Jasper Colville. Then he can fulfil his wife's greatest ambition and become Lord Colville of somewhere or other. Tooting Bec maybe,' de Chassiron said savagely, his contempt for his superior blatant, 'or Clapham Common. But you, Powerscourt,' here de Chassiron leaned back in his chair and ran an arm through his hair, only to find yet again that the incipient bald patch was marching inexorably on, 'you might be trouble. Dead British diplomats, nothing he would like less. Troublesome inquiries with the native authorities, even less welcome. There's nothing His Nibs would like more than to leave Martin under the ice of the Neva river, if that's where he is, and for the body not to be found until he has returned home to take up his new position and his seat in the House of Lords. Once you come to him with something concrete, he won't like it one little bit. Anything that might upset His Majesty's relations with the Tsar of All the Russias not welcome in this Embassy. You could do him real damage if you find out anything really serious about what happened to Martin. We could almost say you've got his future in your hands.'

Now the three men were sitting in the Ambassador's study, drinking English tea and eating cucumber sandwiches. The Ambassador had seen too many of his colleagues fall into the wretched customs of their hosts and forget who and what they were. The Ambassador was seated behind a large desk that would not have looked out of place in a Pall Mall club.

Powerscourt suddenly realized that all the furniture, the sofas, the chairs, the occasional tables, the racks for newspapers, could have been transferred direct from the Athenaeum or the Reform Club in London's Pall Mall. Maybe the British Embassy, like the Russian Tsarina, did its shopping at Maples in the Tottenham Court Road.

Before Powerscourt presented his report on the day's discoveries, the Ambassador graced his little audience with his own view on the diplomatic problems surrounding the strange case of Roderick Martin. The need to be aware of Russian susceptibilities, of their difficulties both with the Japanese War on the one hand, and with the bomb-bearing revolutionaries on the other. The need, of course, for His Majesty's representatives to be aware of the dignity of their own position while not compromising the Russians' room for manoeuvre. The need to be aware, too, of the pressures for information and hard facts from home. Public opinion, although still sleeping on this issue, as everybody had taken great care to keep it out of the newspapers, could easily be roused and might not prove an easy bedfellow. Prejudice against the Russian bear, so prominent a generation ago, in Sir Jasper's view, could easily come lumbering out of the same forest once again. The need for boldness tempered with caution, for restraint married with respect for the Russian perspective.

De Chassiron had been nodding vigorously in agreement with his Ambassador's sentiments. Powerscourt was certain that he was being ironic and, furthermore, that this was a very dangerous game to play. Only when he reflected on it afterwards did Powerscourt realize that de Chassiron knew the Ambassador was so sure of himself that he wouldn't have recognized the irony and the lack of respect if they had sat down beside him in his own drawing room. Powerscourt thought the Ambassador's remarks were nonsense, designed to appeal to everybody and to nobody, to preserve his own position sitting on the fence facing in all directions at once.

His guests paid scant attention to his reports of the visits to the police station and the morgues, though de Chassiron was much taken by the vehemence of the denials that Martin had ever been found by members of that police station. But when he told of the Interior Ministry's insistence on Martin's previous visits, they were astonished. Sir Jasper, anxious possibly to see which way the wind would blow, left the initial reaction to Embassy Secretary de Chassiron.

'Good God man, this is dynamite,' he said, screwing his silver monocle into his eye and inspecting the notes in front of him. 'If Martin came here then he didn't stay in the Embassy, I don't think he even visited the place. I've been here since the year of Our Lord 1899 so I should bloody well know. What on earth do you think he was doing here, Powerscourt? Did your friend in the ministry have any idea what he was up to?'

'The man from the ministry did not vouchsafe any information on that,' said Powerscourt carefully. 'We have to go and see him again early next week for further news. If he was not prepared to tell us all he knew today, I should be surprised if he is going to open his heart to us later on.'

'We, Powerscourt, we?' Sir Jasper was fiddling with a paperknife. 'Have you attained the royal plural or were you accompanied by someone unknown to us?'

'I went accompanied by my translator, a young man of impeccable family and equally impeccable language skills called Mikhail Shaporov, Sir Jasper. He came to me from the Foreign Office in London.'

'Of course,' said Sir Jasper, trying to gloss over the fact that he had been told this information but had forgotten. 'Please carry on.'

'I can only repeat the possibilities I discussed with my translator after our meeting, Sir Jasper,' said Powerscourt, wondering if he too would become pompous after a life in the Foreign Service. 'Martin could have had a mistress here. He could have fathered children out of wedlock whom he wished to visit. He could have come to pay a blackmailer. Or he could have been an agent of the Okhrana, come for a debrief from his masters and a round of fresh instructions. Or he could have come on holiday. The man might have liked the place. It's very beautiful. I'm sure we all know people who make a point of going to Venice or Rome or Paris once a year or so. Martin could have been one of those.'

De Chassiron had a look of anticipation on his face as if he expected some dramatic development at any moment. He was not disappointed.

'Are you telling us, Powerscourt, that you discussed these possibilities with young Shaporov, including the disgraceful accusation that Martin might have been a Russian agent?' Martin might have been rather a lot of trouble to the Ambassador during his life, but he was not going to have the man's service traduced once he was dead. 'I think that was unwise of you, most unwise.'

Powerscourt wondered whether to hit back or not. Probably better not. 'I am sorry if you felt I was out of order, Sir Jasper. I cannot believe there is anything untoward about a young man recommended by the Foreign Office itself. I should say he is very discreet.'

'Nevertheless, Powerscourt, I urge discretion on you. At all times. Nobody working in the purlieus of diplomacy and foreign affairs should forget that. I expect you to keep me informed of your activities, and your . . .' The Ambassador paused for a second or two here as if unsure of the right word. '. . . your speculations every evening from now on about this time.' The Ambassador rose from his seat and headed for the door. 'Thank you, gentlemen, and a very good evening to you both.'

A battalion of cleaners took up their positions on the ground floor of the Winter Palace at five o'clock on the morning of Thursday January the 6th, Epiphany Day. They brought tall ladders with them as well as the usual complement of mops, pails, dusters, soft cloths, feather dusters on long poles. Today was one of the most important days in the calendar of the great palace. Today the Tsar, members of the court and his family and senior members of the Church in St Petersburg processed down from the first floor of the Winter Palace to a special ceremony by the banks of the Neva called the Blessing of the Waters. And the route down from the first floor came down one of the most spectacular sections of this most spectacular of buildings, the Jordan Staircase.

The twin flights of the marble staircase were overlooked by a selection of caryatids, trompe l'oeil atlantes and a fresco of the gods on Mount Olympus. Ten solid granite columns supported the vaults of the staircase. The walls and balustrade dripped with decoration, with gilding, with mirrors. The ceiling, way above the staircase, showed the gods of Olympus besporting themselves in a heaven scarcely less spectacular than the Winter Palace itself. The route upwards was decorated with monumental statues brought from Europe by Peter the Great: Diana, Power and Might. In the great days of the St Petersburg season, before the Japanese War and the threat of terror put an end to the festivities, the rich and the fashionable of St Petersburg would progress up the Jordan Staircase to dance until dawn in the great state rooms on the first floor.

Today it was the route by which the Emperor led his procession to attend the annual service of the Blessing of the Waters at Epiphany in commemoration of Christ's Baptism in the river Jordan. It was an uneasy time in the capital. Workers were on strike against their conditions of employment and their numbers increased every day. Police reported the working class districts as being restive and liable to erupt in violence. For the Blessing a temporary pavilion was set up on the ice of the Neva at a point opposite the northern entrance to the palace. The Metropolitan of St Petersburg dipped a cross in a hole made in the ice and referred to it as 'Jordan'. A small cup was then lowered into the hole and presented to the Emperor who took a sip of the water and handed the cup back to the churchman. Prayers were said for the health of the Tsar and his family, wisely, the more cynical observers thought, in view of the impurities of the river water.

Out on the Neva a detachment of marine police inspected the ice for any signs of suspect activity. The secret police had warned the imperial family that there was a high risk of terrorist activity at this time. The Tsarina and her daughters stayed behind the tall windows of the Winter Palace, staring out at the scene on the blue-green ice. When the proceedings were over there came the sound of a great salute from the guns of the Fortress of Peter and Paul across the river. The more historically minded of the citizens referred to the fortress as the Russian Bastille. Its reputation as a place of incarceration was fearful. Prisoners were said to have died of cold, of hunger, of the terrible beatings they received from the guards. In fact, there were never more than a hundred prisoners in the fortress at any one time and some of them even spent their time reading revolutionary literature without any interference from their jailers.

The fortress was also the necropolis of the Romanovs. Almost all the Tsars were buried inside. And on this Epiphany Day it seemed as if some malignant spirits were intending to increase their number. For these were not blanks being fired from the great guns. This was live ammunition. A policeman standing beside the Tsar fell wounded to the ground, his blood spreading out in strange red patterns against the snow. Shots were fired into the Winter Palace itself, the glass in the windows shattering and flying inside, threatening the flesh of any who got in its way. Other shots ricocheted off the Admiralty Building back into Palace Square. On the first floor in the Field Marshal's Hall shards of glass lay at the feet of the Tsar's mother and sister, but they were unhurt. Out in the snow the Tsar crossed himself and began saying his prayers. Not far from there his grandfather had been driving in his carriage twenty-four years before when a bomb shattered his vehicle, wounded his horses and his companions but left the Tsar himself unhurt. Stepping down from the wreck of his carriage he went to inquire after the wounded. Another assassin ran up and threw a bomb directly between the Tsar's feet. In a huge sheet of flame and metal his legs were torn away, his stomach ripped wide open and his face badly mutilated. Still breathing he asked for what remained of him to be carried into the Winter Palace to die. He left a trail of black blood on the marble stairs while they carried him to a couch for his last moments in this world. Before he passed away, his grandson Nicholas, dressed in his blue sailor suit, came and watched in horror from the end of the bed. Now that grandson, currently Nicholas the Second, Tsar of All the Russias, was hurried, unhurt, into the same palace where his grandfather had died in agony. The word flashed round the great mansions of the capital with astonishing speed. In the bar of the Imperial Yacht

Club, the *fons et origo* of St Petersburg chic, the aristocrats and the generals crossed themselves and prayed for their future. The French Ambassador, holding court by the window, told whoever would listen that the most significant thing in the assassination attempt was the fact that the guns were manned by sailors. These are not the fanatic students who blew up the Interior Minister last year, he said. These men swear a powerful oath to be loyal to their rulers. If they desert the Tsar, what future for the Romanovs? The foreign correspondents rushed from their bar at the fashionable Evropeiskaya Hotel to interview or invent eyewitnesses to the event and telegraph the news, suitably embellished and dramatized, to their employers.

Watching alone by one of the intact windows of the Field Marshal's Hall the Empress Alexandra shivered slightly as she looked out at the snow. She was remembering a prophecy attributed to St Serafim. 'They will wait for a time of great hardship to afflict the Russian land,' it read, 'and on an agreed day at the agreed hour they will raise up a great rebellion all over the Russian land.'

4

Lord Francis Powerscourt decided he had spent too much of his time in Russia listening to people. Listening to the Ambassador and the cynical Secretary at the Embassy, listening to the translations of his young interpreter from policemen and bureaucrats in the Interior Ministry. Now, the day after Epiphany, they were in a rather different waiting room of a very different section of the Russian bureaucracy, waiting for another interview, this time with a senior official of the Russian Foreign Ministry.

The Interior Ministry, Powerscourt had decided, looked rather like one of those vast mental hospitals the authorities built round the fringes of London towards the end of the previous century, enormous complexes where the mad could get lost finding their way back to their own ward, and where a man could forget what few wits he might have left trying to work out how to find the front door. The Foreign Ministry, however, looked like a French Second Empire hotel that had once known better times, a resort that had lost its *raison d'être* perhaps, Vichy without the water, Bath without the spa. The place had certainly once had considerable stylistic ambitions, but now the gilt was falling off the mirrors and the imitation Watteaus on the walls had lost whatever lustre they once possessed, the dancers and the musicians exhausted. Mikhail had told him on the way that while the people in the Interior Ministry saw it as their mission to pacify the interior of Russia, the mission of the people in the Foreign Service was to join the foreigners, preferably somewhere rather warmer than St Petersburg, as quickly as possible. Some of the diplomats, Powerscourt was told, spent almost their entire lives abroad, only returning at the end of their careers to advise on the foreign policy of a country they no longer knew and whose nature they were not now equipped to understand. Combined with the abilities of the Tsar, Mikhail had said savagely, this was a system guaranteed to produce one of the most incompetent foreign policies in the world. Hence, Mikhail shrugged an enormous shrug, the unbelievably stupid decision to go to war with Japan.

A flunkey in a stained frock coat told them in bad French that they were expected inside. The Under Secretary, a man who had risen effortlessly through the hurdles of Deputy and Assistant, greeted them warmly.

'Ivan Tropinin at your service, gentlemen. Please sit down.'

Mikhail had said the man would probably speak French. France after all was the favourite posting of most of these would-be foreigners. It was astonishing, he said, how many little Russian diplomatic missions were peppered along the south coast from Biarritz to the Riviera to Nice and the Italian border. But Tropinin was speaking in his native tongue. Powerscourt wondered if it was to throw him off the scent, whatever the scent might be.

'Please, Lord Powerscourt, your reputation precedes you, we are delighted to see you here.' Tropinin ushered them on to two very decorative French chairs, as uncomfortable as only the French knew how to make them. 'I know you are in St Petersburg about the affair of Mr Martin.' Tropinin was a small thin man with a tiny beard and very delicate hands which he inspected from time to time in case they were going coarse.

Powerscourt nodded. Mikhail was looking intently at the fading portrait of a semi-naked lady on the opposite wall. Perhaps these badges of status came to those who reached the rank of Under Secretary. He wondered what happened when you were promoted above the level of Under Secretary. Maybe there were no clothes at all then.

'I am most grateful,' Powerscourt began, 'for your time. I know how busy you all must be here in the ministry.'

Tropinin laughed. He leaned forward and looked Powerscourt firmly in the eye. 'You will have to talk to many people in this city, my English friend. More than you would like, I suspect. Most of them will be lying to you. I am not going to tell you lies.' Powerscourt had a sudden vision of men from Crete and people telling lies and long undergraduate arguments in his rooms in Cambridge. 'I am going to tell you the truth. Why? Because I like England and I like Englishmen. I have spent some time in your country, Lord Powerscourt. They took me to some of the great houses like your Blenheim Palace. To a Russian, of course, it is scarcely bigger than a hunting lodge, but it is very fine. The park is beautiful. And I know the father and the family of your young translator here. I have known them for years.' The Under Secretary nodded vigorously. Powerscourt wondered if there was some secret code at work, some private language of bribery or obligation he did not understand.

'I am most grateful for your assistance,' Powerscourt put in with a smile, keen to get back to business.

'Of course,' the diplomat said, checking his hands once more. 'Let me come to the point.' Tropinin paused and looked at his two visitors.

'It is a very little thing I can tell you, but believe me when I tell you it is true. Many people will try to tell you that your Mr Martin was not here a couple of weeks ago, that his body was not found by the Nevskii Prospekt, that as there is no body there can be no crime and as there was no Mr Martin, Lord Powerscourt, there is nothing for you to investigate, and as there is nothing for you to investigate you may as well go home and leave St Petersburg to its fate. This is what some people want you to believe.'

'Are you saying that that is not the truth?'

'I tell you, Lord Powerscourt, he was here, he was killed here. That is all I can say.'

'Did you see him, Mr Tropinin? Did you have a meeting with him as you are now having one with us?'

The little man held his hand up. 'I told you I had one thing to say. That was it, I cannot tell you anything else.'

'Do you know why Mr Martin came to St Petersburg? Can you tell us that much?'

'I have nothing further to say.'

'Do you know if he succeeded in his mission, whatever that was, Mr Tropinin?' This was Powerscourt's last throw.

'I cannot help you. I have nothing more to say.'

Lord Francis Powerscourt was standing on the roof of the Stroganov Palace at twelve o'clock on Sunday morning, wearing an enormous borrowed coat in dark grey that brushed the ground as he walked. He liked to think it had belonged to some military man in the distant past, a campaigning Shaporov perhaps, commanding the artillery in battles long ago and far away. On his head he wore a thick Shaporov Russian hat. Beside him, Mikhail was wearing a similar coat and had two very expensive pairs of binoculars wrapped round his neck. By his side, wearing the warmest coat and gloves that London's Jermyn Street could provide, stood Rupert de Chassiron, Secretary to the

British Embassy, who had been invited to share the view and the spectacle from the top of the palace. The three men had come to watch the great march of workers that was going to set out from different points of the city and converge on Palace Square, site of the Tsar's residence, the Winter Palace, where their leader, Father Georgy Gapon, was to hand in a proclamation to the Tsar. While they waited for the marchers to appear, Mikhail told Powerscourt about his recruitment of Natasha and her news from the palace about the boredom and the rituals and the vanishing eggs and the sick little boy.

Below them, diminutive people strolled along the Nevskii Prospekt in their Sunday best. Late worshippers were going in to a service at the Kazan Cathedral to their right, a favourite place for prayer and meditation of the Empress Alexandra. The trams rolled on their tracks towards the Alexander Nevskii Monastery. On their immediate left was the Moyka river and beyond that the great expanse of Palace Square flanked by the General Staff Building, the Hermitage and the Winter Palace, the winter sun glistening off its golden domes. Across the frozen Neva, slightly to the north, the forbidding Fortress of Peter and Paul, burial ground of the Romanovs and prison fortress for their enemies. Further round to the north-west, Vasilevsky Island, home to the university and cabbage soup. To the north-east behind the Finland station, the Vyborg side, home to many factories and unimaginable squalor. To the south-west, beyond the Yussupov Palace and the Mariinsky Theatre, lay the Narva Gates, built to commemorate victory over Napoleon, and behind them the Putilov factories where the current wave of strikes began. From all these different districts the great columns of marching people would be snaking their way towards the heart of St Petersburg.

Today, both Mikhail and de Chassiron had told Powerscourt, might be a key date in Russian history.

'Today could change everything,' de Chassiron said, waving a hand expansively across the city spread out in front of them, glad to be able to embrace historical change in person. 'Autocracy could be banished. The will of the people could bring about a constitution. Of course it depends whether the Tsar pays any attention to them. He's perfectly capable of ignoring the whole thing.' And with that he screwed his monocle back into his left eye and continued his close inspection of the fashionable ladies down below.

'I believe that the Tsar is not even in St Petersburg at the moment,' said Mikhail Shaporov, whose connections with the imperial household were better than most, 'and I don't believe he is intending to come here at all today. Quite what the marchers will do when they hand their petition in to the Chief of Protocol rather than the Tsar of All the Russias, I cannot tell you. I dread to think how cross it could make them, unless, of course,' Mikhail peered over towards the Winter Palace as if the Chief of Protocol might be rehearsing his welcome even now, 'he manages to convince them that the Tsar is inside and will consider their point of view.'

'How do you know that, about the Tsar not being here today?' De Chassiron was on the scent of the source like a bloodhound.

'I can't tell you that, I'm afraid,' said Mikhail cheerfully, 'but believe me when I say it is totally accurate.'

'Can I ask you a question, Mikhail?' said Powerscourt. 'This palace here, the one we're standing on, it belongs to one of your cousins, you say?'

'It does,' said Mikhail. 'My mother came from a very large family so I think we are related to half the aristocracy

107

in the city. My father complains that you cannot drink tea in the Yacht Club without falling over three or four relations, all of them asking you for money.'

Powerscourt saw, to his enormous delight, that the mother Shaporov would have to make the acquaintance of Lady Lucy as quickly as possible. They could start comparing notes on numbers of second cousins and impoverished younger sons.

'And was the Beef Stroganov invented here? That dish with beef and onions and mushrooms and sour cream and so on? Was it so called because the original chef was employed in this palace?'

'It was named after a General Pavel Alexandrovich Stroganov, of the family of this palace,' said Mikhail. 'That must have been about twenty-five years ago. It has made my father very sad.'

'Why is that?'

'My father is very competitive. You will see what I mean when you meet him. "Why should this useless family of Stroganov have a dish named after them", he said, "when they have not done anything for a hundred years except ride their horses and sleep with other people's wives and drink their vodka? We have done lots of things. We are rich. Why should there not be a Veal Shaporov or something like that?"'

The young man shook his head. 'It's all passed now, the obsession for a recipe that would bear the family name. But for a while it was bad, very bad. We had new cooks coming all the time as the old ones whose new recipes did not find favour were thrown out. I was quite young, so I missed out on most of these strange dishes. There was roast chicken with rhubarb and peaches, I remember. Caviar with chestnut and dill sauce. Christ!'

The marchers were intending to meet in Palace Square at two o'clock. In the side streets down below Powerscourt could see groups of soldiers, rubbing their hands together to keep warm, rifles slung across their backs. Some distance away, over by the Admiralty, he could see the cavalry trotting slowly along in perfect formation. What this city needs today, he said to himself, is not soldiers or cavalry but a properly trained detachment of the Metropolitan Police, led by officers with experience in controlling large crowds.

Mikhail was glancing through a roughly printed paper.

'They've written a proclamation, gentlemen, a letter to the Tsar. Would you like to hear some of it?'

Dim memories of great petitions in English history floated across Powerscourt's brain. The Chartists, hadn't they marched to London bringing some great petition with innumerable signatures asking for reform? Hadn't there been a Petition of Right from the Lords and Commons to the King in 1628 that pointed the way to the English Civil War? Not a good omen for the Tsar, Powerscourt thought, King Charles the First in his impeccable white shirt being led to the scaffold outside the Banqueting House in Whitehall.

'I'd love to hear it, Mikhail,' he said, raising his binoculars to his eyes and staring out to the south.

'"A Most Humble and Loyal Address of the Workers of St Petersburg Intended for Presentation to His Majesty on Sunday at two o'clock on the Winter Palace Square,"' Mikhail began. '"Sire: We, the workers and inhabitants of St Petersburg, our wives, our children, and our aged, helpless parents, come to Thee, O Sire, to seek justice and protection. We are impoverished; we are oppressed, overburdened with excessive toil, contemptuously treated. We are not even recognized as human beings, but are treated like slaves who must suffer their bitter fate in silence and without complaint. And we have suffered, but even so we are being further (and further) pushed into the slough of poverty, arbitrariness and ignorance. We are suffocating in despotism and lawlessness. O Sire, we have no strength left, and our endurance is at an end. We have reached that frightful moment when death is better than the prolongation of our unbearable sufferings."'

Way off in the distance Powerscourt thought he could hear singing. He strained his head towards the noise but nothing was clear.

'Christ,' said de Chassiron, peering at the Russian characters over Mikhail's shoulder, 'I shouldn't think anybody's talked to the Tsar in that tone of voice in his entire life. I shouldn't think even his bloody wife talks to him like that. What do you reckon, Mikhail?'

'I'm sure you're right, Mr de Chassiron,' said Mikhail tactfully, his eyes skimming further sections of the proclamation. 'I suspect the great ruler would be furious if he ever read this.'

'I wonder if it isn't always the same question,' said Powerscourt. 'Why this great march now? Why today? Are things much worse now than they were before? Much worse than the day before yesterday or last month? If marches and proclamations today, why not last year? Perhaps you'd better translate a bit more, Mikhail.'

'"And so we have left our work,"' Mikhail was frowning slightly as he spoke, as if the gap between his life and those described here was almost too great to cross, '"and told our employers that we will not go back to it until they have agreed to our demands. Our first request was that our employers discuss our needs with us. But they refused, they would not allow us the right to talk about our needs, because the law does not recognize such a right for us. Our requests also seemed to them to be illegal: reducing the hours of work to eight per day; drawing up a schedule of wage rates for our work along with us and with our agreement; investigating our disputes with the lower management of the factories; increasing the wages of unskilled workers and women to one rouble per day; abolishing overtime; treating us with attention and without abuse."'

Powerscourt thought you could have taken the language and the sentiments and applied them to any industrial dispute in any country in Europe. The poor and the working classes of Birmingham or Bologna or Berlin would feel at home with this proclamation. Truly, Peter the Great's ambition to make Russia European had been realized, but not in ways he would have welcomed. Carried in by subversive pamphlets posted from overseas, brought in by hand by the more daring or least known revolutionaries, maybe even hidden in secret compartments or lining the bottoms of hollow suitcases in the trains and ferries that linked Russia to the West, the seditious thoughts of Europe had come to Peter's capital as surely as the great columns and pilasters of his baroque architects two centuries before.

'Look, Lord Powerscourt!' Mikhail shouted. 'Down there to the south! My God, there's thousands of them!'

Staring through his binoculars Powerscourt could see a great column, led by a priest in a long white cassock carrying a crucifix. He was surrounded by a primitive bodyguard. At the front, just behind the man of God, there marched two young men, one with a portrait of the Tsar, the other with a huge icon of the Virgin. Behind them was a large white banner with the words 'Soldiers, do not shoot at the people!' A new sound rang out to join the singing. The church bells were ringing to bless people on the way to meet their Tsar.

'That's the Russian National Anthem they're singing, Lord Powerscourt.' Up there on the roof Mikhail gave his own special version in an attractive tenor voice.

'God save the noble Tsar!
Long may he live, in power,
In happiness,
In peace to reign!
Dread of his enemies,
Faith's sure defender,
God save the Tsar!
Faith's sure defender,
God save the Tsar!
Faith's sure defender,
God save the Tsar!'

'God knows why you have to repeat the last bit three times, gentlemen,' Mikhail apologized for the reprise, 'but people get very cross if you don't.'

'It's not that different from our own National Anthem, actually,' said Powerscourt. 'God, faith, death to the enemies, all the usual stuff.' De Chassiron was staring through his binoculars at the great column that snaked its way forward behind the priest. Many of them carried their children with them, cradling the little ones in their arms, the fathers holding them on their shoulders for a better view. The old were at the back, shuffling slowly along the ice. They walked with an air of great purpose, as if on this day they walked with destiny. Now Mikhail was tugging his arm again and pointing to the other side of the river. Another vast army from the Petrograd district was approaching the Troitsky Bridge that would bring them very close to Palace Square itself. Further east again the people of Vyborg, behind the Finland station, were also approaching the river. Powerscourt found himself wondering how many of the marchers could be locked up inside the Peter and Paul Fortress. The church bells were ringing out all over the city now for the hour of one o'clock, sixty short minutes before all the marchers were due to arrive in Palace Square. Down below them a group of students, dressed in black from head to foot, were advancing very slowly, taking it in turns to read from the proclamation.

'My God, Powerscourt,' Mikhail was bright with excitement, 'they're not mincing their words, the people who wrote this proclamation. They've dropped all the weasel words and all the weasel sentiments. They're asking the Tsar for the vote. The vote! People have asked for it before but not tens and tens of thousands of them, all heading for the Winter Palace!' He began translating again:

'"Let there be here capitalist and worker, official, priest, doctor, teacher: let them all, whoever they are, elect their representatives. Let everyone be equal and free in their right to vote, and to that end decree that the elections to the constituent assembly be carried out under universal, secret and equal suffrage."' Mikhail stared at Powerscourt. 'Assemblies, votes for everyone, not just the rich, I reckon the Winter Palace will fall down if that petition gets anywhere near it.'

Powerscourt was thinking that these Russian radicals were asking for a wider franchise than that applying in his own country, supposedly a cradle and mother of democracy.

'Do we know anything about that priest? The one leading the column towards the Narva Gates?' asked Powerscourt.

De Chassiron laughed bitterly. 'I have spent quite a lot of time investigating this man, Powerscourt. Forgive me, Mikhail, if I sound unsympathetic to some of your fellow countrymen. It does not apply to you or your family.' He peered over the balcony, small sections of plaster falling off the parapet as he leant forward to inspect the students beneath. 'The priest's name is Gapon, Father Georgy Gapon.' De Chassiron paused for a moment. 'Let's suppose you are the secret police, Powerscourt. You're quite smart in this country if you're a secret policeman. After all, some of the time they're the only thing keeping the imperial family alive. Anyway, you look at all these new factories with their horrible working conditions and their pathetic rates of pay springing up in all the great cities. The lessons from abroad tell you that, at some point, the Russian worker will join a trade union like the German worker or the British worker or the French worker. Fine, you say. Then you have your brainwave. Wouldn't it be much better, a senior secret policeman called Zubarov thought, if we controlled these trade unions, not the radicals or the revolutionaries or the undesirables. Let's have Tsarist trade unions without any of the members knowing about it. So lots of these stooges are put in place all over the country briefed to run the trade unions the way the government tells them. Including Father Gapon here in St Petersburg. It's as if the last French King had not just Danton on his payroll but St Just and possibly Robespierre as well. And what happens? The government gives these Gapons money to set up their union. After a while they go native, or they may go native. They join the opposition. I have reason to believe that our Father Gapon had a meeting with the authorities yesterday but I am sure his heart is with the marchers today. They say he wrote sections of the proclamation after all.'

Down below the student reader changed. A deep bass voice now soared up into the sunlight.

'What we need are, one: immediate release and return for all those who have suffered for their political and religious beliefs, for strikes and peasant disorders.'

'Empty the Peter and Paul Fortress,' Mikhail said to Powerscourt and de Chassiron in wonder, 'bring all those exiles back from Siberia. It's unbelievable.'

114

'Two: immediate proclamation of liberty and inviol-ability of the person, freedom of speech, of the press. Three: universal and compulsory education at the state's expense. Four: equality of all, without exception, before the law.'

Centuries of European protest, of reform movements, of radical parties, of revolutions were distilled into a few pages of Russian and shouted through its capital on a sunny January day. Powerscourt wondered about the dead man, Roderick Martin. Was his death in some way connected to the events of today, or to the causes behind the events? Were there clues to his death down there on the streets, somewhere between the marchers and the military? The column approaching the bridge had burst into song.

'Oh Holy Spirit, One in Power,
With God who reigns in highest heaven,
Come to our waiting souls this hour
And let thy Heavenly aid be given.'

Powerscourt thought to himself that the demonstrators were going to need all the help they could find, divine or human. He was beginning to feel very fearful about the outcome. The marchers were not going to turn round and go home. Would the authorities allow this vast army into Palace Square? He doubted it.

'Thou art light of radiant glow
And thou canst fill our souls with cheer.
Come then thy glorious gift bestow
And with thy presence bless us here.'

They heard great shouts from behind them as Father Gapon worked his column into a religious fervour, using

115

the same tactics he had employed at his mass rallies in the days before the march.

'Do the police and soldiers,' Gapon bellowed, 'dare to stop us from passing, comrades?'

'They do not dare!' hundreds of voices shouted back.

'Comrades, it is better for us to die for our demands than live as we have lived till now!' Gapon again, at full volume.

'Do you swear to die?' he shouted at the faithful.

'We swear!' Hundreds and hundreds of people raised their hands and made the sign of the cross.

The marchers were much closer now. Peering through their binoculars, the party on the roof could make out individual faces very clearly, their unkempt beards, their dirty hair, the rough clothes and even the calloused hands. Most were wearing white shirts. The colour red had been banned by the march organizers as too provocative. The children, sitting on their fathers' shoulders, seemed to think they were as safe as they would be at home. Older children climbed up lamp posts for a better view and screamed encouragement to their parents. Father Gapon's column was probably less than fifteen minutes from Palace Square, the column approaching the Troitsky Bridge a little longer.

Then they heard a different sound. Powerscourt checked his watch. It was twenty past one. At first he did not know what it was but Mikhail had swung round to stare at the marchers from Putilov.

'Oh, my God! Oh, my God!' he said, grabbing Powerscourt by the arm and pointing dramatically to the south. He crossed himself three times. 'It's the cavalry, Lord Powerscourt! By the Narva Gates! They're going to charge! The horses' hooves make a different noise on the ice,' he went on hopelessly, as if that was going to change what was just about to happen. 'And look! Forming up behind them at the top end of Narva Square, lines and lines of infantry with their rifles at the ready.

There's going to be a massacre! God help them all! God help Russia!'

Powerscourt remembered for the rest of his life the strange way the events seemed to unfold to his little party up there on the roof of the Stroganov Palace. He remembered people who had nearly drowned telling him about their lives passing before their eyes in slow motion. The initial charge of the cavalry, sabres drawn to slash at their victims, seemed to take about half an hour. He watched in horror through his binoculars as the dragoons hacked at the faces of the marchers. They seemed to prefer the uncovered flesh to the more obstinate resistance of greatcoats and trousers. Soon the blood, bright and fresh, was staining the ice red. Many were killed on the spot, their heads half hacked off, arms almost severed from their trunks, faces mutilated, necks severed. Some of the marchers turned and fled. Others carried on. Powerscourt thought he could just hear the voice of Father Gapon, shouting through the screams, 'Do you swear to die?' and the answer, still audible in the midday air, 'We swear!' For too many of them, those were the last words they said in their lives. Their last wish was granted. For the infantry, the first rank kneeling in the snow, fired two rounds over the heads of the marchers. Then they lowered their sights. Volley after volley crashed into the protesters. Powerscourt saw one little boy lifted off his father's shoulders and flung back ten or fifteen feet into the crowd, blood cascading from a great wound in his chest. Powerscourt hoped he was dead. He felt his arm being pummelled and the word 'bastards' being shouted over and over again as Mikhail Shaporov wept for the destruction of his city. The commander of the infantry was giving his orders as if he was on parade, 'Reload! Take Aim! Fire!' and every volley brought another round of death to the hallowed ground

117

round the Narva Gates. They might have been built to commemorate Napoleon's defeat in 1812. Today they were present to witness another, less glorious, moment of Russia's history.

Eventually, when Powerscourt thought he could bear it no longer, the firing ceased. The dead and the dying were lying all over the square. Battalions of crows began circling overhead as if they were unsure what sort of carrion might await them down below. The cavalry, not content with the shattered faces dying on the ground, pursued the marchers as they slouched back towards the working class quarters of the city, their own districts where they might hope to find a place of greater safety. Many fell with wounds across their backs or slashed viciously across the neck to die on the bloodied streets of St Petersburg.

Then it was the turn of the marchers approaching the Troitsky Bridge. Mikhail Shaporov was sobbing uncontrollably now, his hand still clasping Powerscourt's arm. De Chassiron had gone pale, almost white. This time the military performed their massacre in reverse order. Volley after volley of infantry fire tore into the head of the column, making its way deeper and deeper into the press of men as the first ranks turned and ran or died where they stood. Then, when the march had turned into a rabble of confused and wounded people, some still trying to advance on the doomed mission towards Palace Square, others wishing to flee back to their homes, the cavalry charged, the lancers screaming their hatred as they cut into the flesh and bones of men of a different class. Powerscourt watched through his binoculars as one dragoon slashed at his victim, cutting him open from his eyes to the chin, and then, his teeth clenched in a grin and the hairs of his moustache standing up on his elevated lip, let out a terrible shriek and spat at the dead man as he fell to the ground.

The remnant of the marchers, those not yet bloodied by the Tsar, and the stragglers of the other columns met up on Nevskii Prospekt, and made a last doomed effort to reach Palace Square. A huge body of cavalry and several cannons had been drawn up at the edge to blast or slash any marchers impertinent enough to reach it into eternity. But the crowd, swollen now by students and onlookers, began to push forward once again. Soldiers were ordered to disperse the marchers using whips and the flats of their sabres. When that proved unsuccessful, they began firing once more. Powerscourt watched in horror as a young girl who had climbed on to an iron fence was crucified to it by a hail of bullets. The screams of the wounded and the dying carried up to the roof of the Stroganov Palace. A small boy who had mounted an equestrian statue was hurled into the air by a volley of artillery. Other children were hit and fell from the trees where they had been perching to get a better view. It was twenty to two, just a few short minutes before their intended rendezvous with the Tsar. The great crowds, sullen now and silent, their anger growing, began to trudge home, many of them helping wounded comrades on their way. Only when the dead lay thick on the ground and the shattered stragglers turned to retreat back up the Nevskii Prospekt did the firing cease. The lancers harried them on their way, slashing the faces of any brave or foolhardy enough to press onwards towards the Winter Palace. Powerscourt watched one cavalryman collect a great mass of papers at the end of his lance. Powerscourt had no idea what he was doing until two of his colleagues dragged a dying man towards the paper. The lancers smeared it with his blood. Then they made a hole in the ice of the Neva and thrust the remains of the proclamations down into the swirling waters beneath. The demands for the vote, for freedom of speech, for a constituent assembly, for equality before the law, all the dreams of Father Gapon and his hundred and fifty thousand supporters ended up stuffed down a hole in the river. The ink would have gone long before the proclamations made landfall, if they ever did.

'They'll never forgive him for this,' Mikhail said. 'Never. As long as this city survives, as long as the last of the marchers survive, as long as their children and grandchildren survive, the people of St Petersburg will remember this day and hate the man who caused all the suffering.' He was still holding on to Powerscourt. His face was wet with tears.

'Mikhail,' said Powerscourt, 'perhaps we could provide some help for the wounded down below. The palace here must have some bandages, we could bring water, vodka perhaps as a disinfectant, whatever the women in the palace think would be best. But I think we should do it quickly.'

And so, as the afternoon wore on, a small party tried to bring what help they could to the dying and the wounded, an Irish peer, a Russian aristocrat and a fastidious diplomat who cared nothing for his appearance as he tried to bring some comfort to the dying. Powerscourt made himself one promise that afternoon: that, whatever it took, he would get to the bottom of the strange death of Roderick Martin.

That evening, out at the Alexander Palace in his village called Tsarskoe Selo, the Tsar did not disturb his routine for the unfortunate events in his capital. He had his afternoon walk, and tea as usual with his family. Then they all spent a busy half-hour sticking their latest photographs into their albums. That evening after supper he read aloud to them from a book his librarian had ordered specially from London. Every evening when he could, the Tsar read aloud to his wife and children. He had not bothered to tell his family about the terrible events in St Petersburg. Much better, he thought, to take their imaginations to a different country altogether, to the West Country of England, to the strange case involving an enormous dog and Mr Sherlock Holmes and Dr Watson and a treacherous bog.

Later that evening there were sporadic disturbances in St Petersburg. Barricades were set up, slogans shouted at the soldiers who continued patrolling the streets. When the workers reached their homes, many of them bleeding to death from their wounds, or carried to their pathetic hovels on makeshift stretchers, they realized the full horror of what had happened. Fathers, husbands, sons, wives, daughters, so many were lost in the massacre. Hope, the hope that had led them on to the streets, the hope that tomorrow might be better than today or yesterday, that hope had died with the blood on the ice. The more perceptive understood that night what else they had lost. Faith in the Tsar, the father of his people, the protector of his flock, the true shepherd of his subjects, all that had gone with the sabres and the bullets and the corpses littering the streets that led to the Winter Palace. A new watchword went out, travelling round the streets behind the Narva Gates where Father Gapon had marched from, to the Vyborg side with its factories and its squalor, to Petrograd and to Vasilevsky Island. Men spoke the slogan only to those they knew they could trust. 'Death to the Tsar!' The marchers had already decided what to call this day. They christened it Bloody Sunday. The blood was the blood of their comrades who lost their lives to death on the Nevskii Prospekt.

That evening the writer Maxim Gorky sent a message to the American newspaper magnate William Randolph Hearst in New York. 'St Petersburg, Bloody Sunday, 9th January 1905,' the message read. 'The Russian Revolution has begun.'

PART TWO

THE TRANS-SIBERIAN RAILWAY EGG

This time has come, a great mass is moving towards all of us, a mighty healthy storm is rising, it's coming, it's already near, and soon it will blow sloth, indifference, contempt for work, this festering boredom right out of our society. I will work and in some twenty-five or thirty years' time everyone will work. Everyone!

Tuzenbakh, Act One,
The Three Sisters, Anton Chekhov

5

Natasha Bobrinsky sat as quietly as she could at the back of the room while the Tsar read *The Hound of the Baskervilles* to his family. Surely, she thought to herself, the Tsar must know what had happened in his city earlier that day. Tsars are meant to know everything. Surely he must have told his wife. Why didn't they tell the children some version of events, however sanitized? The girls would hear about it from the servants soon enough. Word had reached the Tsar's village by about four o'clock in the afternoon. The driver of one of the afternoon trains to Tsarskoe Selo had seen the final massacre on the Nevskii Prospekt and had brought the news with him. Natasha felt tenser than she had ever felt in her life. She knew her face was very pale. This day, she thought, must be a turning point. Nothing in Russia would ever be the same after the day when the Tsar's soldiers mowed down their fellow citizens on the streets of the capital as if they were barbarian invaders from afar. As she listened to that soft voice reading on, about the Stapletons, about the escaped prisoner on the moor and the terrible dangers of the Grimpen Mire, Natasha fell into a reverie where most of the Russian land mass toppled slowly into the Gulf of Finland and St Petersburg, her elegant, sparkling, beloved St Petersburg,

125

began to sink slowly beneath the waters of the Neva, the great spires of the churches and the Admiralty the last to disappear. Maybe the great Hound is the symbol of Revolution, Natasha said to herself as she came round, come to devour the people who look after him and crush their bones in his fearful embrace.

The Tsar read well. His voice was quiet but he knew when to raise it for effect. Natasha wondered if it was true what they said in the servants' quarters, that he was a bad ruler, that his indecision and his incompetence would ruin Russia. As the children filed out and began to make their way upstairs for bed, she felt the touch of a hand on her shoulder.

'Natasha, my child,' said the Empress Alexandra, 'you know something, don't you? Something about what happened in the city today?'

'Yes, Your Majesty,' said the girl. 'I do know something, but whether it is true or not, I do not know.'

'What do you know, child?' said the Empress, drawing Natasha over to sit on the edge of a sofa.

'All I have heard, Your Majesty,' said Natasha, remembering her father shouting at her brothers not to believe every bloody rumour they heard in this rumour-sodden city, 'is that there was a lot of shooting in St Petersburg, and many people were killed by the soldiers.'

Suddenly she wanted to cry for her unknown dead, mown down on a January Sunday.

'They were bad people, very bad people.' The Empress had raised her voice. For one glorious moment Natasha thought Alexandra was talking about the soldiers who had killed the marchers. 'They're all the same,' she went on, and Natasha knew her hopes were false, 'assassins, revolutionaries, bomb throwers, constitutionalists, liberals, seekers after the false gods of freedom and democracy. These are the people who murdered the Tsar's grandfather, and God knows, they have

126

tried to blow us all up enough times since. Why do you think we have to hide away out here, child? I will tell you. It is because the authorities tell us it is too dangerous for the moment to live in Petersburg. Until these people realize who rules Russia, we shall have more crackpot episodes like today. Do you know what they wanted to do, these scum? They wanted to hand over a petition to the Tsar! As if they had any right to tell him what to do! Let us hope that the rabble have learned their lesson today. If not we will just have to shoot more of them next time.'

Natasha bent her head so the Empress might not see her horror.

'On Tuesday, Your Majesty, it is my afternoon off. Could I have permission to go to the city in the afternoon to see my family?'

'Of course you can, my child,' said the Empress. 'I have no doubt you will find opinion in the city even firmer against the rabble than my own.'

Lord Francis Powerscourt was confident enough now of his knowledge of the geography of central St Petersburg to make his own way to the Shaporov Palace to collect Mikhail for their second meeting at the Interior Ministry. Snow had fallen during the night, obliterating the last stains of Bloody Sunday. Bits of clothing flapped about the streets, fragments of hats and caps were stuck on the railings, the front of a shirt, the sleeve of a jacket now shrouded in white. Dogs patrolled the area, still seeking, and occasionally finding, pieces of human flesh. Small scraps of proclamation still fluttered around the Neva. There was a bitter wind and the sun was in hiding. Powerscourt was just turning into Millionaires' Row when two men in dark greatcoats stopped him.

'You are to come with us,' the taller one said in broken English.

'Please,' said the smaller one, though he didn't sound as if politeness was his normal stock in trade.

'I'm terribly sorry,' said Powerscourt, trying to walk on, but finding his way barred, 'I'm going to meet a friend just up the road here.' If he shouted, he thought, they might just hear him in the palace.

'Later you meet friend,' said the taller one, who seemed to be the chief spokesman. 'Now you come with us.'

'Please,' said the smaller one again, 'no trouble. We no want trouble.' Powerscourt felt something hard and round pressing into his side from the pocket of the smaller one's coat. This was trouble.

'Do you mind telling me who you are?' said Powerscourt angrily, as he was frogmarched back the way he had come. 'The British Embassy will hear about this.'

'British Embassy!' The taller one laughed. 'This is St Petersburg, not London. British Embassy go to hell!'

They left him at a tall building on the Fontanka Quai by the Fontanka river that flows through the centre of the city and whose banks are graced by many fine buildings. A bald man shook him warmly by the hand and brought him indoors. 'I think you will find it is warmer inside today,' he said, in flawless English. 'I hope my men did not inconvenience you too much.'

'I have been inconvenienced quite enough,' said Powerscourt, 'and I demand to be released. It is barbaric to go around threatening people like this. And who the devil are you?'

'I thought you might have worked that out for yourself by now, Lord Powerscourt, a man with your reputation as an investigator. My name is Derzhenov, Anton Pavlovich Derzhenov. I am a general in the army of the Tsar, and

Chief of the Okhrana, the secret police charged with the responsibility of defending the person of His Majesty and the integrity of his state. At your service.' He bowed deeply to his visitor.

De Chassiron had told Powerscourt about the many different secret organizations charged with extirpating terrorism, special sections of the police, of the military, of the troops guarding the imperial family, even of the customs. None, in his view, could compare with the Okhrana in the cruelty of their interrogations or their determination to achieve their goals. Not that General Derzhenov looked like a secret policeman. People seldom did. His most distinguishing characteristic was that he was completely bald. Powerscourt didn't think he had ever seen a man so bald. He looked as though he had never had any hair at all. Perhaps, Powerscourt thought, he had been born bald and nothing had ever grown on the top of his head. He was of average height with a small goatee beard and he was conservatively dressed as if he was going to a board meeting. Powerscourt felt he would not have looked out of place in an Inn of Court, relentlessly harrying opposition witnesses and flattering the jury.

'Let me give you a very brief tour, Lord Powerscourt. Our visitors are always curious about what goes on in the Okhrana.' Derzhenov laughed an ominous laugh.

With that he led the way down a flight of stairs to a very long corridor in the basement. Powerscourt saw that the building went back a very long way. There was a series of doors in antiseptic green on either side of the passageway, some with small glass peepholes near the top. There was a very bad smell that might have been rotting flesh. Powerscourt thought he could see a trail of blood oozing out of one of the doors at the far end.

'It's a lot quieter since we taped up all their mouths,

Lord Powerscourt.' Derzhenov spoke as if he was showing a potential purchaser round a desirable residence in Mayfair. 'The neighbours used to complain about the screams. One or two of the guests manage to free themselves of the tapes but not for long.'

He talked, Powerscourt thought, as if he were discussing a new method of producing pig iron or some other industrial process rather than the torture techniques of the Russian secret service. He shivered slightly.

'We've been trying out some new methods,' General Derzhenov went on, peering in through one of the grilles and making approving noises. 'We've recruited a number of former peasants recently. They have a remarkable aptitude for the work.'

The General tapped lightly on the glass and made winding movements with his hand as if he thought the rack or the press holding the victim should be made even tighter. Then he waved happily as if his suggestion had worked.

'Do you know what goes on in the peasant villages, Lord Powerscourt? No? Fascinating, quite fascinating. Some of the miscreants in these places,' Derzhenov went on, walking slowly along his corridor, 'were known to have had their eyes pulled out, their nails hammered into their body, legs and arms cut off, and stakes driven down their throats. We find most terrorists are only too happy to talk before they get to the end of that.' This time Derzhenov beamed happily at his visitor.

Powerscourt saw to his horror that the man was worse than a sadist. He was a connoisseur of torture, discussing its refinement as Johnny Fitzgerald might compare the more expensive brands of Bordeaux.

'Another favourite punishment in the peasant village,' Derzhenov went on, smiling slightly at the cruelty, 'was to raise the victim on a pulley with his feet and hands tied together and to drop him so that the vertebrae in his back were broken; this was repeated several times until the victim was reduced to a spineless sack.'

They were halfway up the corridor now. Powerscourt was feeling sick. Through the door to his left he could hear the swish of a whip. It sounded as if two were being applied at the same time.

'One last example, Lord Powerscourt, one of our most successful imports from the peasant village.' Derzhenov was smiling broadly now, rather like a wolf, Powerscourt thought, as he looked at the dirty teeth of the secret policeman. 'The naked victim is wrapped in a wet sack, a pillow is tied around his torso, and his stomach is beaten with hammers or iron bars, so that his internal organs are crushed without leaving any external marks on his body. Not a single one! Neat, don't you think?'

A single piercing scream came suddenly from the last cell on the right. It was followed by a second, even more agonized than the first. Then Powerscourt heard a terrible thump as if somebody had hit the victim in the stomach with tremendous force. Then the General disappeared into the cell himself. Again Powerscourt heard the sound of whips applied in a frenzy. Derzhenov was sweating slightly as he came out, rubbing his hands together.

'Sorry about that, Lord Powerscourt. Fellow was quite out of order. Now then, pity we've got to leave here but you mustn't be late for your appointment with the Interior Ministry. Come, we'll talk in my office upstairs.'

How, Powerscourt wondered, did the man know about the time of his interview at the ministry? He hoped the General didn't have a torture collection in his room, glass bookshelves perhaps, filled with whips and clamps and racks. He wasn't very far wrong.

'I think I'm going to open a torture museum when I retire, Lord Powerscourt,' General Derzhenov said, taking the stairs two at a time. 'Maybe you'll be able to send me some contributions from England. I particularly like the sound of the Scavenger's Daughter from the time of the Tudors. Very labour-saving, that one, I've always thought. You just fit the hoops on the criminal, making sure he or she is properly bent over, and you can leave them, for days or weeks if necessary. You don't have to go on pulling the bloody levers as they do with the rack.'

The General seated himself behind an enormous desk. There was not a note or a file to be seen. It was as if the General or his staff tidied up every scrap of paper after his day's work each evening. He waved Powerscourt towards a small uncomfortable chair to the side. A great brute of a man with thick black hair and a black beard that almost covered his face slipped into a seat opposite Powerscourt. He was enormous. His hands looked as though they could pull a normal person's arms or legs off with a couple of tugs.

'Colonel Kolchak, my assistant, Lord Powerscourt. He will be helping us in our interview.'

The Colonel growled at Powerscourt who folded his hands neatly on his lap and tried not to look alarmed. The combination of what he had seen in the basement and the presence of the human gorilla across the desk was unsettling, to say the least. It was the General with his intelligence and his obsession with the refinements of torture who frightened him most. He wondered what role the Okhrana might have played in the death of Roderick Martin.

'Perhaps, Lord Powerscourt, you might be able to help us with our inquiries, as your London policemen say.' The General was smiling at his victim, like a headmaster welcoming a miscreant schoolboy to his study for another beating.

'Of course, General,' said Powerscourt, whose brain was beginning to move very fast indeed. 'I am here to inquire into the death of Mr Roderick Martin of the British Foreign Office, who died in this city some days ago.'

'The unfortunate Mr Martin . . .' The General was almost purring. Powerscourt wondered if Martin had been a guest of the Okhrana in one of their bloodstained cells down in the basement. 'Tell us if you can, Lord Powerscourt, we are all friends here after all, do you know what Mr Martin was doing in St Petersburg? He must have come for a reason, such a distinguished diplomat, such a clever man.'

The remains of a scream that had travelled up four floors from an opened grille window in the basement to the General's office temporarily stopped the conversation. Derzhenov grabbed a black telephone and dialled furiously. When answer came he shouted very loudly and very violently in Russian. He began to turn red, so great was his fury. 'My apologies, Lord Powerscourt. I've told the fool down there that if he can't put the bloody tape on properly, he'll be the next victim himself.' Powerscourt wondered if the man had been an older recruit, not one of the recent peasant intake who showed such aptitude for the work.

'I come back to Mr Martin, my friend,' the General went on. 'What did you say he was doing in St Petersburg?'

'I know it must sound strange, General,' Powerscourt was conscious of a continual scowl directed at him from Colonel Kolchak, 'but I don't know. I honestly don't know.'

'Does that mean,' the General said, doodling on a large piece of paper he had taken from one of his drawers, 'that his mission was so secret that only the Ambassador was cleared for it perhaps? I am not sure I would put great faith in your Ambassador myself, Lord Powerscourt, but did he know?'

'No, he did not,' said Powerscourt, realizing suddenly how improbable it all sounded.

'The clever Secretary, Mr de Chassiron, did he know?'

'I know it sounds unlikely, General, but he didn't know either.'

'Let me just get this straight, Lord Powerscourt.' Derzhenov smiled a truly evil smile. 'You expect us to believe that you did not know why Martin was here, Mr Secretary de Chassiron did not know, the Ambassador did not know. Do you have an Embassy cat, Lord Powerscourt? Did the four-legged one know what the two-legged ones did not? This is hard to believe, surely.'

'Sometimes, General, the most unlikely explanation turns out to be the truth.'

'Let me take him downstairs, General.' Colonel Kolchak broke his silence. 'I'll soon get some sense out of him.' The English came very slowly. Powerscourt was astonished by the voice. A man like Kolchak should come with a deep powerful bass. Instead his voice was very high-pitched, almost like a girl's. It made him, Powerscourt felt, more frightening, the thought of those tones shrieking at you for your confession.

'Lord Powerscourt is a most distinguished man, Colonel Kolchak. It is not for us to treat him at this time as if he were a common revolutionary, distributing pamphlets in the university perhaps, or learning to make bombs in some slum on the Petrograd side.'

Powerscourt smiled nervously as the words 'at this time' sank in.

'Let me put a hypothesis before you, Lord Powerscourt, if I may.' The General completed one of his doodles with a great flourish. 'Mr Martin is sent on a mission here. Let us pretend it is a secret mission, as you say.' Powerscourt realized suddenly that the Okhrana might not know any

134

more about Martin's death than he did. In this scenario, he was there to enlighten them. If true, that might work to his advantage. But then, champion chess players are moving pieces in their brains ten or fifteen moves ahead. Maybe he should ask the General how good he was with the rooks and the knights and the bishops.

'Unfortunately for all of us,' Derzhenov shook his head slightly at this point, 'Mr Martin dies. Alas! Poor Mr Martin! Let us not speculate at this moment on how he died or who might have killed him. Let us concentrate on his replacement. Step forward, Lord Francis Powerscourt of Markham Square in Chelsea, sent by the British Foreign Office to fulfil the mission of Mr Martin. Consider, if you would, the visitors attendant on the Lord Powerscourt before he left.'

The General picked a piece of paper out of his desk drawer. 'The Permanent Secretary of the Foreign Office, Sir Jeremiah Reddaway, calls. A junior minister from the same ministry calls two days later. A former Foreign Secretary and Prime Minister, the famous Lord Rosebery himself, also pays a visit from his great mansion in Berkeley Square. And then, orchestrated and organized by Sir Jeremiah himself, the widow Martin in her widow's weeds comes to meet Lady Powerscourt at Markham Square. The purpose of all those visits and all those visitors? Surely, Lord Powerscourt, there can be only one explanation. The Lord Powerscourt is being briefed to carry on the work of the dead man, to take the place of Mr Martin and do whatever he came to St Petersburg to do. So all that remains for you, Lord Powerscourt, is to let us know the outline of what your colleagues told you in Markham Square. The fiction that you do not know what Mr Martin was here for cannot possibly be true.'

It all sounded very definite but Powerscourt thought it might be a fishing expedition, no more. He was astonished that the Okhrana had been watching his house in Markham Square. He remembered de Chassiron telling him, in one of his great tours de force of contemporary Russia, that the Okhrana were the best organized and most sinister secret police in the world. Other states might catch up, he had said, but the Okhrana had a great start. Before Powerscourt could reply there was a knock at the door. A thick-set man wearing a deep blue butcher's apron with dark stains on it spoke briefly in Russian to General Derzhenov. He barked a few words and waved the minion away.

'Fool in the last cell on the right has died on us. Natural causes, the usual thing. Gives us room to welcome another guest.' He looked meaningfully at Powerscourt.

'General Derzhenov.' Powerscourt was aware that there was now less than an hour before his appointment at the Interior Ministry, and that his position might truly be described as precarious. 'You are obviously very well informed about what goes on in London. Now I am going to tell you a story. You are a man accustomed to listening to stories. I leave it up to you to judge whether this one is true or not.

'I have been working as a full-time investigator for over fifteen years. I was involved with Lord Rosebery in one very difficult case concerning the royal family some years back in 1892. We have been very close ever since. Three years ago in 1902 I was asked to investigate some deaths at a London Inn of Court, a legal establishment where barristers have their offices and train up newcomers to their profession. It was a difficult case. At the end I was shot and severely wounded. I very nearly died. I was saved, I believe, by the expertise of the doctors and the love of my family. After that my wife Lucy and I went on holiday to Italy. She made me promise to give up investigating as I had been nearly killed too many times. I agreed, but with some reluctance, I must say. As you gentlemen will know, it is no light matter to abandon one's profession. The procession of visitors your people observed going into Markham Square were not coming to brief me on the nature of Martin's mission to St Petersburg. They were coming to try to persuade me to come out of retirement to investigate his death. Finally, they succeeded. That is why I am here today. But I do not know anything about Martin's mission, any more,' he drew a bow at a venture here, 'than you do. Look.' Powerscourt brought his notebook out of his pocket and began writing names and addresses at great speed. 'Here is Lord Rosebery's address in Berkeley Square, and the barrister Maxwell Kirk's chambers in Queen's Inn. Sir Jeremiah Reddaway, as you know, is at the Foreign Office in King Charles Street. If your agents speak to these people, you will discover very quickly that I am telling the truth.' He handed over the piece of paper.

General Derzhenov looked at him very slowly. He began serious work on another doodle. Peering at the page upside down Powerscourt thought he was drawing people who had lost a limb, in war, or perhaps in his basement. There were spidery figures with only one arm or one leg, or with hands that had disappeared. Two had no heads, perhaps pulled off by Colonel Kolchak in person.

'That is very interesting, Lord Powerscourt. I do believe your story.' The General smiled his wolflike smile once more. 'But I will have our people check it out all the same. I would make just one comment. There is no reason why events could not have taken place as you describe, but with the following exception. That you were also briefed on Mr Martin's visit to Russia.'

Powerscourt laughed. 'You don't give up,' he said. 'Why don't you ask Lord Rosebery about Martin? He doesn't know what the mission was either.'

'But if you were Lord Rosebery, Lord Powerscourt, and a curious Russian person asked you about it, you would say that, wouldn't you?'

'The trouble with you, General, is that you have a very suspicious mind. You see plots and conspiracies where they don't exist.'

Derzhenov laughed bitterly. 'If I did not have a suspicious mind, where do you think Russia would be now? If I did not suspect plots and conspiracies, this Emperor would have gone the way of his grandfather and his Interior Minister and his Education Minister and his Governor of Finland, blown into smithereens by the bombs of the revolutionaries. This is necessary in our country, the whips downstairs, the iron bars to break a man's arms, the water torture, the racks, the burnings, all of it. This is not a safe country for its rulers, Lord Powerscourt. All we can do is try to make it a little safer for them. Russia today is a place where the students learn to make bombs in their science classes, not one where they drift up and down the Backs in punts in your Cambridge drinking champagne and reciting the doubtful verses of A.E. Housman.'

The General shrugged his shoulders. 'You make me grow philosophical, Lord Powerscourt. I need some exercise in the basement to bring me back to reality. Off you go to your meeting. Your young man should be waiting outside. I shall be in touch after I have heard about our discoveries in London. Good day to you.'

The General picked up another of those dark blue aprons from a peg on the back of his door and hurried down his stairs. As Powerscourt left Number 16 Fontanka Quai, he noticed again the disagreeable smell coming from the basement. Very faintly he could hear the swish of the whips and a noise that sounded like a human head being smashed against a wall. He wondered if the General had rejoined his fellow torturers in his own private underworld of pain and suffering.

Shortly before four o'clock that afternoon Powerscourt and Mikhail were back in the Shaporov Palace. Mikhail had brought his friend to the Great Drawing Room on the second floor, a vast chamber with a sprung floor and spectacular candelabra that had originally been intended to serve as a ballroom for the Shaporovs and their guests. Their meeting at the Interior Ministry had been cancelled. The man at the decrepit reception desk had told them in his surliest tones that Mr Bazhenov was not at home. Only when pressed hard by Mikhail had he divulged that there was a message for them. Only when Powerscourt produced a wide variety of papers testifying to his name and existence did the wretch with one arm hand over the envelope. They waited till they were outside the building before they opened it. Mikhail translated fast:

'Interior Ministry, January , et cetera et cetera ... Dear Lord Powerscourt, Please forgive me for not attending our meeting as we arranged. I apologize most sincerely. Something else of great importance to my Ministry has taken me to very urgent meetings elsewhere. More apology, Lord Powerscourt, a paragraph and a half of it. Can you survive without it?'

'Certainly,' said Powerscourt, 'I think I could manage very well.'

'We talked,' Mikhail peered down at some indecipherable piece of Bazhenov handwriting, 'about Mr Martin's visits. I promised to give you some dates of the earlier occasions when he was a visitor to our city. Here they are. 1904, January 5th to 11th, March 21st to 29th, October 15th to 22nd. 1903, January 4th to 12th, March 23rd to 30th,

October 1st to 9th. 1902, January 6th to 14th, October 5th to 12th. We have been unable to find information on previous years. I hope this is useful.

_ 'There's another paragraph of apology, Lord Powerscourt. Translate or not translate?'

'Don't bother,' said Powerscourt, who had filled one sheet of his notebook with the dates in English. 'I think I can manage with what we've got, thanks.'

Now Powerscourt was perched on a sixteenth-century French chair in the Great Drawing Room, thinking his hair should be powdered and his shoes buckled and his legs in tights with a ceremonial sword, perhaps, hanging by his side. Mikhail was opposite him, frowning at the dates.

'Can you attach any significance to the timings of these earlier visits, Lord Powerscourt?'

'Easter perhaps, with your different calendar, Mikhail? Would the man come for Easter?'

'God knows. I think it is more important here than in England. It is the most important religious festival in the Orthodox calendar. Somewhere there's going to be some prayer book or other in this place which will tell us.'

'I think,' said Powerscourt, 'that I should fill you in on what happened in my happy visit to the Okhrana. Then, perhaps, it would be time to review what little we know, Mikhail, and see if we can deduce anything useful for our investigation of the late Mr Martin.' With that, Lord Francis Powerscourt, in behaviour that would have been instantly recognizable to his wife and children, began walking up and down the room. Except that in London his drawing room was the length of his house in Markham Square, while here in St Petersburg the Great Drawing Room was nearly as long as Markham Square itself. Powerscourt spared Mikhail none of the horrors of the basement, the whips, the screams, the General interfering in fury himself.

140

At a quarter past four a young visitor swept into the main entrance of the Shaporov Palace. Mikhail had sent her a note that morning, saying that if she were able to get away, he hoped to be at home by four in the Great Drawing Room. Natasha Bobrinsky had walked all the way from the railway station to the palace, hoping to see some remains of the massacre on the way. She was disappointed, but her cheeks were bright from the walk, her black boots clattered happily over the Shaporov marble and her long fashionable coat kept out the January cold. A dark blue fur hat protected her curls from the freezing air. She resisted all attempts to detain her. The doorman assured her that she could not just march in like this and assume young Mr Shaporov would be able to see her. They had no idea, the servants, what he was doing at this moment. They all had fearful memories of Mikhail's father swearing viciously at them when he did not want to be disturbed, in one case throwing a junior footman right out of the room until he crashed into the opposite wall. Natasha swept past them, ignoring all their pleas to wait.

The geography of the vast Shaporov Palace meant she had to walk halfway along the front of the building before turning right. Then she had to progress down a very long corridor, the Mirror Corridor, created by some late eighteenth-century Shaporov, which connected with the Italian Corridor at the back of the palace, lined with Italian paintings, and led directly to the entrance to the Great Drawing Room, halfway along another corridor.

After her initial escape towards the Mirror Corridor, the butler despatched three groups of footmen to head her off. One was to pursue Natasha up the corridor, trying to persuade her to pause in one of the libraries or sitting rooms off the main route.

'Please, Miss Bobrinsky, please step in here, it'll only take a second . . .'

'I'm sure Mr Shaporov will be only too happy to see you, but we must preserve appearances . . .'

'We could all lose our jobs here, Miss Bobrinsky, I'm sure you wouldn't want that to happen.'

Natasha swept majestically on. The footmen watched helplessly as she turned into the Mirror Corridor. Her back began to multiply as she progressed up the great passage. Soon there were ten, fifteen Natashas reflected in the huge mirrors sent centuries before from the island of Murano near Venice and the St Gobain glass factories in France. Occasional glimpses of black boot, multiplied ten or twenty fold, reduced the footmen to a moonstruck combination of admiration and lust. At the top of the corridor the underbutler watched the marching army approaching his position at the turn of the two corridors. All the Natashas he could see wore expressions of great determination. Every now and then there was a defiant toss of twenty beautiful heads as she approached the corner. The underbutler withdrew his two colleagues and himself to the opening of the rear corridor just before she reached it. He formed his little band up, arms linked, across the corridor, stretching almost to the opposite wall. Behind them a dazzling array of Raphaels and Botticellis and Andrea del Sartos guarded the entrance into the Great Drawing Room. But not a single Natasha arrived. She dived through a side door, hurried down three flights of stairs, found the lift that connected with the side door into the room three floors up and presented herself in the Great Drawing Room where her young man was deep in conversation with the man from London they called Lord Francis Powerscourt.

'Natasha! How nice to see you!' Mikhail Shaporov seemed to cover the hundred yards or so between his chair and the lift in a couple of seconds, switching effortlessly into their common language of French. 'Have you just arrived in St Petersburg? How are they all out there in Tsarskoe Selo?'

Natasha strode imperiously across the drawing room and sat down on a French chaise longue next to Powerscourt while Mikhail made the introductions. Powerscourt and Natasha had not met before. 'Never mind all of them out at Tsarskoe Selo,' she said briskly, beginning to peel off her black leather gloves, 'what has been happening here in St Petersburg? My family are away in the south of France, as you know, so I rely on you to keep me informed, Mikhail. What took place here on Sunday? We heard rumours of marches and hundreds of protesters shot dead by the Tsar's troops. That can't be true, can it?'

Mikhail Shaporov sat down beside her. The pair of them, Powerscourt thought, looked absurdly young, absurdly innocent, absurdly ill equipped maybe to cope with what was happening in their country.

'We watched it all from the roof of the Stroganov Palace,' he began, 'Lord Powerscourt and I and a colleague of his from the British Embassy.' He told her of the marching columns, of the singing of the National Anthem, of the hymns rising up into the sunshine, of the children on their parents' shoulders, of the portraits of the Tsar and the icons of the Virgin. He told her how all the different columns began to concentrate on Palace Square where they hoped to hand in their petition with its absurdly optimistic demands for the vote, for free elections, for a constituent assembly, for laws to regulate the wretched lives of the wretched workers in their wretched factories. He told her of the charges of the cavalry, sabres slashing into innocent faces, lances cutting into innocent backs. He told her of the round after round of infantry fire, smashing into the bodies of the marchers, reducing them to random chunks of flesh bleeding to death on the streets. He told her of the red blood staining the ice and the shattered remains of one hundred and fifty thousand protesters whose journey had started with hope and ended in total despair. He told her of the pathetic attempts the three of them had made to help the wounded as they lay dying on the Nevskii Prospekt. He told her of the aftermath, the corpses waiting for the carts to take them away, the pathetic children's toys broken on the ground from the gunfire, the waves of hatred that had flown across the city.

'How many?' said Natasha at the end, her face the colour of ivory.

'Nobody knows,' said Mikhail gravely. 'The foreign newspapers have talked of thousands and thousands of martyrs. The authorities here, the police and so on, talk of a couple of dozen terrorists accidentally killed in a revolutionary incident. Lord Powerscourt, who has seen a number of battles in his time, thinks we shall never know the true figure, but it is probably a thousand or so. And, of course, hundreds and hundreds more wounded. Russia will never forget Bloody Sunday.'

They all fell silent. The only sound in the room was the ticking of a Sèvres clock at the far end of the room. Mikhail took the girl's hands and held them in his own. Powerscourt wondered what the Russian for 'no longer wanted' might be.

'I know what I meant to tell you, Lord Powerscourt,' said Natasha suddenly. 'It's only just come back to me. You remember Mikhail asked me to listen out for any mention of the name Martin out there in Tsarskoe Selo? Well, I have heard two mentions!'

The girl paused as if she expected instant congratulations. 'How very interesting,' was the best Powerscourt could manage. Inwardly he cursed himself for his English reserve in the face of all this Russian intensity. 'How did you come to hear it? Who was speaking?'

'The first time was the day before the march,' Natasha said. 'That must have been on the Saturday evening. I was passing the door of the Empress's mauve drawing room and I heard her talking to some official or other.'

'How did you know it was an official, Natasha?' said Mikhail.

'Well, I couldn't work out how I knew it at first. Then I realized the man kept referring to her as Your Majesty.'

'And the second?' Powerscourt this time.

'The second time was Sunday night, quite late. We'd heard the latest episode of *The Hound of the Baskervilles*.' She stared at the looks of incomprehension of the two men. 'Oh yes,' she said bitterly, 'in the Tsar's Alexander Palace in Tsarskoe Selo it is more important that the inmates hear the latest fictional exploits of Mr Sherlock Holmes than they should hear the facts about what is going on in their own city.' Natasha paused and concentrated hard, trying to ensure that her memory was perfect. 'I'd been talking to the Empress Alexandra and I'd left my bag in the hall,' she went on, staring intently at Mikhail as if he could help her remember, 'so I crept downstairs to collect it. Nicholas and Alexandra were having the most frightful row in the drawing room. I didn't dare stop because I could hear a sentry coming along the corridor. She was shouting at him about following the path of his father and his grandfather, about how autocracy was the only path the Russians would ever understand and the path to Western fantasies of democracy and constitutional government was bound to be a total disaster.'

Natasha stopped, listening perhaps to the voices replaying in her head. 'And what did he say?' whispered Powerscourt after a moment or two of silence.

Natasha drew herself up to her full height. 'He said, I think this is right, how many dead did she want lying on the streets, how many members of their own family had to be buried in St Petersburg, before she followed the path of the Englishman Martin.'

6

Outside the windows there came the noise of an enormous steam whistle, like some mighty vessel in pain. Powerscourt stared hard at Natasha. He had no idea what the words meant and, for the present, no idea how he was going to find the answer. Over fifteen years as an investigator, however, had taught him that often you just have to wait for the answers to appear.

'Natasha, Mikhail,' he said cheerfully, trying to convey a confidence about affairs he did not actually feel, 'I would very much like to talk some more about Mr Martin, the late Mr Martin. But it must wait for an hour or so, if you will forgive me. I must send some messages to London. I should have done so before.'

Mikhail stared at Powerscourt. 'Forgive me, my lord, I –' He broke off suddenly and looked desperately at Natasha, wringing his hands together.

'Is there something you would rather I did not hear, Mikhail?' said the girl. 'Some male secret that we women are not allowed to listen to?'

Her tone was jocular but Powerscourt thought she was on the verge of anger. Mikhail seized the nettle.

'I should have told you this before, Lord Powerscourt. I forgot. If you want to send a confidential message to

London, I would not recommend the orthodox routes. The Okhrana are now able to decode the telegraph traffic from all the major embassies in St Petersburg. They circulate the key points round the people guarding the Tsar and the ministries if they think it's relevant. That is rather a great secret, and I would ask you not to tell your Embassy just for the moment.'

'Traffic one way? Traffic coming in? Or traffic going out as well?'

'Traffic going in both directions, my lord. They employed some eccentric mathematics professors and a couple of grand master chess players to work out how to do it.'

'May I ask how you know this, Mikhail? If you are able to say, that is.' Powerscourt managed not to use words like 'one so young'.

'My father told me,' said the young man.

Mikhail's father was beginning to assume legendary proportions in Powerscourt's mind, somewhere between a Russian J.P. Morgan and George Bernard Shaw.

'Does he have a couple of tame maths professors and the odd grand master to hand as well, so to speak, Mikhail?'

'I'm sure he's got lots of those,' said the young man loyally.

Powerscourt smiled. Mikhail thought he was enjoying some scheme forming in his brain.

'So,' said Powerscourt, 'if I could send a message to people in London by a different route, warning them that the orthodox channels were being broken, we could then send a whole lot of false or inaccurate information to the Okhrana and its customers, secure in the knowledge that they would receive it without knowing that we knew what was in it and that it might be false.'

'Exactly so,' said Mikhail, gazing hungrily at Natasha and wondering if there might be a time for love as well as a time for secrets.

'And how, Mikhail, do I send a secure message to London from here?'

'Well, my lord, if you give it to me I shall send it by one of my father's messengers or by his telegraph machinery. It's perfectly safe. There is a messenger leaving at half past seven tonight, as a matter of fact, and the telegraph is working all the time.'

'That would be splendid,' said Powerscourt. 'I shall go and attend to my business at the Embassy. Let me make a suggestion. I am sure you two have important matters to discuss. How would it be if I returned,' he paused briefly to look at his watch, 'in a couple of hours' time, at half past six? We could discuss Mr Martin briefly and then I should be delighted to take you both out to dinner.'

'Thank you very much indeed,' Natasha and Mikhail said in unison and laughed happily at the accident of their response.

'Take care, Lord Powerscourt,' Natasha called after him, 'we don't want you ending up like poor Mr Martin.'

Mikhail waited until Powerscourt had gone and then he smiled at Natasha.

'Do you know what this room was designed for, Natasha?' he asked.

The girl's eyes flashed back at him, bright with anticipation. 'For dancing, of course, silly. Do you think earlier Bobrinskys danced across these boards with earlier Shaporovs?'

She pulled him to his feet and they waltzed at ever growing speed across the floor. Natasha thought how nice it was to be held in these arms and how much more pleasant life would be in this palace than in her place of exile at Tsarskoe Selo. She could hear the music spinning in her head. She wanted it to go on for ever. Mikhail held her ever tighter, one arm pressing firmly in the small of her

148

back. They stopped in front of a huge French tapestry of Bacchus and Ariadne. Mikhail kissed her, very gently at first, then with a growing passion as he felt her respond. Natasha thought she would like it here on Naxos, with the raging seas outside and the smell of the wild flowers on the mountainside and your lips being caressed by Dionysus.

Lord Francis Powerscourt was not thinking of love on a desert island, or even romance in a Russian palace, as he climbed the stairs to de Chassiron's office on the first floor of the British Embassy, looking out over the frozen city. He was trying to work out how to exploit the fact that he knew the Okhrana were reading the outgoing and incoming traffic to and from the British Embassy. He felt sure he and Johnny Fitzgerald had devised some scheme to exploit a similar situation years ago in the Punjab. Not for the first time he wished Johnny was with him. After Johnny had carried out the requests he was going to send by the Mikhail Shaporov message service, he, Powerscourt, would ask Johnny to join him. That would please Lady Lucy too.

De Chassiron's enormous desk was covered with telegraph cables, lying in unorganized heaps on the dark green leather. De Chassiron himself was stretched out on the sofa, one hand behind his back, the other doodling notes on a pad in front of him. He was still very pale, as if suffering from shock.

'My dear Powerscourt,' he said, the words slightly slurred, 'how good to see you on day three of the Russian Revolution. Will you join me in a glass of Georgian brandy? They say it is good for the nerves.' He bent to the floor and half filled a tumbler. 'And how have the travails of the empire struck you today? Have you witnessed any more massacres? Cavalry charges in the poorer quarters? The Tsar in person with a sabre on a black horse?'

Powerscourt realized that the diplomat was slightly drunk. He must have been drinking for most of the day, for Powerscourt recalled on previous occasions how much alcohol he had been able to consume without showing any ill effects at all. He told de Chassiron about his encounter with the Okhrana. De Chassiron was fascinated.

'As far as I know, you're the first Englishman to go in there at all, Powerscourt, never mind come out again alive. Congratulations.' He didn't seem to take on board the subtler points about the dead Martin.

'I've been a bad boy today, a bad, bad boy,' de Chassiron went on, shaking his head slightly now. 'Been told off by His Nibs. He didn't like my account of what happened on Sunday. Asked me if I thought I was working for the *Daily Mail* with lurid and sensational' – he just about managed to get the word out – 'accounts of the slaughter of the innocents. He said, the silly old fool, that I was exaggerating what had happened. His Nibs doesn't seem to realize that some of us here,' the drunken diplomat was close to tears at this point, 'do actually care what happens to this bloody country, that we can't bear to see it being disembowelled in front of our eyes on such beautiful streets with such beautiful buildings. Our brother in Christ, the French Ambassador, usually well informed, says the people will probably all go on strike now. Whole country going to close down while the Tsar plays charades with the family at the Alexander Palace out at Tsarskoe Selo.'

De Chassiron bent down and refilled his glass. Powerscourt thought he should help him upstairs to his rooms quite soon so he could sleep it off.

'I told His bloody Nibs I'd seen it all,' he went on, waving his glass at Powerscourt, 'that I'd held the hands of some of these poor people as they lay dying. No good. Useless. Ambassador says whole thing has been exaggerated by the liberals. Man in Foreign Ministry had told him so. Foreign newspapers are talking of thousands dead. Italians chief ghouls as usual. Six thousand dead, some rag in Rome says. Mind you, if they'd had their way, those bloody Italians, Our Lord would have fed fifty thousand rather than five on that holy mountain in those bloody Gospels. It's the old story,' de Chassiron polished off about half of his glass in one enormous gulp, 'Foreign Office in London meant to represent interests of foreigners. Foreign embassies meant to represent view of the countries they're stationed in to His Majesty's Government, not the other way round.'

'De Chassiron,' said Powerscourt, knowing that there was limited time to get any sense out of his colleague, 'I've got to send a message to London, to Lord Rosebery and the Foreign Office. How do I do that?'

'All messages to London have to be cleared by Head of Station, His Nibs,' said de Chassiron, rising slowly to his feet. 'Telegraph room's down the corridor from here. Turn left out of my door, second door on the right. Operated by helpful youth called Crabbe, Ricky Crabbe.' During this little speech, de Chassiron had risen slowly but steadily to his feet. 'Going upstairs now, Powerscourt. Don't tell His Nibs you've seen me. Mum's the word.'

As Powerscourt made his way towards the telegraph room, he wondered if de Chassiron had managed to send any cables to London that day. And, if he had, what they would make of them at Okhrana headquarters at 16 Fontanka Quai.

Ricky Crabbe, guardian and master of the telegraphic equipment, looked to Powerscourt to be little more than

151

twenty years old. He was clean-shaven, painfully thin and had very clear blue eyes.

'You must be Lord Powerscourt, Lord Powerscourt,' he said, holding out a rather dirty hand with surprisingly elegant long fingers. 'Sorry about that, my lord, I've not been myself these last two days and that's a fact.'

'Where did you watch the events from?' asked Powerscourt.

'I was over with my friend Harrison Wisebite Junior at the American Embassy, my lord,' said Ricky Crabbe. 'They had a near perfect view of the massacre at the Narva Gates. Then the Americans began sending telegrams to Washington and New York as soon as the first volley was fired. My friend Harrison said it was to tell their friends and their brokers to start selling their Russian stocks and bonds as fast as they could. Anyway, my lord, how can I help you? I think you knew my elder brother, my lord, Albert Crabbe, served with you in Army Intelligence in South Africa?'

Powerscourt looked closely at the young man. Then an elder version of Ricky came to him, again very slim, very cool in action, this one, sending telegraphs out right up to the last moment when the post had to be abandoned before the arrival of the Boers.

'Albert Crabbe!' said Powerscourt. 'Known as Quick-Fingered Bertie to his friends! The finest and the fastest telegraphist in the British Army! What has become of him?'

'Well, sir,' said Ricky, delighted to hear the praise of his brother, 'he got bored with peace. No point staying on at army rates of pay to send out all that routine stuff, Albert said. He went to work for one of those big banks in the City, my lord. He's in charge of all their telegraphs and telephones and heaven knows what all now. Making a packet of money now, our Albert, always on at me to join him.'

'We'll talk about this another time, Ricky,' said Powerscourt, looking at the clock, wondering if the Okhrana's decoders worked twenty-four hours a day. 'I've got to send a couple of messages to London. Is the Ambassador fussy about length, number of words and so on?'

'Don't think His Nibs knows how the machines work at all, my lord,' said the young man cheerfully. 'He's supposed to see all outgoing messages, but you just write yours out and I'll send it off for you.'

As Ricky Crabbe checked the inner workings of his machinery, Powerscourt composed his messages with great care. To Sir Jeremiah Reddaway: 'Proceeding with mission. Please expect inquiry from Russian sources about our meeting in Markham Square. They merely seek confirmation that you were trying to persuade me out of retirement. They have some silly notion that we discussed Martin and the nature of his mission. I hope to have made them see the truth but your help would be most welcome. Powerscourt.'

He sent the same message to Rosebery, via the Foreign Office. He wondered if Rosebery's delicate nostrils might tell him something was slightly wrong in the wording of the message.

Ricky Crabbe bent over his code book. His right hand produced a new, completely unintelligible version of the messages which he proceeded to send to London at breakneck speed.

'You're here about that Mr Martin, aren't you, my lord,' he said to Powerscourt as his hands continued to tap out the code, 'trying to find out what happened to him, isn't that it?'

'You're absolutely right, Ricky,' said Powerscourt, remembering what hotbeds of gossip places like embassies could be. 'Do you know anything about it? You must have all kinds of secrets passing through your hands in such a sensitive and important post as this.'

Ricky Crabbe frowned. 'Do you know something, Lord Powerscourt? You're the first person who's ever asked me that.' He paused and stared at the last two lines of the despatches to London. 'There's just one thing, my lord. I'm sure it's nothing, nothing at all.' He paused again, and then hit about six of his keys in rapid succession.

'There, they've gone. Now then, where was I? Mr Martin, that's it. I'm fairly sure, my lord, but I couldn't prove it, that at some point round about the time of Mr Martin's disappearance, somebody used these machines here without my knowing. There were only two times over those days when I wasn't here on duty – once I had an urgent signal to take immediately to His Nibs, and the other early the following evening when I was summoned for a drink in his office for Christmas. I didn't know the summons was social, if you know what I mean, I thought it was just to pick up a message, so I ran as fast as I could. Now I think about it, my lord, that was the time when the lock on this door broke and we couldn't find a Russian to come and fix it for about three days. They were all drunk. So I tried to do what I could but I suppose somebody could have walked in here and sent a message.'

'Assuming they knew how to send one, that is,' said Powerscourt.

'Indeed, my lord, there's none of the diplomats here know how to do it.'

Powerscourt wondered again if Martin had been a spy. Suddenly he remembered Sir Jeremiah Reddaway telling him that Martin had been trained in the use of the telegraph. These machines would hold no mystery for him. 'What made you think, Ricky, that somebody else had been on your machines?'

'Two things,' said Ricky Crabbe promptly. 'I always put the cover back on when I'm not actually using it.' He took a dark cover off the machine and replaced it quickly. 'When I got back, the cover was off.'

'And the other thing?'

'Well, that's hard to explain, Lord Powerscourt. Telegraphists would find it easier to understand. I've got what they call a light hand, my lord, I don't press down very hard on the keys. Whoever used it when I was away, if somebody did, had a much harder fist than me, so the key felt different for a little while when I got back. It had just got used to the other fellow, don't you see.'

Endless possibilities were spooling out of Powerscourt's brain. He suddenly realized how much it must have taken the young man to tell him this.

'Ricky,' he said, 'I cannot tell you how grateful I am for this news. It may make a substantial difference to my inquiries. Naturally I do not have to remind you to keep all of what has passed between us this evening as confidential.' He smiled happily at Ricky. 'I can see that you are going to be as valuable a member of my team here as your brother was in South Africa!'

Ricky Crabbe turned pink with pleasure. 'Thank you, my lord, thank you. I tell you what, my lord. I'll keep all your messages here for you unless you want them sent round, if that would be a good plan.'

'Excellent,' said Powerscourt.

'And there's one other thing, my lord,' said Ricky, as Powerscourt prepared to take his leave. 'If you want to send a really private message to London, one nobody knows about, just let me know. Me and my brother have been experimenting with secret codes and things. I can certainly send you a message nobody else will be able to read.'

'I'm delighted to hear that,' said Powerscourt, shaking the young man's hand. 'Thank you very much indeed. And what is the appeal for your brother in his bank of these kind of messages, Ricky?'

Ricky laughed. 'He says we could make our fortune, my lord. These banks, he says, are so obsessed with secrecy they'd pay a king's ransom to be certain no other bugger was reading their messages.'

'Hindustani Rules at the Embassy.' Powerscourt was beginning his message to Johnny Fitzgerald, perched on the edge of de Chassiron's desk, a sea of telegrams floating off to his right. He wondered if he should repeat the phrase and decided against it. Johnny was sure to remember the time he and Powerscourt had been reading the ingoing and outgoing messages to and from a rebellious Hindustani chieftain, allowing the British authorities to mount a deadly and devastating response to a rebellion the Maharajah had thought was entirely secret. Hindustani Rules would be enough to tell him that all formal traffic to and from the British Embassy was being decoded and read elsewhere. This message was going through Mikhail's father's telegraph machines to Johnny Fitzgerald via Powerscourt's brother-in-law William Burke's bank. 'Urgently need information on Martin's movements,' Powerscourt's message continued, 'supposed to have been in St Petersburg on following dates: 1904, January 5th to 11th, March 21st to 29th, October 15th to 22nd. 1903, January 4th to 12th, March 23rd to 30th, October 1st to 9th. 1902, January 6th to 14th, October 5th to 12th. Please check via FO, FO travel agents, possibly Rosebery butler for unorthodox routes.' Lord Rosebery's butler, a man called Leith, was famous throughout Rosebery's wide acquaintance for his encyclopedic knowledge of United Kingdom and European boat and railway timetables. If there was a coal steamer to Hamburg, connecting to a timber transport to Riga or Tallinn with virtually unknown railway links to St Petersburg, Leith would know about it. His admirers claimed that his greatest coup was to have spirited abroad, for a fee of five hundred pounds, a man not only wanted by the police, but watched for in person at every port and railway station in Britain. 'Please check Martin financial situation with William Burke. Debts? Gambling? Women? When inquiries launched please proceed to St Petersburg as fast as possible. Could be preliminary reconnaissance for Birds of Northern Europe. Love to Lucy and the children. Looking forward to seeing you. Francis.'

Mikhail Shaporov and Natasha Bobrinsky were sitting demurely in front of the fire, drinking tea, when Powerscourt returned to the Great Drawing Room shortly after six thirty. He thought there was something slightly different about their clothes as if they might have been readjusted in a hurry or even taken off during his absence but he made no comment. He remembered that he was to have the pleasure of taking the two of them out to dinner in one of the Nevskii Prospekt's finest hotels. He handed over his message to Johnny Fitzgerald.

'It's to my greatest friend,' he said, smiling at the two of them. 'We have been together on all my investigations.'

'And will you ask him to join you here?' asked Natasha, pouring Powerscourt a cup of tea.

'Yes, I have,' Powerscourt smiled.

'I will take the message to my father's telegraph office this evening,' said Mikhail, 'but come, Lord Powerscourt, we were going to talk about Mr Martin and how to find out if he has been here.'

'Do you know why he came here?' asked Natasha.

Powerscourt took a sip of his tea and fingered a long thin biscuit. 'Well, Miss Bobrinsky,' he began.

'Please call me Natasha,' said the girl with a smile that could have launched a few hundred ships or more on the route to windy Ilium. 'Miss Bobrinsky makes me sound like a governess or an old maid.'

'I'm sure that any family in Europe,' now it was Powerscourt's turn to smile a pedestrian, humdrum smile that could scarcely have launched a rowing boat, 'would be overjoyed to have you as daughter or governess, Natasha. However, let me return to Mr Martin.' He took a mouthful of biscuit and stared earnestly into the fire.

'I can think of any number of reasons why Mr Martin should have come to St Petersburg in those earlier years,' he began. 'He could have had a second wife here. I do not imagine the authorities in St Petersburg check with the authorities in London to ask whether a man has been married before. Or he could have had a relationship with a woman here and not been married to her. He could have had a child or children with either of the above and come to visit them. He could, more fancifully, have been a devotee of Russian church music and come here at Easter and the other times to satisfy his passion. In case you think that is unlikely,' he turned and smiled at Mikhail and Natasha, 'I was once involved with a case in England where a man wrongly arrested for murder was going round the cathedrals of England attending Evensong, or Vespers as I think it would be called in the Orthodox rite.'

'How many did he get through?' asked Mikhail.

'How many services? Or how many cathedrals? Same thing, really,' Powerscourt replied. 'I think it was about seventeen. He was over halfway through. Anyway, on another tack, our friend Martin could have been here because of gambling debts. I gather people here do gamble in rather a big way, palaces, estates, entire stables wagered away in the course of an evening. Perhaps he ran up enormous sums and came back when he could to pay them off. I know it sounds unlikely, but I don't think it's impossible. Then there's blackmail. Perhaps he was being blackmailed and came back at these intervals to settle another tranche of his debt.'

Natasha was entranced. Mikhail had told her Powerscourt was clever. Now, she felt, he was trailing his brain in front of the two of them like a matador with his cloak in the bull ring.

'Perhaps,' Powerscourt went on, unaware that he had been despatched to the Plaza del Toros in Pamplona or Madrid on what might prove to be his last mission, ' though even I think this is unlikely, perhaps he had Russian ancestry somewhere and had come to search for his past. Perhaps there was a great fortune, some vast estates maybe, waiting way out there beyond the snows and the route of the Trans-Siberian. Or, more sinister of all, perhaps Roderick Martin was a spy. A spy not for the British but for the Russians. Perhaps he came here to report back on his previous period of treachery in the service of the King Emperor and to be briefed for the months ahead in his service of the Tsar of All the Russias. Perhaps the confusion between the ministries about whether Martin was here or not was caused by the fact that only one of them knew he was a spy. The rest thought he was what he said he was, an English diplomat. Perhaps, and this is my last thought, Martin was a kind of conduit for messages that were too important or too sensitive to go through normal diplomatic channels. There is little diplomacy that does not have its back channels, secret routes for the passing of information. Maybe Martin, according to these dates, had been doing this dangerous work for years.'

As Powerscourt stopped Mikhail gave him a loud cheer and Natasha leant over and kissed him on the cheek. 'Bravo, Lord Powerscourt! A tour de force!'

'Superb,Lord Powerscourt!' The laughter rang out across the Great Drawing Room. Powerscourt suddenly felt the world was a better place and that he was a younger man.

'We have been thinking while you were away,' said Mikhail earnestly, still smiling, 'and we have two suggestions.' Powerscourt was glad there had been time for thought in his absence. 'You have a photograph of Mr Martin, maybe two or three, I think,' the young man went on.

'I have half a dozen, I believe,' said Powerscourt.

'With one or two of them,' said Mikhail, 'Natasha and I will go to the Yacht Club and ask around. I think we just have to say he is a relative of ours who has gone missing. But everyone who is anybody in St Petersburg goes there. We will spend several days there and see what we can find.'

'And the other thought?' said Powerscourt, admiring the slight flush in Natasha's cheeks from the fire.

'That involves my granny,' said Natasha happily. 'I think you'd better come along too, Lord Powerscourt. I'm sure my granny would approve of you. You see, at the times we have for Mr Martin's presence in St Petersburg, at the start of the year, those are the great times for balls and parties. All of St Petersburg gets involved. Almost everyone attends one of these balls or soirées or supper parties or dancing parties or whatever they are called. My granny must be the only person in Russia who has attended every single function for years and years and years. And she never forgets a face, never. The only slight problem,'

Natasha began to giggle rather disloyally here, 'is that now her memory is beginning to go. So, she'll say of course I know who he is, I met him at the Oblonskys' in '95. But it may take some time to remember the name nowadays. I think we'd better give her plenty of notice before we go and see her so she can get her thoughts in order.'

'I look forward to meeting her,' said Powerscourt, wondering if Natasha's granny had been a beauty in her youth. 'This all sounds very promising.'

'I'm not sure, you know,' said Mikhail seriously. 'This will only work if Mr Martin moved in our sort of world. What happens if he didn't, Lord Powerscourt?'

'We'll just have to wait and see,' said Powerscourt.

'And there's something I forgot.' Natasha Bobrinsky looked very serious all of a sudden. 'I thought of it on the way here. Lord Powerscourt, Mikhail told you about the missing Fabergé Easter eggs, the Trans-Siberian Railway egg and the Danish Palaces egg?'

'He did,' said Powerscourt. 'What of them?'

'Somebody said the other day that they'd both gone abroad.'

'Just abroad? Not London? Not Paris or Rome or New York?'

'Just abroad,' said Natasha. 'Do you think they could have been trying to send somebody some sort of a message?'

For the next three days visitors to St Petersburg's most fashionable location, the Imperial Yacht Club, were greeted at some point during their stay by Mikhail, or Natasha when she could get away, or occasionally both together, asking if, by any chance, they recollected meeting the person in the photograph. It was, they assured their

161

victims, a question of an inheritance, a rather large inheritance, always a subject dear to an aristocrat's heart. Powerscourt was invited in from time to time to witness these encounters and was most impressed with the seriousness with which the young people took to their task. They worked well in harness, Mikhail taking all the women and Natasha taking all the men. Mikhail would look at the women with great devotion, Natasha managed to give the impression that she, in person, might form part of the inheritance.

Powerscourt regretted that he did not have a wider choice of photograph. The Foreign Office had been in such a hurry to send him to St Petersburg that he had accepted the first clutch of photographs he had been offered. They were identical. They all showed Martin in a rather nondescript suit, with an undistinguished shirt and a dreary-looking tie with a stain near the top of it. He was seated in a garden chair with a wide expanse of lawn behind him. Powerscourt happened to know that the lawn was the lawn of Martin's house, Tibenham Grange, in Kent. Had the photographer turned his subject round one hundred and eighty degrees, the spectator would have seen the moat, the fifteenth-century square building, the little tower, maybe from the right angle, the tiny courtyard within. Tibenham Grange was one of the finest small moated houses in England, much praised by the American novelist Henry James when he came to stay. With the Grange behind him, Martin would have looked like a man of substance, a man of discernment in his choice of property, possibly even a little eccentric to have bought such an ancient specimen in a modern age of continual progress towards a better world. But with the anonymous lawn behind him, he could have been a civil servant or, perhaps, a local government official in the lower ranks.

Not that there was any shortage of identifications of Roderick Martin from the blue-blooded clientele of the Imperial Yacht Club. He was, an elderly dowager informed Mikhail, undoubtedly the man in charge of the sleeping cars on the Moscow to St Petersburg express. She had had dealings with him only the week before. This was the fellow, a red-faced colonel told Natasha, who counted out the money for you in the Moscow Narodny Bank further up the Nevskii Prospekt. The colonel would put money on it.

Nonsense, said a society beauty, dazzling Mikhail with her most flattering smile, everybody knew this man: he was a senior official in the Ministry of Finance who had entered into a sensational wedding with an heiress some years before. The marriage, alas, had not lasted. Ability with figures, the beauty told Mikhail sadly, was not sufficient for a happy union. Powerscourt actually wondered if that might be true until he was told that the lady was a notorious liar.

The most plausible identification came from an elderly man who drank champagne faster than anybody Powerscourt had ever seen. 'Dobrynin!' he said. 'Blow me down, it's bloody Dobrynin! Haven't seen the bugger for years!'

While Natasha waited for further enlightenment, the man downed the rest of his glass and held it out absentmindedly for a refill. A Yacht Club waiter seemed to be in permanent attendance solely for the purpose of replenishment.

'Well, I'll be damned,' the elderly gentleman said. 'Has somebody killed the bastard at last? Surprising he's lasted as long as he has really.'

Natasha did not mention that somebody had actually killed the bastard.

'Who is he, sir?' she asked in her most innocent voice.

'Who is he?' snorted the man, holding out his glass for yet another refill. 'I should think,' the man said, peering round the room, 'that a large number of the people in this club have been through his hands. And I mean literally through his hands! A very large number indeed!'

The old man nodded as if he had solved the problem. Natasha waited. The old man peered at the photograph again.

'Bloody man!' he said again, memories coming back fast, probably speeded on their way by the Dom Perignon. Natasha looked at the old gentleman once more.

'All right, all right!' he said. 'Women wouldn't know about him. Bastard Dobrynin was head of mathematics in the lycée out at Tsarskoe Selo, place where Pushkin went to school,' the last bit said condescendingly as if even a flibbertigibbet like Natasha must have heard of Pushkin, 'and if you didn't get your sums right, he would beat you and beat you and beat you until you did. Very painful subject, mathematics, for most of his pupils, even to this day.'

He peered again at the photograph. 'Dead, did you say? No? Pity. Lost, that's nearly as good.' His arm shot out once more. Natasha moved away. So seriously did they take this witness that Natasha checked with the school when she was back at the Alexander Palace in Tsarskoe Selo. There had indeed been a Mr Dobrynin at the lycée. He was retired now, she was told. But he still lived in the village, just a few minutes' walk from the palace. If Natasha or any of her friends needed help, Mr Dobrynin still offered coaching in mathematics.

7

They left Roderick Martin in the Imperial Yacht Club. Or rather they left his photograph, attached to the noticeboard with a message and quite a large reward for accurate information about him. Mikhail Shaporov's father had been responsible for the reward, apparently telling his son that it would be enough for a down payment on somebody's gambling debts.

Powerscourt was delighted about the replies to his messages to London. From Sir Jeremiah Reddaway, for the present, there was no news. From Johnny Fitzgerald there was a cheerful message, saying that he looked forward to working with his friend again. It would, he said, be like the old days up Hindustan way in India. Powerscourt had already cleared Johnny's arrival with the Ambassador and de Chassiron. He had also sent a note to all the ministries where he had called, to the Interior Ministry, the Foreign Ministry, even the Okhrana, advising them of Fitzgerald's coming.

But it was Rosebery who excelled himself in the despatch of messages to the Okhrana. Rosebery the politician had always been touchy, difficult, mercurial. He was notorious for it. He would angle for high office and then agonize for weeks over whether he would accept the position or not.

Scarcely had he sat down in his Cabinet Ministry than he would be thinking of resigning. Indeed, his critics said that he took more pleasure from leaving office than most normal people did in accepting it. Morbid, over-sensitive, ever quick to take offence, prone to long fits of depression, Rosebery was said to be more highly strung than his strings of racehorses. But on this occasion he had served his friend well. Powerscourt wondered if he had divined that he was writing, not to the Foreign Office or to Powerscourt, but to the Russian secret police.

His message was addressed to the Foreign Secretary himself, with copies to Sir Jeremiah Reddaway and to Powerscourt at the British Embassy.

'Dear Foreign Secretary,' he began. Powerscourt suspected he had no intention of paying any attention to government directives about the high costs of international telegraph messages. 'Please forgive me, as a previous holder of your distinguished office, for troubling you in these difficult times. I find, yet again, that my role in events just past is being misinterpreted, and that my position on some delicate events of recent weeks is in danger of being misconstrued.'

Nine out of ten on the pompous scale so far, thought Powerscourt with a grin. In his role of injured party, this was vintage Rosebery.

'I propose to place on record my role in the unfortunate affair of Mr Roderick Martin for the elucidation of posterity and lest there be any misunderstandings in the present. The facts are clear. I was informed of the demise of Mr Martin by the Prime Minister and by yourself, as you will recall, at a meeting in Number 10 Downing Street late last year. On that occasion I was not told anything of Mr Martin's mission or of his intentions in St Petersburg. To this day I know nothing of either of those matters. Rather

I was consulted about the likelihood of Lord Francis Powerscourt being persuaded out of retirement to inquire into the death of Mr Martin. I undertook to use whatever capital and whatever credit I possessed in that quarter on the Government's behalf.

'To that end, I called, not upon Lord Powerscourt himself, but on his wife, who I believed was the principal obstacle to his returning to his former career as an investigator. I pointed out to Lady Powerscourt that she was hindering her husband in his career and probably making him a sceptic to the question of his own courage: that men of quality in the public sphere have no right to refuse to carry out their work merely because it might be dangerous: furthermore, that the nation would be ill served indeed if men like her first or her second husbands were to cower at home because of the off-chance of a bullet abroad. I believe my arguments may have had some purchase with Lady Powerscourt. She grew agitated and asked me to leave. At no point in our conversation did we discuss Mr Martin. That was not the point of my visit.

'That, in short, is a full recapitulation of my role in this unfortunate affair. It grieves me more than I can say when it is rumoured abroad that I had inside knowledge of Mr Martin's objectives or of his mission to the Russian capital. These rumours are an insult to the dead and an affront to the living. I had no such knowledge. I trust, nay, I have every confidence, sir, that you will do everything in your power to ensure that the truth prevails and that the reputation of the British Foreign Office and its servants for upright and honourable behaviour is upheld with as much vigour today as it has been in former times. Yours sincerely, Rosebery.'

Powerscourt smiled as he read the telegraph for the second time. He had, he felt, advanced a knight into the heart of the Okhrana defences, and the knight was well protected. He wondered what General Derzhenov would make of it when his decoders finally presented it. He wondered idly if they operated on a daily basis, the mathematics professors and the chess masters, transcripts of Embassy messages available to read on the day they arrived in St Petersburg. Would this be enough to persuade the old sadist Derzhenov, as Powerscourt mentally referred to him, that he, Powerscourt, knew nothing of what had brought Martin to St Petersburg?

Two days later Natasha Bobrinsky and an Embassy guard called Sandy escorted Powerscourt to the Bobrinsky household and the Bobrinsky grandmother in Millionaires' Row near the Embassy. Ever since Powerscourt's abduction by the Okhrana thugs, the Ambassador had decreed that he should be accompanied wherever he went. Natasha, looking very demure in her lady-in-waiting clothes, told Powerscourt a brief life history of her elderly relation on the way.

'She's my mother's mother, Lord Powerscourt, so she started life as a Dolgoruky back in 1830 or something like that.' Powerscourt thought the girl made the date sound as if it belonged to a different era altogether, Iron Age rather than Bronze, as it were.

'She married quite late by Russian standards, Elizabeth Nicolaievna,' Natasha went on. 'She must have been twenty-three or twenty-four. Her husband was a cavalry man, very tall, very handsome, they say. My granny says to this day that he was the best-looking soldier in St Petersburg.' The girl fell silent, as if trying to remember her grandfather.

'What became of him?' asked Powerscourt.

'It's all rather sad, Lord Powerscourt. They had two children, my mother and her sister, and then my father was killed in a training accident. Some explosives went off when they shouldn't have done, just when he was inspecting them in fact, and he was blown to smithereens.'

Powerscourt thought, but did not say, that it sounded as if her grandfather had encountered by accident the same fate that was now being meted out on purpose to the ruling elite by the revolutionaries.

'Anyway, Lord Powerscourt, there she was, this Elizabeth, with two little girls, heaps of relations to help with the children, and plenty of money. I'm sure she looked quite hard for another husband, though she would tell you, if you dared to ask, that she was far too busy looking after the children.'

They had entered the Bobrinsky Palace now, a slightly smaller version of the Shaporov, but with the same profusion of enormous mirrors and paintings on the walls. Sandy, the Embassy guard waited in the entrance lobby. 'What she did, my granny,' Natasha went on, 'was to pursue an interest in etiquette, who stands where on military parades, what kind of dances are suitable for the unmarried, all that sort of stuff. Soon the foreign embassies were asking her for advice. Her library grew bigger and bigger with books of deportment and all that junk. Then the imperial courtiers began checking things with her. By fifteen years ago she was the unquestioned expert on decorum and etiquette in St Petersburg, invited to every social function in the calendar. That's why she may be able to help. If our friend Mr Martin showed up at any of those dances or parties, she'll have seen him. Let's just hope she remembers him. She's bedridden now, poor old thing, I don't suppose she'll go to any more grand balls in this life.'

Natasha was now knocking firmly on a pair of very solid double doors. As they obeyed the instruction to enter, Powerscourt saw that they were in an enormous chamber, with three sets of huge windows looking out towards the Neva. Two vast fires were burning in enormous grates, set in elaborate and ornate marble fireplaces. At one end, at right angles to the river, stood a huge bed, surrounded by tables with books and newspapers, tables with drinks and cigarettes and one table totally covered with small notebooks which Powerscourt suspected might be the records of the balls or the diaries of the social years gone by.

'Natasha, my dear, how nice to see you, and you, young man, you must be Lord Francis Powerscourt, come from England to share in our troubles.' Elizabeth the grandmother had a thin voice that cracked from time to time. She was sitting up, resting on a profusion of pillows, in the centre of the bed. She was wearing what might once have been a white lace gown, with elaborate work at the cuffs and around the neck. On top of that she had a dark grey jacket and her throat was circled with pearls. Elizabeth's face was lined now, the grey hair receding slightly across her forehead and tied in a bun at the back, each hair clearly visible under the surrounding lamps and reminding Powerscourt of an old lady's hair under a white cap, painted by Rembrandt, that he had seen in a gallery in Amsterdam some years before. It seemed appropriate in this most elegant of cities that life should imitate art.

Natasha's granny pointed firmly to a tall silver jug. Natasha refilled the old lady's glass, carefully avoiding Powerscourt's eye as she did so. Powerscourt wondered if she drank all day, lying here with the view and the flames in the fire and her memories.

'Now then, Natasha, show me the picture of this man you want identified. You know him as Mr Martin from

170

London, but he could be called anything here in St Petersburg.'

'Well remembered, Granny,' said Natasha, and drew the photograph from her bag. The old lady inserted a long Turkish cigarette into her holder and sucked in the smoke as she inspected her victim.

'Pity he's wearing his gardening clothes, my dear,' she said, frowning at the nondescript features. 'You don't have any more, I suppose?'

'I'm afraid not, Grandmama,' said Natasha.

'Young man,' the old lady took a fearsome swig of her glass, and peered closely at Powerscourt, 'have you ever been to any of our grand balls or court balls here in St Petersburg?'

'I regret to say I have not had that privilege,' said Powerscourt, bowing slightly.

'I am going to have to paint a picture for you,' the old lady said, taking in a further lungful of smoke, 'a picture of what they're like, to remind myself, and to see if I can remember your gardener.'

She took another deep draught from her glass and waved at Natasha for a refill from the jug.

'He was here in January last year and the two years before that, according to your information, this man Martin, Lord Powerscourt. Forget the dates of his other visits for the moment. Something tells me he is dead, but we will leave that for a moment. Now, then, close your eyes, I want you to imagine Palace Square at night in January, my children. All of the three vast blocks of the Winter Palace are blazing with light. Up above you can see the stars in a clear night sky.' Elizabeth Bobrinsky held up her hands as far as they would go. 'Around the Alexander Column in the centre of the square, braziers are burning in defiance of the winter cold. There is a vast queue of

171

carriages arriving in an unbroken line in front of the Winter Palace, and open sledges bringing the young officers who do not fear the cold, their horses' harness covered with blue netting to stop the snow blowing into their passengers' faces. And from across the square, my dears, you can just see the silhouettes of the women as they hurry across the few steps between the arriving carriage and the entrance to the Winter Palace. Everywhere tonight there is fox, sable, silver fox, arctic fox, all are on parade with their human friends. Up the staircases of white marble they go, the male guests in their uniforms of cream and scarlet, spreadeagle helmets of gold and silver, Hungarians and Caucasians bright in their national dress, diamonds and emeralds and pearls glittering on the princesses and the beautiful women.'

The old lady paused, absentmindedly polishing off her glass. Powerscourt suspected it was some form of vodka cocktail. She peered out at the flames in the fire opposite. 'I cannot see him yet,' she said, 'but I have not given up hope. Even a gardener may dance with a princess after all.' There was another pause. She began to screw up her eyes in concentration and waved rapidly at her glass with her right hand. Natasha poured the refill.

'There are so many sorts of balls, my children, but let us pretend for a moment that this is a *bal blanc* such as my Natasha might attend, one for the young ladies who are not married with rows of chaperons like me lining the walls, watching to see that no girl dances twice with the same partner.' The old lady cackled suddenly. 'Many times I have broken the rules in these *bals blancs*. I would do it for you, Natasha, if you wanted, but don't tell anyone I told you. I can't see him here, your gardener, at a dance where waltzes are forbidden, the two-step is regarded as not quite proper and most of the evening is spent in quadrilles with the young people advancing and retiring and forming circles over and over again. No, I'm sorry, Mr Martin is not here.'

Silence, save for the crackle of the flames, filled the great room. 'Would you like to have a rest, Granny?' asked Natasha.

'Rest, child? I've only just begun. I'm just getting into my stride. I think my glass is empty, mind you.' The old lady closed her eyes and stared as hard as she could into the past. 'There were all sorts of balls at the Winter Palace, of course, concert balls and Hermitage balls.' She paused. 'I danced with the Tsar, not the present one, his father, a great bear of a man but very light on his feet, every year from '87 to '92 at a Hermitage ball. There was a young Dane with lashings of blond hair, I remember, attached to the Embassy, who danced with me at a concert ball in 1900, the best dancer I ever knew in my entire life. I even danced with Bismarck once, my children, at a Nicholas ball in the 1880s. He trod on my feet. I can still remember that.' She stopped, waiting, perhaps, for the memories to keep coming.

'Some things were always the same of course, the flowers, the baskets of orchids, the thousands of palm trees, the exotic plants from the Crimea, the masses of lilac and tulips and roses sent specially from the Riviera.' She paused again, the look on her face abstracted as she swept through her recollections. 'The food, the elaborate pastries, the special ices to cool the dancers down, the plates of cold sturgeon, the chicken creams, the stuffed eggs, the three different kinds of caviar, the great blocks of ice standing about with holes cut in them filled with tubs of champagne . . . And sometimes, when the numbers weren't too big, you could walk with your partner away from the ball, my children, and go deep into the empty rooms of the Winter

Palace. The gentleman would take his partner on his arm – a famous admiral took me once – ' Elizabeth Bobrinsky smiled at the memory of her naval escort, 'and you could wander through countless empty suites and end up in magical half-lit rooms with only the odd orderly officer to be seen somewhere in the distance, and those enormous windows, as high as a cathedral, looking out over the Neva sparkling in the cold and the moonlight with maybe a light fall of snow come to dust the outside of the Winter Palace.'

Powerscourt and Natasha dared not speak a word. They waited. Elizabeth took another absentminded gulp of her vodka.

'Where is he? The gardener?' She spoke very fast, looking around her now, as if some faint memory was stirring. 'He was here in St Petersburg in the January of 1903, that's not very long ago. Natasha, my dear, do you remember the famous ball of 1903? It was the two hundredth anniversary of the founding of St Petersburg and that was the last ball held in the Winter Palace what with these common little assassins blowing up Ministers of the Interior and the war with those horrid yellow Japanese.'

She stopped suddenly as if she had lost her way. A sad, abandoned look came over her face as if she was six years old and lost in a strange park.

'Natasha?' she said quietly. 'Natasha? Are you still here?'

'Of course I'm still here, Grandmama,' said the girl gently, reaching out to take her grandmother's hand, 'You were just telling us about the anniversary ball in 1903. Maybe Mr Martin was there.'

Elizabeth Bobrinsky paused once more. She looked as though she might have used up all her strength. 'Early January,' she said, speaking very slowly now, 'there was a performance of *Boris Godunov* in the Hermitage, then, two days later, the costume ball in the Nicholas Hall in the

174

Winter Palace. Three thousand people, marshalled by those giant troopers of the Chevalier Guards in white, silver and gold at every entrance and along all the staircases, and Cossack Life Guards in their crimson and blue, the Negro footmen dressed in scarlet from head to foot.' She stopped again and took a tiny sip of her drink. 'Half past eight, the ball started. The guests were waiting in the Nicholas Hall as the Grand Master of Ceremonies appeared and tapped three times on the floor with his ebony staff, embossed in gold with the double-headed eagle of the Tsar. The crowd fell silent as the great mahogany doors, inlaid with gold, swung open and the Ceremony man called out "Their Imperial Majesties!" and fifteen hundred ladies curtsied in unison.'

Powerscourt noticed that she had changed tenses as if what happened twenty or thirty years ago was so vivid it came to her in the present, while events of two years before were consigned to the past.

'Everybody there was wearing seventeenth-century court dress. The Tsar was turned out as Alexis, the second Romanov Tsar, in a rich red caftan embroidered with gold thread and Alexandra was dressed as his wife Maria, in a sarafan of gold brocade with a silver design inlaid with emeralds, pearls and diamonds. Everywhere you looked there were velvet gowns and gleaming golden head-dresses, dangling festoons and flashing ribbons.' She smiled again at Natasha. 'Do you know, child, I danced with four Grand Dukes that night! I haven't danced since, mind you. Now I'm going to have a serious look for that Martin.'

Elizabeth closed her eyes. There was a deep furrow of concentration on her brow. Powerscourt could hear strange leaden notes of music being hummed by the old lady. It sounded as if they were out of tune. An old hand, the skin on the back like rumpled parchment, began to conduct an imaginary orchestra. Natasha was making dancing gestures at Powerscourt, swinging her arms round an imaginary dance floor between the tables and the window. They thought they could hear her mutter No from time to time. Then the hand and the humming stopped. She seemed to frown even harder. The hand came up, stayed steady for a few seconds or so and then conducted the tuneless humming into a dance that Powerscourt thought was a polonaise. This was followed by a waltz. Powerscourt suddenly realized that for their benefit the old lady was conducting this titanic effort of will and memory, that, very probably, he and Natasha were witnessing this evening the last dance of Elizabeth Bobrinsky. He wondered how many dances the old lady could hum out of tune and suspected the answer ran into thousands. He settled back for a long wait. Natasha, he noticed, had her arm on her grandmother's shoulder and looked close to tears. Suddenly the old lady's left hand began scrabbling frantically round the tables. Natasha placed the photograph of Roderick Martin between her fingers. She opened her eyes and stared hard at the image, as if she wished to lock into her memory every section of the photograph. Then she closed them again. Join us again for another evening of your favourite dance tunes with the Winter Palace Orchestra . . . Powerscourt was lapsing into London music hall announcements. But not for long. With a loud shout of 'Yes! There you are! You can't hide from me, Mr Martin!' Elizabeth Bobrinsky opened her eyes and slammed her fist on the table. 'I always had the feeling I'd seen him before. I'd forgotten that at the costume ball we didn't have national music only for the two hundredth anniversary. We had the usual stuff, waltzes and things as well for the non-Russians, diplomatic corps, military attachés, visiting professors, those sorts of people. I saw that Mr Martin just now dancing a waltz with Tamara Kerenkova. I've just remembered, he may look like a gardener, but he's a beautiful dancer.' She saw her granddaughter exchanging looks with the Englishman. 'It's not "is", is it?' she said suddenly, realizing the truth behind those glances. 'Poor Mr Martin's dead, isn't he? Poor man, he'll never dance again.'

'You've done incredibly well, Grandmama. I'm so proud of you. Now tell us about Tamara Kerenkova,' said Natasha.

'I will when you've run and fetched us all some champagne, my child.' Elizabeth Bobrinsky's success had brought a flush to her cheeks and new energy to her demeanour. 'I've always said that vodka is a drink for peasants and factory workers. Did you know Mr Martin, Lord Powerscourt?'

'I'm afraid I did not,' Powerscourt replied. 'He was an English diplomat. I have been sent by my government to find out what happened to him.'

'I don't think I want to know about that,' said the old lady. 'Look at the trouble I got into for knowing poor Mr Martin in the first place, all this rootling about in my memory like an old dog in an attic. Ah, the child has brought some champagne.'

As they toasted the old lady in Taittinger, Powerscourt waited for Natasha to ask the question. He hadn't thought it fair to pursue it while she was out of the room.

'Tell us about Tamara Kerenkova, Grandmama,' she said.

'She was a Bukilov before she married. I knew her people a little. Clever family, artistic rather than military.'

'And what happened to Mr Kerenkov?'

'He was a naval gentleman, I think. Maybe he still is. He

was probably away at the time of the ball.' Powerscourt thought that the Kerenkovs would not be the first naval couple to embark on manoeuvres while the husband was away. And he was quick to observe that there was no whiff of censure or disapproval of a married woman attending a ball without her husband.

'You wouldn't know where she lives, this Tamara, would you, Grandmama?'

'Give me till tomorrow, my child, I'm sure old Maria Bukilov will tell me in the morning.'

Powerscourt suddenly remembered the words of the first Detective Inspector of the Metropolitan Police he had ever worked with in a case of a corpse with no name. 'Give me a name and I'll get you an address. Give me an address and I'll get you people who knew the dead man. Give me people who knew the dead man and I'll get you a murderer.'

8

Johnny Fitzgerald had decided to tidy up his study before he began work on Powerscourt's queries. The study was Johnny's special sanctum, a large room at the top of his house, twenty-eight feet by twenty-four, with fine views over the gardens of South Kensington. Very few people were allowed in. At this point Johnny was approximately halfway through the writing of his third book about British birds, *The Birds of the West*, which covered the country from Devon and Cornwall, north into Somerset and Glamorgan and onward into North Wales. Johnny reckoned he had stayed in all the cheap hotels he ever wished to see, though he remained resolutely cheerful to the landladies. A visitor to this room would have found it hard to tell whether there was carpet or rugs on the floor or even whether there was any floor at all. Papers covered it as the waters had covered the earth in Noah's flood. They were stacked several layers high at the corners of the room. Ranged around the centre were drawings of some of the birds Johnny had encountered during his research, great birds of prey in flight across moorland or coastline, delicate warblers and finches and chaffinches to be found in the hills and the wooded quarters inland, gulls and cormorants and skuas that patrolled the cliffs and the sea. If asked, Johnny would have said that he loved them all, with a love so simple and pure he could not imagine transferring it to the more perilous world of human relationships. And, oddly enough, if you had asked him, he could have told you the exact whereabouts of every piece of paper he had worked upon. He had charted their position as accurately as any vessel surveying the waters of the great oceans of the world. He stood for some time, this January morning, wondering how to strike his camp. He looked rather sadly at some of the drawings, particularly of the seabirds, as though he was going to miss them. Then he got down on his hands and knees and made a series of piles of paper running in sections down the room. When they were all together he tied each one firmly with string and lined them up in order of assembly on a gap in his bookshelves. Johnny reckoned he could reproduce the chaos more or less as he had created it.

Johnny had already written to William Burke outlining Powerscourt's concerns about the finances of Roderick Martin. He had launched inquiries in travel arrangements to and from St Petersburg with Rosebery's butler. Now he was going to read all he could about Russian politics in a local library where they kept back copies of the newspapers. He didn't want to sound ignorant in St Petersburg. It would, he thought, be bad enough with them all talking in Russian all day. Johnny had had a low opinion of Russian and Russians ever since he discovered they used a different alphabet. Different words were bad enough in his view, but different letters were beyond the pale. Like the bloody Indians, he said to himself. And after his session with the press, he was going to take tea with Lady Lucy Powerscourt and her family. Johnny Fitzgerald was godfather to the boy twin, Master Christopher Powerscourt, now almost three years old. He took his responsibilities very seriously, Johnny, specializing in crawling races across the floor and piggy-back rides up and down the staircase.

At around the same time Mikhail Shaporov, Natasha Bobrinsky and Lord Francis Powerscourt were having an urgent meeting to discuss what to do about Tamara Kerenkova, dancing partner of the late Roderick Martin. They had secured an address for her from Natasha's grandmother's connections near the Alexander Nevskii Monastery at the far end of the Nevskii Prospekt. Now what were they to do? Natasha was for immediate action.

'We must go at once, all three of us, and call on her. We can't afford to waste time. There is not a moment to lose.'

'I'm not sure all three of us barging in on the poor woman would be a very good idea,' said Mikhail. 'It might put her off.'

'Off what?' said Natasha angrily. 'Off telling us the truth?'

'Well,' said the young man, trying to be tactful, 'how would you feel if three complete strangers were to call on you and ask you about your intimate relations with some strange Englishman? You'd have to ask some pretty delicate questions too.'

Such as, was he your lover? Powerscourt thought. And if so, for how long? If the affair collapsed, did you kill him? Or did your husband kill him? And where is your husband now, madam?

'Lord Powerscourt,' said Mikhail, 'could you give us the benefit of your experience here?'

'Well,' said Powerscourt, smiling at the two of them, 'first of all we do not know if she is still at this address. And however much we might all want to meet the lady, I do not think three of us is a good idea. I have had some experience of dealing with people in these tricky situations.

The most important thing is to make sure that they do not feel threatened. In London I used to invite them to come to my house rather than my going to theirs. I felt they would feel less vulnerable in my home. Their own house with all its connotations and memories would not be contaminated by this awkward and difficult knowledge. So I think the first thing to do is to send Mrs Kerenkova a note asking her if she would like to come here for morning coffee or afternoon tea. And, I'm sorry, Natasha, I think Mikhail and I should see her in the first instance so he can translate for me. When we see how that goes we can bring you in later.'

Natasha laughed. 'It's all right, Lord Powerscourt,' she said, 'I thought three was going to be too many whatever happened. Anyway, I've got to get back to Tsarskoe Selo.'

'Please remember,' said Powerscourt, 'how incredibly important anything you might find out there would be to our cause. And please be careful. I cannot over-emphasize that.'

As she skipped off to catch her train, Powerscourt and Mikhail began to compose a letter to Tamara Kerenkova, inviting her to call.

Lady Lucy Powerscourt embraced Johnny Fitzgerald on his arrival in Markham Square. The twins attached themselves to his lower legs like limpets on manoeuvres. Johnny knew how worried Lady Lucy must be, with Francis away on his dangerous mission. He was only too aware how one dead Englishman on some foreign shore could easily turn into two, particularly in a place as febrile as St Petersburg.

'Have you heard from Francis, Lucy? Did he seem well? You can't say much in messages on those telegraph machines.'

She smiled a huge smile. 'I've had two letters from him so far. He spent most of his time describing the people in the Embassy. There's a diplomat he rather likes called de Chassiron, I think. He doesn't care very much for the Ambassador. And he says dealing with the Russian ministries reminds him of the bureaucracies of the states run by the Indian maharajahs, incredible torpor for days and days followed by sudden, inexplicable bursts of activity.'

'The news is terrible, with all those people shot the other day,' said Johnny tactfully, displaying a small fraction of his new knowledge, 'but I don't suppose that's got anything to do with the death of Mr Martin.'

The twins at this point released themselves from Johnny's legs and demanded that he organize running races round the dining-room table. The memory stayed with Johnny a long time, two small children doubled up with laughter and giggles as they bumped into table and chair legs and each other, and their mother watching from the side with a look of great sadness in her eyes.

Lord Francis Powerscourt felt sure he had been taken up to heaven like one of those people in Renaissance paintings. It was surprising, he thought, how white everything was. He knew, of course, that white was the colour of purity and of cleanliness and as such might be expected to feature heavily in any celestial colour scheme, but not, surely, to the detriment of everything else. He remembered vaguely the words of the Christmas carol about how we would wait around in heaven, all dressed in white. God himself, he recalled from the Book of Revelation, had a head and hairs that were white like wool, as white as snow. Powerscourt wondered how long you had to wait before you were called to action. Maybe there was no action at all up here, maybe the waiting was all. Better to be a doorkeeper in the house of my God than to dwell in the tents of the ungodly. He wondered if there might be any detective work to be carried out in heaven. He was sure any decent investigator would be able to throw light on the motives of Pontius Pilate and the precise nature of the activities of Judas Iscariot. Powerscourt had always been doubtful about the thirty pieces of silver. Maybe he should ask William Burke to find out the exchange rate and the conversion tables so that the money that betrayed a son of God and started a world religion could be seen in the cold currency of English pounds. Then he told himself he was being remarkably silly. Surely God knew all that. He knew everything. Of all people in all places this was the last one to need investigators. Never mind. He would be a doorkeeper. He would watch out for the ungodly. It was, he reflected suddenly, rather noisy up here in heaven. He had thought that the engines of torment were down below rather than up here. There was a terrible screech and the St Petersburg to Volkhov train shuddered to a halt, its engine shrieking like a wounded animal.

Powerscourt looked up and checked his watch surreptitiously. He had only been asleep for a couple of minutes. Beside him Mikhail Shaporov was locked into his reading of Joseph Conrad's *Nostromo*. Their destination was Volkhov, to the east of the capital. For they had discovered, by a complicated series of messages over a period of ten or more frustrating days, that Tamara Kerenkova was not in St Petersburg but currently resident on her husband's estates some fifteen miles north of Volkhov, and that she would be happy to meet Lord Powerscourt and his interpreter early on the afternoon of Monday January 31st. 'Exiled', had been Mikhail Shaporov's verdict – probably, Powerscourt thought, after a conversation with his father: 'Bloody husband doesn't want her parading round St Petersburg with the wretched Englishman, so he packs her off to the ancestral fields out in the back of beyond. Nobody to talk to. People go off their heads with boredom out there, they end up as characters in Chekhov plays for God's sake, forever whining on about going to Moscow.'

Gradually the engine lurched back into life. Everywhere you looked outside, fields, hills, trees, all were white. There was nothing visible that was not white. Inside the long train various military men paraded up and down in their red and black uniforms, naval and army officers returning home on leave perhaps from the Russo-Japanese War. In the third class nobody was going to war but they seemed to have brought ample supplies with them, cooking pans, plates, food, vodka, all to sustain them on their journey. He remembered suddenly his conversation with de Chassiron the day before. Powerscourt had asked him what rules, if any, governed affairs between members of the aristocracy in St Petersburg.

'Rules?' de Chassiron had said, unscrewing his monocle with great care. 'Rules? I'm not sure I know the rules, my friend, but I'll try. I've never been involved in one of these affairs myself, they send us home on the first mule they can find if we do.

'Let me put it like this, Powerscourt. You know the rules, the conventions, that govern what goes on in some upper class house parties in England. Not in all of them, of course, but the ones where almost all the guests are sleeping with other guests they're not married to. Often involving the King when he was Prince of Wales, and presumably, continuing now he's King, only more so. Adultery by Royal Command. Everybody knows where everybody else's bedroom is – some hostesses, I believe, leave out a sleeping plan with the occupants of all the

185

bedrooms named like a seating plan for dinner – so at a certain point the guests peel off and creep round the upper floors till they've found their lover. Much creaking of floorboards, squeaking of doors, seeking of nocturnal happiness and so forth. All very gentlemanly. No challenges. No duels. No pistols at dawn. All caused by a leisured class with too little to do where adultery becomes the sport of choice. Most dangerous option on offer after all. I think it's probably the same here, more or less. Former Ambassador, man much more interested in human behaviour than the current one, swears he once overheard three young men at a party discussing which of five different men might have been their fathers. It's a long time now since Pushkin went to his death in a ludicrous duel over his wife's honour.'

'I see,' said Powerscourt. 'But if all that is true, and I'm sure it is, why is the Kerenkova no longer in Petersburg? Why has she turned into the chatelaine of the family estates miles from anywhere?'

'I can only guess, Powerscourt, maybe the husband has banished her. Maybe it had all got too serious – these affairs are tolerated, on the whole, because the rules stipulate that at some point everybody will go back to their husband or wife. Not necessarily for ever, but until the music starts again.'

Sitting in his railway carriage, with the white world flying past, Powerscourt suddenly wondered about the husband. They knew nothing about him. He would have to ask this Tamara not only about her lover, if he was her lover, but about the man she married as well.

A light snow was falling over the Alexander Park at the Tsar's Village, Tsarskoe Selo. Natasha Bobrinsky and the four Grand Duchesses, daughters of the Tsar, each pulling a toboggan, were by the west side of the Toboggan Hill. The girls never tired of pulling their vehicles up this hill and hurtling down it as fast as they could go. The most daring, the most reckless was the third daughter of the Tsar and the Tsarina, Marie Nicolaievna. She persuaded her elder sister to push her as fast as she could on the top of the hill before she began her descent. This meant she travelled even faster going down. The light was beginning to ebb. The soldier on duty to their right seemed to have drifted off. Marie was embarking on what must, surely, be her last or her second last run of the day. Then it happened. Natasha said afterwards that it must have been because of the fading light. She had total faith in the girl's ability to control herself and her machine. As the toboggan and the girl hurtled down towards the bottom of the hill Marie swerved suddenly to avoid a stone or some other obstacle in her way. The angle was too sharp. The toboggan turned over and Grand Duchess Marie was flung out, hitting her head on a tree trunk hidden in the snow and rolling over several times before she finally stopped.

'She's dead!' shrieked Anastasia, the youngest.

'She's bleeding,' shouted Olga, the eldest, wailing piteously, hunting in her pockets for a handkerchief to staunch the blood.

'They'll blame us for what happened!' yelled Tatiana. 'They'll never forgive us if she dies!' And she proceeded to cry and sob as though her heart would break.

'Marie's not going to die,' said Natasha, trying to take control of the situation.

'Girl! You!' A young soldier rushed out of the bushes in front of the Krasnoselskie Gates. 'Mind my place till I get back!' He pointed to a small shed just inside the palace grounds. 'I have been trained in first aid. I will take the girl to the Palace.' With that he bent down and picked up Marie and held her tight. He began running towards the palace in great strides, shepherding the other girls beside him, telling them to be calm and not to cry.

Natasha reached the shed and went inside. There was a rough desk facing visitors and a large book sitting on it. Outside the gates, by the great wall that ran right round Tsarskoe Selo, was a security station. Here, visitors to the palace had to show their papers and were searched if the guard thought it necessary. The Captain of the Guard came for a brief word with Natasha.

'I saw what happened, miss. You'll have to wait here till he comes back or he'll be dismissed the service for dereliction of duty. And you must enter the name and purpose of visit of anybody we send through in that big book.' With that the captain returned to his post, aware that he too could be dismissed for dereliction of duty. Quite soon the Tsarskoe Selo piano tuner came through. Natasha smiled cheerfully at him and put his name in the book.

Then she looked out into the gloom that stretched towards the Alexander Palace. She checked that the captain and his men were all in their positions. Then she began turning back the pages of the visitors' book. Faster and faster she went, in case the soldier returned. Her hand began to shake. Now she was back to the beginning of January, now back to the last days of December. Natasha thought her knees were knocking against each other. The light was really bad and she didn't know where the lamps were kept and she didn't think she had time to look for them. The handwriting changed with the year and the old 1904 script was much more difficult to read. Natasha wished she was one of those sensible people who go around with matches in a side pocket. December 31st, nothing there. December 30th, no. Is there anybody coming? Not yet. Her hands were really shaking now. Yes! At last! Here it was! December 22nd, British diplomat, Roderick Martin, time of arrival nine thirty in the evening, time of leaving, not there, purpose of visit, meeting with the Tsar. Meeting with the Tsar! The Tsar on his own! Nobody else! No diplomats, no heads of protocol, no members of the Imperial Security Service, no Foreign Minister. Natasha knew by now just how rare that was. She felt her heart was going to come right out of her chest as she turned the pages back to the present day. Hadn't Lord Powerscourt said how important her role here was? And hadn't she proved him right? Mikhail might swan about the city interpreting senior government officials, but she had found the pearl without price. She didn't think she could bear the wait to pass on her news. As Natasha made her way back to the palace, having handed the sentry post back to the soldier, one further thought struck her.

Mr Martin hadn't gone out through the Krasnoselskie Gates. Or if he did, they had taken care not to write it down. Had he left by some other route? Or had he never left at all? Had he been killed here and his body carried back to the frozen waters of the Neva?

'You must be Lord Powerscourt! And you must be Mikhail Shaporov! You both must be cold and hungry after all that travelling. Come in and we'll have some tea.'

Tamara Kerenkova greeted them on the porch of her house, bowing slightly as she addressed her visitors. The house was old, many of its external features hidden by the snow. She showed them into a long room with tall windows looking out into a garden. Powerscourt thought he saw rows and rows of cherry trees in the distance, their boughs laden with snow. There was a great fire blazing in

189

the grate and a young borzoi asleep on one side. A liveried servant came to take their coats. Mrs Kerenkova disappeared briefly to organize tea and refreshments. Powerscourt knew there was something unusual but he couldn't put his finger on it. It was Mikhail Shaporov, laughing, who filled him in.

'You'll get it any second now, my lord,' he said.

'Get what?' Powerscourt replied.

'Now then.' Tamara Kerenkova had come back. 'Please tell me how I can help you. Thank you for telling me about the death of Mr Martin in your letter, Lord Powerscourt. I am so glad you saw fit not to wait for personal contact.'

Powerscourt wanted to laugh but felt the circumstances were inappropriate. She was speaking perfect English, this Russian lady, she could have been conversing in a Mayfair drawing room. He didn't need an interpreter. But then, remembering previous encounters of this sort in previous cases, perhaps he did. But he needed an interpreter of the female heart rather than of the Russian language.

'May I compliment you on your English, Mrs Kerenkova?' said Powerscourt. 'Here I am with my excellent interpreter Mikhail and he's not needed at all.'

'I'm sure,' said the lady with a smile, 'that a young man of such wide education and such an excellent family will always be useful to you, Lord Powerscourt.'

She must have been about thirty, Tamara Kerenkova, of average height with very delicate features, a small nose and pale blue eyes that held you in their gaze. Her hair was blonde, falling in ringlets down the sides of her face, and every now and again she would toss her head to clear her face. Powerscourt couldn't work out whether the gesture was natural, affectation or flirtation. Did she shake her locks like that when she was on her own? he asked himself. He didn't know the answer.

'We had an English nanny, Lord Powerscourt,' she went on, 'Mrs Harris, all the time we were growing up. Part of her job was to teach my sister and me English. She came from Brighton, our Mrs Harris. If you wanted to distract her from a boring spelling lesson, you could always ask her about the pier. For some reason she was mad about piers. If you were lucky she would draw the sea front and the chain pier for you in your art book. It might take up all the time allotted to the spelling! Mrs Harris always laughed when she realized what had been going on. Maybe she didn't like spelling either.'

Powerscourt had a strange vision of two little Russian girls in a vast schoolroom up in a draughty St Petersburg attic learning English with a woman from Brighton who liked piers.

'I'm afraid, Mrs Kerenkova, that some of the questions I may have to put to you may seem rather distasteful. May I offer my apologies in advance for any queries that may seem prurient or inappropriate.'

The young woman laughed. 'Don't worry, Lord Powerscourt, you don't have to sound like the family solicitor. I'm sure we'll get along very well.'

'Could you tell us first of all how you met your husband?' Powerscourt had decided in the train that it would be easier to start with Mr Kerenkov rather than Mr Martin.

'My husband?' Tamara sounded surprised but she carried on. 'I met him nine years ago at a ball just before Easter. He was in the navy. He still is, as a matter of fact. We were married the following year.'

'May I ask if you have any children?'

'You may. We do not. Not yet anyway. There is still time.' The slightly pained look with which Mrs Kerenkova began her reply was replaced with one of defiance at the end. Powerscourt wondered how much hurt lay behind the words. He wondered too if Roderick Martin had seemed to offer some sort of solution.

'Ah, tea,' said Mrs Kerenkova, as a footman entered with a tray, glad perhaps of the break in the interview. 'Some cake for you, Lord Powerscourt? And a hefty slice for you, Mikhail – growing boys need plenty of food.' She gave the interpreter a gargantuan piece of cake, spilling out over the edge of the plate, which he proceeded to demolish with amazing speed.

'And Mr Martin?' Powerscourt took a small sip of his tea. 'Might I ask when and where you met him, Mrs Kerenkova?'

Tamara did not hesitate. It was as if, Powerscourt was to reflect later, she had been rehearsing her answers before they came. 'We met in Berlin in 1901. In the autumn. My husband was on the staff of the naval attaché there at the time.'

Powerscourt thought that in certain countries naval attaché meant little more than spy. Regular visits to naval dockyards, earnest interest in the latest techniques of propulsion or navigation or armaments – all could be displayed as examples of naive enthusiasm when in fact they were merely cover for espionage.

'Did you meet him at some diplomatic function? Some grand occasion at the Wilhelmstrasse, the Imperial German Foreign Office perhaps?'

'We met at a ball, Lord Powerscourt, a ball given by the Austrian Ambassador.' Tamara Kerenkova's eyes drifted away. 'It was fitting really. You see, my husband hated dancing. He didn't really like parties of any sort, come to that. Roderick and I were dancing less than a minute after we were introduced. We got to know each other on the dance floor. He was such a beautiful dancer, Roderick, very formal one minute, then breaking all the rules and sweeping you right across the floor the next. It was so exhilarating. I think we fell in love on the dance floor, Lord Powerscourt, dancing a waltz or a two-step or a polonaise, it doesn't matter now. One of the reasons he came when he did, at the beginning of all those years, was that January was the season for the great balls in St Petersburg. They were the grandest of their kind in Europe. Roderick and I were never happier than when we were dancing. The sprung floors beneath your feet, the beautiful women with their jewellery sweeping past, the men in their finest clothes, the officers in their gaudiest uniforms, and the arms of the man you love holding you tight as you whirl around the floor – time is simply annihilated as your lover guides you through the steps. Inside the form and the rhythm of the dance your mind and your heart can float away to a different world. Do you believe that, Lord Powerscourt?'

It was then that a truly terrible thought struck Powerscourt, one that was never to wholly leave him for his entire time in Russia. Suppose you were the espionage chief of the Okhrana, he said to himself, the spying equivalent of the terrible Derzhenov who was in charge of counter-terrorism. Suppose you had a spy in your employ, a really useful spy who could bring you the secrets of one of the Great Powers of Europe. So often with spies the problem lay with the sending of messages, the transmission of information. Powerscourt remembered the story in Herodotus of Histiaeus who wanted to send a message from the Persian court to his son-in-law Aristagoras, the tyrant of Miletus, urging him to revolt. But Histiaeus suspected that any message might be intercepted with fatal results. So he shaved the head of his most trusted slave and tattoed the message on to his scalp. When the hair had grown back he sent the slave to Aristagoras with a message that he needed a haircut. In modern times there might not

193

be enough room on a single scalp for the message. Elaborate systems of deception were often set up for the spy to meet and to debrief his handler. But suppose the handler was a woman and that she met her lover at the great balls of Berlin or Vienna or St Petersburg. Secrets could be whispered as they twirled round the room in the Viennese Waltz. Pages of information could be popped into a handbag or slipped down a décolletage during a two-step. The next rendezvous for the next exchange of information would be an innocent-sounding conversation towards the end of the evening about the next ball where they would see each other again. As a system, as cover, it was perfect. And, looking at Tamara Kerenkova, he thought she was cool enough to carry it off.

'I am sure you are right about the appeal of the dance, Mrs Kerenkova, the poets have been enthusing about it for centuries.' Powerscourt felt annoyed again at the contrast between Russian passion and English reserve. 'Forgive me for asking a personal question, but where did Mr Martin stay when he was here?'

The young woman laughed. The borzoi awoke and shuffled over to the tea trolley. 'Why, he stayed with me. My husband was away with his ship, most of those years. He would be away now, in Japan, fighting that terrible war, but he had to come back with a badly damaged ship that needed repairs.' She broke a piece of cake into small pieces and gave the dog his tea. He seemed to like the cake. Mikhail Shaporov stroked his white coat as he listened to the conversation. He sensed that some dramatic thought had gripped Powerscourt a few minutes before but he had no idea what it was.

Powerscourt gave no sign at all of excitement now. 'Do you mean that Mr Kerenkov is in St Petersburg right now, attending to the repairs?'

'Why, yes, Lord Powerscourt, he has been here since the middle of December.' She smiled at him. Powerscourt thought that naval officers must be pretty good shots with a revolver. Not a problem to shoot a foreigner in the heart and dump his body on the Nevskii Prospekt. He thought the young woman was daring him to ask the next question. He asked it.

'Might I ask, Mrs Kerenkova, why you are here at the family estate when your husband is in St Petersburg?'

She laughed again and now she too began to stroke the borzoi. 'See what questions they ask us, Potemkin,' she began by addressing the dog. 'I could say,' there was another of those tosses of the head to clear the face of that blonde hair, 'that I came here to prepare things for his coming a little later. But that is not the truth. Things are not very good between us just now. I am sure, Lord Powerscourt, that even in England the aristocratic husbands and their wives sometimes do not get on as they should. Is that so?' Powerscourt nodded, betraying an entire class in an afternoon. 'At first Vladimir did not care about me and Roderick. He thought it was just an infatuation, that it wouldn't last. Even when we met up for all those Januarys he didn't seem to mind.'

'So what happened?' asked Powerscourt. 'How did he come to change his mind? I presume he sent you out here because of some family disagreement?'

Tamara laughed bitterly. 'Disagreement? I suppose you could call it that. You see, Lord Powerscourt, I'd always told Vladimir when Roderick was coming. Always, so it wouldn't be a surprise. Then,' she stopped as if trying to fix a date in her mind, 'round about the middle of last month he heard Mr Martin was coming, coming to St Petersburg. He didn't believe me when I said I didn't know. And I didn't, you've got to believe me, Lord

Powerscourt. Of course I'd have told him if I'd known, I'd have told all of St Petersburg that he was coming to take me dancing once again, I'd have been so happy.'

Powerscourt was growing used to the shocks now. 'I believe you, of course I believe you, Mrs Kerenkova,' he said quickly, and he did, 'but could I confirm something you just said? You said your husband knew Mr Martin was coming to St Petersburg round about the middle of last month? Is that right?'

The young woman nodded. 'That's right. I might be a couple of days out, I can't remember exactly. Is that important?'

'It might be,' Powerscourt replied, 'but could I just get one thing clear in my mind? Did your husband send you out here because he felt you deceived him about Mr Martin's visit? Or was there another reason as well?'

Potemkin growled as if he didn't like the question or the tone. Mikhail scratched his head once again.

'There was another reason, Lord Powerscourt,' said Tamara Kerenkova. 'Vladimir said it wouldn't have mattered if Mr Martin hadn't been English. Russian naval people are very annoyed with the English at present. I think our ships sunk a couple of British fishing boats on their way to Japan and the Russians thought the British were making too much fuss. Who cares about a couple of bloody fishermen anyway, was what Vladimir said. He said my affair with Mr Martin could make him very unpopular so he wanted me out of the way for a while.'

'Quite so,' said Powerscourt. 'Did your husband give any idea how he learnt Mr Martin was coming to St Petersburg?'

'I'm afraid he did not. Could I ask you a question, Lord Powerscourt? Do you know what Mr Martin was doing here, why he came to St Petersburg?'

Now it was Powerscourt's turn to smile. Potemkin padded off to inspect the snow falling in the garden. 'If I knew the answer to that question, my dear lady, I would be well on my way to solving the mystery. At the moment, I have no idea.'

'Can I give you my theory? I believe he must have been sent here on government business. I'm sure your Foreign Office told him he was not to breathe a word to a single soul. Otherwise he would have told me.'

'How did he usually let you know he was coming?' asked Powerscourt. Visions of messages in a bottle, of coded signals hidden in the advertisement pages of *The Times*, of slaves with shaven heads, flashed through his mind. He had visions too of a mythical elderly relative living in a distant part of Britain perhaps, a sort of Scottish Bunbury in Martin's life, who had to be visited every year in early January.

'You're thinking of some romantic roundabout way of letting me know, Lord Powerscourt, I can tell from the look on your face. It was perfectly simple. He wrote to me, that's all, usually a couple of months in advance.'

'Did he ever mention Mrs Martin, Mrs Kerenkova?'

'Very seldom. She had him, Roderick, I mean, for eleven and a half months of the year,' Tamara Kerenkova said bitterly. 'I don't think she knew what she had. I wouldn't have let him wander off like that if I'd been married to him. Anyway, he wouldn't have wanted to.'

'Forgive me this question, Mrs Kerenkova.' Powerscourt was staring straight into those pale blue eyes. 'Would you have said your husband was a violent man?'

'Violent?' Those pale blue eyes opened very wide suddenly. 'Of course he is violent. All those naval people are violent, very violent. They're in charge of enormous guns that can sink a ship in a couple of minutes and drown a thousand sailors. I think that's a rather naive question, Lord Powerscourt.'

'I do apologize, Mrs Kerenkova, I wasn't referring to his professional life.' Powerscourt said no more. The young woman flushed.

'If you mean what I think you mean, it is did Vladimir kill Mr Martin, or was he capable of killing Mr Martin? I must tell you the answer is No.'

'You're sure about that?' asked Powerscourt crisply.

'Lord Powerscourt,' the young woman said, laying a hand on his arm, 'I should say that at some point in your life you have been a soldier. I should say that if you were faced, in your professional life, with a charge of your country's enemies, all racing towards you at full speed like those Zulus with their spears at Rorke's Drift our governess used to tell us about, you wouldn't hesitate for a second before you killed as many as you could. But in your personal life, I don't believe you could kill anybody, unless perhaps it was in defence of your family.'

Powerscourt bowed slightly. Suddenly Potemkin launched into an enormous fit of barking. He raced out of the room towards the front door. There was a tremendous ringing of bells.

'Please excuse me, gentlemen, I must go and see who that is. Forgive me. I shan't be long.'

'Mikhail, what do you think?' said Powerscourt. 'Do you believe this Tamara person?'

Mikhail cut himself another piece of cake now the coast was clear. 'I think she's a very good actress,' he said. 'I think she's been rehearsing this part for days and days. And I'm sure she's holding something back but I have no idea what it is.'

Potemkin charged back into the room and sidled up to Mikhail. 'My uncle used to give his dogs very strange names, Lord Powerscourt. He had a retriever called Raskolnikov once and then he had a pair of hunting dogs called Nicholas and Alexandra, after the Tsar and his wife.'

'Were they any use?' asked Powerscourt.

The young man laughed. 'He had to get rid of them in the end. Said they couldn't make up their bloody minds which way to go.'

'Forgive me, gentlemen.' Tamara Kerenkova was back, smiling at her guests. 'Those, believe it or not, were my nearest neighbours, only ten miles away, dropping by to invite me to a party at their house next weekend. Now, where were we, Lord Powerscourt?'

'I am most grateful to you for your time, Mrs Kerenkova. It is nearly time for us to go and catch our train. Let me ask you this though: did Mr Martin ever talk to you about his work at all?'

She paused and looked at the fire. 'Roderick wasn't one of those men who have to tell you everything they've done during the day the minute they walk in the door. He used to talk to me about his work sometimes at the balls. I was amazed at how many people he knew at these functions, ambassadors, politicians, lawyers, financiers, all sorts of people.'

'I didn't so much mean at the grand functions,' said Powerscourt, 'rather when you and he were alone together.'

'Pillow talk, do you mean?' said the girl, laughing, and then something snapped inside her and her laughter turned into tears, tears which she could not stop.

'I'm so sorry,' she said, wiping away the tears with Mikhail Shaporov's handkerchief, 'I'm so sorry. You see, I told myself I had to be brave for this meeting and I've practised it for days in my head. I've tried to lock out of my mind the fact that he's not here, that I'll never see him again. It's hardly any time at all since I heard of Roderick's death, you see.' She broke down again. The two men waited. Potemkin came to snuggle up beside his mistress. 'I wanted to be cheerful and happy and English stiff upper lip and now I've let myself down.'

'You haven't let yourself down at all, Mrs Kerenkova,' said Powerscourt in his most emollient tones. 'You've been very brave. Please compose yourself and we'll take our leave of you.'

The young woman made a desperate effort to control herself. 'I just want to answer your question, Lord Powerscourt. About Roderick talking to me about his work.' She blew her nose loudly on the Shaporov handkerchief. 'It was one day last summer. We'd just gone to bed. He'd been very worried all day and he wouldn't tell me what it was. I went on and on at him, the way women do about a secret. I was amazed when he told me. "Tamara," he said at last, "my government are about to do a very foolish thing. They're going to make an alliance with France and they're going to call it the Entente Cordiale." "Surely that's a good thing, making alliances with your neighbours," I said, not that I cared very much who was allied to whom, nothing like as interesting as who's married to whom. Roderick sat up in bed and looked very solemn. "There is only one reason France wants allies," he said, "and that's to find other countries to fight Germany. One day we will have to fight Germany because of this alliance with France and it will be terrible." Then he went straight to sleep.'

She looked up at Powerscourt, her eyes still red, her cheeks still stained with tears.

'If there's anything else you remember later on,' said Powerscourt, rising to his feet, 'you have Mikhail's address in St Petersburg. And thank you so very much for being so helpful. '

'Not at all,' she said, 'thank you so much for coming. I hope I was of some use.'

Potemkin raced their carriage down the drive until it turned the corner by the side of the cherry orchard. Powerscourt was wondering what other high diplomatic secrets might have been divulged between Roderick Martin and his mistress in between the sheets. Another thought struck him when Volkhov and the Kerenkov house and the borzoi Potemkin were far behind. He remembered the question he should have asked. Suppose there was an estrangement between Martin and Tamara, a falling out, maybe an end of the affair. She suspects him of being involved with another woman. That could be why he has not told her of his latest visit. And when she hears of his impending return to St Petersburg, does she borrow her husband's revolver and return to the city in a fit of Russian passion to shoot the man who had been her lover?

As they headed back towards St Petersburg, out at the Alexander Palace at Tsarskoe Selo Natasha Bobrinsky was pacing up and down her room in stockinged feet, desperate for the time to pass. It was, she had decided, much much worse than waiting for a lover. There were still days to go before she could be released from her palace prison to tell Mikhail and Powerscourt what she knew, that shortly before his death Mr Roderick Martin of His Majesty's Foreign Office had been received, alone, in his study quite late at night, by Nicholas the Second, Tsar of All the Russias.

9

The note was waiting for Powerscourt at the Embassy a couple of days after his return from Tamara Kerenkova. 'Please join me for a small private tour of the Hermitage this evening. My man will call for you at six thirty. Derzhenov.' Mikhail Shaporov was checking various coastguard offices in case they had custody of the body of Roderick Martin. Natasha Bobrinsky was still locked up at the Alexander Palace. Rupert de Chassiron, reading volumes of cables that had come in overnight, was sceptical about his cultural expedition.

'It seems fairly absurd, Powerscourt, with the whole country in ferment, possibly on the edge of revolution, that you and the head of the secret police should be gallivanting round the galleries of the Hermitage late at night when there's nobody about. Do you suppose he's got a stash of pornography hidden away up there?'

'God knows,' said Powerscourt wearily. 'Tell me something, de Chassiron. Who would you say has the best intelligence system here in St Petersburg?'

De Chassiron's customary look of weary boredom left him for a few moments.

'Do you mean best intelligence system about the foreigners or about the natives?'

'Both,' said Powerscourt.

'Well . . .' De Chassiron bent down to retrieve a recalcitrant cable that had fallen on to his carpet. 'The best intelligence system about the foreigners is run by the colleagues of General Derzhenov whom you are going to see this evening. As for the best intelligence about the natives, the Americans are too crude in their approach, too liable to barge in and ask people to tell them what is going on, that sort of thing. We British are more interested in intelligence from Berlin than we are from here, more prepared to spend money there. Cousin Willy more interesting than Cousin Nicky perhaps. My own knowledge is based on the local papers, a lot of reading, a number of local contacts, and, frankly, diplomatic gossip. I could talk for hours about the Russians but my knowledge is pretty thin. The best informed people are the ones with the longest cultural links with this country, the ones who provide a home from home for the local aristocracy in Paris or Biarritz or on the Riviera. The French, I should say, are the best informed. And there is one further reason why they need to know precisely what is going on.'

'Which is?' said Powerscourt.

'Money,' said de Chassiron. 'French loans have paid for the modernization of Russia – well, not entirely, but without them it wouldn't have happened on this scale. The Russians need another loan fairly soon. If they don't get it, there are fears that the economy could collapse. If the revolutionaries don't get them,' de Chassiron visibly cheered up at this point, 'then the bankers will. That is why the French are the best informed.'

'And I presume,' said Powerscourt, feeling his way through, 'that the centre of that intelligence, the brains and the knowledge, would be in Paris rather than St Petersburg. It would be too dangerous to concentrate the knowledge here. Am I right?'

'You are,' said de Chassiron. 'And why, pray, this interest in the best intelligence about Russia?'

'My friend,' Powerscourt laughed, 'I cannot be expected to amass a detailed knowledge of this country in a week or ten days. I may need to tap into somebody else's brains.'

'I don't think our lords and masters at the Foreign Office will be very pleased to hear that their star investigator is crawling off to the French secret service. His Nibs will have a fit. Maybe worse.' De Chassiron grinned like a schoolboy at the thought of his Ambassador losing his temper.

'I've no intention of consulting His Nibs, de Chassiron. You and I have never had this conversation. A man could stop off in Paris on his way back to London after all. You see, I'm beginning to have a theory about why Martin was killed. It's very flimsy, on the surface very unlikely. I should just like to bounce it off somebody and I don't want to burden you with it right now in case it's too preposterous.'

'It's your investigation,' said de Chassiron cheerfully. 'I'm happy to help any time I can.'

A large body of soldiers were marching across Palace Square as Powerscourt made his way towards the Hermitage. He looked forward to going inside, even in such nauseating company, for he had long been keen to see the finest art gallery in Europe. A footman in blue and scarlet took his coat and gloves as he entered. A tall, rather sombre waiter offered him a glass of clear liquid from a silver tray. Maybe it was going to be a combination of cocktail party and art viewing, Powerscourt said to himself.

'My dear Lord Powerscourt! Please do me the honour of taking a glass of this special vodka! It is of exceptional purity. Now then, do bring your glass with you. Have you been to the Hermitage before? No? Well, I'm afraid most of it is closed but I have my own humble section to show you.'

Derzhenov, his bald head shining like a small light, led the way up an enormous marble staircase, decorated with huge pillars and monumental mirrors.

'We must not forget our business, Lord Powerscourt, about that poor Mr Martin. Such a shame!' With that Derzhenov opened an enormous door and led them through a series of interconnected rooms full of Italian masterpieces of the Renaissance. They were hard to see in the gloom, and Derzhenov had now got so far ahead that only the odd word drifted back across the marble floors. 'Leonardo room . . . such a treasure trove, Raphael room . . . what a privilege . . . Raphael's Madonna Conestibale . . . what a painting.' Powerscourt suspected that the man knew very little about art but was perfectly capable of enthusiasm in spite of ignorance about the Old Masters. Such characteristics, after all, are not confined to St Petersburg.

Then they turned left and Derzhenov opened another enormous door. It gave on to a long corridor, lined with tall windows that looked out across a courtyard to the opposite side of the building. The Okhrana man pressed a button and rather feeble, yellow, museum-strength light came on to illuminate the pictures.

'All of these are of special interest to me, Powerscourt. The Hermitage authorities have allowed me to mount my own little private collection within the larger whole. Such a privilege! And now to have you with me to share its delights!'

Derzhenov had positioned himself in such a way that only one painting was so far visible. 'What about this one, my dear sir? Sixteenth-century Spanish if you please. Not just one saint but three! And Christ and the Virgin and God Almighty too!'

Powerscourt saw that the painting was called *St Sebastian between St Bernard and St Francis*, completed in 1582, by the Spanish painter Alonso Sanchez Coello. It existed on three separate layers. On the bottom of the picture Sebastian was tied, rather loosely, to a tree. He was naked except for a white loincloth fastened at the waist and he was leaning outwards on his right hip which curved in to meet his trunk. He was pierced by a number of arrows, one in the leg, one which had gone right through his right arm and five to his stomach, waist and shoulder. There was no blood from his wounds and the saint had a rather dreamy expression on his face as if he expected to levitate up to heaven fairly soon. To his left St Francis, clad in a brown habit, appeared to be pleading with him on some undisclosed saintly business. On his other side St Bernard knelt with a crook clasped between his hands. Behind the saint shadowy figures could be seen, with mountains and a lake in the distance. On the next level, Christ, in a similar loincloth to the saint but with a red robe, and the Virgin appeared to be discussing possible rescue missions or preparing to welcome him home. And on the topmost level, God, in a golden light, surrounded like an elderly and benevolent headmaster by hosts of misbehaving and mischievous putti, gazed down on the scene, the world in his hand, and released a dove of peace.

'Well,' said Derzhenov, taking a large swig of his vodka, 'what do you think of it?'

'As a work of history or as a work of artistic composition?' said Powerscourt, feeling rather like a new and junior curator at the National Gallery being interrogated by the Director.

'None of those! God in heaven, Powerscourt! Have you no idea what my interests in these pictures are likely to be?' He strode forward and tapped Sebastian on the heart.

'Look, man! They're meant to be killing this fellow, for Christ's sake! And they're pathetic! If this was an archery contest, the heart would be here in the very centre of the ring.' Derzhenov drew a series of imaginary circles like an archery ring outwards from St Sebastian's heart. 'Anybody shooting an arrow or anything else into the centre in there would get maximum points. But look at this! Not a single shot near the heart! Not one! No points for the archers. No blood either. The fools are not shooting hard enough, for God's sake. Bloody arrows are going far enough to penetrate the skin but not hard enough to do any real damage. No proper management of those archers, that's what I say. If they'd behaved like that under my command I'd have crucified every third one of them! Even our new peasant intake when we bring them here can see the bloody archers are a lot of old women.'

Powerscourt shuddered when he realized that Derzhenov must be conducting courses in torture here, bringing his minions to learn what lessons they could from the works of the Old Masters.

Derzhenov had moved on to another canvas. 'And what about this one? By that Italian fellow who got everywhere, Titian,' he demanded angrily. 'See any improvement?'

This, Powerscourt saw immediately, was a very different sort of St Sebastian. He was flanked by no companionable saints. Neither Christ nor the Virgin nor God nor his putti offered comfort from the layers above. You could just see that the saint was attached to a dark tree, barely visible behind him, a white loincloth round his waist. The background was unclear, a turbulent impasto of dark purple, broken and illuminated in places by yellow or gold patches that might have been sunshine or the lights of a great city or the campfires of a distant enemy. The saint himself was lit from the front so his trunk was in pale gold. The arms and legs were paler, with the head and the right arm in shadow. There were two arrows piercing his right arm and three in his torso. The expression on his face was of long suffering, of acceptance of his fate.

'Well?' snapped Derzhenov, as Powerscourt finished his preliminary inspection of the painting. 'What do you think?'

'Well,' said Powerscourt gingerly, 'it's a much greater painting than the other one, much simpler, more powerful.'

'Powerful? Poppycock!' Derzhenov tossed off the remainder of his vodka. 'Do I need to remind you what was wrong with the first one? Inaccurate archery fire again. Nowhere near the heart, for God's sake. Arrows not drawing blood. Pathetic. Sebastian should have been dead long before if they could have fired straight, those Mauretanian archers. Know what I think, Powerscourt? It's a serious failure of duty by the counter-terrorist forces in Rome. Couldn't be tolerated here in Russia. Third century AD, all this stuff with arrows and loincloths and so on, I think. Roman history not my strong point, but this Sebastian had been clearly discovered by the authorities giving comfort and sympathy to Christian revolutionary elements. Enemy of the state. Should have been disposed of quietly in some Roman basement like our own. No bugger would ever have heard of him then. No bloody paintings either. Instead the archers are so bad the man survives! He was rescued, for God's sake, by some other terrorist sympathizer called Irene and nursed back to health. Fellow only dies when he shows himself to the Emperor who has him stoned or cudgelled to death, can't remember which. Terrible failure by the security services, that's how I portray it to our students.'

Powerscourt was saved from the need for speech by the reappearance of the waiter with the vodka tray who glided in almost invisibly from a door hidden by a tapestry.

'Splendid, splendid,' said Derzhenov, downing one glass and taking another. 'Let me lead you to our next pair of pictures, Lord Powerscourt. These I always take care to show our new recruits. Can I interest you in a couple of Flagellations on the way?' Derzhenov had moved away to the window and was looking at the snow falling fast on the courtyard outside. 'Both remarkable examples of how not to whip a man? No? A couple of heads of John the Baptist, perhaps? One a Caravaggio where the mouth of the beheaded prophet seems to carry on speaking after death? My own favourite depiction of violence, the blinding of Samson, a quite remarkable early work by Rubens? No? Well, before we step along to the last two, perhaps we could speak of Mr Martin.'

Powerscourt had known this must be coming. He wondered if the violent paintings had been meant to soften him up. Well, he thought to himself, he had seen far worse things in battle. Then, he told himself, so too had Derzhenov.

'My assumption, Lord Powerscourt,' the Okhrana man continued to stare out at the snow, deliberately avoiding eye contact in the manner of an Old Bailey barrister, 'is that you have not found the answer to the death of Mr Martin. If you had, you would have gone home by now. Is that right?'

'You will understand, General, that I am not at liberty to discuss the case with you, however much I might want to.'

'Nonsense, Lord Powerscourt, don't give me that rubbish. If you thought I could help, you would have been begging for my assistance.'

'And you must understand, General, my belief that if you had the information you seek, you would not be questioning me at all.'

Not so much chess as fencing, Powerscourt felt, unsure of his ground. He wondered if the Okhrana man had read Lord Rosebery's cable by now.

'You have been to speak to that mistress of Martin's, I believe, Lord Powerscourt. Did she have anything to say for herself, apart from the names of all the waltzes they ever danced together?'

'I'm sure you have spoken to Mrs Kerenkova in your time, General. You would have been remiss if you had not. She told me what I am sure you already know, that her husband is here in St Petersburg, supervising the repairs on his ship.'

'I did know that, but thank you for being prepared to tell me. Anything else?'

Powerscourt thought it might help his cause if he flung unimportant titbits in front of the Russian. 'Only that he knew Mr Martin was coming, sometime round about the middle of December,' he said. 'Do you find that odd?'

The Russian shrugged his shoulders. 'The military, be they army or navy, are always close to the intelligence services, I think. They talk, they gossip. So you are staying for a while longer, Lord Powerscourt?'

'I hope so,' was the reply, 'unless something terrible happens, or you decide to throw me out.'

'Thank you for being so co-operative, Lord Powerscourt. Let me just show you my last two treasures.'

They passed beyond a couple of severed heads, sitting incongruously on silver salvers, and a couple of flagellation scenes where the action was too dark to see properly. Then Derzhenov stopped. 'My second favourite,' he said solemnly. '*The Flaying of Marsyas*, by Titian,' he went on reverentially. 'For anyone who needs to extract information from the unwilling, it is an inspiration.'

Powerscourt looked at the painting. It told the story of the flaying of the satyr, half man, half goat, called Marsyas who challenged Apollo to a musical contest, Marsyas on his pipe, Apollo on the lyre. When Apollo won, some said by challenging his opponent to play his instrument upside down as Apollo could his lyre, his reward was to have Marsyas flayed alive for his insolence in challenging a god. The action took place in a wood or a forest towards the end of the day and the colours were a study in flesh tones up through various shades of brown to a pale pink. There was no blue or green or red to be seen. Marsyas had been tied upside down to a tree. Bits of an improbable pink ribbon could be seen fastening the ends of his legs to the branches. His hands at the bottom of the painting were tied together. The dark brown and occasional white of the fur on his satyr's legs contrasted with the hairless trunk and chest beneath. His arms formed a circle round his head. To the left of the painting a young woman was playing the violin, another stringed instrument that would mock the satyr in his agony. To the right were some spectators, a naked man carrying what looked like a bucket of coal, possibly for a fire to heat up the flaying devices, an old woman sitting with her hand on her chin, a child and a couple of dogs. A naked man with a black woollen hat was working on the goat part of Marsyas with a silvery instrument. A section of goat fur had already been removed from around the knee. A young woman, scarcely more than a girl, was attacking the skin on his upper chest with a silver knife. Marsyas himself seemed to have passed out. All the participants looked as though this was a perfectly normal routine that happened every day in the forest, hanging a satyr upside down and cutting the skin off his body.

'Just suppose, Powerscourt,' Derzhenov had that cruel smile again, 'that this Marsyas was a terrorist, a revolutionary, a maker or a planter of bombs rather than a stupid satyr with a pipe. How long do you think he would last out before he talked under this treatment? Ten minutes? Half an hour? You would have to be very tough indeed to last much longer than that. They say the French used this technique on Spanish guerillas in the Napoleonic Wars. The painter has failed once again, of course. How they shied away from the sight of blood, these sensitive Venetians!' Derzhenov waved his right hand expansively at the upside-down figure of the satyr. 'The whole area round the body of Marsyas here would be drenched with blood. This section of the forest would be like a small abattoir, don't you think, Lord Powerscourt?'

Powerscourt nodded feebly. By his calculations there was only one more painting to go. He remembered suddenly seeing the Rubens called *The Blinding of Samson* some years before in Amsterdam. It was one of the most terrible paintings he had ever seen, Samson held down inside a cave while a group of soldiers in armour assault him. A big soldier on the left of the strongman has a great rapier, pointing directly towards Samson's face. The viewer thinks at first that this sword is going to do the terrible deed. Only on closer inspection does it become apparent that another, less obtrusive, soldier, crouching by Samson's side, has this very second driven a dagger into Samson's right eye and the first spurts of blood are beginning to shoot outwards and upwards. What on earth was this last one going to be like? What horrors had been committed to paint by some unfortunate artist working to fulfil a sadistic patron's fancy?

'Here we are,' said Derzhenov, rubbing his hands. 'What a pity we are about to run out of time. I am going to be late for my appointment with the Foreign Minister. Never mind. It's another martyr. I do like martyrs.' He giggled slightly as he said the words. 'St Lawrence this time, not, I'm told, one of the crème de la crème of Christian martyrhood, but a significant figure all the same.'

At first sight the painting, by a French artist called Jean Valentin of the early seventeenth century, looked innocuous enough compared to Derzhenov's previous compositions. St Lawrence, Powerscourt recalled, was an early Christian martyr of the third century AD, sentenced to death shortly after his Pope. On the far left of the painting a Roman soldier was holding back a crowd. On the far right were a couple of young men carrying buckets with what looked like fish in them. A Roman captain on a horse looked preoccupied. Seated on a table were two or three figures who seemed to be supporters of St Lawrence. The light was dark everywhere except for the bottom half on the left-hand side. There, St Lawrence, clad only in a loincloth, was being fastened on to a gridiron. Another man, naked to the waist, seemed to be supervising the fire underneath it. The flames were clearly taking hold below. It was obvious that in a few minutes St Lawrence would be totally bound to his gridiron and that his fate was to be burnt, grilled or roasted to death. The saint himself was calm, if a little apprehensive as his fate drew near.

'I suppose you're wondering what the appeal of this one is, aren't you, Lord Powerscourt? All looks a bit tame, bit peaceful?'

'Oh, I think the appeal is perfectly obvious, General,' said Powerscourt. 'It's the waiting, the suspense, not knowing how long your death is going to take that appeals to you, I think.'

'Well done, Lord Powerscourt, well done indeed. Suppose you were our friend the bomb maker or some other form of revolutionary vermin. The arrows could despatch you in a couple of minutes if they were properly controlled. The flaying would probably despatch you pretty quickly, unless,' he giggled suddenly as if the thought had only just occurred to him, 'unless, of course, you took things really slowly, one cut every half an hour maybe. But the gridiron! The gridiron! You could turn the temperature up and down just as you could on a domestic oven at home. Very slow roasting could take hours and hours before the victim is killed. Very fast and he'd exchange one form of hell for another in a couple of minutes. The interrogator has total control, you see. Wouldn't you talk and confess all after a couple of hours of the leisurely cooking, the slow roast, Powerscourt? I know I would. That's why I think this is one of the finest, it's most likely to get a confession. Heaven knows why the wretched French got so excited about the guillotine. Nobody had time to tell the authorities anything at all when the blade was shooting down towards their necks.'

Derzhenov collected his vodka tumblers and checked that all the paintings were hanging properly. 'I forgot to tell you, Powerscourt,' he said as he led the way out of their long corridor, 'that someone in the Catholic hierarchy must have had a warped sense of humour. Do you know what he's patron saint of, among other things, our mutual friend St Lawrence here? Guess.' Powerscourt had no idea. 'Prepare yourself, my friend,' said Derzhenov, smiling broadly. 'After all he went through on his gridiron, St Lawrence is the patron saint of cooks!'

Two days later Natasha Bobrinsky was off duty at the Alexander Palace. She kept telling herself to be calm. I may have this very important piece of news which is a very great secret, she said to herself as the train carried her the fifteen miles or so from Tsarskoe Selo to St Petersburg. In her fashionable bag she held the note from Mikhail inviting her to tea in the Shaporov Palace. Some older people might say I am only eighteen years old, she thought, but I am a woman of the world, a friend and colleague of a great investigator sent from London to look into a mystery, and the lover of one of the most eligible young men in St Petersburg. Natasha was wearing a dark red coat of her mother's today with a black fur hat. Her friends said it set off her dark hair and her green eyes. It was two years since she had borrowed the coat, and she was not sure she had actually told her mother about the loan, but it served very well.

As she set out from the station to walk to the Shaporov Palace, she was so lost in her own thoughts that she had not time to notice a soldier, who had been sitting in the next carriage staring blankly out of the window. The soldier, wearing the normal uniform and greatcoat, seemed to look into the distance on the steps of the railway station as if he expected a sign or a signal. Then he followed Natasha, about fifty yards behind. She was not to know that all sections of the Russian security services, police, Okhrana, maritime and customs, imperial protection units, all favoured military personnel for the work of following and trailing persons of interest. It was the uniform, they would have said, if pressed. Uniforms are so much more anonymous. So when Natasha went into the main entrance of the Shaporov Palace, the soldier backed away into a doorway some seventy yards distant. He lit a cigarette and checked in his pocket for the half bottle of vodka. He settled down to wait. Most of the people he was asked to follow were middle-aged men. A pretty girl made a delightful exception. The man in the doorway wasn't a soldier at all. He had been recruited into the ranks of the watchers and proved reliable. Out on the Vyborg side his wife and family were grateful that he was in work and much better paid than he would be in one of those terrible factories.

Natasha tried to look unconcerned as she walked into the little Dutch sitting room. It was called the Dutch sitting room because it had a multitude of Dutch and Flemish

215

paintings crammed on to its walls, Rembrandt portraits, Rubens landscapes, seascapes by Van de Velde. Powerscourt didn't think General Derzhenov would care much for any of them. Natasha was wearing a long black skirt with an elaborate shirt of white lace fastened to the neck on top. Mikhail was translating for Powerscourt from a navy newspaper that carried details of ship repairs, including Tamara Kerenkova's husband's ship, the *Tsarevich*. Powerscourt rose to shake Natasha by the hand. 'Unless I'm very much mistaken,' he said with a smile, 'you have something important to tell us.'

'How did you know?' said Natasha, slightly cross. 'I thought I was being frightfully grown up and reserved about it.'

'You were, my dear Natasha,' said Powerscourt, feeling rather like her great-grandfather, 'but sometimes people have a sort of glow about them if they're excited. Why don't you tell us all about it.'

Natasha folded her hands together in her lap as her governesses had taught her. Although she had rehearsed this little speech about fifty times by now, she suddenly felt it slipping from her memory once the moment of revelation had come.

'It was the beginning of this week,' she began, looking alternately at Mikhail and Powerscourt. Mikhail was wondering if they would have a chance to be alone together on this day. Powerscourt was wondering just how much danger the girl was in. 'All the girls, the Tsar's daughters, I mean, were out in the park with their sledges by Toboggan Hill. Toboggan Hill was built years ago to provide a good slope to run down in the snow. The girls all love it. The little boy was sick, he was in bed at the house with his mother and three doctors from St Petersburg fussing over him.'

Powerscourt thought it might be advantageous at some point to find out exactly what was wrong with Alexei, the Tsarevich.

'They're all very good with their toboggans,' Natasha went on, 'though the two elder ones are quite cautious. The third child, Marie, is easily the most gifted at it, but she is also the most reckless. This is what happened.'

Natasha paused briefly to concentrate on her memories. Already the afternoon seemed like a dream from long ago. 'It was growing dark,' she began.

'Sorry to interrupt,' said Powerscourt, 'but were there just you and the girls there at this point, no security police, no soldiers?'

'There had been a soldier,' Natasha said, 'but he seemed to have disappeared. I think he may have gone to relieve himself in the bushes. They're always doing that. Anyway, it was very nearly dark and I thought there was only enough light for two more descents of Toboggan Hill. Marie got one of her big sisters to push her across the top so she had a good head of speed when she began her descent. Then it all went wrong. Her toboggan hit a stone or something and she was thrown out, hitting her head on a tree trunk hidden in the snow. She was flung off through the air. All the other girls started screaming and wailing. I was just going to try to calm them down when this soldier appeared from a sort of shed by the Krasnoselskie Gates not far away. He seemed to know what he was doing. He told me he knew about first aid and things, and that he would carry Marie back to the Alexander Palace. He picked her up and collected the other girls as well. One thing he did say, was that I had to mind his shed until he came back. I've thought since that he must have assumed, as a soldier or guard or whatever he was, that he would get a reward for bringing the girls back.'

Natasha paused and took a drink of tea. Mikhail looked at her admiringly.

'The shed was very crude, Lord Powerscourt. There was a sort of writing ledge with a big book on it. The Captain of the Guard from the far side of the gates told me I had to write down the name and purpose of visit of anybody coming in. The only person who came in my time was the piano tuner. But here comes the bit that will interest you, Lord Powerscourt. I turned the pages back to the days when Mr Martin was in St Petersburg. On the evening of December the 22nd last year, Mr Martin came to see the Tsar alone. If people are coming in a body, all their names are entered together. Mr Martin was there on his own. He probably saw the Tsar when the rest of the household had retired for the night.'

'Bloody hell! Well done, Natasha!' said Mikhail.

'Indeed,' Powerscourt chimed in, 'extremely well done. Natasha, are you sure nobody saw you looking at the back entries?'

'Well, I can't be certain. But the captain and his men were all on the other side of the gates. He's not even meant to come inside the park at all. And the soldier who carried Marie to the palace didn't come back for a good ten minutes or so.'

'This is easily the most significant fact we have learnt since the start of the investigation, and I am eternally in your debt,' said Powerscourt, staring vaguely at some fishing boats in the Scheldt estuary on the wall. 'Can I ask you another question, or rather another two questions, Natasha?'

'Of course,' said the heroine of the hour, wondering dreamily about romantic interludes with Mikhail. 'Ask whatever you like, Lord Powerscourt.'

'My first question relates to the missing Fabergé eggs, the Trans-Siberian Railway egg and the Danish Palaces egg,' he began. 'Would you know if any of the children were particularly attached to those particular eggs?'

'Why, yes, I do know the answer to that one. The two youngest girls were very devoted to the Danish Palaces egg. I suppose they remembered visiting some of the places in their summer holidays. Tatiana, the second daughter, was also devoted to the railway. But the real fan was the little boy, the Tsarevich. I only saw him watching the tiny train move across the carpet once. There were servants and big sisters everywhere making sure he couldn't get near it in case he did any damage. But Olga told me the week after it went how upset he would be if he ever found out. He once watched it cross the carpet twenty-nine times in succession, she told me, and even then he could only be brought away by the offer of ice cream and chocolate in the kitchen.'

'And have any more things disappeared, Natasha?' Powerscourt asked quietly.

The girl looked at him in astonishment. 'How did you know? Or how did you guess? A couple of bulky things seem to have disappeared in the last month or two. A rocking horse that all the children have played with in their time seems to have gone missing. And an old, very heavy dolls' house that used to belong to the girls' grandmother has vanished. They all used to play with that from time to time.'

Natasha was on the point of asking Powerscourt how he knew to ask about these things when there was a fierce rap at the door.

'Come in,' said Mikhail.

One of the Shaporov butlers drew himself to attention right there in the doorway and bellowed out his news.

'Message for Lord Powerscourt.' Mikhail and Natasha translated Russian into French virtually in unison. 'Message from Mr de Chassiron at the British Embassy. Will he please return at once. There have been most significant developments, not for his inquiry, but for Russia.'

Once again Natasha and Mikhail translated together. Powerscourt did not know how they might all three be received at the Embassy, but he felt sure he could not just abandon them here. Mikhail they knew, and Natasha would, he felt sure, go down very well with de Chassiron. Maybe she would bewitch the Ambassador with her beauty.

'Come on,' he said, 'let's go and find out what's happening. I have a great urge to speak once more to the Embassy telegraph officer.'

Rupert de Chassiron had made a valiant job of tidying up his cables. There was now one very large pile of them, neatly shaped, at the far end of his table. There was another much smaller pile in front of him. He glanced down at it anxiously from time to time as if he thought it might leave the room. He seated Powerscourt opposite with Mikhail and Natasha on either side. Natasha he had greeted gravely with a severe bow almost to the floor.

'Thank you for coming,' he began. 'The news is bad. It comes from Moscow. Let me tell you first of all what we know for certain.' He paused and riffled through his pile of cables, finally selecting one that seemed to contain a very short message indeed.

'This comes from the British Consul in Moscow. Grand Duke Serge, Governor General of Moscow, uncle and brother-in-law of the Tsar, has been assassinated. Revolutionary elements blew him up with a bomb by the Nikolovsky Gate on the way out of the Kremlin this morning. Death was instantaneous.'

Ricky Crabbe the telegraph operator came in with some more cables to add to de Chassiron's pile. He nodded cheerfully at Powerscourt and stared long and hard at Natasha before returning to his post.

Nobody spoke. 'There is other, unconfirmed information. The Grand Duke, as you know, was one of the most hated members of the imperial family. People said he boasted that he never slept in the same bed in the Kremlin for two nights running in case the revolutionaries came for him. He was a most determined opponent of the granting of any reforms whatsoever. According to some of the other reports, the bomb was thrown straight into his carriage. The coachman was mortally wounded but he took some time to die. The Grand Duke was in the epicentre of the explosion. His clothes were ripped off his body, his head was gone, all that was left of him was a hand and part of a foot. He was scattered into hundreds of fragments of blood and muscle and bone, some of them sticking to the walls of the gateway. There was a rumour that students from Moscow University hurried to the scene and carried tiny pieces of the Grand Duke's flesh away as souvenirs.'

Outside the watcher in soldier's clothes wondered how much longer the young lady was going to stay inside the British Embassy. He felt sure he would be well rewarded for this information. And though he wanted to be home he knew he could not desert his post now. He pulled his vodka bottle from his pocket and settled down to wait.

Natasha Bobrinsky had gone pale. 'He was married to the Empress Alexandra's elder sister, this Grand Duke, wasn't he, Mr de Chassiron?'

The diplomat nodded.

'I met him shortly after I'd gone to work for the Romanovs,' she said sadly. 'And to think of him now reduced to hundreds of pieces of flesh and blood, like minced meat. The Empress came to her sister Ella's wedding to this Grand Duke years ago in the Winter Palace chapel. She told me about it just before Christmas, the great pillars in the chapel, the singing and chanting of the choir, the clergy in their rich vestments, and the jewels all over the society ladies. Alexandra said she felt like a German pauper.'

'What do you think the reaction will be, de Chassiron?' asked Powerscourt, wondering how it might affect his investigation. Anything that made Derzhenov and his thugs less interested in the strange death of Roderick Martin was to be welcomed.

'It'll make the imperial family even more security conscious than they are already. There's a rumour that nobody is to be allowed to leave Tsarskoe Selo for the funeral when the body is brought up here from Moscow. They're to remain inside the Alexander Palace, cowering behind the walls. God only knows what kind of example that sets their subjects if you're unwilling to be seen burying your dead.'

'But will there be reaction or reform?' Powerscourt had scarcely asked the question when Ricky Crabbe burst in without knocking and handed a cable to Powerscourt.

'This has just come from the Foreign Office for you, my lord. From Sir Jeremiah Reddaway, my lord.'

Powerscourt expected some freshly discovered details about Martin's past or his financial affairs. Nothing had prepared him for this.

'Corpse found lying in water at Tibenham Grange with severe head wounds consistent with fall from the tower of the house or assault and battery with blunt instrument. Body positively identified as Mrs Letitia Martin, wife of late diplomat, Roderick Martin. Please return soonest. Reddaway.'

10

Two more deaths, Powerscourt thought bitterly. The one in Moscow would surely bring more hatred and division to a country that already suffered from a surfeit of both. The one in Kent might bring an end to the family Martin, for, as far as Powerscourt knew, there were no children of the marriage. De Chassiron was scrabbling through a little booklet brought out from one of his desk drawers. Ricky Crabbe was hovering with intent by Powerscourt's side, as if expecting a telegraph message to materialize almost instantly.

'How terrible,' said Natasha Bobrinsky. 'Two more dead people. Will it never stop?'

'I presume you will have to go back to London, Lord Powerscourt?' asked Mikhail. 'Would you like me to accompany you? It can be a long and tedious journey.'

Powerscourt managed not to say that he had no need of an interpreter in his own country. 'That's a very generous offer,' he said, 'but you need to stay here and keep watch over Natasha. I know you think I'm being absurdly old and fussing, Natasha, but I am sure you could be in very great danger if your employers or some of their staff find out that you are in touch with me and the British Embassy.'

'Here we are!' said de Chassiron suddenly, holding up a battered copy of a railway timetable. 'There's an express to Berlin in two and a half hours, Powerscourt, you'll be able to pick up a connection there easily enough.'

'Thank you,' said Powerscourt, his brain a long way away. 'Could you bear to hold on here for a minute while I compose a message or two for the Foreign Office with Ricky here.'

With that Powerscourt followed the young man into his telegraph room. 'I have a number of questions and messages for you, Ricky,' he began. 'The first is the least important. I presume that if I send a message to the Foreign Office, and you turn it into code, that it could be read at the other end within minutes of arrival?' Powerscourt was thinking of the Okhrana at this point rather than the Foreign Office.

'Correct, my lord,' said Ricky Crabbe.

'Something like this then,' said Powerscourt. 'Terrible news death of Mrs Martin. Returning London via 19.30 to Berlin.'

In less than half a minute, Crabbe had coded the message and sent it off to London.

'Now then, Ricky, I want to try your secret system to your brother. This message is to be sent to Mr Burke, whose address I am writing for you on this piece of paper. "Returning London because of death of Mrs Martin in mysterious circumstances. Please inform Lady Lucy I leave today, Friday, on the 19.30 from St Petersburg to Berlin. All love, Francis." There was nothing in the message that needed to be kept secret, but Powerscourt wanted to test this secure channel of communication in case it was needed for more important messages in the future.

'That's going to cheer up your wife, my lord, knowing you are coming home.'

'Never fear, Ricky, I shall be back here very soon. Now I want to ask you about keeping records of the telegraph messages and things like that. I've suddenly realized that it could be very important.'

'Fire ahead, my lord,' the young man said.

'When you send messages out, Ricky, do you keep a copy?'

'I have to, my lord. Normally I have the piece of paper with the original message, handwritten by the Ambassador or Mr de Chassiron. Then I code it, sometimes on the bottom of the same piece of paper, sometimes on a different sheet. The Foreign Office Telegraphy School, my lord, is adamant that all outgoing messages, copies and originals, must be filed.'

'I'll come back to that in a moment, if I may. Tell me about the incoming messages.'

'Same thing, really, my lord. We have to write them down. Sometimes we have to decode them. Other times we can bring the message to the recipient as taken down. But even before I leave this room, I have to make a copy. If the traffic goes on increasing at current rates, my lord, we're going to have to rent a warehouse to keep all the stuff.'

'Do you file the messages under subject matter or under day of the month?'

'Day of the month, my lord, with the subjects subfiled in alphabetic order. Messages from Bucharest ahead of those from Vienna, as it were.'

'Now then, Ricky, I come to the point. You told me before that it was possible that Mr Martin could have sent a couple of messages out of here when the office was empty. What would have happened to them?'

Ricky Crabbe looked at him keenly. 'Well, I don't think he would have left any copies lying around for me to file, my lord. He'd probably stuff the message in his pocket and get rid of it later. As for the far end, it may have gone to the Foreign Office, though if it had they would have surely told you about it, my lord, or to some telegraph office at a local train station or in a town. God knows whether they'd keep copies, probably they would until it had been collected.'

'And if it had gone to the Foreign Office, would he have sent it in code?'

Ricky Crabbe paused and stared at his machinery. 'I doubt if he would have sent it in code at all, my lord. He might have done. But not even Mr de Chassiron knows how to use the codes.' Suddenly Ricky stopped staring at his wires and buttons and turned slightly pale. 'Do you think, Lord Powerscourt, that he could have sent a message to his wife saying he'd found the Crown Jewels or whatever else he had found out? And because of what he knew, one lot of Russians killed Mr Martin here, and another lot could have killed Mrs Martin in Kent if they knew what was in the message? Or if they tortured poor Mr Martin till he told them what was in the message?'

Powerscourt nodded. 'Well done, that is indeed what I am wondering. Please don't tell anybody else about it, Ricky, you were very quick to work that out.' Powerscourt looked at his watch. An hour and three quarters left before his train. 'Could I ask you one further favour, Ricky? Could we have a look at the incoming traffic from the Foreign Office over the five days before I came here?'

Ricky pulled a series of files down from his shelves. Once they were properly sorted he read with growing astonishment Sir Jeremiah Reddaway's very full accounts of the Foreign Office's efforts to make him change his mind and return to detection. Now for the first time he realized the importance of the visit of Lord Rosebery to Markham

Square. One mystery at any rate was solved, even if a whole lot more awaited him in London. General Derzhenov didn't have battalions of spies lurking behind the trees in Markham Square to know the details of Powerscourt's visitors come to persuade him out of retirement a month before. He just read Sir Jeremiah's telegrams.

'Ricky,' he said, shaking the young man's hand, 'thank you so much for your help. If anything important should happen in my absence, please send a message to Mr Burke on your secure channel with your brother. Don't go near the Foreign Office. If I need to get in touch with you I'll go through your brother.'

'Mr Burke's office will have the address by now, my lord. Can I say I hope we see you back here soon? And that your mission to Kent is successful?'

Powerscourt wondered if there was a suggestion that his visit to St Petersburg had been unsuccessful. As he walked back to de Chassiron's room, he decided to write a series of very short letters. He wrote to Mr Bazhenov, Deputy Assistant Under Secretary at the Interior Ministry, to Mr Tropinin, Under Secretary at the Foreign Ministry, to General Derzhenov of the Okhrana in his torturer's lair on the Fontanka Quai and to Mrs Tamara Kerenkova, one-time mistress of the late Roderick Martin. He informed them as a matter of courtesy that he had been recalled because of the sudden, mysterious death of Mrs Martin. He thanked them for their assistance during his stay and said that he looked forward to renewing their acquaintance on his return. With Mikhail and Natasha he was as optimistic as he dared be in the circumstances.

'I'll be back as soon as I can,' he said. 'It may be that the second death makes it much easier to solve the first. Depend upon it, I have often known that happen in the past. Natasha,' he smiled at her, 'please take very great care. I know I've said it before but I dread to think what might happen to you if they ever found you out, those people at the Alexander Palace. Mikhail, I fear we shall never find the body now, but please keep trying. And if you need to get in touch, Ricky Crabbe has his own methods of reaching me in London.'

'Why do you think the body will never be found, Lord Powerscourt?' asked Mikhail.

'I suspect that somebody doesn't want us to see what happened to Roderick Martin before he died. He may have been tortured because he wouldn't tell his captors what they wanted to know. Or he may just have been killed because his captors didn't want anybody else to know what he knew. Or he may have been killed in frustration because he wouldn't tell them what he knew. I just don't know. Martin's body was left out on the Nevskii Prospekt in the middle of the night and then spirited away. Something tells me that whatever his secret, the people who wanted to find it still haven't done so. At least one of them, the Okhrana, hope I will lead them to it.'

There were over twenty people out in the night air, men and women, standing in the clearing in the forest, dressed in home-made white robes. Three bonfires marked the limit of their territory. In the centre of the area stood a man called the Pilot, the leader of the group and the Master of Ceremonies for this evening. Beside him was his wife, known as the Blessed Mother. Behind them a group of drummers beat out a rhythm of ever-increasing frenzy. Each person carried a candle and as the candle burnt down they began to dance, slowly and reverently at first and then with more vigour. The Pilot noticed that the stranger who had come to his house earlier that day and soothed his sick daughter was dancing particularly wildly, his dark head rolling vigorously as if he was drunk. As the delirium grew and the dance grew wilder yet, the celebrants flung their robes to the ground and knelt before the Pilot to be whipped with birch rods. Then they began to whip each other with the birch rods, the *khlysti* that gave their name to the sect, the drums beating faster still, the candles flung to the ground, their terrible hymn broadcast into the forest air.

I whip, I whip, I search for Christ,
Come down to us, Christ, from the seventh heaven,
Come with us, Christ, into the sacred circle,
Come down to us, Holy Spirit of the lord.

At the point when hysteria was about to engulf them all, the Pilot grabbed a woman and dragged her to the ground. According to the rules of the sect it was impossible for anybody to refuse a member of the opposite sex at these orgies. The Pilot was followed by the other *khlysti* members until there was a mass of groaning, shrieking couples on the ground. There were more women than men. The unfortunate just had to wait their turn. The Pilot noticed that the stranger seemed to be giving himself generously to the business. The drums beat on, calling the faithful to their duty. This was the first necessity of their belief system. Without sin, there could be no repentance and no salvation. Without first indulging in these rites of darkness there could be no entry into a state of grace. The Church frowned on these practices and they had been declared illegal by the state, even though there were said to be over a hundred thousand *khlysti* members across Russia.

The stranger left early next morning, looking refreshed rather than exhausted by his exertions the night before.

'Are you going back home now?' asked the Pilot.

229

'No, I am continuing my journey,' the stranger replied.

'May I ask where are you going to?' the Pilot continued.

'I am going to St Petersburg,' said the stranger.

'Will you tell me your name, in case we meet again?' said the Pilot, holding out his hand for a farewell handshake.

'One day,' said the stranger, 'everybody in Russia will know my name. I am a priest. I am called Rasputin, Father Grigory Rasputin.'

Powerscourt wondered if Lucy would come to meet him at Victoria station as his train arrived in the middle of the morning. As he strode down the long platform, packed with porters and passengers, he peered at the crowd of welcomers at the far end. There was the usual collection of especially tall people only found at the great railway termini who blocked the view for everybody else. And Lucy was not particularly tall. Then he saw the head of a small figure raised aloft on shoulders he could not see. There was a shout of Papa! three times and two tiny people hurtled towards him as fast as their legs would carry them. Powerscourt was amazed at how effectively they dodged in and out of the surrounding traffic, navigating their way past porters with vast trolleys and elderly ladies of uncertain gait. He waved vigorously from time to time even when he couldn't see them to give the twins something to steer for. Then, laughing with excitement, Juliet and Christopher were upon him, demanding to be lifted up at once for a better view of the station. They were both uncontrollably happy, peering into Powerscourt's face from time to time to make sure he was really home and giggling cheerfully when their inspection was proved right. So it was a heavily laden husband, with a twin on each shoulder and a porter carrying a suitcase and a large shopping bag in each hand, who was reunited with his wife at the bottom of Platform 14, Ashford, the Dover Boat, Calais and Paris.

'Francis, my love,' Lady Lucy said, 'I don't think I've ever been so happy to see you home.' She squeezed whatever bits of her husband she could find. 'They've been frantic, these two,' she nodded at the twins, 'ever since they heard you were coming back. They promised to be good if they were brought to the station to meet you, and they were, staying ever so still, not fighting, not running round at all. I was quite taken in! I relaxed my guard, you see, so when I lifted Juliet up I didn't have a firm hold on Christopher and then they were off!'

'Never mind,' said Powerscourt, taking hold of a section of his wife's shoulder and holding it tight. 'We're all here and we're all fine.'

Forty-five minutes later the twins were still coiled round their father as he tried to have a conversation with Lucy over tea in the drawing room in Markham Square. She asked him about his investigation. He remembered that these were perilous waters.

'It's been very sedate stuff really, Lucy. Lots of meetings with Interior Ministry people, diplomats from the Foreign Office, long conversations with a very clever Englishman in the Embassy, a Russian princess, a very beautiful Russian princess who works as a lady-in-waiting to the Tsar's family and discovered that our friend Mr Martin appears to have met the Tsar shortly before he died.'

Lady Lucy had a vision of Russian sirens, seductive in fur, come to lure her Francis to his doom. 'How old is this female, Francis?'

Powerscourt laughed. 'Natasha? She's about eighteen, but I think she's falling in love with my translator. He's all of twenty-five and works in London most of the time. I don't think you need to be concerned about the fair Natasha, my love.'

All this time Powerscourt had been conducting tickling and pushing games with Christopher and Juliet. Then he remembered something. He put the twins on the carpet in front of him and looked at them as severely as he could.

'Juliet! Christopher! I want you to stand still for a moment. Still! Now then. I have brought a present for each of you back from St Petersburg. I want you to go downstairs and bring up that brown shopping bag I had at the station. It's by the suitcase in the hall.'

With whoops of Present! Present! the twins shot off down the stairs. Powerscourt grinned. 'It's hard to imagine them ever being sort of stationary, isn't it, you know, reading a newspaper, looking at the wallpaper, anything like that. I'm going to tell you all about the investigation this evening when Johnny's here, my love. He is coming to dinner this evening, isn't he?'

Lady Lucy smiled. No investigation of her husband's would be complete without Johnny Fitzgerald. 'He is coming, of course he's coming. He asked me to give you a message, Francis. He said he's going to concentrate on the village and leave the house to you. He'll meet you at the station for the train nearest to seven o'clock this evening.'

'Very good,' said her husband, thinking how meticulous Johnny had been. There was the customary sound of a minor earthquake, large animal in distress, small football crowd in pain that heralded the arrival of the twins, dragging the bag along the floor.

'Very heavy, Papa,' said Juliet. 'Big bag,' agreed Christopher.

Powerscourt placed the bag on his knees and began to rummage around inside it. 'That's funny,' he said after a while, 'I'm sure I packed those things before I left.'

He continued searching. The twins looked slightly less hopeful than before. 'They must be down here in this corner, behind their mother's present,' he went on. 'No, they're not there either. They must be on the other side.' The twins were beginning to look rather anxious. Maybe their Papa had forgotten to put the presents in the bag. Lady Lucy was trying very hard not to smile.

'They're not that big, well, they're not that small either. Could they have slipped out of the bag when I put it on the luggage rack? That carriage must be halfway to Dover now if it goes back the way it came.'

Visions of new possessions they had not yet seen heading back all the way to St Petersburg appalled the twins. They looked at each other sadly. Their faces fell. If he had been heartless, Powerscourt might have wanted to place a bet on which one would burst into tears first.

'Hold on!' he said with the air of a man remembering at last where he has buried the treasure. 'I know what's happened. They're stuck between Thomas and Olivia's presents!' One final delve into the bag which might, Lady Lucy thought, have indicated to a cynical observer that Powerscourt knew all along where the presents were, and he produced two packages cocooned in thick brown paper.

'Oh dear,' he said, looking at the expectant faces of his children, 'I'm not quite sure which one is for which child.' He began feeling the presents. The twins were growing more impatient by the second. Then something seemed to make his mind up. 'This one is for you, Juliet, and this one is for you, Christopher.'

There followed the normal rending and tearing sounds as the paper was ripped to shreds and thrown on the floor. Juliet had a wooden doll with four smaller dolls inside. Christopher had a Russian Imperial Guardsman in full battle kit, a defiant moustache emphasizing his superiority.

Powerscourt would not have confessed to anybody in the world that he had actually bought the things at Berlin Lichtenberg station. But his present for Lucy had been purchased at a very fashionable shop on the Nevskii Prospekt itself.

'I must go to Kent, my love,' said Powerscourt, looking at his watch and at the twins who appeared to be arranging an assignation between the smallest of the dolls and the guardsman. 'I was going to give you this tonight, but with all these presents going round . . .'

He handed Lucy a rectangular parcel, a book well covered in stout wrapping paper and string. There was a drawing of a very beautiful woman on the cover. The writing was in Russian. Lucy looked at him.

'I know it's in Russian, my love,' said Powerscourt gently, 'but I don't think it will matter when you know what it is. That,' he nodded reverentially at the book, 'is a first edition of Tolstoy's *Anna Karenina*. Do you remember you used to have that coat I called your Anna Karenina coat when we first met? I remember meeting you wearing it one day in St James's Square. '

Lucy flicked through the pages, pausing now and then to look at the illustrations. 'Oh, Francis!' was all she could say. 'Oh, Francis!'

The road down to Tibenham Grange was steep, twisting and turning its way through the woods. Powerscourt noticed two other dwellings on the way down. At the bottom of the hill was a large lawn, big enough for croquet or tennis, with a lake on a raised level behind it. To the left was the house itself, a near perfect medieval moated manor house, described by some historians, Powerscourt recalled, as one of the finest of its sort in England. As he paid off his cab, arranging for a pick-up at six thirty to return to the station, he saw a tubby police constable of middling years eyeing him suspiciously.

'This house is closed to visitors at present,' the constable said, 'even to architects. Especially to architects.'

'I'm not one of those,' said Powerscourt cheerfully, drawing on long years of experience with the various layers of the police force. 'My name is Powerscourt. I'm an investigator. I believe the Foreign Office will have told Inspector Clayton I'm coming.'

'My apologies, sir, forgive me, please. Constable Watchett at your service, sir. I'll bring you to the Inspector now, sir.' Watchett led Powerscourt over a stone footbridge that crossed the moat. 'I don't hold with these houses with water all around them myself,' said the constable, glancing down into the depths. 'Damp must come in something rotten and everyone knows damp can be bad for houses, very bad.'

Constable Watchett shook his head as he showed Powerscourt into an elegant library, divided into sections by bays of bookshelves set at right angles to the windows. The Inspector was at the far end. He was a tall, thin Inspector with a slight limp as he made his way down the library to greet his visitor. His hair was a light brown and his cheerful blue eyes showed that his calling had not yet completely destroyed his faith in human nature. 'Andrew Clayton, Lord Powerscourt,' he said, holding out his hand. 'What a pleasure to meet you at last! I trust you have recovered from your journey.'

'Well recovered, thank you,' said Powerscourt, staring intently at the young man. 'Delighted to make your acquaintance. Have we met somewhere before?'

'Only by reputation, my lord,' said the Inspector, 'in South Africa. I was wounded rather badly in a skirmish during your time there. Our colonel said that if it hadn't been for the intelligence provided by your department, we would have all been killed. I joined the police force after that.'

'I'm sure it was nothing,' said Powerscourt. 'Quite soon we must have a long talk about South Africa, but for the moment, as you know at least as well as I do, we have urgent business.'

'Of course,' said Clayton, leading the way back to his end of the library. He pointed out a comfortable armchair next to his own. 'Could I make a suggestion, Lord Powerscourt? My first inspector, when I was a humble sergeant, used to lay enormous stress on organizing the evidence, such as it was, in chronological order. D follows C which follows B which follows A, he used to say. It got rather monotonous after a couple of cases, but still. I know the Foreign Office have an interest in this death here, my lord, and I know you have been in St Petersburg looking into the passing of this poor lady's husband. So perhaps you could tell me first about the Russian end, as it were, and then I can take it up from here.'

'Very good,' said Powerscourt and paused momentarily to organize his thoughts. He left nothing out: the despatch of Martin on his ultra secret mission to St Petersburg with only the Prime Minister knowing the purpose of his visit; Martin's late night meeting with the Tsar shortly before his death; the discovery of his body by a police station which later denied all knowledge of him or his corpse; the Foreign Ministry's conviction that he had never been in St Petersburg at all; the Interior Ministry's knowledge not only of his current but of his previous visits in earlier years; the sinister presence of the Okhrana with its torture chambers in the basement of the Fontanka Quai and its master's collection of sadistic paintings in the Hermitage; Martin's mistress in exile out in the country who remembered her dancing days with Mr Martin in years gone by and whose husband told her he was coming to the city yet again. He threw in, almost as an afterthought, the telegraph messages decoded by the Okhrana and his own possession of a secret channel outside their knowledge. He spoke of his inability to decide if Martin was killed because of what he knew, or because he wouldn't say what he knew and therefore had to die in case that information passed into the wrong hands; of his uncertainty over whether Martin had sent any telegrams, and if so, to whom; of the complete absence of the body of the dead Martin.

'I don't envy you that lot, my lord,' said Clayton. 'May I ask one very silly question from a country policeman in Kent not used to the ways of the big cities?'

'Please do,' said Powerscourt.

'It's this, my lord,' said Inspector Clayton earnestly. 'We're always reading how unstable these Russian places are. Only last month, I read in the paper the other day, there were hundreds of Russians killed by their own soldiers and that in the centre of St Petersburg itself. Mightn't Mr Martin just have met a load of ruffians who robbed him and killed him because he was a foreigner?'

'Nothing is impossible, Inspector,' said Powerscourt, reluctant to say he thought they were playing for higher stakes than robbery and casual killing.

'Anyway, my lord, that's as may be. Now it's my turn.' Clayton looked down briefly at the papers on the little side table beside him, as if he had written out what he was going to say. 'Mrs Martin died from a fall from the tower of this house into the moat below. She hit her head on the stone wall of the footbridge on the way. That, according to the doctors, was probably what killed her. As far as we know, on the day of her death Mrs Letitia Martin was alone in this house. There is a housekeeper cum cook, married to a butler cum handyman cum coachman, who live in one of the little cottages opposite the tower you'll probably have seen on your way in, my lord. Kennedy, they're called. Their daughter in Tonbridge has just given birth to their first grandchild so Mrs Martin gave permission for them to go and spend two days and nights with the new arrival. We can find no record of anybody else coming to visit her. Constable Watchett, who is an expert woodsman, is checking through all the surrounding area to see if he can find any traces of any intruder. So far, not a thing.'

Inspector Clayton paused for a moment. 'We know,' he went on, 'that she was in the habit of reading, or writing letters or working on the household accounts in the next library bay to this one, the one with the rope across it, my lord. We can have a look in there in a moment. We know from the doctors that she probably died somewhere between three and six in the afternoon. We have no idea if she went up to the tower on her own, or if some unknown visitor came with her. The unfortunate thing is that Mr and Mrs Kennedy went away on the Tuesday. Poor Mrs Martin died on the same day. The Kennedys did not come back until early evening on the Thursday. As they were the last people to see her alive, so they were the first to find her dead. They thought she had slipped. They said she sometimes went up there to look at the view or watch the birds. She could have slipped. But after his contact with the Foreign Office, my lord, our Chief Constable quickly discarded that theory. Or she could, of course, have jumped, the despatch of the Kennedys to the new grand-daughter a perfect pretext for an uninterrupted suicide. But come, enough of this speculation. Let me take you up to the tower before the light goes, my lord.'

Inspector Clayton led the way up one flight of stairs at the end of the library. 'Constable Watchett probably told you he doesn't approve of houses on water, my lord,' he said, continuing along a corridor that led into a bedroom and then a small chapel, perfectly equipped with pews and altar and crucifixes. 'He doesn't approve of higgledy piggledy houses either, as he puts it, houses where all the stairs aren't in the one place.'

They had now entered a long elegant drawing room with French tapestries on the walls and one or two expensive-looking pictures. Looking out of the window Powerscourt saw the moat again, from a different angle this time, beguiling, seductive, mysterious. Inspector Clayton had stopped at the bottom of another staircase, this one in stone.

'We don't know, my lord,' he said, 'if she came the way we have just come, or if she came in from the other direction with the big bedroom, but she must have gone up this stone staircase.'

He made his way up the steps, pausing to push open the wooden square at the top.

'Was this locked normally?' Powerscourt asked.

'No, it wasn't, my lord. There seemed little point, really. Nobody could reach the tower without going through the house and if anybody came with a young family Mr Kennedy would always lock the door before they arrived.'

Now they were out on top of the little tower, on a platform not more than twelve feet square. To the west lay the cottages and other outbuildings that came with the estate. To the north, the large lawn and the lake behind. To the east and the west, the woods that formed part of the Weald of Kent. Clayton tiptoed across to the point where the West Bridge lay almost directly beneath them. 'The doctors think this is where she must have gone from, my lord,' said the Inspector, peering down at the water. 'The parapet is dangerously low, as you can see. I expect the coroner will say something about it at the inquest. They're always very good at trying to close stable doors after the horses have bolted.'

'Do they think she stood on the parapet and jumped? Or toppled over and fell?' Powerscourt was feeling the pull of the water again. Heights, even heights as low as this, had always unsettled him.

'They don't think it would have mattered. Her body would have crumpled – the doctor's words, not mine – and the head would have shot forward to strike the stone wall that is the side of the footbridge. They think that is what killed her.'

'You mean the doctors aren't sure?'

'The poor woman was in the water for over forty-eight hours. They think the blow from the bridge did for her, but she drowned as well, if you see what I mean, just to be on the safe side, perhaps. She was floating face down in the moat when the Kennedys found her, Kent's answer to Ophelia.'

Powerscourt looked closely at Inspector Clayton. Police inspectors were not, in his experience, known for familiarity with the works of Shakespeare and the paintings of Waterhouse and Millais. He wondered suddenly if Letitia Martin had known about Tamara Kerenkova, waltzing round the state rooms of St Petersburg with her, Letitia's, husband. Had that, perhaps, been resolved between them? Or had Martin's return to the Russian capital, in his wife's view, been the final betrayal of their love? Had the terrible irony been that Martin had, in fact, kept true to this imagined promise of fidelity to his wife? For he had not been in touch with Tamara on his return to St Petersburg, a fact that had given Tamara considerable disquiet. Powerscourt stared down into the water for answers that never came. He tried to imagine the despair Letitia Martin might feel if she thought Roderick had returned to her, only for him to betray her once again.

'You look very pensive, my lord,' said Clayton. 'Does anything strike you about the circumstances up here?'

'Only how short a distance you have to fall to kill yourself, Inspector. She could have slipped, of course. Or, as we both know, been pushed. I was trying to imagine how Mrs Martin might have felt about her husband going back to Russia. She probably knew about the mistress, not necessarily the name but of her existence. Wives usually do. Now, it seems, he is going back to her. Any stories he tells his wife about the extreme secrecy, only the Prime Minister knowing the full story and all that, will all sound like special pleading to her. After he goes, and then dies, she grows increasingly miserable. It's a double betrayal, first his going off to see that woman again, and then not being alive to be reproached for it. Her unhappiness deepens,

> '. . . for many a time
> I have been half in love with easeful Death,
> Called him soft names in many a mused rhyme,
> To take into the air my quiet breath:
> Now more than ever seems it rich to die,
> To cease upon the midnight with no pain.'

'John Keats, my lord,' said Inspector Clayton proudly. 'Stanza six if my memory serves me.'

'It serves you very well, I think, Inspector,' said Powerscourt. 'Let me step back a little, as it were, from this fanciful speculation about Mrs Martin's state of mind. Was it wet that day? Would the stones underfoot have been slippery?'

'It was wet, my lord. If there had been two people up here the rain would have washed away any traces of their feet, if you see what I mean. Do you wish to stop up here a little longer, my lord? Or shall we go down and I'll see if I can persuade the constable to make us some tea?'

Powerscourt took another look at the view from the little tower. He felt sure he would be up here again. 'Some of Constable Watchett's tea would be excellent, Inspector. There are a number of points I would like to raise with you back in that splendid library, if I may,' he said, making his way down the stairs and back the way they came. Once again the water in the moat, its shifting elusive surfaces, the way it shimmered one minute and was absolutely still the next, fascinated him. Maybe the Powerscourt family could go and live in a house with a moat. He could sit by a window and pretend to read a book while watching the changing behaviour of the surface of the water. He checked himself when he realized that somebody would have to be on call twenty-four hours a day to pull the twins out after they fell in, which they surely would, several times a day.

Inspector Clayton removed the rope that had guarded Mrs Martin's bay in the library and pulled up a couple of chairs. Constable Watchett had found some tasty fruit cake to accompany the tea.

'Will?' said Powerscourt, the word muffled by the cake.

'Will who?' said Clayton, wondering if Powerscourt had discovered another suspect.

'Sorry,' said Powerscourt, washing his mouthful down with some of the constable's excellent tea, 'do we know if Mrs Martin left a will? Or,' he said after a pause, 'come to that, Mr Martin?'

The Inspector sighed. Powerscourt seemed to have touched a sensitive point. 'I have to confess, my lord,' he began, 'that I feel bad about this will business, very bad. The family solicitors are Evans Watkinson and Ragg over at Tonbridge. When I started this case, I'll be honest with you, my lord, I had a mass of work to finish off from two other cases. So I asked Constable Watchett to write to them on my behalf.' Powerscourt wondered if the letter had been laced with home-spun wisdom better suited to the local pub than to a solicitor's office. 'Anyway, my lord, a letter came back, addressed to me, suggesting I remember my duties, which include liaising with the deceased's solicitors, before asking ill-qualified members of the constabulary to address their betters. I have written a letter of apology, but they have still not replied. It was not well done, my lord, and now my Chief Constable asks about the wills every other day.'

Powerscourt smiled at the Inspector. 'Don't worry,' he said. 'I remember similar problems of bureaucracy and administration in South Africa. Give me the address for Evans Watkinson and Ragg before I go this evening, and I will call on them tomorrow.'

'Thank you, my lord, thank you very much. I may say that I found no sign of any wills in the desks of either Martin, but they could have decided to keep them with the lawyers for safety.'

'Let me ask you something else, Inspector, something that I think might have led to Mrs Martin's death. Is there any sign that she received any letters or cables from her husband while he was in Russia?'

'Cables? Not that I have seen so far, my lord.'

'This is going to sound preposterous, Inspector, so please make allowances for a tired investigator whose wits may have been sapped by prolonged exposure to the Russian temperament and the Russian climate.' Powerscourt took another draught of the Watchett tea and promised himself a further piece of cake if he could make his proposal believable.

'It goes something like this. Martin, you will remember, saw the Tsar in his country palace about fifteen miles from St Petersburg. Furthermore, Martin saw the Tsar on his own. That means the questions under discussion must have been of the utmost importance, questions of the highest national policy, questions so sensitive that Tsar Nicholas didn't want anybody else to hear about them. Let us suppose, however, that somebody else in the entourage gets an inkling of what they talked about. They pursue Martin back to St Petersburg. Before they find him he sends a message to his wife, telling her what he knows. When the somebody else and his colleagues catch up with Martin, they torture him until he tells what he knows, including the fact that he has passed the information on to his wife. They kill him, and dump the body on the frozen river. A few weeks later, they come here and kill his wife, leaving the body in the moat. By the time the Kennedys find Mrs Martin, the killer or killers have reached Hamburg or Berlin on their journey back to St Petersburg.'

Inspector Clayton peered outside at the fading of the light. Soon it would be dark and he always found the place oppressive then.

'There's only one query I have with that premise, my lord,' said Inspector Clayton, eyeing Powerscourt carefully as he tucked in to another slice of fruit cake. 'If you are being tortured, not that I am an expert, mind you, but suppose you have told your enemies what you know. Why do you need to tell them you have sent a message to somebody else as well?'

'That's a very fair observation, Inspector,' Powerscourt replied. 'Let me try to answer it. The answer, I believe, lies in the psychology of torturer and tortured, if you follow me. The torturer believes that there is always one further piece of information to be extracted from his victim, no matter how much he has dragged out of him already. And the tortured man thinks he would have attained relief by disclosing the most important thing he knows. But he hasn't. Why can't they leave him in peace? So he throws

244

them one more titbit, in the hope that the pain will finally stop. By this stage, that is probably all he can think of.'

'Thank God we live in a civilized society where these things don't happen,' said the Inspector. 'There are a couple of things you need to be aware of, my lord. I've just heard your cab coming down the hill, so I'll be brief. The first I have no direct knowledge of, merely station gossip. There is or there was some feud about the ownership of this house, Lord Powerscourt. There was a long court case between different branches of the Martin family before Roderick and Letitia took up residence.'

'And the second?' asked Powerscourt, hoping for a sympathetic lawyer under the age of seventy-five on the morrow.

'Johnny Fitzgerald told me about it this morning, my lord,' said Inspector Clayton, 'and no doubt he will have more details for you this evening – he told me he was dining at your house. It seems that Mr Martin may not have been the only one to have strayed from the holding the betrothed from this day forward, for better for worse, for richer for poorer, in sickness and in health, to love and to cherish, till death us do part. Mrs Martin was very friendly with a Colonel Fitzmaurice, a retired military man from over Ashford way. They went away together, my lord, though nothing else has ever been proved.'

'And what of the gallant Colonel, Inspector? What does he have to say for himself?'

'That's the problem,' said the Inspector, raising a hand to ask the cabbie by the door to wait a moment longer. 'Unless Johnny Fitzgerald has had some luck today, the Colonel has disappeared, vanished off the face of the earth. My Chief Constable believes he may have gone to join the Martins on the other side.'

245

11

The last dishes had been cleared away. The candles had burnt halfway down. A great-great-grandfather of Lady Lucy's, resplendent in a scarlet coat with enormous moustaches and a chest covered with medals, painted by Lawrence, was standing to attention over the fireplace, surveying his descendants. A bottle of claret and a bottle of port awaited the gentlemen's attention. Lady Lucy was sitting at the head of the table with Francis on her right and Johnny on her left. She felt so proud to have Francis home. Olivia had confided to her at bedtime that they were now a proper family once again, and while Lady Lucy might have questioned the assumption that she couldn't cope on her own, she was largely in agreement.

Once again Powerscourt presented his account of his investigation so far. It was, perhaps, less full than the one he had given to Inspector Clayton that afternoon. He would, he said, confine himself to the facts in the first instance. When they had heard Johnny's report on Mrs Martin, he might speculate. He made no mention of the torture chambers in the basement of the Okhrana head-quarters or of the grisly paintings in the special section of the Hermitage. He stressed two things, the differences between the various Russian ministries and the secret service, and the fact that Martin had actually seen the Tsar. He mentioned the tapping of the Embassy telegraphs by the Okhrana and the private system operational between the brothers Crabbe in St Petersburg and London. He said he thought the investigation would now assume less and less importance in the eyes of the Russians. Their thoughts and their agencies would be increasingly devoted to the threat of terrorism and the broader political dilemma of repression or reform. He told of the affair between Roderick Martin and Tamara Kerenkova and the circumstances surrounding her banishment at the time of his last visit. The single most important thing in helping solve the problem, he said gravely, would be an interview with the Tsar. But then, his, Powerscourt's, fate might be the same as Mr Martin's. He said he had tried to think of a message to the British Embassy, ostensibly sent to de Chassiron, but designed to be read by the Okhrana, which might precipitate events that would unlock the mystery. So far he had failed. In any case, he pointed out, he wasn't sure the Okhrana knew any more than he did. He looked forward to hearing Johnny's report but unless there was some firm evidence from the solicitors or the telegraph company, he feared that the death of Mrs Martin would remain a mystery. If they could discover more about the telegraphs sent from the British Embassy on the evening or the night of Martin's death, the situation might become clearer. For if Martin had sent a message to his wife, and if the message contained compromising material, and if the Okhrana read it almost immediately, then that might account for Martin's death, assuming the message was sent after his visit to the Tsar. It would also explain the death of Mrs Martin, killed for the same reason as her husband. They were killed to keep their knowledge a secret. Martin could, he admitted, have sent a message earlier in the day once he knew his

247

business would be concluded by his interview with the Tsar. He also looked forward, he said, to hearing the views of Lucy and Johnny. The only firm plan he had at present, he told them, was to stop off in Paris on his way back to St Petersburg and speak to somebody high up in the French secret service. He passed on de Chassiron's judgement that they were the best informed organization in Europe about Russia and the court of the Tsar.

Johnny Fitzgerald began his account with the answers, as far as he knew them, to Powerscourt's queries sent from St Petersburg. William Burke, he said, had reported that there were erratic swings in the balances of Martin's bank account, consistent, Johnny now realized, with the visits to Russia and the possible purchases of treats and other delights for la Kerenkova. Martin's train tickets for his various expeditions to the Russian capital had not been bought through the Foreign Office, but through a branch of Thomas Cook round the corner. That was perfectly proper as he was going on private business, or, possibly, spying business. Then he moved on to the life and times of Mrs Letitia Martin in her own village of Tibenham with a very large swig of his port. Johnny looked round happily at his friends. 'I've got one surprise for you all,' he said, 'but as in all the best stories, I'm going to save it to the end. The first thing to say about Mrs Martin is that she was very popular. She always arrived in the village on her horse, never on foot, never in a carriage. The natives seem to like that. She was well known in the few shops. The vicar spoke warmly of her as a regular participant at Communion and a generous giver to the fund for the restoration of his church spire. Stood for four hundred years, could fall down next week, give generously today, as the vicar's sign outside the church proclaims. There's just one slight crack in this perfection. Mrs Martin was always very late in paying her bills. Sometimes, the butcher told me when his shop was completely empty, her suppliers might have to wait over a year to be paid.'

'Had this been going on for a long time, Johnny, or was it a recent development?' Powerscourt was fiddling with a fountain pen.

'It had got very bad in the past few years, they said. Even the vicar had heard about it, for God's sake. But it may tie in with William's information about the fluctuating bank balance.'

Johnny seemed to regard discreditable information that reached the ears of the Church as especially trustworthy, almost as reliable as Holy Writ.

'What about the Colonel, Johnny?' said Lady Lucy. 'I'm very keen to hear about the Colonel.'

'The Colonel, the Colonel, I'm just coming to the Colonel, Lucy,' said Johnny with a grin, virtually singing the words "the Colonel" as if it were the refrain in a ballad. 'Colonel Peter Templeton Fitzmaurice, formerly of the Irish Rangers, one-time resident at Castleford Lodge, some ten miles from Tibenham, nine miles from the Grange. I have to say, ladies and gentlemen,' Johnny looked at his hosts in turn, 'that the hard evidence for any sort of relationship between those two is, well . . .' Johnny paused, searching for the most appropriate phrase, 'flimsy might be the right word. Or thin. Certainly inadmissible in a court of law. It started in the lounge bar of the Coach and Horses. I don't mean any affair started there, but my information did. It was ten minutes or so before opening time and the landlady, a handsome woman in her early thirties, years younger than her husband, referred to them. "Of course, there's that Mrs Martin and her special friend the Colonel," she said, nodding vigorously at the word "special". The same process then began to repeat itself. You know, Francis, you know those people who go about studying strange tribes in remote places and asking them questions – anthropologists, are they called? – they could have a field day down in rural Kent. Communication by non-verbal means, they could call it. I don't think a single person used words like affair, close friendship, love, certainly not love. There was the serious nod, making the recipient of the nod complicit in the knowledge of the nodder. There was the tap, or even the double tap on the side of the nose. There was the rolling of the eyes. There were phrases like no better than she should be, carry on, carry along even. The lad who drives the little fly to the station and back was regarded as a priceless witness for the prosecution because he had once seen them standing together on the station platform With Luggage. No evidence that they were necessarily travelling together With Luggage, of course, but grist to the mill all the same.'

'Was there any truth in it, Johnny? As far as you could discover?' Lady Lucy smiled at him.

'Well, yes, I think there is. Or was. You see, I took a trip over to Castleford Lodge earlier today. The Colonel is not in residence. The housekeeper is. I don't know why, but housekeepers for some reason are much more forthcoming than butlers in my experience.'

'It's because you're male,' Powerscourt cut in.

'I don't think you should undermine a fellow investigator's talents in that way, Francis, I really don't. It's quite uncalled for. She didn't know Mrs Martin was dead, the housekeeper. Her face fell and she looked very pale when I told her. "The master would be so upset if he knew that," she said, "he was so fond of that lady, he really was. When she came here to stay he'd be happy for days afterwards." Then she burst into tears. I didn't think it politic to inquire about the sleeping arrangements at that precise moment, so I left.'

250

'Isn't it curious,' said Lady Lucy, 'how the words could apply to her master alive or dead. I find that very strange. So which is he, Johnny, the amorous Colonel? Is he alive or is he dead?'

'I don't know. The housekeeper doesn't know. I've nearly finished,' said Johnny, eyeing his still half-full glass of port. 'We know she was popular with the locals. We know she was hard up, sometimes very hard up. I don't think she was mean. We know she was having a relationship of some sort with the Colonel, dead or alive. And . . .' Johnny paused melodramatically, like the conjurer finally about to produce a hatful of rabbits or the Queen of Sheba, 'we know that a week or ten days before her death she received a visit from a foreigner. A rather unusual foreigner.' And Johnny tapped the side of the nose in the manner of the Tibenham residents he had described a few moments ago.

'Stop teasing, Johnny,' said Lady Lucy. 'Who was it, Hottentot or Zulu, Afghan or Bedouin?'

'Russian,' said Johnny. 'The lad in the fly brought him to and from the station to Tibenham Grange. When he asked the stranger where he came from – the man was wearing an astrakhan coat, for God's sake – he said Russia. And then he smiled, apparently.'

'Pretty big place, Russia,' said Powerscourt. 'Any city, by any chance? Kiev? Archangel? Moscow? Minsk? St Petersburg?'

'I'm afraid he didn't say and the lad didn't ask. Pretty remiss of him, but there you are.'

Powerscourt started walking up and down the dining room, running his hand along the backs of the chairs. 'Damn! Damn! Damn! I hate to say it but the really infuriating thing about this case is that so many people are dead. Both Martins for a start. We can't ask them a thing.'

251

'You know what happens in those circumstances, Francis,' said Johnny flippantly, 'there's one lot of dead people and another lot of live people who want to find out what happened. The live lot send for some investigators to find the answers. That's why we're here, Francis, to find out why the other buggers are dead, isn't it?'

'Of course, Johnny, you're right. I'm being stupid,' said Powerscourt with a smile. 'But there are so many things a Martin could answer if only they were here. Who was this Russian? What was he doing here? Had he come from the Embassy to offer his condolences? Had he come from the Okhrana with a final message? Or had he come to find out if Mrs Martin had received a message from her husband in St Petersburg? Or was he the spy Martin's handler in London, come to see Mrs Martin with messages of sympathy and large bundles of cash? I know I'm supposed to be offering suggestions as to what has been going on. I don't discount the spy theory at all. Maybe the Okhrana asked Martin once he was in St Petersburg to perform some final, unbelievably dangerous act of treachery. He refuses. They kill him and create this smokescreen which has baffled me ever since.'

A disconsolate Powerscourt sat down and began to run his fingers through his hair.

'Don't worry, Francis,' said Lucy, 'you've had cases as difficult as this in the past and you've always solved them in the end.'

'It wouldn't look too good,' her husband said bitterly, 'if I allowed myself to be brought out of retirement for a case I couldn't solve. I'd be finished then, as an investigator, totally finished and hung out to dry.'

'Francis, Francis,' said Johnny Fitzgerald, leaning over to refill his friend's glass, 'you are forgetting one of the most salient facts of this investigation, if you can have a most salient fact. What is that? I hear you ask. Quite simply this. You have been operating on your own. Single. Unaided. Achilles without Patroclus. Aeneas without whatever he's called, the faithful Achates. Wellington without Blucher at Waterloo. You have not had me at your side to offer sympathy, friendship, intelligence, common sense and alcohol on your journey through this vale of tears. But I am here now. Oh yes, Johnny Fitzgerald is now on the case. So why don't you make all our lives easier by offering up your thoughts as to what might have happened to the late Roderick Martin. And,' he added as an afterthought, 'to his wife, if you have formed any theories yet in that department. You don't usually wait for the facts to get in the way of the theories.'

Powerscourt smiled. Lady Lucy felt relieved and stood up to give her husband a quick kiss on the cheek. 'When you're ready, Francis,' she said, 'we're ready when you are.'

'I said earlier,' Powerscourt began, 'that I would speculate about what has been going on in this case. I don't think I feel capable of speculation yet, so what I would like to offer you are some questions to which I don't know the answers.' He gazed at Lady Lucy, suddenly realizing that the shape of her mouth and her chin were identical to those of their twin daughter Juliet. He found the thought cheering, knowing that a partial replica of Lucy would be at large in the world long after the original had gone.

'Question Number One,' he said, Lady Lucy fascinated to see that he was not, for once, emphasizing his point by tapping the index finger of one hand into the palm of the other, 'may seem obscure, but it would help enormously if we knew the answer. Why did Martin not tell his mistress Tamara Kerenkova that he was coming to St Petersburg? He had always told her before. Why not this time? It was, after all, about to be the season for balls and dancing, even if the balls were not as magnificent as in years gone by on account of the Tsar not providing any entertainment because of the war with Japan. Did Martin know that her husband was in St Petersburg? But then that didn't seem to have bothered either of them before. Has anybody any suggestions?'

'Is it possible,' said Lady Lucy, 'that Martin had broken it off as you implied earlier? He promised his wife he would not see her and he kept to his word.'

'And surely it's equally possible,' said Johnny, 'that her husband did not know about any giving up on Martin's part. Kerenkov killed him. He told the local police about the body and then his naval friends made it disappear. Isn't it possible that we're not dealing with high politics at all, Francis, but with the old story of the revenge of the jilted husband?'

'Perfectly possible,' agreed Powerscourt, 'but that wouldn't explain the interest of the Russian secret service in Martin and his movements. The biggest unanswered question is Martin's meeting with the Tsar. Who arranged it? The British? Possibly. Or the Tsar? What in God's name were they talking about that was so sensitive it had to bypass the Ambassador and the diplomats and the diplomatic protocol and the diplomatic bag? Military matters? Something to do with the naval conflict in the Far East? Were the British offering to break their treaty with the Japanese and ally themselves with the Russians? Unlikely, I should have thought. Were the British looking to extend their alliance with France to include France's ally, Russia? The normal channels might be a trifle stormy just now after the sinking of those fishing boats, but the Tsar could take a long view. He needs all the allies he can get against his cousin Willy in Berlin, after all.'

'Why are you so sure it had to do with high politics, Francis?' asked Lady Lucy.

'Because,' he replied quickly, 'I can't think what else it might have been. The Tsar doesn't need a man like Martin to get him an invitation to Cowes Week or to Ascot. He's got teams of flunkeys to look after that side of things. If his wife wants some more furniture, they'll send for a man from Maples, not a man from the Foreign Office. And it looks as if Martin was sent from London on a mission which included, or perhaps mainly consisted of, seeing the Tsar. I'm sure it had to do with politics, Lucy.'

'And the third question, Francis?' Lady Lucy was well used to questions in her husband's investigations that came in numbers now, numbers sometimes quite small, unrolling themselves like the platforms in some great railway station, on other occasions growing into large numbers that taxed her ability with figures.

'I think,' Powerscourt began, 'that the last question has to do with the inability of the various bits of the Russian bureaucracy to agree with each other. Why weren't they all singing the same tune about Martin's death? Why didn't the Foreign Ministry know about Martin's previous visits to St Petersburg? Come to that, why didn't the Okhrana? I think there may be a perfectly simple explanation that has to do with the nature of bureaucracies whether they're in modern Russia or ancient Rome. They're all competing with each other in a spirit of Darwinian struggle if not for the survival of the fittest, then certainly to be the part of the system with the best information for their master. De Chassiron told me that all sorts of the imperial protection units had their elite corps looking after the Tsar, the police, the household troops, the customs, the navy and so on. One of them is going to know what happened to Martin, I'm certain of it. As to which one, I simply haven't a clue.'

Powerscourt got up and poured himself another glass of claret. 'There's another possibility, actually,' he said. 'I've only just thought of it. You know I've always wondered if Martin was a double agent, a man really working for the Russians rather than his own side. He'd be a perfect recruit with his brains and his career prospects. Imagine having the British Ambassador in Washington or Berlin reporting direct to the Tsar in the Winter Palace. But suppose the British find out. They decide there's only one thing to do with him. They kill him. And they send a message to his masters in St Petersburg that they know what has been going on by dumping his body, or appearing to dump his body, on the most famous street in the Russian capital. I'm just a distraction, a means of trying to persuade everybody that Martin is really a good British man after all.'

'I'll say one thing for you, Francis,' said Johnny, 'you may have been away from investigations for a year or two but the brain hasn't got any slower.'

'I should hope not,' said Lady Lucy loyally, wondering, as she had all evening, how much her husband was not telling her about what went on in St Petersburg.

In his little office at the back of the Alexander Palace Major Andrey Shatilov of the Imperial Guard, Royal Palaces Security Division, was reviewing the reports on Suspect No. 28,487B. This was only one of the hundreds of such files that passed through his office every day. The Major was only concerned with the St Petersburg district. Other officers had Moscow and the provinces, especially the royal palace at Livadia in the Crimea, under their control. Shatilov saw that Suspect No. 28,487B was employed as a lady-in-waiting in the Alexander Palace. This made him immediately suspicious as many of the waiters and the footmen and the grooms and the maids were already on the payroll of the Imperial Guard. There were, in the Major's view, few finer places to obtain accurate first-hand intelligence on the imperial family. And 28,487B's activities outside Tsarskoe Selo were equally suspect. She was consorting with a rich young nobleman called Mikhail Shaporov, whose father was suspected of links and contacts right across the political spectrum from the Social Revolutionaries on the extreme left to even more dubious cells on the far right. Shaporov *père* would not, the Major reflected grimly, be the first one in uncertain times to take out as many insurance policies as possible. Then there was the Englishman, Powerscourt, with whom she had been observed in three separate locations, including one at the Imperial Yacht Club where they had been inquiring about the dead man, Martin. Powerscourt, the Major saw on his file, had returned to England but was expected to come back to St Petersburg in the near future. He was some sort of an investigator, despatched to look into the death of the wretched Martin. Soon, Major Shatilov said to himself, soon we shall have Miss Natasha Bobrinsky in for questioning. That way we shall also send a message to this fool Englishman come to meddle in other people's affairs.

The offices of Evans Watkinson and Ragg were in a handsome eighteenth-century building at the end of Tonbridge High Street nearest the church. A collection of prints of clippers, elegant vessels with greyhound lines that used to speed across the Atlantic or the tea routes to China, adorned the reception area, manned by an ancient greybeard who looked as if he might have begun his career during the Crimean War. Mr Ragg, Mr Theodore Ragg, Powerscourt was told, would attend to him, if Lord Powerscourt would step this way up to the first floor.

Ragg was about fifty years of age, with a small well-trimmed moustache and suspicious brown eyes. He was wearing a brown suit that his wife might have told him was slightly past its best. Powerscourt wondered if there was a Mrs Ragg and decided that there probably was. Lucy could always tell about these things.

'You're here about Mr and Mrs Martin, I understand, Lord Powerscourt?' Ragg's voice sounded to Powerscourt as though he disapproved of investigators as a class, and even more of ones who were lords.

'Yes, I am,' said Powerscourt brightly. 'I was asked by the Foreign Office to look into the death of Mr Martin in St Petersburg, you see.'

'Indeed,' said Ragg. 'I would point out, however, that this is Tonbridge rather than the Russian capital. How may we assist you here?'

Powerscourt realized that brevity might be the order of the day. 'Did either of them leave a will?'

'No,' said Ragg.

'To whom does the estate pass in that case?'

'I am not sure I am at liberty to tell you that, Lord Powerscourt.'

'Tell me, tell me not,' said Powerscourt quickly, 'but if you do not tell me you will have the police here this afternoon, and they will take up even more of your valuable time, Mr Ragg. Are you competent at shorthand? Some of the London forces are like lightning with it. I have never cared for it myself. But the chances are that a policeman taking very slow shorthand could take up most of your afternoon. And if by any chance you should decide not to co-operate with the police, you would have the Foreign Office lawyers to deal with instead. Charming, the

258

Foreign Office lawyers, of course, but pretty brutal, I think you'd find.'

'As far as we know, Mr Samuel Martin, some sort of cousin,' said Ragg, with considerable malice.

'Address, Mr Ragg, address?'

'I'm not obliged to give you that.'

'For God's sake, man. We're talking about one or possibly two murders here and you are refusing to hand over an address. It's not credible.' Suddenly a dark suspicion flitted across Powerscourt's mind. 'You don't represent Mr Samuel Martin too, do you, Mr Ragg?'

'No, I don't. 128 Hornsey Lane, London N is the address you seek.'

'I also understand,' said Powerscourt, 'that there was something resembling a family feud concerning the ownership of this house and estate the last time they changed hands. Is that so?'

'It is so, and a very interesting case it proved to be, Lord Powerscourt.'

Theodore Ragg seemed to have softened suddenly. Powerscourt wondered if it was the legal subtlety of the case or the size of the fees and the length of the affair that caused the sudden change in his temperament. The answer was soon apparent.

'Fascinating case, my lord, fascinating,' said Theodore Ragg with a faraway look in his eyes. 'It went on for over five years before it was finally settled in the House of Lords.'

Five years of fees, Powerscourt thought, noticing also that Thedodore Ragg's gums seemed to be bleeding slightly. The man was having to swallow constantly to stop drops of blood escaping down his chin. Maybe this accounted for his earlier ill temper. Maybe he didn't like dentists.

'Old Mr Martin, the dead Mr Martin's benefactor, was very ill at the end, Lord Powerscourt, this must have been over twenty years ago now,' said Ragg. 'His mind was going, you see. Mr and Mrs Roderick Martin were abroad on Foreign Office business, they were very young then, so Mr Samuel Martin and his wife came to stay to look after the old gentleman. If my memory serves me, Mr Roderick Martin was first cousin, and Mr Samuel Martin second cousin, twice removed. We used to have their family trees all over the offices here in those days. The Samuel Martins tried to get rid of the old man's own doctor, Dr Morgan, but he, the doctor, didn't like the look of what was going on. He kept coming back to see the old man whenever he could. The staff used to let him in the back door. Then the Samuel Martins brought in another doctor, a man nobody liked, by the name of West, Barnabas West. And when the old gentleman finally died, the Samuel Martins produced another will, signed two weeks before he passed on, leaving the house and the estate and the money to the Samuel Martins and witnessed, among others, by the doctor, West. Then the Samuel Martins promptly moved into Tibenham Grange and took charge of their inheritance. When Roderick Martin came back, he said the other will was a forgery. He went to court with the original will, signed some ten years before and kept here in our safe. Originally the lawyers said that the later will had to take precedence and it was up to Mr Roderick to prove otherwise. Well, my lord, we used to say it would become like Jarndyce versus Jarndyce, Martin versus Martin, new counsel being instructed every six months, new judges in the Court of Appeal who didn't know the background. Eventually it was proved that the signatures of one of the witnesses were forgeries and that was an end to it.'

Ragg sank back a little, obviously tired by his narrative. Powerscourt wondered if his entire career had been a disappointment after that. 'What a fascinating time it must have been, Mr Ragg. Did the two sides of the Martin family bury the hatchet in the end?'

There was a cackle from the solicitor. Now at last, Powerscourt thought, blood was going to escape from the unfortunate man's mouth. But with a Herculean effort, swallowing hard three times like a seabird swallowing a fish, Theodore Ragg kept his dignity. 'Bury the hatchet, Lord Powerscourt? The only way either side would have been satisfied would have been to bury the hatchet in the other party's neck. I'm sure that's still true today.'

Suddenly Theodore Ragg looked exhausted. He began to look anxious like a man who thinks he might miss his train or fail to make his connection. Powerscourt wondered if the blood was an omen of something rather more sinister than bad gums. He remembered a previous President of the Royal Academy coughing blood into a series of perfectly laundered white handkerchiefs and dying not long afterwards.

'I must leave you in peace, Mr Ragg,' said Powerscourt, looking into the sad brown eyes of the solicitor. 'Just one last question. How old would Mr Samuel Martin be now?'

'About fifty or a few years more,' said Ragg. 'Forgive me if I was rude earlier on, Lord Powerscourt. I was feeling particularly unwell.'

'Think nothing of it,' said Powerscourt, rising to his feet and heading for the door. 'There's nothing to forgive, you have been most helpful.'

As he made his way towards the front door, he understood what an enormous effort Theodore Ragg must have been making during their conversation. The coughing in the room behind him began like a slow rumble far off, then it turned into a great hacking shriek, and finally it ebbed away into sounds of weeping. Powerscourt could hear doors opening and closing as the partners went to offer help and comfort to their dying colleague.

The telegraph office was but a hundred yards away down the High Street. Powerscourt was shown into the office of the manager, a dapper young man by the name of Charlie Dean, who looked as if he and his clothes would have been happier in Finsbury Circus or Leadenhall Street in the City of London. He was quick to grasp the import of Powerscourt's visit and the importance of any possible messages from St Petersburg.

'How long would we keep a message, you ask, my lord. Three months.'

Fine, thought Powerscourt. If Martin had sent any message to his wife here, and if, for some reason she had forgotten to collect it, the message should still be somewhere in the system.

'And what kind of authority would you need before you handed the message over to somebody, Mr Dean?'

'Company rules say we have to try three times to deliver to the recipient in person. Well, we tried and failed three times in this case so now it could be handed over to anybody with a proof of connection with the address. If you're thinking what I think you're thinking, Lord Powerscourt, I don't think anybody has been in here asking for cables they have no business with. We know most of our customers in a place like this, you see.' Charlie Dean sounded rather sad as he said that. Powerscourt thought he would be much happier somewhere very busy in the metropolis where every customer was a perfect stranger, a new challenge, offering possibilities of fresh messages and fresh romance.

'And suppose you wanted to send a message the other way, Mr Dean. Would you have a copy of anything Mrs Martin might have sent to Russia?'

'That would be before she was killed, I suppose,' said Charlie happily, glad to welcome murder to the Tonbridge telegraph office. 'Well, there should be a copy of that too. If you wait here, my lord, I'll just go and make some inquiries.'

The walls of the little office were adorned with prints of great cricketers like C.B. Fry and Ranjitsinghi, interspersed with modern photographs of ancient telegraphic equipment. Powerscourt was reflecting that a man who scored as fast as Fry could probably transmit a telegraph message at record speed when the manager returned, in a very excited state.

'Look, Lord Powerscourt, it's a message! From Russia!' He handed Powerscourt the thin envelope used to protect the cable. It came from St Petersburg, dated December 22nd, possibly the very date of Mr Martin's death.

'Has this been here ever since? Nobody has asked for it or anything like that?' said Powerscourt.

'It's been here ever since,' said Charlie Dean. 'Aren't you going to open it? The fiendish killer might be unmasked right here in this office, my lord.'

Powerscourt grinned. He wondered if Charlie was a regular reader of the adventures of heroes like Sexton Blake with their emphasis on excitement and melodrama rather than detection and analysis. He looked at the envelope.

'What are you thinking, my lord? Do you feel you may have the master criminal in your hands?' Powerscourt was feeling rather nervous. This could be the answer to all his problems. It could mean that he would never have to go back to St Petersburg. Above all, he thought of Roderick

Martin. Did he send this message before he saw the Tsar or after? If it was after, had he put in the cable the news that was to kill him, and might have killed his wife too? The message, after all, might have been in the hands of the Russian security services inside the hour. Plenty of time to prepare an expedition to Tibenham Grange and push a widow into the moat beneath. And, maybe more important yet, how much longer did Martin have left to live when he wrote it?

Charlie Dean's eyes were burning bright. His brain seemed to have taken off to some fictional Valhalla. 'Maybe he's going to tell of the deadly fight on the ice floe with the Russian killers, my lord. Maybe the chief villain behind Mr Martin's murder is going to be exposed at last!'

Powerscourt opened the envelope. He looked rather sadly at the message. He handed it over to Charlie.

'Coming home tomorrow, Thursday,' it read, 'should be back in three or four days.'

'It must be in code, my lord,' said Charlie feverishly. 'Tomorrow probably means enemies vanquished and Thursday means, well, coming home Thursday.'

'I think we'll find,' said Powerscourt, folding the message carefully and putting it in his pocket, 'that the message is more useful than might first appear.'

'You mean there is a secret code, my lord?' Hope died hard in Charlie Dean's heart.

'Not exactly,' said Powerscourt with a smile, 'but think about what the message says. He must have done, or been about to do, whatever he went to St Petersburg for, don't you see, Charlie? Otherwise he wouldn't be so confident about coming home tomorrow. Mission accomplished, that's how I read that bit.' Privately, Powerscourt wasn't so sure. It could mean, this has all been a complete disaster, so I'm coming home tomorrow, he said to himself, though he wasn't convinced. And had he sent it during the day? Or in the evening when Ricky Crabbe thought somebody else had been using his machines? And why – Powerscourt's brain was circling round the problem like a bird of prey – hadn't Mrs Martin come to pick it up? Maybe her husband wasn't in the habit of sending messages. After the shock of his death it could have passed completely out of her mind as she mourned for her husband.

'And the other thing, Charlie,' said Powerscourt, keen to bring as much excitement as possible to the young of Tonbridge, 'is that sending this may have been one of the last things he did alive.'

'What do you mean?' asked Charlie. 'Did the Cossack monsters charge in and drag him off the telegraph machine to his death?'

'Not quite,' said Powerscourt, 'but he could have been killed very soon afterwards, outside in the snow.'

'I'll never forget this morning, Lord Powerscourt,' said Charlie. 'For me, it's been so exciting. I know I read too many of those detective stories, but this has been like a look through the door of one of them. I'm ever so grateful, my lord.'

'I tell you what I'll do, Charlie,' said Powerscourt with a smile. 'When I know what happened, what really happened, I'll let you know. I tell you what, even better, I'll send you a telegram.'

Forty minutes later Powerscourt was climbing up the little stone staircase that led to the top of the tower at Tibenham Grange. Of Inspector Clayton, or Constable Watchett, keeping the property free of visiting architects, there was, at present, no sign. As he stood on the top once more Powerscourt gazed intently at every single stone in the

265

surface, in case they had all overlooked a vital clue. He stared into the woods, imagining a fifty-five year old man, bent on revenge for what had happened all those years before, inching his way towards the Grange. He saw him helping himself to a weapon in the kitchen and presenting himself in front of an unsuspecting Mrs Martin in her favourite bay in the library. Then he saw her marched at knifepoint through the house she loved towards the tower from where she would see it no more. He saw the man creeping back through the woods towards a train to London, secure in the knowledge that this time his claim on the estate would surely win the day. He was woken from his reverie by a loud shout from Inspector Clayton who had appeared suddenly on the lawn.

'Thank God you've come,' yelled the Inspector. 'See you in the library.'

There a panting Inspector delivered his message. 'You're to return to London, my lord, as soon as possible, your wife says. There's news from Russia. Lady Powerscourt didn't say what it was, but it surely concerns the investigation.'

Before he set off for the station Powerscourt told Clayton all he had discovered about the earlier court case from Theodore Ragg, and he showed him the telegram from St Petersburg.

'I wish that message had been more help to you, my lord,' said the Inspector. 'Do you think it likely that this old family feud has come to the surface?'

'I don't know,' said Powerscourt, 'but I'm sure we have to look at it closely. If we can eliminate the other Martin, as it were, we're still left with the original three contenders.'

'Three?' said Inspector Clayton.

'Three,' Powerscourt replied firmly. 'Did she fall, did she jump, or was she pushed? Something tells me we may never find the answer.'

Powerscourt was lucky enough to secure a whole compartment to himself on the way back to London. He sat by the window and stared out over Kent. He hoped, he prayed, that the news from St Petersburg was not what he feared it might be. He wondered if he should take Johnny Fitzgerald back with him or leave him working on the death of Mrs Martin. He wondered how upset Lady Lucy would be if he disappeared into dangerous territory once again. He wondered, less seriously, if he should buy more dolls and soldiers for the twins.

The message was brief, sent by Mikhail Shaporov via his father's private system to William Burke. 'Natasha due to meet me at four o'clock yesterday,' it said, 'but she did not appear. Nor has she come today. What should I do? Mikhail.'

Powerscourt swore violently to himself. It was what he had feared, that something would happen to the girl. Had she fallen into the hands of the Okhrana? Would she live to survive her incarceration? Was Natasha Bobrinsky, young, beautiful and clever, about to meet the fate of Roderick Martin on the ice of the Nevskii Prospekt?

12

Powerscourt had composed his reply on the train. 'Suggest no, repeat no activity for the present. There may be some domestic crisis at the Alexander Palace. Leaving London for return to St Petersburg tomorrow. Regards. Powerscourt.' He sent it off to William Burke's office in the City and began pacing up and down his drawing room. He was debating with himself the sending of a rather different cable to the Russian capital, one that would precipitate a crisis in his investigation. It might also, he reflected grimly, kill him. He thought of Lady Lucy and knew that, for once, he could not ask for her advice. The one person he could ask, Johnny Fitzgerald, was not in London, although he might be later. He consulted a train timetable as a diversion and discovered that if he left London that evening he would have time for a meeting in Paris in the morning and still connect with the service to St Petersburg. Then he found his mind made up and he set off for the Foreign Office. Sir Jeremiah Reddaway was able to squeeze him in between a meeting of the Ottoman Empire working party and afternoon tea with the Icelandic Ambassador.

'God bless my soul,' was the mandarin's first reaction to Powerscourt's request. 'I've never heard of such a thing before. It's quite unconstitutional.' Powerscourt refrained from pointing out that as there was no written constitution it was difficult to break it. 'Are you sure about this, man? What do you think you will gain from it?'

'I need to test a theory about Martin's death, Sir Jeremiah.'

'But what's wrong with us here at the Foreign Office, Powerscourt? What's wrong with me, for God's sake?'

Once again Powerscourt held his tongue. 'I want to speak to the best informed person I can find about Russia and the court of the Tsar. Our Embassy in St Petersburg' – he did not name de Chassiron – 'believe that the best informed person is the head of the French secret service. The French Ambassador in St Petersburg is well informed, but M. Olivier Brouzet is the man I wish to see. With your approval, of course, Sir Jeremiah. We are allies with France now, after all, are we not?'

The diplomat snorted. Rosebery had observed long ago that concluding an alliance of friendship with another country virtually guaranteed that relations would begin to deteriorate immediately.

'All right, man. I'll sanction it,' said Sir Jeremiah with bad grace. 'If I didn't, I presume you'd just go ahead and make the appointment anyway.'

Powerscourt made no comment. Ten minutes later he made his way to the telegraph office and dictated a message to go at once to de Chassiron in the Petersburg Embassy.

'Returning St Petersburg tomorrow. Believe I should be in a position to know what happened to Martin in a week or so. Please request audience with Tsar for me on Martin related business. Kind regards. Powerscourt.'

The real recipient was not de Chassiron. It was the Okhrana. Powerscourt hoped Mikhail Shaporov's information about reading the messages was correct. He felt elated suddenly, as a man might who is gambling with his life. The message might smoke Derzhenov out and force him to reveal what he knew about the death of Martin. And if he were granted an interview with the Tsar, it might also produce the same result as before. Powerscourt could join Martin in a cold and icy grave.

The normal pattern of life at the Alexander Palace was in turmoil. The routine, the patterns by which this most regular of families lived their lives had been thrown into chaos. The heir to the throne, His Imperial Highness Alexis Nicolaievich, Sovereign Heir Tsarevich, Grand Duke of Russia, was sick, very sick, and none of the doctors sent from the city could cure him. It began with a haemorrhage which arose without the slightest cause and lasted for three days. Bandages were applied which sometimes showed blood. Then a bruise ruptured a tiny blood vessel beneath the skin and Alexis' blood began to seep slowly into surrounding muscle or tissue. The blood did not clot as it would in a normal person, it went on flowing for hours, leading to a swelling the size of a grapefruit. Natasha Bobrinsky was now looking after the four girls virtually on her own. She had no time to visit the city or even to write letters. She went with the girls on their visits to their infant brother and ushered them out a few minutes later. She noticed that the parents were reluctant to conduct any conversation with the doctors in front of the princesses. This is the future of Russia, Natasha said to herself, standing by one of the nurses at the end of the crib and watching the infant toss from side to side, this child, this tiny Romanov holds the fate of the empire in his hands. Should he die, the Emperor and Empress might never recover. When she wasn't by her son's side the Empress was praying, on her knees in front of her icon of the Virgin, beseeching the cruel God who had done this to her child to take pity. Earthly sinners are urged to repent, she told herself, God can repent too and take back whatever dreadful fate he has handed down to my Alexis, the awful horrors of joints that bled and would not stop, the terrible cries of pain from the child that could not be assuaged. Natasha would sink to her knees beside her Empress when she could and join her in her prayers. She felt that this family were being asked to suffer too much. The thought of a lifetime punctuated by these bouts of illness and uncertainty was more than she could bear. Late one afternoon Natasha accompanied two of the doctors from the sick room to the front door and the carriages that were waiting to take them back to the city. She heard the word whispered between them when they thought nobody was looking or listening, only some servant girl. Natasha didn't know what the word meant but she could look it up in the library when she got a chance. She felt sure that Lord Powerscourt would like to know.

Only one thought offered faint consolation to the Empress. All through the illness she had prayed that the faith healer Philippe's prophecy to her might be fulfilled, that he was only a messenger for a greater healer due to follow him. The Montenegrin sisters had sent word that a new staretz, another holy man, a man with extraordinary powers of healing had arrived in the capital from Siberia. Maybe this man would be the answer to her prayers.

Powerscourt had letters to write on his return to Markham Square. He wrote to Lord Rosebery asking him to make a very particular request from the Private Secretary to the King. He asked him not to elaborate, not to give any hint of why he was making this peculiar inquiry. If pressed, he could say it was to do with national security and the death of a British diplomat. No details could be given of where the Foreign Office man had met his doom. When Rosebery had the answer – and the question was of considerable urgency – he was under no circumstances to send the cable via the Foreign Office. He was to send one word, Yes or No, to be transmitted to Powerscourt through the house of Shaporov in St Petersburg from the offices of William Burke in London. He, Powerscourt, thanked Rosebery most sincerely for his help and promised to fill him in on the details on his return. Then he wrote to Johnny Fitzgerald. When he, Johnny, had satisfied himself that he knew all there was to know about the death of Mrs Letitia Martin, he was to come to St Petersburg. But only after a strange journey to the East of England. Once more Powerscourt enjoined his friend to total security. Once more he requested that a one-word answer be sent to the Shaporov address. One look into the eyes of the people he was going to see, Powerscourt told his friend, and Johnny would know if Powerscourt's guess was correct. He wrote one final letter to Lady Lucy. He sealed it carefully and wrote her name in bold letters on the envelope. He placed it in the front drawer of his desk so it could be easily found if he did not return. 'Lucy,' it said, 'I love you so much. I always will. Francis.' Then he went to have a farewell cup of tea with her before he set off for the Dover boat.

The Place des Vosges, Powerscourt remembered the next morning, was, according to devotees of Paris, the most beautiful square in the city, and therefore the most beautiful square in the world. On a bright February morning, with only the pigeons taking their rest on the gravel in the centre, the thirty-nine tall houses made of stone and red brick stared impassively outwards as they had for the previous three hundred years. In the arcade that ran right round the square the cafés and the galleries were setting out their wares. Victor Hugo had lived here, Powerscourt remembered. So had Richelieu for a period of ten or twelve years. A plaque on the front of Number 32 announced the European Art Exchange, the cover story for the French secret service. M. Olivier Brouzet, Director General of the organization, had his office on the first floor, looking out directly on to the square. He might have just reached forty, Powerscourt thought, and was perfectly dressed in a grey suit with a cream shirt and a pale blue tie. He was tall and slim and looked as though he might have been an athlete in his youth. He had a very small painting behind his desk that could have been a Watteau, and eighteenth-century tapestries on his walls.

'It is, Lord Powerscourt,' he said after the introductions had been carried out and Powerscourt was settling himself down opposite the Frenchman at his eighteenth-century escritoire. 'It is a Watteau, I mean. The Louvre were kind enough to let us have it on loan. Now then, how can I be of help to you? I am so pleased to see co-operation between our two countries on intelligence matters. Some of your compatriots, I suspect, might not be so keen.'

His English was perfect. Powerscourt was to learn later that Brouzet had spent three years at Harvard after his time at the Sorbonne. Powerscourt explained his mission, the missing Martin, the missing body, the different accounts of his activities from the different ministries, Martin's affair with Tamara Kerenkova, the fact that he had met the Tsar. He included his meetings, but not their accompanying delights, with Derzhenov. He repeated his belief that the French secret service was the best informed organization about Russia in the world.

'Derzhenov the primitive!' the Frenchman said. 'Does he still take time to torture his victims in person down in that frightful basement in the Fontanka Quai?'

'I'm afraid he does.'

'Let me be frank with you. I think we should be as open as possible with each other. One of us, as surely as night follows day, will want to keep something back, but so be it. Let us help each other where we can. We knew about Mr Martin in this office and his love trysts with la Kerenkova. Some of my colleagues here wanted to elect him an honorary Frenchman for the way he carried out his affairs. We have many sources of information, as you might imagine, Lord Powerscourt. There are the émigrés all around us here in Paris and on the Riviera. Three times now I have applied for extra funds to put a man on permanent station in the casino at Monte Carlo. Never, I tell my superiors, are Russian aristocrats more likely to tell the family secrets than when they have just lost all their money at blackjack or on the roulette table. Always they refuse me at the Quai d'Orsay. I say they must be damned Presbyterians or Quakers or some other form of terrible American Puritan. Never mind. We also have many agents in St Petersburg, in the banks, among the servants of the aristocracy, and most of all, at the imperial court at Tsarskoe Selo. That is how I know about your visit and your two Russian colleagues. All the reports I have seen about Natasha Bobrinsky incidentally, tell me she is very beautiful. It is true?'

Powerscourt wondered what kind of world left you permanently speculating about the physical attributes of your informers or the people they informed against.

'Oh, yes, M. Brouzet,' he replied, 'she is very beautiful. Quite headstrong, I should say. Might be rather a handful.'

'Some day,' said the Frenchman darkly, 'they will release

me from this office and let me out into the real world. Even Mrs Kerenkova must be worth a look, I would have thought. Now then, enough of this, sorry, Lord Powerscourt. Let me come back to your colleague Mr Martin. I knew he had been killed. I presumed somebody had killed him, whether for what he knew or what he refused to tell, I do not know. And I know he had been to see the Tsar. That, my friend, must be the key to the whole affair, that meeting.'

'Did you know, M. Brouzet, that not even the Foreign Office or the British Ambassador in St Petersburg knew why he was there, that his mission was a complete secret, known only to the Prime Minister?' Powerscourt could hear Sir Jeremiah Reddaway fussing with fury at this piece of intelligence being given away. Powerscourt hoped that if he gave up an ace he might at least be offered a king.

'I did not know that, Lord Powerscourt, how very helpful of you. Did you know, incidentally,' – something was coming his way, Powerscourt thought. Was it a knave or a valet as the French call the jack, or a queen or a king? An ace even, perhaps? – 'that Kerenkov was seen at the station late on the night Martin was probably killed? I mean the St Petersburg station where the Tsarskoe Selo trains come in. You can guess the rest, I am sure.'

Queen, Powerscourt said to himself, maybe king. 'I just have this problem, M. Brouzet, about Kerenkov killing Martin. Why do it now? Why not before? He'd been home lots of times in the past after Martin had left his visiting cards with the fair Tamara, after all.'

The Frenchman shrugged. 'The affairs of the heart, love, revenge, jealousy, Lord Powerscourt, are not susceptible to the rational analysis you and I carry round in our heads. Let me return to the meeting between Martin and the Tsar with this new piece of knowledge you have given me.'

He paused briefly and stared out into the square. A number of people were now making their way across it, one or two of them tourists, earnestly consulting their guidebooks.

'I always say in my mind to these damned tourists, Lord Powerscourt, forgive me if many of them are your fellow countrymen, that they should read their wretched Baedekers in their hotel rooms or in the cafés or even when they go home. In this square, of all squares, they should look at the buildings and soak in all the beauty. Maybe then they can carry some of it home to Boston or Birmingham or wherever they come from. Forgive me, I digress again.'

Powerscourt smiled. He thought that if he had to choose a man to work for, His Nibs, say, or Reddaway or even de Chassiron, he would prefer this slim Frenchman.

'Let us put our brains together, Lord Powerscourt,' Olivier Brouzet continued, 'and think about this meeting. Consider first of all the subject matter. Of what do emissaries from Prime Ministers speak to autocrats like Nicholas the Second? Of money? Unlikely, it seems to me. The Tsar doesn't understand his own domestic finances, let alone those of his empire. Mind you, I'm sure we could find bankers in this city who would argue that understanding your own finances would be a crippling handicap in coping with your government's. However, with the greatest respect, my lord, it is France, the old ally, that provides most of the Russian loans, not the English. So I think we can rule out money as a topic for the meeting.'

Powerscourt had two cards he had not put in play. He thought of them as the eight and nine of trumps, no more. But because he was not sure if they were real information, or just a guess, he did not introduce them. Over the next two days as he travelled across eastern France and most of the German plain he was to wonder if he had been right not to do so.

'A new treaty, do you think that possible, my lord?' Olivier Brouzet smiled quizzically at his guest.

'It's possible,' said Powerscourt, 'but in that case why are there no Foreign Office ministers present?'

The Frenchman laughed. 'Think of the psychology of the Tsar, my lord. He has to appoint all these damned ministers, Finance, Interior, Education and so on. If they are any good, they make the Tsar look a fool for being so bad at the rest of his job. If they are bad, he reassures himself that as the autocrat of Russia he must have been better than they were in the first place. There's nothing he would like more than to conclude secret treaties behind the back of his Foreign Ministry. He'd be boasting about it to that old cow Alexandra for weeks afterwards. After all, he concluded some bloody treaty with the Kaiser without telling any of his ministers. They had to spend years wriggling out of it.'

'That's all very well for the Tsar,' said Powerscourt, 'but I find it hard to see a British Prime Minister carrying on like that.'

'More difficult for the British, but not impossible,' said Brouzet cheerfully. 'I'm sure Lord Salisbury wouldn't have turned a hair. Well, that's treaties as one possible subject of the meeting. Do you have any other thoughts as to what they might have talked about?'

'Just one,' said Powerscourt, hanging on grimly to his eight and nine of trumps. 'What about the little boy? What about the Tsarevich and his terrible illnesses? We, the British, or it might equally well be the French, will send you three, let us say, or four of our finest children's doctors, to see if they can find out what is wrong with Alexis. That's certainly the kind of thing you'd want to keep very quiet.'

'All arriving with false beards and fake moustaches, mind you, Lord Powerscourt, dressed as if they were going

277

to an undertakers' convention. Think of the outrage in London if the boot was on the other foot, and three Russian doctors were coming to sort out the health of the Prince of Wales. The rumpus in St Petersburg would be enormous, especially since they hate that bloody woman so much. But it is quite likely, certainly. Do you know what the illness is, Powerscourt?'

'I don't,' said Powerscourt,

'Neither do I,' said Brouzet smoothly, and Powerscourt wondered if that was the French secret service's eight and nine of trumps. 'But I hope to know fairly soon. Let us consider, finally, the dynamics of the meeting, if we may.'

'The dynamics?' asked Powerscourt, wondering if he was wandering into some French metaphysical territory.

'Let me explain,' said the head of the French secret service. 'Suppose the original idea comes from the British. They send Martin to St Petersburg. He sees the Tsar. For someone to kill Martin it seems likely to me that the Tsar said Yes, rather than No, to whatever proposal it was Martin brought. If he said No, it was merely reverting to the status quo, after all. Martin could be left alive as nothing had changed. That says Treaty talk to me, I think. Or it's the other way round. The Tsar has the original idea. He sends for a British agent. Somebody doesn't like what the Tsar is offering to the British and kills Martin before he can take the message home.'

'But the message could have been sent by cable before Martin was killed,' said Powerscourt.

'Pedant,' said the Frenchman.

'Or,' said Powerscourt, 'think of it like this. Suppose we've got the order all wrong. The original idea comes from the Tsar. He sends a message to London. Martin comes, not as a man with a message, but as a man with an answer, the answer to the original idea or question from the Tsar. That's what he conveys to the Tsar out there in the Alexander Palace. That's what somebody overhears, or maybe the Tsar is indiscreet. That is what kills Martin. As a matter of fact, I have requested an audience with the Tsar on business related to Martin but I doubt if he will see me.'

'But the message, Lord Powerscourt, what did it concern, this message from London?'

'I wish I knew, M. Brouzet.'

'I do like that last theory, Lord Powerscourt. But look, you must be on your way, or you will miss your train.'

As they shook hands at the front entrance and Powerscourt looked out once more at the glories of the Place des Vosges, the Frenchman put his hand on his arm. 'Will you promise me, one thing, Lord Powerscourt? Tell me the true story if you can, when you have found it. I am sure you will find it, you see. God speed and good luck!' As he went back into Number 32, Place des Vosges, with his escritoire and his Watteau and his tapestries, Olivier Brouzet resolved to help his English colleague in one important respect. He would ask the French Ambassador to St Petersburg, the most respected man in the St Petersburg diplomatic community, to use his good offices at court to obtain for Lord Francis Powerscourt an interview with Nicholas the Second, Tsar of All the Russias. On his own. Just like Mr Martin.

Even at the entrance gates, some hundreds of yards from the dockyards themselves, the noise was deafening. It was, Powerscourt felt, as he waited with Mikhail Shaporov for a guard to take them inside, a harsh, clanging, brutal sort of noise. In times gone by the wooden ships would have been built to gentler tunes in wooden dockyards without this harsh screeching of modernity. But Krondstadt was where some Russian ships were built, Krondstadt was where the battleship *Tsarevich* was being repaired, Krondstadt was where Lieutenant Anatoli Kerenkov would be found. The earlier unease about Natasha Bobrinsky had gone, to be replaced with concern for her health after such a long sojourn looking after the Tsar's daughters and helping out with the sick little boy. She had written a very short note the day after the cable was sent to Powerscourt, explaining why she had not been able to leave the Alexander Palace. A further message said she would be with them at lunchtime the following day.

A very dirty sailor came at last to escort them to the Lieutenant. His face and hair were filthy and it took some time to work out that his straggling coat must once have been green. A foul-smelling cigarette hung from his lips. Powerscourt decided he must work in the engine room. He led them on to a sort of viewing platform high above a vast open hangar of a dock. Lying on a huge metal cradle was a ship, shrouded in scaffolding. Men the size of tiny dots scurried along the planks, some making minor repairs to the sides or the hull, others, higher up, beginning to apply fresh coats of paint. At the further end of the vessel, the prow, a huge crane was hovering some twenty-five feet above the deck. It was holding a vast grey gun, destined to be lowered into place to serve as a warning and a siren of destruction for Russia's enemies. A man in a red hat was directing the operations with a series of enormous bellows, punctuated, Mikhail whispered to Powerscourt, with terrifying threats about the fate of anybody who caused the gun to miss its appointed place. Beyond the prow, just visible through the smoke of the various smithies, were the pale blue waters of the Gulf of Finland. And on the southern side, eight or ten miles to the south-east, was a group of buildings as different in spirit as it was possible to be from this industrial furnace and floating factory of death, the graceful eighteenth-century palace of Peterhof, built as a summer residence for earlier Tsars, famed for the glory of its fountains and cascades that bounced the water down the hill towards the sea, a place where water nymphs danced in marble glory and the gods who had presided over past Russian victories stared out into eternity.

'You are Powerscourt?' a short bearded man in blue uniform greeted them. 'Kerenkov.' He was powerfully built with very dark eyes and a permanent scowl playing about his features. He looked like a close associate of Blackbeard or one of the fabled pirates of the Caribbean, equally adept at storming treasure ships by day and their owners' wives and daughters by night.

'How kind of you to spare us the time, Lieutenant,' said Powerscourt, eyeing the gun handle that protruded from the man's trouser pocket. 'You must be very busy.'

Mikhail was translating very fast this morning, as if he was on especially good form, or frightened.

'Derzhenov told me about you,' said Kerenkov.

Powerscourt wondered what the sadist had said about him.

'Do you work for Derzhenov?' Powerscourt asked.

'Sometimes,' Kerenkov replied with a scowl. 'Do you?'

'I do not. At present I am working for the British Government trying to find out who killed Mr Martin, as you almost certainly know, Lieutenant Kerenkov.'

Kerenkov spat viciously into the sawdust at their feet. 'I did not kill the man, Powerscourt. He is not important. There are other people we Russians have to kill. Japanese for a start. If we do not kill them they will kill us. It is now eleven months since my ship was damaged, barely able to limp home with its survivors. We threw fifty-seven Russians into the sea on our way home, dead from the

281

wounds they received, gone to enrich the ocean rather than the peasant earth of their motherland.'

Kerenkov paused and pointed at the hanging gun, now a mere fifteen feet from the deck. He planted a rough hand on Powerscourt's shoulder. 'Do you see that gun, man? It looks pretty impressive, doesn't it, you'd think it's going to be a real help in the battles with the Japanese. Stuff and nonsense!' He launched a vicious kick at the planks on the side of their platform.

'It's virtually a waste of time sending it over to Japan,' he went on, 'bloody thing is obsolete even before it's fitted. One of my jobs out there in Port Arthur was to make a report on the Japanese navy. I tell you, those little yellow fellows have speedier ships, quicker guns that fire further and faster than ours, nastier torpedoes, more efficient shells, the conflict should be banned under the rules of war as a totally uneven contest. Everybody back in St Petersburg thinks we must win, we'll win when our Baltic Fleet finally sails halfway round the world for a lasting victory, we'll win because we're European, or our elites are European, we'll win because we're a superior race. That's all nonsense.' He paused, Mikhail's young voice stopped a couple of phrases later, and Powerscourt felt for the man, a patriot without the means to defend his country.

'Now I think about it, there's a bloody ship of yours, Powerscourt, a British frigate, wandering about the Gulf of Finland. It's been going up and down for weeks as if it's taking a holiday cruise. Do you know what the damned thing is doing here?'

'I have no idea,' said Powerscourt.

'Do you know any history, man?' Kerenkov seemed to be changing tack.

'A bit,' said Powerscourt, anxious not to give offence.

'Do you remember that damned Crimean War?' Powerscourt nodded.

'I've been reading lots of history books lately, from then on,' said the unlikely scholar. 'We lost that war because we were so backward. So from then on Russia must be able to defend itself. Russia must be able to produce the latest weapons, Russia must become modern, Russia must have huge capitalist factories to produce the guns and the bullets and the giant pieces of artillery that could fire a shell across the Gulf of Finland. But that's not Russia, Powerscourt, capitalists and middle class and workers replacing tsar and aristocrats and peasants. Our poor country is being torn apart by the battle between conservatism and modernity, between change and not change, between the old and the new. I don't like the new very much, Lord Powerscourt, the only thing is that it's not as bad as the old.'

An enormous crash heralded the arrival of the gun on to the deck. Sparks and dust temporarily hid it from view. The man in the red hat surpassed himself in the volume of his shouts. Various dots at the front of the vessel seemed to be waving their hands in the air. Kerenkov peered forward to check it was success rather than a catastrophe. 'Thank God that's landed safely,' he said. 'Let's pray we meet some wooden Japanese ship from the middle of the last century in the next battle.' Maybe the safe arrival of the gun mellowed him slightly. 'Sorry for boring you with my views,' he said. 'I just care about what's going on.'

Powerscourt thought now was the time to ask his questions.

'Forgive me for asking you, Lieutenant, about your relations with the late Mr Martin. Did you ever meet him?'

'I did not, sir. I could see little point in shaking the hand of a man who has had intimate relations with my wife.'

'Quite so, Lieutenant, quite so. I think on this last occasion you had advance warning of his coming to St Petersburg, is that not so?'

'I did,' said Kerenkov, 'lots of people knew he was coming.'

Powerscourt suspected this was not true, but felt there was little he could do about it. 'And why do you think, Lieutenent,' he went on, 'that Mr Martin kept away from your wife on this occasion? He never had before, after all. Did you warn him off?'

Kerenkov looked at him blankly. He did not reply. 'You were seen, you know,' Powerscourt went on, 'at the station, on the evening Martin was killed. Were you waiting for him to come back from Tsarskoe Selo? Were you waiting to take him off to the Nevskii Prospekt? And then to kill him?'

Kerenkov turned red suddenly. Veins began throbbing in his temple. His hand moved ominously towards his pocket. 'Look here, Powerscourt, I know I'm a rough sort of a fellow,' he began, restraining himself with difficulty. 'My profession is killing people, rather as yours is finding out who killed them. But the people I want to kill are Japanese. My country is at war with them. We are not at war with England. Some people think I had every reason to kill Martin but in today's St Petersburg that sort of morality has long gone. It's melted away like the snows in spring. I didn't kill him, please believe me, and I have no idea who did.'

'I do believe you, Lieutenant,' said Powerscourt with a smile, 'but could you set my mind at rest about one thing?'

'What's that?' Kerenkov asked, staring down below at the worker ants engaged on painting the sides of the ship.

'Your presence at the railway station the night Martin was killed.'

For the first time Kerenkov laughed. 'I'm not quite sure how to put this, Lord Powerscourt. Following the example of my wife perhaps? When in St Petersburg carry on as the St Petersburgers do? I was waiting, Lord Powerscourt, for a lady who is not my wife.'

Successful voyage round the inner islands, Powerscourt said to himself as they set out back towards the city. Pirate strikes gold.

PART THREE

THE TSAR'S VILLAGE

❦

All Russia is our orchard.

Trofimov, Act Two,
The Cherry Orchard, Anton Chekhov

13

Natasha Bobrinsky was feeling confused as she sat in the train carriage bringing her back to St Petersburg. For well over a week she had been more intimately involved with the royal household in Tsarskoe Selo than ever before, taking care of the four daughters, helping with Alexis, trying to provide care and support for the Empress Alexandra. Strange fragments of news filtered into her part of the Alexander Palace. Natasha heard whispered conversations about strikes and industrial disputes, about the lack of enthusiasm for the monarchy, about peasant unrest in the provinces. The previous evening the Empress seemed to have cracked. She did not sink to her knees in private prayer once she had emerged from caring for the sick baby as she usually did. She stared at Natasha as if she didn't know who she was and began attacking the aristocrats of St Petersburg. Vain, worthless, godless, hopeless, selfish, arrogant, self-indulgent, drunk, were some of her kinder adjectives. None of them, according to the Empress, were fit to serve the Tsar, none of them truly fit to speak for the soul of Mother Russia. And on the peasants she bestowed the blessings of the beatitudes: blessed were the poor in spirit for theirs was the kingdom of Heaven, blessed were the meek for they should inherit the earth, blessed were the merciful for they should obtain mercy. These peasants, according to Alexandra, were the true supporters of the monarchy. They knew instinctively about the sacred relationship between Tsar, peasant and God that sustained the Romanovs on their throne and kept the wheels of Russian society turning properly.

It was, perhaps, regrettable that Alexandra should have sounded off in this fashion, for Natasha had been feeling a growing sympathy for the Empress. Now, she thought, as the Tsar's countryside rolled past her windows, she was not so sure. Maybe it was unfortunate that Natasha's parents chose to spend more of their life in Paris and on the Riviera than they did in Russia. Natasha could see the appeal. Nobody said that her father, a man devoted to the joys of the table and the wines of Bordeaux, on which, indeed, he had written a short monograph for a Russian publishing house in Paris, had to spend his time in St Petersburg or Moscow. A career in the public service, ascending the slow steps on the ladder of bureaucratic advancement, he would have regarded as beneath contempt. And as for Natasha's mother, she had never heard her speak of the Empress with anything other than a withering scorn about her German ancestry, her lack of social graces and the vulgarity of her personality. Natasha would never have claimed to be an expert on the peasants. But one of her brother's friends at university, in a fit of misplaced zeal for the general advancement of mankind, had gone with some like-minded souls to live with a group of peasants, to try to improve their lot and welcome them into the joys of civilization. Their reception showed little of the spirit of the meek or the merciful and plenty of that of the poor in spirit or, more precisely, poor in worldly goods. One of Natasha's brother's friends had been beaten up so badly he had to be taken into hospital, their money and valuables were all stolen by the peasants, even their clothes were taken from them. Such people might embody the Tsar's support in his wife's view, but Natasha wanted nothing to do with them.

She was carrying the one word she had heard from the doctors to pass on to Mikhail and to Powerscourt. She had looked it up in the big dictionary in the Tsarskoe Selo library and felt as she read the entry that this particular page had been visited many times in recent weeks. As she left the station and set off to walk to the Shaporov Palace, the man in soldier's uniform followed her once again. Hello, missy, he said to himself, I haven't seen you for a week or more, welcome back. And as Natasha crossed the street with a toss of her head, the soldier grinned. You haven't grown any uglier while you've been away, missy, that's for sure. I do hope they're not going to do anything nasty to you when they read another of my reports.

'Haemophilia,' said Natasha firmly when she and Mikhail and Powerscourt were all seated on their eighteenth-century French chairs in the Shaporov library.

'What on earth is that, Natasha?' said Mikhail.

'Is that what the little boy has? The Tsarevich, out there at the Alexander Palace?' Powerscourt had turned pale.

'It is,' said Natasha, slightly cross that anybody could have guessed her secret so quickly. 'How did you know, Lord Powerscourt?'

'It was a guess, Natasha. You said the word with so much meaning it obviously had to be something very important. But please, please, don't tell a single soul about it apart from the two of us. It could be fatal. It may already have been fatal.'

'But what does it mean?' asked Mikhail, feeling slightly left out.

Powerscourt nodded slightly to Natasha as if to indicate that she should provide the definitions.

'Basically, it means that your blood won't clot,' she said. 'If you're bruised from a fall, Mikhail, your blood will clot quickly and the flow will stop. But if it happens to Alexis, the blood keeps on flowing and ends up making a big swelling which can be very painful.'

'What happens if he cuts himself?' asked Mikhail. 'Will he bleed to death?'

'I'm not sure, I'm not an expert,' said Natasha, 'but I think I heard them say that if the bandage is very tight, the cut will heal itself.'

As the girl regaled her lover with the details of her time with Alexis, Powerscourt was wondering if this one word, eleven letters long, held the key to his dash across Europe in the quest for Martin's killer. Had Martin learnt that the baby had haemophilia? Had he, somehow, tricked the Tsar into confirming it? Had he been killed because he knew of the terrible secret at the very heart and future of the Romanov dynasty? Or had he been killed because he refused to tell what he knew? Could he, Powerscourt, now go home?

Mikhail's questions went on. 'Do you die of it? Die early, I mean?'

The girl looked lost. The dictionaries had provided no help on this one. 'I don't think you're likely to live as long as anybody else,' said Powerscourt. 'However many precautions you take, one accident could still prove fatal. It's a royal disease. Lots of royal houses have had it, including quite a lot of Queen Victoria's relations. It's a nightmare for any royal family though. Do you assume that this child will grow up to succeed to the throne? Or do you have to resign yourself to the fact that he will be gone before he can assume the crown? In which case the child may find out that his own parents think he will be dead before he's twenty-one, hardly a vote of confidence. You don't dare try to have any more children. To have one haemophiliac son might be regarded as a disaster. To have two would be a catastrophe.'

Before he could elaborate any further the door opened and one of the oldest men Powerscourt had ever seen came into the room very slowly, leaning heavily on a stick. He was quite bent, remarkably slim, and with a cascade of dandruff flowing down one side of his black jacket.

'Messages, my lord,' said the greybeard, holding out a small silver tray for Mikhail. 'Just come. Sent over from the British Embassy.'

'Thank you, Borodino,' said Mikhail. 'You may go now.'

As the old retainer shuffled off, his stick clicking regularly on the floor like the beat of a metronome, Mikhail handed the messages to Powerscourt. The door closed as he peered at his correspondence.

'Did you really call that old gentleman Borodino, Mikhail?' asked Natasha sharply, as if she thought a reprimand was in order.

'Yes, I did,' said Mikhail. 'What of it?'

'Don't you think it's rather rude, naming him after a battle?'

Mikhail laughed. 'Calm down, Natasha,' he said, smiling at her. 'When my brother and I were small he looked very old even then; my father told us he had fought at the battle. General Kutuzov's right-hand man, he was, or so my father said. So he's been known as Borodino ever since.'

'Well, well,' said Powerscourt, looking up from his mail, 'I have some interesting news. My great friend Johnny Fitzgerald will be joining us tomorrow. God knows how his telegram took three days to get here. Maybe the Okhrana held it up. Anyway, Johnny Fitzgerald and I have served, well, almost as far back as Borodino itself!'

Amid the laughter he did not disclose the precise contents of his telegrams. From Lord Rosebery, asked to make certain specific inquiries of the royal household, there came a one word answer. Yes. And from Johnny, apart from the details of his arrival, Mrs Martin most likely suicide. More later. Eastern England, you cunning old serpent. Answer Yes. At last, thought Powerscourt. At last bits of this puzzle may be starting to fall into place.

'Natasha, Mikhail, forgive me,' said Powerscourt, rising anxiously to his feet. 'I must go and warn the Embassy to prepare another bed. Perhaps I could buy you supper later?'

'That would be lovely, Lord Powerscourt,' said Natasha. 'I don't have to be back in Tsarskoe Selo until tomorrow.'

As Powerscourt left, his feet tapping out a slightly faster rhythm down the great corridor than Borodino's, Mikhail looked anxiously at Natasha. He felt that he must make the most of the little time they had left before she returned to the palace. But he also felt that she did not realize just how dangerous her new knowledge might be.

'Natasha,' he began.

'Mikhail,' she countered, thinking this was the forerunner of some romantic advances and wriggling into a more comfortable position.

'Be serious for a moment, please, Natasha, I don't think you understand how serious that knowledge is. I think you could be in great danger.'

'Haemophilia, Faemophilia, Mikhail, I don't care. I know Lord Powerscourt said it could be fatal, but I don't see how. They'll deny that there is anything wrong with the little boy until the last breath in their bodies.'

'All the same,' said Mikhail, 'they're not exactly advertising the fact that a Romanov has got haemophilia, are they? Even the doctors were whispering the word when they thought nobody else was listening, weren't they?'

'I don't see what all the fuss is about, Mikhail. And you know I've got to be back there tomorrow.' Natasha twisted herself round until she was in what she thought might be a more alluring position. There wasn't much room to display yourself to best advantage on these French chairs, she thought.

'I think you shouldn't go back there at all,' said Mikhail. 'I think you should write in and say you're ill and can't go back in case you infect anybody.'

'I'll come and infect you in a minute, Mikhail Shaporov,' said Natasha, rising to her feet at the lack of any advance from the Shaporov quarter. 'Wasn't it on this floor you said there was that little room with the naughty Caravaggios?'

Mikhail decided to beat a tactical retreat. 'Very well,' he said, 'very well for now. Let me take you to this little room, Natasha. I think you'll like it. The only thing is, there's hardly any room to sit down in there.'

'Why is that?' asked Natasha at her most demure.

'Most of the space is occupied by something other than a chair or a sofa.'

'I've no idea what you mean, Mikhail Shaporov,' she said, laughing at him with her eyes and taking him by the hand. 'Perhaps you'd better show me.'

Powerscourt was just a few hundred yards from the British Embassy when he felt a touch on his arm. There was that bald head again, complete with the ingratiating smile beneath it. Powerscourt thought he would rather have walked all the way to Siberia than have another meeting with this face.

'Lord Powerscourt,' said Derzhenov, the Okhrana chief, 'how delightful to meet you again. Perhaps you would do me the honour of accompanying me to my humble abode? I have something to tell you and something to show you. Both will be of interest, my dear friend.'

Powerscourt felt himself being steered away from the sanctuary of the Embassy and de Chassiron's Earl Grey in the direction of the Fontanka Quai and its revolting basement. He wondered if Derzhenov had any more torments to show him down there. He rather suspected he had.

'Have you been seeing much of that charming Natasha Bobrinsky lately, Lord Powerscourt? Such a beautiful girl.'

'I have seen her recently, as a matter of fact, Mr Derzhenov. She was in good spirits.'

Derzhenov looked shiftily around him, as if he were under surveillance from some of his own operatives. 'I should tell her to take care, Lord Powerscourt, if I were you, to be very discreet. Some of the other organs of state security have been keeping an eye on the fair Natasha and they might not like what they see.'

Powerscourt felt lost in the thickets of the Russian intelligence chess game, a pawn surrounded by marauding knights and bellicose bishops. Why on earth, he said to himself, is Derzhenov telling me this? Surely he is on the same side as this other organ of state security, whatever that might be, wherever it might be found. Relief came from the unexpected quarter of the basement of the Okhrana headquarters and a couple of guards saluting their master and his foreign visitor. On the way down the steps Powerscourt was assailed once again by the smell, a putrid compound of sweat, dried blood and human waste that rose to greet the visitors. The noises too were the same as before, the groans and smothered grunts of men whose lips are sealed and have no way to express their agony. Further up the corridor there was the familiar sound of whips meeting human flesh. But Derzhenov was drawing Powerscourt towards a door that led into a small courtyard outside. What he saw there took his breath away.

On the left-hand side, nearest to the wall, a soldier was holding back a couple of people whose filthy faces and bloodstained clothes showed they must be prisoners pressed into service as extras. On the far right were a couple of young men carrying buckets with coiled whips in them. Seated on a table were two or three more prisoners, spectators of the scene beneath them. A young woman was trying to hide behind them. The light was dark everywhere. On the right-hand side of the scene a prisoner, clad only in a loincloth, was being fastened on to a gridiron. Another man, naked to the waist, seemed to be supervising the fire underneath it. Powerscourt could see the flames taking hold below. He could hear the hiss as they leapt from coal to coal. Powerscourt thought it was probably the most obscene sight he had ever witnessed.

'Do you not like my artistry, Lord Powerscourt? Do you not admire the echoes of the martyrdom of St Lawrence I showed you in the Hermitage? The prisoner in the loincloth, he even looks a bit like the dead saint. My two boys with the whips in the buckets – so much more appropriate than the fish in the original, don't you think, Lord Powerscourt? – are under orders to set to work if they think the man may talk.' Derzhenov paused briefly and shouted something in Russian. The man supervising the fire bent to his task with greater vigour than before. The two guards fastening the man on to the gridiron strapped him down.

'We think this fellow on the gridiron has links with the people who blew up Grand Duke Serge in Moscow,' Derzhenov went on. 'We've got a couple of the gang here. They're a bit squeamish down there in the Kremlin. The unfortunate Grand Duke was shattered into hundreds of pieces by the bomb. Our friend here' – Derzhenov pointed to the prostrate figure, his mouth gagged, his face already contorted into a rictus of pain – 'is only being burnt a little. All he has to do is to tell us all he knows and he will be released.'

Derzhenov inspected his little tableau. 'Oh, Lord Powerscourt, I almost forgot. You see the girl at the back there, hiding behind the men? That is his sister. We thought she might enjoy the show.' Derzhenov laughed a blood-curdling laugh. 'If he does not talk, Lord Powerscourt, maybe we will swap them over. The young man can watch his sister take on the role of St Lawrence, that should loosen his tongue.'

Derzhenov steered Powerscourt back towards the corridor. 'Would you like to join us in a bet, Lord Powerscourt? We take bets, you see, on the time the prisoner will talk or the time he will die. You can take your pick.'

Powerscourt shook his head and wondered how much more he could take. There was always a double-edged quality to Derzhenov's displays of torture. One side of it showed how ruthless he and his colleagues could be. The other was a warning to Powerscourt. If you don't co-operate, then you'll be next on the skewer or underneath the whips or fastened to the gridiron.

'We must take one very quick look at one of the cells near the end here,' Derzhenov said, almost licking his lips in anticipation. 'It is, dare I say it, another of my combinations of art and interrogation!'

Powerscourt had visions of rows and rows of real cruci-fixions mounted in the style of Rubens and Caravaggio and Tintoretto and the etiolated saviours of El Greco. What confronted him in Cell 24 of the Okhrana basement was worse.

On the back wall of the cell somebody had painted a forest scene in the evening. There were occasional shafts of light visible in the gloom. In front of this sylvan idyll a great tree trunk had been fixed with chains. And hanging upside down was a prisoner, his legs secured to the upper branches. His hands at the bottom of the tree were bound with rope. His arms were locked in a circle round his head. Standing by the prisoner's left side was a young woman, almost naked, her bare right breast not far from the victim's chin. In her right hand she carried a knife and she was peeling the skin from the prisoner's chest in slow deliberate movements. Kneeling on the floor a male guard, also equipped with a deadly knife, was peeling the skin from his lower legs. The prisoner's body was totally covered in blood.

'The flaying of Marsyas, Powerscourt, do you not think it fine? And the girl at work on his chest, maybe arousing the final pangs of desire from the victim in her déshabille? My own special touch, I must confess. Really, I am not sure which I am fonder of, this Marsyas in here, or the Martyrdom of St Lawrence without. It is so hard to tell.'

The prisoner uttered what must have been a scream. The gags on his mouth made it sound like a small groan. 'We thought this one was going to talk about half an hour ago,' Derzhenov went on, 'but when we took the gag out he just spat in the eyes of his captors. But come, upstairs, I have news for you.'

This time the Okhrana chief took him, not to his office, but to a small sparsely furnished sitting room on the third floor. The only decorations on the walls were a painting of a monastery and a silver crucifix. Any notion Powerscourt might have had about a religious side to the Russian secret service was swiftly dispelled.

'Forgive me, Lord Powerscourt, they may be using my office for interrogations shortly so I thought we had better find alternative accommodation. We have a tame priest or two on the books here, you might be surprised to hear. Often some prisoners will talk more easily to them. This is the room we give the priests.'

So that explains the monastery and the cross, Powerscourt thought. He wondered briefly if it was the famous monastery Dostoevsky used as a model in *The Brothers Karamazov*.

Derzhenov was coughing significantly in the chair to his left. 'I promised I had news for you, Lord Powerscourt. And what exciting news it is! Can you guess?'

Powerscourt wondered briefly if he was to be taken on a special tour of all the Okhrana torture rooms in Russia from Moscow to Archangel with specially adapted carriages on the Trans-Siberian Express, soundproofing for screams a speciality, and specially adapted facilities for carrying passengers half in half out of their compartments, being torn apart by the speed and the wind.

'I cannot imagine, General Derzhenov,' he said, his mind suddenly very alert. He remembered the rash message he had sent to the Embassy from the Foreign Office in London saying that he hoped to solve the mystery of Mr Martin within a week. He had thought at the time that he might catch something with that message. He felt sure Derzhenov had read the cable. Had his catch now arrived? Was he the catch?

'I expect notice of this audience is awaiting you at the Embassy, Lord Powerscourt, indeed I'm certain of it. But it gives me great pleasure to be the first to tell you in person. Your request, Lord Powerscourt, your request for an interview with the Tsar has been granted! You are going to meet with the Autocrat of All the Russias! Tomorrow evening! To think that I will not be there to see it.'

'This is excellent news, General Derzhenov. Thank you if your good offices have had anything to do with it.'

'One must always do one's humble best to help one's friends, that's what my dear mother used to say, Lord Powerscourt.'

Powerscourt tried to imagine what Derzhenov's mother must have been like, monster, harpy, she-devil, tutor and mentor to the Borgias and to Lady Macbeth, ogress, fiend, but words failed him. He wondered if she were still alive. Better not to ask.

'I don't suppose you know the time for the meeting?' asked Powerscourt. If it were late then Johnny Fitzgerald might be able to accompany him.

'Nine thirty,' said Derzhenov, beaming with his knowledge and his ability to convey good tidings. He paused for a moment before dropping in, 'Same time as the unfortunate Mr Martin, oddly enough. And that was on a Wednesday too.' The Tsar at nine thirty. Death by half past one.

But if he thought Powerscourt might be superstitious, there were no signs of it. 'There is just one small thing I would ask of you, Lord Powerscourt, one very tiny favour.'

'Of course, General, ask away.' Inwardly Powerscourt prayed that the good Lord would forgive him this and all his other sins.

'If you could see your way, Lord Powerscourt, to telling me the gist of your conversation with the Tsar, insofar as it has to do with Mr Martin, I would be most grateful.'

Powerscourt thought he disliked the Uriah Heep Derzhenov even more than the earlier Attila the Hun Derzhenov. And he wondered, not for the first time, about the strange fascination Martin's meeting with the Tsar had for his secret service. Certainly Derzhenov seemed to have no idea what was discussed or what was resolved.

'General Derzhenov,' Powerscourt went on, relieved to know he had a slightly better hand than he thought he might have had five minutes ago. Derzhenov had to keep him alive until tomorrow evening at least. 'I am sure you know the responsibilities of a man in my position towards his government, particularly when the death of a senior diplomat is involved. And the discretion involved. But rest assured, if I can see my way clear to helping you in the manner you request, I shall certainly do so.'

And may the Lord have mercy upon my soul, he said to himself.

Derzhenov had one last card to play. 'It so happens that I shall be in these offices tomorrow night when you return from Tsarskoe Selo. Perhaps you could pop in then, if it was convenient.'

Had Martin, too, popped in at Fontanka Quai on his way back from the Alexander Palace? Had that been the last place he had seen alive? Powerscourt didn't feel happy.

'I fear my Ambassador will want to hear my news first, General Derzhenov. But the next morning, have no fear.'

As he made his way out of the building, Derzhenov trotting by his side, Powerscourt thought he smelt something particularly nauseous rising from the basement. It was, he decided, after a couple of discreet sniffs, the smell of roasting flesh. Or, to be more precise, roasting human flesh. St Lawrence was being offered up as a sacrifice to his God once more.

His hair was dirty. His fingernails were black and extended far forwards like the claws of an animal or the talons of a bird. His beard was untrimmed. He smelt of the country-side, of the filth of the peasants, so alien to the salons of the capital. The most remarkable thing about him were his eyes, deep-set, grey, that seemed to disappear into pin-pricks of light when he spoke. The self-styled Father

Grigory Rasputin was the latest sensation to burst into the jaded world of the seance takers and the psychic-loving circles of St Petersburg. He claimed to possess two of the attributes of the *staretz*, the traditional holy man said to come from the purer world of Siberia to cleanse the capital of its decadence. Holiness Rasputin certainly thought he possessed. Had he not walked the length of Russia not once but twice, and been on pilgrimage to the Holy Land? And could he not cure people of their illnesses? There were many witnesses to his ability as a healer. People said he could even reverse the flow of blood, to direct it away from a wound, for example.

It was the Montenegrin sisters, Militsa and Anastasia, both Grand Duchesses, who introduced Rasputin into society as they had introduced the Frenchman Philippe Vachot years before. Within a short time women of all classes were flocking to his dirty apartment in search of an audience with him, or more. Rasputin had one unique advantage for a holy man who might be a fraud. He offered a threefold package to his women admirers, in the shape of sin, redemption and salvation. Before they could be saved, Rasputin assured the gullible and the neophytes, they had to commit sin. If they cared to step with him into his bedroom, soon known as the Holy of Holies, he would be happy to provide the sin in his role as another weak and humble servant of God. Then, in his role as Holy Father, he could offer redemption from their transgressions. Finally he would bless them and see them through to the final stage of their journey to salvation. The Montenegrins spread his fame. To the rich women of St Petersburg, they said, he brought the promise of carnal and spiritual satisfaction at virtually the same time. To those nursing the sick and the afflicted, they stressed his healing powers. The messages sent to the Alexander Palace stressed that here was a mighty healer. They reminded Alexandra of the words of Philippe Vachot that he, Vachot, was but the forerunner of one greater and more powerful than he. Rasputin, they implied to the beleaguered party in Tsarskoe Selo, was the Christ to Vachot's John the Baptist.

Johnny Fitzgerald was very taken with St Petersburg. He liked the great buildings, he like the huge squares, he confessed most of all to having developed an enormous liking for the vodka on the train.

'There I was, Francis, minding my own business, when these two fellows came in and joined me. They were pretty well gone by this stage but they offered me a choice of three varieties of vodka as if I was their long-lost relative. I'm sure I will be able to find some more of the stuff round the place.'

Powerscourt was delighted to be able to tell him that the Ambassador, of all unlikely people, had a small cellar devoted to vodka and might be persuaded to open up. More seriously, Johnny was able to tell Powerscourt of the latest discoveries in the case of Mrs Martin. None of the police inquiries, he reported, had produced any sightings of strangers going up or down the path to the house. Furthermore, a note had been discovered in the bureau in the study of Colonel Fitzmaurice's house, apparently in Mrs Martin's hand, addressed to her in-laws but not posted, saying that she could go on no longer. There was no further news of the mysterious Russian visitor, who seemed to have vanished into thin air. The Colonel, possible paramour of Mrs Martin, had not disappeared at all. He had taken himself to the south coast to recover from the excitement and wrestle with the treacherous winds and very fast greens of Rye Golf Course. On a normal day

Powerscourt would have been asking for more details, checking on the handwriting, inquiring what the police view was and generally making himself a nuisance. But today the affairs of the late Mrs Martin and the little tower at the top of Tibenham Grange seemed very far away. Today was a day for her husband, the late Mr Martin. Was not he, Powerscourt, going to have an evening audience with the Tsar on exactly the same day of the week as Martin? Might today not be the day when he would find Martin's killer? Or perhaps, he wondered, it would be the day when Martin's killers killed him too. The Ambassador had only ever had two private audiences with Nicholas the Second since he took up his post and he regarded it as slightly unfair that a mere upstart, a hired hand rather than a member of the proper Foreign Office, should enter the imperial presence after a couple of weeks or so.

A party of six set off to escort Powerscourt to his audience. He was accompanied by Johnny Fitzgerald, Mikhail as interpreter, secretly hoping for a quick glimpse of Natasha, the coachman, a sergeant from the Black Watch and Ricky Crabbe the telegraph king who had expressed such pathetic longing to see the Tsar's palace that even the Ambassador could not resist him. Powerscourt had a brief conversation with de Chassiron about the interview before he left.

'House rules?' de Chassiron had said, placing his beautifully polished shoes on his coffee table and fiddling absentmindedly with his monocle. 'Not much different from school, really, going to see the headmaster. Sorry, Powerscourt, that wasn't helpful. Just like going to see the King really, big handshake, bow, don't interrupt him, however stupid the things he says, all these damned monarchs since Louis the Sixteenth have thought they were cleverer than they actually were. If you're lucky there won't be a flunkey there during the interview, though they may be listening at the doors. Flunkeys in my experience get very irritated if they think their master is carrying out business behind their back. It's almost a criminal offence.'

'And how should I think of him when I talk to him, de Chassiron? Foreign Office official? Adjutant of regiment? Manager of a small bank out in the country?'

De Chassiron smiled and lifted his feet off his table in one quick, elegant movement.

'Not the first, Powerscourt, not the second, maybe the third. How about this though? Think of him as a rather dim Captain of Cricket at school, chap who can barely add up, can't remember much history, hopeless at languages but very popular with the boys and a good batsman. You must have met plenty of those, Powerscourt.'

Powerscourt agreed that he had. As they travelled the fifteen miles out to Tsarskoe Selo, Mikhail was bringing him up to date on the latest number of strikes that were slowly strangling the country. Johnny Fitzgerald was peering out into the darkness as if Russian birds, previously unknown to him but of fabulous size and plumage, were flying in formation around their carriage. Ricky Crabbe's fingers, Powerscourt noted, were still tapping messages out on to the frame of the carriage widow. Maybe he did it in his sleep. The sergeant from the Black Watch went to sleep.

The Alexander Palace was made up of a centre and two wings. All the state apartments and the formal reception rooms were in the centre. The imperial family's private apartments were in one wing, the ministers of the court and the attendant staff in the other. Ricky Crabbe decided to remain with the coachman. He would, he said, take a peep inside a bit later. In reality, he was rather overwhelmed by the grandeur of the surroundings, the troops

of horsemen riding round the walls of the park on permanent patrol against terrorists, the soldiers and policemen
who stopped the carriage at the entrance gate and peered
carefully into all their faces before writing their names
down in a book, the sentries in their long coats striding up
and down the outside of the building at regular intervals
as if they were mobile flower boxes.

Powerscourt and his two companions were guided on
their journey to the Tsar by a symphony in gold braid and
a footman with a plumed hat. Through the audience rooms
they went, through the Empress's private drawing room,
down a long corridor leading to the private apartments. In
the last room at the end of the corridor the Tsar's personal
aide-de-camp indicated that Johnny and Mikhail were to
wait there with him. He began an animated conversation
with Mikhail on the virtues of the capital's most expensive
restaurants. Powerscourt felt his mind going far away to
the ice on the Nevskii Prospekt where a fellow countryman
lay dead, ignored and forgotten by the authorities. A
strangely clad Ethiopian was on guard outside the Tsar's
door. As he opened it the symphony in gold braid coughed
slightly and announced in perfect English:

'Your Imperial Majesty! Lord Francis Powerscourt from
His Britannic Majesty's Foreign Office!'

14

The first thing Powerscourt noticed about Nicholas the Second, Tsar and Autocrat of All the Russias, was that he was quite short for an Autocrat. He must, Powerscourt thought, have been about five feet seven inches tall. His father, Powerscourt remembered, had been a great bear of a man, capable of bending pokers into circles and other feats of strength guaranteed to impress small children. The second thing was a quite remarkable similarity to his cousin George, Prince of Wales, second son of King Edward and Queen Alexandra. There was the same neatly trimmed beard, the same shape of face, the same hair greying slightly at the temples. Nicholas had lines of strain running across his forehead, not surprising, Powerscourt thought, when you were presiding over an empire in chaos, even less surprising when you thought of the haemophiliac son and heir, possibly bleeding to death even now in some upstairs nursery.

The Tsar was wearing a simple Russian peasant blouse, baggy brown trousers and soft leather boots. Standing in front of his desk, he ushered Powerscourt into an armchair. The room was quite small with one window. There were plain leather chairs, a sofa covered with a Persian rug, some bookshelves, a table spread with maps and a low bookcase covered with family photographs and souvenirs.

'Lord Powerscourt, welcome to Tsarskoe Selo,' said the Tsar. His English would not have been out of place in an Oxford quadrangle. 'How may I be of service to you and your government?'

'I am not in the service of my government, sir. I am an investigator employed by the British Foreign Office to look into the death of a Mr Martin. Mr Martin, sir, was on the staff of the Foreign Office. He came here to see you at the end of last year. Then he was killed.'

'I heard that sad news, Lord Powerscourt. Tell me, you say you are an investigator. What, pray, do you investigate?'

Powerscourt thought the Tsar made investigating sound like a most disagreeable profession. Perhaps he imagined investigators scouring the files of his ministries for examples of administrative incompetence or worse, looking into the inefficiencies of his armies, or, saddest of all, creeping round his household for long enough to tell his subjects that their future sovereign Alexis the Tsarevich might have bled to death before he was one year old, never mind attaining his majority.

'I am not alone in being an investigator, sir. There are a number at work in London at present. I only operate when people ask me to. Usually they ask me to investigate murders.'

The Tsar sounded faintly relieved to hear Powerscourt and his ilk were not contemplating opening a branch office in Moscow or St Petersburg. 'Do you think Mr Martin was murdered, Lord Powerscourt?'

'I most certainly do, sir.'

'And,' the Tsar went one, 'do you expect me to know who killed him?'

'No, I do not, sir,' said Powerscourt, wondering if the

Tsar did actually know but wouldn't say, 'but I would find it very helpful to know what you talked about with Mr Martin.'

'I cannot help you there, I'm afraid, Lord Powerscourt. The matter was confidential.'

Confidential enough to get a man killed, Powerscourt thought bitterly. Confidential can mean fatal on a bad day in the Tsar's palace at Tsarskoe Selo.

'I fully appreciate that, sir,' said Powerscourt, looking at a photograph of three very happy little girls draped round their papa on a yacht, 'but I would like to appraise you of what I propose to tell my government about your conversation with Mr Martin on my return.'

'And why should that interest me?' said the Tsar rather shortly, as if he had had enough of investigators.

'It should interest you, sir, because it will contain my account of what transpired between you and Mr Martin. I give you my word that if you wish to correct my version in any way, I shall not tell a single soul who provided the information. Come, sir,' Powerscourt smiled suddenly at his host, 'come on a little adventure with me. Put aside the cares of state for ten minutes or so. Join the ranks of the investigators!'

The Tsar lit himself a cigarette. He returned the smile. 'Very well,' he said, 'for the moment I am your Mr Sherlock Holmes of 221b Baker Street. Sherlock Romanov perhaps. I shall consider what you have to say. Begin please!'

Powerscourt drew a deep breath. Now was his opportunity. From Markham Square to Tsarskoe Selo, via the British Embassy, Kerenkov's shipyard, Kerenkova's dacha, the eyes of Natasha Bobrinsky and the torture chambers of Okhrana boss Derzhenov was a long and complicated journey.

'When I first began investigating the death of Mr Martin,' he began, trying to be as honest as he could with the Tsar, 'I thought that he had been sent here by the British Government with some proposal or other. A new treaty perhaps, an alliance with the French against Germany, maybe. It was possible, I thought, that he had been killed because somebody didn't like the proposal or didn't like your response to it. That all seemed perfectly possible.'

'But you changed your mind, Lord Powerscourt. Why did you do that?'

'I spent a lot of time, sir, trying to work out the dynamics of the meeting, who summoned who, that sort of thing. After a while I decided that the most likely sequence of events was rather different. The first event was you sending a message to England, to the King, I think, with a request that he should only discuss it with his Prime Minister. I think the request was in the form if not of a question, then something very like it. You see, sir, I began to think that the meeting had more to do with family than it did with affairs of state. That would explain why the conversation, if you like, began as monarch to monarch rather than minister to minister. And the need for confidentiality, for secrecy, if you will, explains why a man had to come from London rather than going through the British Embassy here.'

'I was going to ask how you arrived at that conclusion but I shall save my questions for the end of this fascinating piece of investigation, Lord Powerscourt!' Sherlock Romanov finished his cigarette and immediately lit another. Powerscourt noticed that some of his fingers were deeply stained with nicotine.

'The second event,' Powerscourt went on, 'was Mr Martin arriving here with the answer from London. Again I can only guess at what the answer was. And I can only speculate as to why up until now no action has been taken.'

311

'And what was the answer, Lord Powerscourt?' The Tsar was now surrounded by a penumbra of smoke, his hand emerging from time to time to knock off the ash at the end of his cigarette.

'I think, sir, that the question sent by you or your agents to London went something like this: Would the British royal family, and by extension, the British Government, be happy to welcome the Tsar's wife and children to England while the present unrest in Russia continues. And,' Powerscourt was reluctant to divulge this piece of news, 'were there doctors in London who were experienced in the treatment of haemophilia.'

'God bless my soul!' The Tsar had turned pale.

'And the answer, brought by Mr Martin,' Powerscourt carried on relentlessly now, 'was Yes, as long as the Russian royal family were content to live quietly in the country and didn't expect to be taken round London on a never-ending quadrille of state banquets and ceremonial balls. A suitable place could be found for them in Norfolk, close to the Royal Family establishment at Sandringham.'

The Tsar looked at Powerscourt with considerable pain in his eyes. His question now had a slightly desperate air. 'There is a flaw, of course, in this theory of yours. Do you see what the flaw is, Lord Powerscourt?'

'I am not sure it is a flaw, sir. I presume you refer to the fact that your wife and children are still here in Tsarskoe Selo, St Petersburg, not in Norfolk, England. But I do not believe that invalidates any of the rest of the theory, sir. There has been a British frigate on patrol in the waters off the coast here for a number of weeks now. People are beginning to talk. It seems possible to me, sir, that a number of factors could have intervened to modify the situation. The Empress might not have liked the plan. She might have preferred to stay with her husband in his hour of duty and help him fulfil what she saw as his obligations as ruler of Russia. The Tsar's advisers, if they heard of the plan, might have thought it an unhelpful act to send the Tsar's family and his heir out of the country. Hostile elements in society, not just the bomb-throwing fraternity, might have branded it cowardice, a vote of no confidence by the Tsar in the Tsar's own administration. And finally, sir,' Powerscourt thought he must stop very soon, 'if security is so bad at present that you cannot attend the funeral of one of your own relations, blown to smithereens by the Kremlin walls, it might also be too bad to permit a party of six with all their attendants to make their way from here to a main-line railway station or to the English frigate.'

The Tsar crossed his legs and stubbed out his cigarette. 'You will be interested to hear, Lord Powerscourt, that almost all of what you said is true in one sense or another. I congratulate you. But I have two questions for you. How did you know we were thinking of sending the children to England? And how did you know about my son?'

Powerscourt thought fast. He knew that if he mentioned the disappearing toys or the vanished Trans-Siberian Railway egg, Natasha would be in trouble. He did not dare rely on her testimony for the haemophilia either. He decided to take a huge gamble, not with the first question, but with the second.

'I have a politician friend, sir, who is intimate with members of the British royal family. Forgive me if I do not mention his name. I asked him to inquire among his contacts to see if preparations were being made for the possible reception of a party of Russian royalty. His inquiries revealed that the answer was Yes. He also told me that inquiries were made about whether London had doctors skilled in the treatment of certain diseases. No name was given to the disease but it was clear from the descriptions given that it was haemophilia. The disease is all too well known to London doctors, unfortunately. Queen Victoria was a carrier.' So far so good, Powerscourt thought, looking at the Tsar closely, now for a diversion. 'When I considered where the British royals would be likely to accommodate Russian royals, I felt London would be inappropriate. Too public, too many prying eyes from the journalists and members of the public. Windsor Castle? Large enough, certainly, but there's rather a lot of gloom and not much privacy. Sandringham is where they would send them. And when I asked a colleague to go and make inquiries in the area about any plans that might have been made to receive a group of foreign royalty, the answer was Yes. No nationality was known, but a party of foreign royals including a number of children was expected, had indeed been expected for some time.' Powerscourt smiled faintly, as if apologizing for knowing too much, for being too well acquainted with the Tsar's affairs.

'I see,' said Nicholas the Second, 'I see.' He looked like a man playing for time. Powerscourt remembered de Chassiron saying that the Tsar had plenty of charm but very little in the way of brain. 'This is all very interesting, Lord Powerscourt, but please enlighten me as to how it helps your investigations with Mr Martin, the dead Mr Martin.'

Powerscourt prayed that Nicholas was not going to look at his watch. That, the Ambassador had told him, in what must, Powerscourt thought, have been the only piece of useful information ever imparted by His Nibs, was a certain sign that the Tsar wished the interview to end.

'Let me try to explain, sir.' Don't patronize the man, for God's sake, Powerscourt said to himself, don't let him see I think he's rather dim. 'Suppose you have two friends.

You know they have met for a conversation. Almost immediately afterwards one of them is killed. Anybody trying to solve the mystery would wish to know what the two men talked about. It might have a bearing on the reasons for their murder. The same thing applies to Mr Martin.'

'Do you,' asked the Tsar, possibly returning to the Sherlock Romanov mode, 'have a list of suspects, as it were, for the killing?'

'I do, sir, but forgive me if I do not put names to them,' Powerscourt said. 'I would not want you to carry round in your head a collection of possible murderers who might be totally innocent. It would be as unfair on you as it might be unjust on them.'

'And do you think, Lord Powerscourt, that this conversation we have just had will make it easier for you to catch the murderer?'

Powerscourt noted that the conversation had now reverted to the past tense. He did not tell the Tsar that he believed his best chance of finding the murderer still lay in the three or four hours immediately after this interview.

'I do, sir, and I am most grateful to you for your time and your patience in listening to my theories.'

'I wish you good luck in your inquiries, Lord Powerscourt. Perhaps we shall meet again some day.'

'I hope so, sir, I sincerely hope so.'

The interview was at an end. The symphony in gold braid and the footman with the plumed hat collected Powerscourt and the rest of the party and escorted them to their carriage. The symphony wished them Good Evening. The plumed hat bowed slightly at the departing foreigners. Not too near the palace, probably just outside the park, Powerscourt expected the carriage to be stopped and that he and Mikhail would be taken away. This was the gamble he had taken when he sent his message to the Embassy about being in a position to solve the mystery of Martin's death inside a week. Whatever happened to Martin had happened after he left the Tsar. Somewhere between Tsarskoe Selo and St Petersburg he had been killed.

They heard their adversaries before they saw them, a rattle of horses' hooves hurrying across the snow. Then a party of six men came into view, all in some elaborate Russian army uniform Powerscourt didn't recognize, all with rifles slung across their backs, the leader with a pistol in his left hand. Powerscourt remembered an old army instructor telling him years before that left-handed shots had to be treated with great care as they were often more accurate than right-handers.

'You!' the left-hander barked at the coachman. 'Follow us.' A very young soldier took his place beside the coachman on the box seat and stuck a gun in his ribs.

'What do you think is going to happen now, Francis?' whispered Johnny Fitzgerald.

'I think they're going to haul me off for questioning, Johnny. If they take me on my own that probably means it's Derzhenov. He doesn't need an interpreter. If they want Mikhail to come too, it's a different collection. Whatever happens, I don't think it's going to be good for my retirement prospects to stay with these gentlemen long, whoever they may be.'

The coach had turned out of the park and was now passing down the main street of the village. At the very end of the built-up area they turned left into the grounds of a rather dilapidated house. Faint lights could be seen in a room on the ground floor. The paint seemed to be peeling from the pillars by the front door. There was some discussion between the men who had captured them. Then Powerscourt and Mikhail were ordered out of the carriage and marched roughly into the house. Four men stayed on guard by the coach, scowling at the English and smoking strong-smelling cigarettes.

Powerscourt and Mikhail were shown into what had once been a handsome room with high ceilings and sash windows. There were a couple of battered armchairs in the middle of the room. Two wooden chairs had been placed in front of a rickety table at the opposite end from the window. Powerscourt noticed to his dismay that there were a number of stout sticks and a couple of Russian knouts or whips lying casually in the corner of the room. Opposite the chairs was a pale officer in his mid-forties with a great scar running down the lower side of his face. Most people, Powerscourt thought, would have grown a beard to hide the injury. Not this man. He flaunted it like a badge of honour. His hair was grey and his eyes were a dull brown.

'Major Andrey Shatilov of the Imperial Guard, Royal Palaces Security Division,' he said crisply.

'Lord Francis Powerscourt, attached to His Majesty's Foreign Office,' Powerscourt replied, 'Mr Mikhail Shaporov of the Shaporov Bank, acting as my translator. Pray explain to us why we have been taken prisoner in this fashion. I shall report this to my Ambassador here.'

Powerscourt wondered suddenly if the world of conventional diplomacy, with its notes and its niceties, its protocols and its levees, was somehow alien even in St Petersburg. Peter the Great may have been trying to civilize a nation when he built his capital here on this isolated spot, but after two hundred years he still had not succeeded. These people here, the Major with his scar and the rough soldiery outside, belonged to some alien world, the world of the peasants perhaps, tucked away in the great empty vastness of Russia with only their women and their violence for company. Russian generals, he remembered, had always been careless with the lives of their men. There were so many of them, endless reservoirs to make up the numbers when the first drafts had perished.

Shatilov's voice was crisp. 'It is not for you to inquire why you have been taken into temporary custody by the local authorities here, Powerscourt or whatever you say your name is.'

Powerscourt said nothing. Two of Shatilov's thugs were lounging on the chairs in the middle of the room. One of them was fiddling with a very long piece of rope.

'My request is quite simple,' Shatilov said, managing to imbue even those innocent-sounding words with a charge of venom. 'All you have to do is to tell me the nature of your conversation with the Tsar.'

Powerscourt paused for a moment. 'Don't translate this bit,' he said to Mikhail, speaking very fast, 'I want to make him lose his temper. My conversation with the Tsar was confidential,' he went on more slowly. 'It is not my business to tell you of his business any more than it would be for me to tell you of any discussions I might have with my King in London. What right do you think you have to make such a request?'

Shatilov was beginning to warm up nicely, Powerscourt thought. His fingers began strumming on the table.

'Those of us in charge of the security of the imperial family are entitled to know all of his conversations! All of them. For his own safety! Now will you please tell me the nature of your conversation!'

Powerscourt wondered suddenly what would happen if it became known that the Tsar was planning to send his children abroad. It would say, as surely as if he had signed a proclamation, that he was not in control of events, that he had lost faith in the ability of his regime to protect his

318

children. The Emperor himself would be announcing that he has no clothes. The myths and façade of autocracy, built up over nearly three hundred years of Romanov rule, would vanish like mist on a summer morning. Maybe the monarchy would fall and the Tsar would have to follow his family to England to stick family photographs into English albums and watch an English sea lapping at an English coast. The alternative, of course, might be worse, the Tsar's children blown into minute fragments by a terrorist bomb, or murdered in their beds. It was, they had said to him in London before he left, a matter of vital national importance. Well, Powerscourt thought, looking absently at the Major's scar, it certainly was for Tsar Nicholas the Second. And for King Edward the Seventh? The presence of the Tsar's family in England would surely lead to an alliance with Great Britain. Confronted by the vast forces of France, Russia and the British, surely even the Kaiser would not risk a war, particularly when those other English-speakers, the Americans, might join the battle on the side of the Allies. A matter of vital national importance in London as it was in St Petersburg.

'I would like you to tell me about a different conversation, Major Shatilov, a conversation you had, possibly in this very room, with a predecessor of mine, a man called Martin who came to St Petersburg, who saw the Tsar on a Wednesday evening, and who was found dead on the Nevskii Prospekt later that night or very early the next morning. Did you come across Mr Martin, Major? Did he perhaps sit in this very room with you and your thugs?'

There was a quick muttering from the pair in the chairs. 'I know little or nothing of this man Martin,' said Shatilov. 'I repeat, before my patience runs out, tell me what happened with the Tsar!' He looked meaningfully at the whips in the corner.

319

Now it was Mikhail Shaporov's turn to speak very fast. 'We weren't meant to hear it, but one of the chair people said, "Mind the same thing doesn't happen to you,"' and then he went on to translate the rest of it.

Powerscourt wondered how much longer Johnny Fitzgerald and the man from the Black Watch were going to be. He had no doubt that they had begun working on a rescue mission as soon as he and Mikhail had been taken away. He too looked with some suspicion at the whips in the corner. Whatever happened he had no intention of betraying the Tsar. He wondered how painful it might be.

'Did you kill Martin? Here in this room?' He spoke with as much hostility as he could muster.

'Shut up about Martin!' shouted Shatilov, half rising now out of his chair. 'I want to know about the Tsar!'

'Did you kill Martin?' If Powerscourt had wanted to make the Russian Major angry he had certainly succeeded.

'Shut up about Martin! For the last time, I want to know about your conversation with the Tsar!'

Powerscourt was certain the man was lying about Martin.

'Did you kill Martin?' Powerscourt shouted for the third time. Mikhail Shaporov raised his voice to the same pitch.

'That's it! That's it! I've had it. Vladimir! Boris! Tie them up!' Shatilov had turned bright red.

'The full treatment, boss?' one of the soldiers asked.

'Not yet, tie them up first,' said Shatilov, going over to the corner and picking up a whip.

'Sorry about this, Mikhail,' said Powerscourt.

'Don't worry, we'll be all right in the end,' said the young man cheerfully.

By now the two men were tied securely to their chairs. Powerscourt found he could just about move his arms. If there was a deus out there somewhere, he said to himself, he wished he would hurry up and get out of his machina. Shatilov was pacing up and down behind the chairs, brandishing the whip in his left hand. Powerscourt felt there appeared to be a poverty of imagination in Russian torture methods, whips, whips and more whips.

'Do you see this, Lord Powerscourt?' Shatilov was showing him the leather thong. 'In a moment, this is going to tear into the bare flesh of your back. After a while there won't be any flesh left. All you have to do is to tell me the nature of your conversation with the Tsar and nothing will happen to you.'

'Is this what you did to Martin? Whip him till he died?'

'Cut his coat off!' Shatilov was shouting to his assistants. Powerscourt felt his jacket being ripped away from his back.

'You can keep your shirt on to start with, you bastard,' yelled Shatilov, and the whip whistled through the air to bite deeply into Powerscourt's back.

'Tell me about your conversation with the Tsar,' Shatilov shouted. 'You've got ten seconds before I whip you again. After that your shirt comes off. Ten, nine, eight, seven, six –'

On the count of six there was a tremendous crash as Johnny Fitzgerald and the sergeant from the Black Watch rushed into the room, pistols in their right hands. They made straight for the two soldiers who had left their guns by the chairs in the centre of the room. But it was Ricky Crabbe who was the real revelation in the rescue party. Powerscourt was to say later that he had seen David as in David and Goliath reborn in a dingy house on the outskirts of the Tsar's Village. He had bestowed about his person a number of large stones. The first of these, less than a second after Johnny had entered the room, he despatched with remarkable accuracy at the head of Major Shatilov. It took him right in the centre of his face and he collapsed to the ground, blood pouring from his face, hands searching amidst the blood for what might remain of his nose.

'Fantastic shot, Ricky!' said Powerscourt as Johnny Fitzgerald released them from their ropes. 'I am so glad to see you all! Now, let's tie them up. I want to have a word or two with the Major here when he's strapped to the chair.'

The Black Watch sergeant was expert at binding the prisoners in ways they would not be able to escape from. Shatilov was spitting blood down his uniform as he was locked in position. Powerscourt took a pistol from Shatilov's pocket and pulled up a couple of chairs next to him.

'Can you make this sound as bloodthirsty as you can, Mikhail? He's got to believe that I mean it when I say I'm going to kill him.'

'Of course,' said Mikhail.

'Now then, Major, let me just explain the rules now we're in charge.' Powerscourt laughed what he hoped was a bloodthirsty laugh. The Major seemed to find it difficult to talk. 'All you have to do is to tell us what happened to Mr Martin. Then everything stops. Possibly including you. I haven't decided on that yet. But what you need to understand is that there are a number of ways in which we could help you talk, and there are a number of us to do it. The sergeant,' Powerscourt pointed to the six feet four inches of the man from the Black Watch, 'is very keen to see what happens with one of your knouts on a bare back. Death perhaps by whip. Ricky, our expert marksman here, is anxious to see what happens when people are pelted with stones from different distances. Death maybe by stoning. A biblical death for you, Major. Johnny Fitzgerald is a great believer in the sticks or canes you keep in the corner of the room. Another death by beating. I, believe it or not, Major, believe in the pistol as the means of making you talk. I have made a rough count of the number of bullets available here for this particular gun and I have so far counted fifty-four. I am curious to see how many wounds the human body can sustain before it actually dies.'

There was a sort of gurgle from the chair. Ricky's stone had certainly left its mark.

'So,' said Powerscourt, pointing his pistol absent-mindedly into the middle of Shatilov's wounded face, 'let us begin. Why don't we start with the moment Mr Martin was brought here at about a quarter to ten in the evening. Why don't you take it on from there, Major?'

There was another gurgle from the Major. Powerscourt turned the pistol to the ground and fired it six inches from Shatilov's left foot. The noise was deafening. The two soldiers twitched in their ropes as if they thought they might be next.

'Perhaps that might help your concentration.' Mikhail was sounding very fierce as he translated the ferocious Powerscourt, the Powerscourt hungry for wounds and thirsty for blood.

There was another gurgle. Powerscourt now placed the barrel of the gun in the middle of Shatilov's bloody mouth. He could feel the teeth rattling inside. 'I don't have to use all the fifty-four bullets, Major. I could kill you now, rather like, I suspect, you killed Mr Martin and took his body away. Now it's my turn to count to ten. You'd better start talking before I get to ten, Major, or your mouth will disappear. Probably not quite enough to kill you as long as I avoid what passes for your brain. One, two, three . . .'

There was a lot of rustling about in the Shatilov chair. He was trying to shake his head.

'Four, five, six . . .'

Shatilov's hands were tied behind his back so he could not point. 'I think he's trying to ask you to take the gun out of his mouth, sir,' said Mikhail.

323

Powerscourt peered closely at the Major. 'Seven,' he said. He withdrew his gun from Shatilov's mouth. 'Eight.'

'It was all an accident,' Shatilov began, the words slurred and heavy as if he were drunk, and Powerscourt thanked God he hadn't had to reach ten. He wasn't at all sure what he would have done.

'I don't want to know whether you think it was an accident or not, Major. I'm sure the scribes and Pharisees would have described Christ's death on the cross as an accident, given half a chance. Just tell me when and how things happened.'

The Major looked at Powerscourt with pleading eyes. Please don't kill me, they seemed to be saying. Powerscourt was remaining pitiless for the time being. His quest was nearly over.

'The man Martin,' Shatilov began, 'was brought to me here after his interview with the Tsar. He refused to tell me what their discussions were about. He said it was a matter for diplomats, not for secret policemen who weren't intelligent enough to be employed by the Okhrana.' That tribute to the intelligence of his staff would have pleased Derzhenov, Powerscourt thought. But he doubted it would have gone down too well in this room with the scarred Major.

'So what did you do when Mr Martin refused to tell you the nature of his conversations?' Powerscourt was dangling his gun ostentatiously in the general direction of the Major's private parts.

'Well,' said the Major, glancing down anxiously, 'we – we thought – we decided to take measures to persuade him to talk.'

Powerscourt took a brief walk up to the end of the table and back, gun in hand, always pointing at Shatilov. 'What measures?' he shouted, his face a few inches from the Major.

There was a long gap. Powerscourt wondered if he should start counting again. 'We beat him,' whispered the Major.

'With what?' asked Powerscourt.

'The whip.' Shatilov was virtually inaudible now.

'Ordinary whip? Or Russian whip?'

'Russian whip.' The Major began to whimper now, like an injured child.

Powerscourt hadn't finished yet. 'When you say we, Major, do you mean you yourself, or your men or a combination of the two? And if you try to tell a lie I shall pull every last tooth out of your head.'

'It was me,' said Shatilov, trying unsuccessfully to rock in his chair.

'And how long did it go on for?' asked Powerscourt, feeling waves of pity suddenly for Roderick Martin, owner of Tibenham Grange, lover of Tamara Kerenkova, one of the brightest stars in the bright firmament of the Foreign Office, passing away here under the vicious care of a Russian sadist. He remembered somebody telling him years before that above a certain number of lashes, was it fifty or was it eighty, a victim of the knout would be sure to die. Certainly that death would be a welcome relief.

'Until he died,' Shatilov whispered, trying to draw back from Powerscourt.

'And how long did that take?' asked Powerscourt sadly, certain that some pedant in the Foreign Office would want to know the answer.

'Less than half an hour. Maybe twenty minutes? The man must have had a weak heart or something.'

Powerscourt narrowly avoided the temptation to shoot all the Major's teeth out, one by one. He was nearly finished.

'And what did you do with his body?'

'We dumped it on the Nevskii Prospekt and told the police to make a note. Then we put the body through a hole in the ice.'

Somewhere out in the Gulf of Finland, Powerscourt thought, a mutilated body was floating with the fishes. Maybe the weals on Martin's back might have eased a little after their passage through the salt water. Even now, he felt sure, there would still be enough wounds on the battered corpse to tell whoever might find him, be they Balt or Finn or Estonian, that this man did not have an easy passage to the other side. Martin had served his King and country well. He had kept faith to the end, even at the cost of the most terrible pain. Now Powerscourt understood why they had never known how Martin had died, whether he had been shot or strangled. Shatilov could not let the police report say he had been tortured to death.

Somehow, Mikhail seemed to sense that the interrogation was at an end.

'What are you going to do with him, Lord Powerscourt? This disgrace here.' He nodded contemptuously at the figure of Shatilov, whimpering like one who thinks his last hour has come.

'What indeed?' said Powerscourt. 'Part of me would like to kill him here and now. He murdered a compatriot of mine in the most horrible way. He is an appalling human being. I don't think he deserves to live. But I can't kill him. I'm not a Russian court or a Russian judge or a Russian court martial, though God knows what any of those would do with him. I'm not a Lord High Executioner.'

'But your mission here, Lord Powerscourt, the quest to find out what happened to Mr Martin, the nature of his conversations with the Tsar, you know all that now. Your work here is done, is that so?'

'Who knows?' said Powerscourt. 'Sergeant,' he said to the man from the Black Watch, 'can you make sure these people are properly tied up? So they won't escape for days? And gag them so they can't make a noise,' he added, thinking incongruously of the victims of Derzhenov's basement. 'When you've done that, let's go home.'

15

'Francis.' Johnny Fitzgerald had been inspecting the cupboards in and around Shatilov's quarters and had collected a burglar's haul of hammers, screwdrivers, spanners, jemmies and other tools. It looked as though he was expecting trouble.

'There's something you should know.'

'What's that, Johnny?' asked Powerscourt, his mind still focused on the late Martin.

'We don't have a coach any more,' said Johnny.

'We don't have a coach any more?' replied Powerscourt.

'We don't have a coach any more,' Johnny Fitzgerald repeated. 'Two of those bastard soldiers stole the horses. And we don't know where they took them.'

Powerscourt started to laugh. 'Sorry, I know it's serious, but I was just thinking of the Ambassador, not the most popular man in the Embassy, having to tell Mrs Ambassador that the coach which used to take her round fashionable Petersburg has disappeared. Is the actual carriage worth keeping?'

'We've hidden it in an outhouse for now,' said Fitzgerald. 'But the problem is this. These people we've just tied up, the Imperial Guard, Royal Palaces Security Division, whatever they're called, guard all the roads and all the railways round St Petersburg. If our friend Shatilov is found and released before we get back to the Embassy, we'll be joining your man Martin as food for the fishes.'

'What's the fastest way to get back? Apart from the horses we don't have?' Powerscourt was beginning to grapple with this new problem.

It was Ricky Crabbe who provided a possible solution. 'There's a goods train coming through at eleven o'clock, my lord, going to St Petersburg. God knows where it ends up. The last passenger train is half an hour after that.'

'I don't like goods trains,' said Powerscourt, who had been locked up in a goods carriage in India for an entire afternoon at the hottest time of year with a herd of incontinent cows for company, 'but I'm happy to try again if people feel that would be better.'

'Once you're in one of those damned carriages,' said Johnny, 'you're a sitting duck. If they lock the humans in like they lock the animals in, you can't even jump off the bloody train.'

Shortly afterwards a small but determined group were lurking in the shadows at the end of the platform of Tsarskoe Selo station. Johnny Fitzgerald had been making small experiments with his new tools. He disappeared at one stage into a siding full of unwanted carriages. Various grunting and swearing noises announced that he was still of the party. Ricky Crabbe had appropriated a couple of stout bags which he was filling very methodically with large stones. Powerscourt was trying to learn and amplify a basic message in Russian: I am from the British Embassy, we all have diplomatic immunity. Mikhail was assuring him that if he set his mind to it he could be fluent in Russian in six months. The coach driver, saddened by the loss of his vehicle and possibly his livelihood, had taken delivery of a large number of roubles from Powerscourt and set off in search of the missing horses. He said he would be able to buy them back if only he could find the thieves. The sergeant from the Black Watch was looking out at the distant road, waiting to see if the enemy would appear.

The train was late. Local trains in Russia, Mikhail informed Powerscourt, were often late. Powerscourt practised saying I am from the British Embassy, we all have diplomatic immunity to Johnny Fitzgerald but it failed to have any impact.

'You could be saying put all your money on Shatilov in the two thirty at Doncaster for all I know, Francis,' he said cheerfully, 'and I think you should sound a little more guttural, if you know what I mean. But carry on practising. It may turn out useful sooner than we think, if only the bloody Russians would understand what you're saying to them.'

Maybe it was the mention of Shatilov that brought their problems. To their left they could hear, approaching at a good speed, their train, gusts of smoke almost matching the colour of the surrounding snow. To their right the night air was rent with whistles and the sounds of shouting men on the other side of the platform, hurrying to reach the station before the train could leave. Somehow or other Shatilov's men must have been alerted to the flight of the English party. Maybe, Powerscourt shuddered as he thought of it, he was leading this revenge mission in person, whip conveniently stuffed into a coat pocket. Powerscourt did not rate his chances very high if he met Shatilov again. The train was drawing to a halt at the little station. There were half a dozen carriages with a guard's van at the rear. There were more passengers than you might have expected. The sergeant was swearing viciously under his breath.

'Do we take the train or not, Francis?' asked Johnny.

'We go,' said Powerscourt, 'last carriage before the guard's van. If we stay here we're marooned, miles from anywhere.'

The whistles were very close now. The train driver would have to be deaf not to hear them. The five men bent double so their heads would not protrude above the height of the carriages as they raced into the train. They could hear feet running up the platform. Powerscourt hung briefly out of the window in time to see a party of twelve men marching into the front carriage behind the driver. The last man aboard, his face wreathed in a series of bloodstained bandages, with a pistol in his left hand, was Major Shatilov, with a face, Powerscourt reported to his friends, like thunder.

'Never mind, Francis,' said Johnny Fitzgerald, fiddling with some giant spanner in his stolen bag, 'you can say to them as they come through the connecting door that you're from the British Embassy and we all have diplomatic immunity. That should do the trick.'

Everybody laughed. Their compartment had a dozen wooden benches with a party of four middle-aged Russian women at the front. Mikhail placed himself on sentry duty at the connecting door where he would be able to see any soldiers coming on their way down the train. The sergeant kept him company, fingering one of the Russian guard's pistols in his pocket as he stared up the carriage. 'Can you get on to the tops of these coaches, Johnny?' asked Powerscourt. 'Did you have time to see as the train came in? And could you jump from one to another?'

'The answer to both of these questions is Yes,' said Johnny, returning the spanner to his bag, 'particularly if you come from the British Embassy and have diplomatic immunity.' Ricky Crabbe was fingering the stones in his

David's pouch, selecting the ones he liked best and putting them in his coat pocket. Powerscourt checked that he had the gun and the bullets from the Shatilov villa. Not for the first time that evening he regretted that they had not been able to bring any weapons with them but Powerscourt was certain that anybody trying to enter the Alexander Palace with a gun would have been in Siberia inside a fortnight if not trussed up and gagged in one of Derzhenov's basement cells.

'This is what I think we should do,' Powerscourt said, looking anxiously at the four middle-aged women. 'We can't stay here in this carriage with the ladies. I don't want to retreat into the guard's van. Johnny, I think you and Mikhail and the sergeant should get on the roof now and move forward as far as you can, all the way into the first carriage. That way you'll be behind these soldier people. If things get really rough, you could attack them from behind. Ricky and I are going to be Leonidas and the three hundred Spartans at Thermopylae here for a while but I don't think we'll hold them very long. Then, unlike Leonidas, we're going to bolt too. Mikhail,' Powerscourt recalled the young man from his sentry duty, 'can you get rid of these ladies here?' As he pointed to them Mikhail paused briefly, then a look of great seriousness appeared to descend on his young features. He began speaking loudly to the women. After a while he pointed vigorously up towards the front of the train. One of the women appeared to ask a question. Mikhail shouted back and pointed again. Looking with horror at the three Englishmen, the four Russian ladies grabbed their belongings and shot out of the carriage.

'What on earth did you say to them?' asked Powerscourt.

'I told them, I'm afraid, my lord, that the three of you were just about to begin unnatural sexual acts right in the

332

middle of their compartment. I said that these acts of depravity would continue until the end of the journey. I said it was their patriotic duty to go and tell the driver in person, whatever obstacles they might find in their way, that these Satanic practices were happening in his train. For myself, I said, I was going to keep an eye on the situation so I could make a full report to the authorities later on. Even when the four ladies were halfway down the next carriage, they could still be heard complaining of this insult to the Russian railways and their country's honour.'

'Well done,' said Powerscourt. 'Now then, you and your colleagues had better be off.'

Ricky was now the sentry. As he took up his position, he told Powerscourt that the best place in the carriage for the despatch of his weapons was behind one of the benches, about two thirds of the way down. Powerscourt tried to work out how long they would be able to hold out in this compartment. He worried about how exposed they would be making their way along the roof before the enemy showed up behind them. Gunfights on the roof would be fatal. A lot depended on how effective these soldiers were going to be. If they were well-trained killers, he and his little band were probably finished. But if they were recent recruits, mere rabble in uniform as a colonel in one of Powerscourt's regiments had once described his opponents, they might lose heart after a few rocks from David's sling and a couple of well-aimed pistol shots.

'They're coming, sir.' Ricky Crabbe was grinning as he went into his first battle. 'The women are holding them up. Looks like they're getting a right lecture, sir.' Ricky positioned himself behind his bench, eyes peering through the slats. Powerscourt, further back, almost at the door to the roof and the outside world, could hear footsteps overhead as Johnny and Mikhail and the sergeant made their way along the train. Powerscourt hoped the noise wouldn't travel to the next carriage.

The young man who opened the connecting door couldn't have been more than eighteen or nineteen. He had joined the military as a better alternative to life in his peasant village. It was almost certain that he had never heard of the story of David and Goliath. Ricky's missile caught him almost in the centre of his right eye. For a moment the Russian soldier blundered about thinking he was blind. Then he whimpered and collapsed on to a bench, holding his face. The soldier behind him gazed in astonishment at his colleague. He hadn't seen the stone. Then he too received a present from Ricky Crabbe, smack in the centre of his teeth. He reeled backwards and blocked the doorway. 'Now!' said Powerscourt, and fled towards the open air. He knew that the next thing likely to come through the doorway was a stream of bullets. He had given his gun to Ricky to give himself one last burst of covering fire before he disappeared upwards. If Ricky was as good a shot with a pistol as he was with a stone or a rock, Powerscourt imagined he would hit the bull's eye at two hundred yards with a gun in his hand. Now Powerscourt began to climb towards the roof. There were eight rungs to go. Still no sound from down below. Maybe the Russians were demoralized. Maybe the Major was giving them a pep talk.

Powerscourt was now walking uncertainly along the roof. The train was travelling at about twenty-five miles per hour. Light snow was beginning to fall. He saw that the gap between the two carriages was only four or five feet, not too hazardous a leap even for a person who was terrified of heights and regarded the roof of a Russian train as being about the same height as a skyscraper in Chicago. Then he heard it. There was a volley of shots down below, followed by a small cheer. Five seconds later there were four rounds from the pistol, followed by two screams and the sound of Ricky Crabbe coming up the steps and along the roof. Powerscourt thought there might be a pause down below while the wounded were attended to. Perhaps the other three were dead. As he jumped across to the top of the fourth carriage he saw that Ricky was now lying flat, waiting for the first Russian head to surface on to the roof of the carriage before he blew it away. Telegraph transmission seemed to be a good training ground for war. For the first time Powerscourt began to hope that they might survive this escapade. He had done what he was called on to do. He had fulfilled his mission. He dared not imagine what Lady Lucy would think of him cavorting about on top of a Russian train in the middle of the night, pursued by a gang of Russian soldiery. Lady Lucy, he realized bitterly, would be even less pleased with him now. For Nemesis had arrived at the other end of the third carriage. Johnny Fitzgerald and Mikhail must have descended back into the train before Nemesis began his climb.

Major Shatilov was looking at Powerscourt, delighted with his prey.

'Good evening, Major.' Powerscourt was trying to sound calmer than he felt. 'A very good evening to you.'

The Major was standing right in the centre of the roof of the carriage. He took a gun from his pocket and shook his head. He shouted at Powerscourt in Russian. Then he pulled a whip from his other pocket and waved it vigorously towards his enemy. After a while he cracked it a couple of times. The thong seemed to Powerscourt to travel through the air at incredible speed. Then Shatilov pointed to his watch and his right hand went round many many times. It's going to be a long-drawn-out affair,

Powerscourt thought, death that might take a week or maybe two. Shatilov shouted some more. Powerscourt remembered the dreadful stories of Russian criminals sentenced to a thousand birch lashes in the terrible punishment known as running the gauntlet. When the victims collapsed after three hundred lashes or so they were carried off the parade ground. But when they had recovered they were merely restored to the gauntlet at the point where they had stopped on the previous occasion. Second time around most of the prisoners dropped dead long before they reached the thousand blows.

Powerscourt wondered if Ricky Crabbe could hear the crack of the whip or the sound of Shatilov's voice. Maybe it was lost in the wind. He wondered if he should jump off the train and take his chance with a broken leg on the hard ground. He thought of his children and said a prayer for Lady Lucy. Maybe he should never have accepted this assignment and should have remained with the transepts and clerestories, the chantry chapels and the sarcophagi of England's cathedrals. The Major was still fingering his whip, feasting his eyes on Powerscourt and his plight. Then Powerscourt saw hope. He saw more than hope. He saw Nemesis coming this time for Major Shatilov, as long as he didn't look around. Powerscourt began talking to hold his attention. He pretended to plead for mercy. He sank to his knees, his hands raised in supplication. All the time his brain was calculating speed and distances and the time he would have to act unless he was to meet the same fate as the Major. On and on he went with his pleading. Already he had worked out what to do when the last moment came. It was nearly here. Shatilov was still looking at him. Now! Now! Powerscourt flung himself down and pressed his head and his body as tightly as he could into the roof of the carriage. The full force of the

336

centre of the brick bridge hit Shatilov between the shoulder blades and broke his back. He was flung on to the roof of the carriage and his body scraped along the top of the bridge's arch for a while before he toppled over the side. He was further mangled by the wheels of the train as they passed over him and rolled on into the night.

Ricky Crabbe crawled over to Powerscourt. 'I had him covered, sir, but I didn't want to shoot in case I only wounded him and he shot you. I've seen off one of those soldiers coming up to the roof. Don't think the rest will be in any great hurry.'

A couple of minutes later they were dropping down into the first carriage, nearly stepping over Johnny Fitzgerald who was lying flat on the floor with a pair of enormous spanners in his hand. The sergeant was by his side, his tunic removed, his shirt sleeves rolled up, ready for some enormous feat of physical exertion.

'Am I glad to see you, Francis. The peasants pretending to be soldiers are all down at the back of the train. We're all here now, us and the four ladies.'

Powerscourt saw the women huddling together as if for warmth right in front of the door into the driver's compartment. Mikhail stood between them and the door. God only knew what debauchery they expected now there were four of the foreigners to play together. Powerscourt told Johnny about the Major's end. 'I bet you were glad to see the end of him, Francis. Killed at the bridge eh? Like Horatius he asked, "Now who will stand on either hand And keep the bridge with me?" No answer in both cases. Now, if you'll stand back, I'm going to try this. I've nearly finished but I had to wait till you showed up, Francis. All my life I've wanted to do this.'

Johnny took one of his enormous spanners and bent over the divide between the first and second carriages.

There was an enormous grunt, then another, closely followed by a screech of metal. Then he and the Black Watch sergeant lent all their force into pushing the second carriage away from the first. As Powerscourt stared at the second carriage he saw a wounded soldier enter it at the far end. But as the man began to walk towards the front of the train, he seemed to be getting, not closer, but further and further away. They could see a look of astonishment on the man's face as he realized he would never reach the front of the train, that he would not reach the doctors of St Petersburg on this journey. Johnny had decoupled the engine and the first carriage from the rest of the train. What remained of Shatilov's pathetic army would soon be stranded in the middle of the countryside with no engine. They would probably block the line until they could be towed away. As Powerscourt looked round his little band, Johnny with grease on his hands and his arms, Ricky Crabbe, his clothes filthy from crawling along the roof, Mikhail with a great bruise on his forehead from bumping into the rungs up to a carriage roof, the sergeant trying to get the dirt off his arms, he felt very proud of them. Johnny was still staring out the back, rubbing his hands together in his delight, rejoicing in his severed train. It was Mikhail who spoke.

'I've managed to convince the ladies, Lord Powerscourt, that you at least are a respectable person. I've told them you can reassure them in Russian. They're going to ask you now.'

With that Mikhail had a brief conversation with the four women. One of them stared hard at Powerscourt and fired a rapid salvo at him in Russian.

'I am from the British Embassy and we all have diplomatic immunity,' Powerscourt replied in what he hoped was his best Russian and trying to remember where

Mikhail had told him to put the emphasis. There was another blast from the four ladies. Powerscourt looked inquisitively at Mikhail.

'What have we here?' he asked.

'They say,' Mikhail laughed, 'that you're nothing better than a damned horse thief and they're going to report you to the authorities the second this train reaches St Petersburg.'

Before he went to bed that night Powerscourt drafted a letter for the Ambassador to send in the morning. It was addressed to the Tsar and outlined in considerable detail what had happened to him and his colleagues, the theft of the horses, the beginnings of torture, the total lack of respect afforded to citizens of the United Kingdom and a man attached to its Foreign Office. How would the Russians feel, he asked rhetorically, if a member of their diplomatic staff on a mission to the King in Buckingham Palace was hijacked on his way out and taken to be stretched on the rack at the Tower of London? Powerscourt made no reference to their escape and the little battle on the train. Nor did he say anything about the substance of his conversation with Nicholas the Second. He doubted very much if the letter would reach the Tsar himself. Some court official would doubtless read it, but even that, he felt, should be sufficient to put a stop to the activities of Major Shatilov's successors. In that assumption he could not have been more wrong.

For at eleven o'clock the following morning a distraught and tearful Mikhail presented himself at the British Embassy. Natasha, he told a weary Powerscourt and de Chassiron, resplendent in a new shirt from Paris, had disappeared. A friend of hers was in the city that morning. Natasha had told her, Mikhail reported, that she thought she was being followed by some of the soldiers of the guard. Perhaps they had taken her prisoner. Perhaps they were going to mistreat her.

'She disappeared once before, didn't she,' asked Powerscourt as gently as he could, 'and she came back again, didn't she?'

'That was because the little boy was ill, my lord,' said Mikhail. 'He's not ill now, at least not for the present.'

De Chassiron saw how upset the young man was. Anybody might fall in love with Natasha. He himself could easily have fallen in love with her. Perhaps the entire squad of soldiers in the Alexander Palace had fallen in love with her.

'You don't suppose,' Mikhail was tormenting himself now, 'that they will take revenge on Natasha for what happened to the Major and the others last night?'

That thought had crossed Powerscourt's mind some moments before. He looked at his watch. The engineless train should have been discovered by now. Perhaps Shatilov's mutilated body had also been found. It would take some time, he thought, to work out how he had met his end. The presumption would be that he had been killed by one of the Englishmen rather than destroyed by a bridge. He stared hard at a print of King's College Cambridge behind de Chassiron's desk, the Chapel standing out like a bulwark or a beacon of man's love of God in a sceptical and scientific city. He could see de Chassiron lounging about on the grass in his gown, arguing with the dons. Powerscourt wondered if the print followed him on all his postings, a travelling reminder of the glory of youth accompanying him into the shallows of middle age.

It must have been the print that made up his mind, he told Johnny later. For when he turned his gaze back to de Chassiron he knew exactly what he was going to do.

'There's only one thing for it,' he said. 'The Ambassador

has, I hope, sent on the letter I drafted for him last night. That made no mention of the little battle on the train or the death of the ghastly Major. Any references to those events would, it seems to me, be likely to have the most unpleasant consequences. Who are these English people anyway? What is their business here? They are spies. Of course they are spies. And what happens to the heroic defenders of the person of the Tsar and the integrity of his realm when they apprehend these villains and try to extract information from them by traditional Russian methods? Why, the heroic Major is slain doing his duty. Powerscourt and the rest of his English rabble are murderers. To the cells with them! Death to the traitors! Long live the Tsar!'

'You could have a point there, Powerscourt,' drawled de Chassiron. 'At the very least you could be locked up for years before any case came to trial. Last night you were up on the roof of a railway compartment. Maybe in view of the fact that these people guard the roads and the railways you'll have to leave on another.'

'I'm damned if I'm going to crawl out of this country like a criminal,' said Powerscourt. 'The important thing at the moment is to rescue Natasha. I'm going to rouse Johnny Fitzgerald and then he and I are going to pay a visit to General Derzhenov at the Okhrana headquarters on the Fontanka.'

'And what are you going to do when you get there? Pop yourself into one of those nice cells they have in the basement?' De Chassiron looked as if he thought his friend had gone mad.

'Let me try to put it into diplomatic language for you, de Chassiron. I am going, on behalf of the British Government, to conduct a negotiation aimed at the speedy release of Miss Bobrinsky who has been a great friend to the British Foreign Office and the British Government.'

'That makes her sound like a spy, an English spy,' said de Chassiron. 'That might not do her any good at all. I think you have to let events take their course. There's nothing we can do. Talk of going to the Okhrana is so much pie in the sky. Why should they lift a finger to help us?'

'I think you are wrong there. In fact I'm sure of it. Derzhenov has already asked to see me to discuss my conversation with the Tsar. I propose to tell him something, but not necessarily all of what was said, in exchange for the immediate release of Natasha.'

'But he's not going to interfere with another of Russia's intelligence agencies.' De Chassiron sounded very certain.

'My dear man,' said Powerscourt with a smile, 'this is one of the problems of having competing intelligence agencies. They usually hate their rivals far more than they hate their enemies. I bet you the Okhrana loathe the late Major Shatilov and his organization. Anything they can do to bring them into disrepute brings more power to the Okhrana.'

'And how much do you propose to tell him? More than you propose telling our Ambassador here, or myself? That would be rather treacherous conduct.'

'That's unfair,' said Powerscourt angrily. 'You know perfectly well that I am specifically instructed to give the results of my investigation to the Prime Minister and to him alone. At present, however much I might want to fill you in, de Chassiron, I just can't do it. Anyway, we shall see,' said Powerscourt, rising from his chair. 'Please come too, Mikhail, Derzhenov speaks very good English but I have no idea who else we might meet on the way.'

Derzhenov was alone in his office on the fourth floor. The villainous Colonel Kolchak, Powerscourt thought, must be kicking people to death in the basement cells.

'How good of you to call, Lord Powerscourt!' the head of the Okhrana purred. 'And you must be the famous Johnny Fitzgerald. And Mikhail, of course, in case I forget my English. You come just as you said you would, Lord Powerscourt, the morning after your interview with the Tsar. How kind! How very kind!'

Powerscourt felt as though a month had elapsed since his interview with the Tsar. 'Now then, my friend,' Derzhenov went on, 'I understand you have had some interesting adventures since your interview. Is that not so? Interesting adventures?'

'I will tell you about those in a moment, if I may, General Derzhenov. But most of all I want to ask for your assistance.'

'My assistance, Lord Powerscourt? How can the son of a humble schoolteacher possibly be of assistance to the representative of the greatest empire on earth?'

Powerscourt felt that American or German historians might take issue with the last statement but he did not think the time or the place were appropriate for a discussion on the rise and fall of empires. 'It is a very simple matter, General. It concerns a young lady called Natasha Bobrinsky. She is a friend of Mikhail. She has been helping us in a general sort of way, in the inquiries about Mr Martin, for example. She has done nothing whatsoever to harm or betray her country. She is employed part-time as a lady-in-waiting to the Empress at the Alexander Palace at Tsarskoe Selo. For the past few days she felt she was being followed by members of the Imperial Guard, Royal Palaces Security Division. This morning she has disappeared.'

Derzhenov frowned deeply at the mention of the Imperial Guard. 'And you would like my help to find her?' he asked. 'Is she one of the – how do I put it? – the Bobrinsky Bobrinskys?'

'She is,' said Powerscourt, 'and with your help I am sure she would be released by lunchtime.'

Derzhenov laughed a rather alarming laugh. 'I'm not sure about that, Lord Powerscourt. I think you are exaggerating my powers. But tell me,' Derzhenov began running the tips of his fingers together, 'what information do you bring me this morning, the morning after your interview with the Tsar?'

What was Natasha Bobrinsky worth? How much should he tell the head of the Okhrana? None of it? Some of it? All of it? Powerscourt had been running these questions through his mind on the way to the Okhrana headquarters. He still had no answers. He knew nothing that would endanger British national interests. In fact, some of what he knew damaged Russian national interests rather more than his own. Yet somehow he found the prospect of telling his secrets to the head of a foreign intelligence agency who was not allied to Great Britain very hard to take. It would have been different if it had been the urbane head of the French secret service, weaving elegant plots with his Watteau in the Place des Vosges.

'If I tell you, General, will you secure the release of Miss Bobrinsky?' said Powerscourt, hoping to be saved by the non-specific nature of his statement. But Derzhenov was too wily a bird to fall for that one.

'I'm afraid, my friend, you will have to do better than that. I might promise to secure the release of the young lady – if I can – and you would tell me nothing. Why don't you tell me what transpired and then I will tell you what I might be able to do to release the young lady.'

'But then,' now it was Powerscourt's turn, 'I could tell you all I know and get nothing in return. Assuming,' he smiled at the General, 'you were an unreasonable man. Which you're not.' Oddly enough, Powerscourt was certain that this man opposite, who whipped his prisoners for fun, who had the more unfortunate of them killed in ways that replicated classical paintings, would, nevertheless, keep his word.

'We could go on like this all day,' said Derzhenov. 'I suspect that in our careers we often have. Lord Powerscourt, I ask you to trust me. If you tell me what happened and I think you are telling the truth we will see what can be done with this Natasha Bobrinsky. If you do not trust me, then I suggest you leave now. That way you will not compromise yourself or your mission. Your knowledge will remain with you. Miss Bobrinsky will remain locked up. But I hope you do not leave.'

There was a pause. Neither Johnny Fitzgerald nor Mikhail spoke. Then Powerscourt held out his hand. One part of his brain said, You're shaking hands with a mass murderer. The other part said, 'Very good, General. I accept what you say. Let me begin with the original nature of my mission to St Petersburg, the question of who killed Roderick Martin.' Powerscourt saw that Derzhenov had begun taking copious notes. Perhaps he and his information were going to end up as dusty footnotes in the Okhrana files. Information supplied by the English investigator Powerscourt.

'The last we knew of him was that he left the Tsar at about ten o'clock. The Tsar declined to say anything at all about the nature of their conversation. Martin appeared to vanish until the appearance of his corpse on the Nevskii three or four hours later.'

Powerscourt paused and poured himself a glass of water. Water shall wash away their tears, he said to himself. 'I now know what happened to him. He was apprehended by members of the Imperial Guard, Royal Palaces Security Division under the control of a Major Shatilov.'

'This Major Shatilov, Lord Powerscourt, have you seen him lately? A little bird tells me he has gone missing.'

'I'm not sure I have anything to add to that,' said Powerscourt blandly. 'As I say, Mr Martin was taken into custody by the Major in a house on the outskirts of Tsarskoe Selo.'

Derzhenov was still writing. Powerscourt waited patiently until he had finished before he went on. 'Major Shatilov was most anxious to know the nature of Mr Martin's conversation with the Tsar, almost as anxious as yourself, General. It's strange how all the intelligence agencies should want the same piece of news, it really is.'

There was a cackle from Derzhenov. 'Just get on with the story, Powerscourt. What did Martin tell him?'

'He didn't tell him anything.'

'So what did Shatilov do then?'

'He beat him to death with a knout, General.'

'Is that so, Lord Powerscourt?' Derzhenov looked up from his scribbling. 'That's very bad management,' he said, shaking his head, 'people shouldn't die from a single session with the whip.'

'Maybe he had a weak heart, General Derzhenov. Maybe it was because members of the British Foreign Office don't live in a world where people are beaten to death with whips. They're not used to it.'

'You could have a point there, Lord Powerscourt.' Derzhenov was back writing again. 'And you are sure the man Martin said nothing before he died?'

'Not a word, General.'

'Not a word? I see. But tell me, what is your source for this information? Where does it come from?'

'Why, General,' said Powerscourt, trying to look as innocent as possible, 'it came from Major Shatilov himself.'

'Really?' said Derzhenov with great emphasis. 'Was this the last action of the Major before he disappeared? Do you expect him to turn up early one morning on the Nevskii, rather like Mr Martin before him?'

Powerscourt had decided some moments before precisely what he was going to tell the Okhrana man. He was going to tell him about Martin's death as he had done. He was going to tell him about the last conversation Martin had with the Tsar in the sense that it now seemed that a flight to Norfolk was less likely. He would, if he had to, tell him about the death of Shatilov and the skirmish on the train. But he would not, out of a sense of loyalty to the Tsar, disclose anything about the haemophilia. He felt sure the Tsar would want that to remain private.

'I wouldn't know about that,' said Powerscourt, reluctant to be drawn into detailed discussion on the man's death. Though it was the bridge that killed him, a hostile prosecutor could easily make out a case against Powerscourt and his men.

'I see, Lord Powerscourt,' said Derzhenov, temporarily chewing on the end of his pen and looking closely at the Englishman. 'Maybe we shall come back to this later. But tell me, what of Martin's conversation with the Tsar?'

So Powerscourt told him: the original approach from the Tsar to the English King asking if his wife and family would be welcome in England, the despatch of Martin, bearing the answer that they would be welcome in Norfolk, Powerscourt's discovery of the place where they were to be accommodated, the final reluctance to take up the offer, for reasons as yet unexplained.

'Did the Tsar tell you this himself, Lord Powerscourt? Were there just the two of you at the meeting?'

'There were just the two of us, General,' said Powerscourt, 'and no, the Tsar did not tell me, I told him.'

'You told him, Lord Powerscourt? But how did you know? You weren't even there!'

'Let me put it this way, General, I worked it out. I don't want to say anything more about my methods, if you don't mind. But the Tsar confirmed that it was more or less true.' There's no point, he said to himself, in rescuing Natasha Bobrinsky from the frying pans of Major Shatilov, heated to unbearable levels, no doubt, before being applied to stripped flesh, into the fires of the Okhrana, gridirons and reproductions of the martyrdom of St Lawrence a speciality.

Derzhenov suddenly seemed to make up his mind. He stopped writing and carefully screwed the top back on to his German fountain pen. 'Lord Powerscourt, I think there is more that you are not yet telling me. I believe you know more than you let on about the death of Major Shatilov. Let me just ask you one question on that subject, if I may. If he were to be found dead, would you say – assuming you were a guessing man, you understand – that he was killed in a fight or by accident?'

'Being completely ignorant of the facts, General, I would not like to make any comment at all,' said Powerscourt, beginning to sweat slightly.

'I forgive you,' said Derzhenov, smiling at his visitor. 'There is one piece of information you have, I believe, which you are not telling me about, but I know it already. Fear not. I respect you for not telling me. Now then. Miss Bobrinsky, how shall I put this? You could tell her friends to expect her back in St Petersburg this afternoon.'

And with that a beaming Derzhenov led them down the stairs and out into the fresh air. He shook them all warmly by the hand. For once there were no noxious smells or sounds of horror coming from the basement.

'What on earth,' said Johnny Fitzgerald when they were a good hundred yards clear of the building, 'was that last bit about?'

'The bit about I know what you're not telling me but I don't mind? He means, I think, that he knows about the haemophilia. Quite how he knows, I can't imagine. I just hope his organization is quite secure or the whole bloody Russian Empire will know about it before the end of the year.'

16

Lord Francis Powerscourt was sitting next to Rupert de Chassiron in the back row of the seats in the University of St Petersburg's theatre at four o'clock the same afternoon, waiting for a play to begin. Natasha Bobrinsky had indeed been released from captivity and had gone home to recover from her ordeal. She and Mikhail and Powerscourt were to meet for dinner at a hotel on the Nevskii Prospekt where they had dancing in the evenings. Johnny and Ricky Crabbe had disappeared on an outing to some distant place where the local birds could be seen to best advantage, way out near the tip of Vasilevsky Island. Afterwards, Powerscourt had learned to his horror, Ricky was going to take his new friend back to his own quarters and introduce him to a range of different vodkas. De Chassiron was slightly apologetic about the play.

'Don't expect anything fancy like you would see in the West End, Powerscourt. Don't expect anything very much at all. The students are all on strike – the English Department only got permission to put this on because it is not part of the course. The English professor is very keen on drama and he has translated this play himself. He put on another one by the same author last year and I came to see it. This one's called *The Cherry Orchard* and it had its first performance last year in Moscow.'

'Should I have heard of this author, if the professor is so keen on his work? Is he famous?'

'He's not famous, not yet anyway,' said de Chassiron, 'he's dead now, poor man. He was a doctor called Chekhov, Anton Chekhov. He was still quite young when he died.'

If they had been back in London such an amateur production would probably have irritated both Powerscourt and de Chassiron. The professor's translation appeared to be more than competent, but some of the student actors seemed to have been spending more time on revolutionary activities than they had on learning their lines. When you added the fact that the prompter appeared only to have a copy of the play in Russian rather than English, the difficulties, for Powerscourt at least, were compounded. And some of the cast had a less than perfect grasp of the English language so that much of the dialogue passed him by.

Nonetheless he thought he had the hang of the main points of the story. The Cherry Orchard belonged to a Mrs Ranevskaya who is returning home from Paris at the beginning of the play. The estate and the Cherry Orchard will have to be sold to pay off the family debts unless she agrees to cut all the trees down and build villas for the new middle class on the site of the orchard and live off the rental income. A local merchant, risen from the ranks of the former peasants, offers to help her do this, but she refuses. There are two of her daughters, one adopted, and her brother in the cast, all going to be affected by the sale. There is an aged servant called Firs who regrets the passing of the old days of the serfs when everybody knew their place. There is a perpetual student called Trofimov who boasts of not being thirty yet. All of these characters, Powerscourt felt, were out of place. They didn't seem to belong to their own time, to their own space. They were displaced persons in what had become, for them, almost a foreign country. They floated precariously between the old world of the Ranevskaya estate and the different world they would inhabit when it was gone. Very near the end the stage was empty, with the sound of all the doors being locked with their keys, and all the carriages leaving. The silence was broken by the striking of a solitary axe against a tree, a rather melancholy sound. The old servant appears. He has been forgotten, left behind. Suddenly Powerscourt felt very strongly that the Cherry Orchard, for Chekhov, was Russia. The old order of long ago, of masters and serfs, has long gone. Nobody is sure what is going to replace it. Russia is being sold off to the new capitalist class, who will cut down the cherry orchards and build the villas while the previous owners complete their abdication of responsibility by going back to their lovers in Paris.

'Life has gone by as if I hadn't lived,' says the eighty-seven-year-old Firs at the very end, 'you've got no strength left, nothing, nothing.' There is the distant sound of a string breaking, as if in the sky, a dying melancholy noise. Silence falls and the only thing to be heard is a tree being struck again with an axe far off in the orchard. The final curtain falls. The old order is being cut down. Powerscourt wondered what Dr Chekhov would have made of Bloody Sunday and the current paralysis in his country. Would he have any prescriptions? Or would he be content to describe the symptoms?

'Can you tell me one thing, Lord Powerscourt?' Natasha Bobrinsky and her young man Mikhail and Lord Francis

Powerscourt were waiting for coffee at the end of their dinner in the Alexander Hotel halfway along the Nevskii Prospekt. Their table was hidden away at the end of the dining hall, decorated like a London club, a rather expensive club with valuable paintings all over the walls. To their right a small orchestra could be heard tuning up for the dancing which was due to commence in fifteen minutes. Two servants were lighting enormous candles on the walls of the ballroom.

'Of course, Natasha, whatever you like,' said Powerscourt.

'Well,' said the girl, leaning forward to address Powerscourt more closely, speaking in her near perfect French, 'I think I understand most of what has been going on when I've not been there. Mikhail told me all about the wicked Major and what happened to him and what happened to Mr Martin and I think you were all very brave about that. I know about the little boy.' She paused briefly to look at a couple of violinists making their way towards the stage, tugging vaguely at their instruments. Powerscourt was impressed that she had chosen not to name the disease.

'But there are two things I don't understand.' Her long fingers began tapping out some unknown musical beat on the white linen tablecloth. Waltz? wondered Powerscourt. Foxtrot? Mazurka? He suddenly remembered Natasha's grandmother in that great bed, humming her way through the dances of her youth, trying to salvage Martin's name from the depths of her memory. 'Why didn't Mr Martin tell Tamara Kerenkova he was coming? He'd always told her before.'

'I'm not absolutely sure about that,' Powerscourt replied, 'but remember, the previous times he came he wasn't working, if you see what I mean. He wasn't representing Great Britain or the Foreign Office, just himself. This time he was on business, very important business, and the Prime Minister must have told him he couldn't even tell the church mouse a thing about it. I think Kerenkov knew Martin was coming because the Okhrana read the telegrams from the Foreign Office giving the date of his arrival and told Kerenkov about it in some ploy of their own.'

Natasha Bobrinsky nodded. 'I see. My second question has to do with that meeting. How did you work out what happened between the Tsar and Mr Martin? How did you know that there was a plan to send the family to England?'

Powerscourt smiled. It was difficult not to smile at Natasha, she looked so pretty this evening. 'Part of the answer lies in the information you brought from the Alexander Palace, Natasha.' He paused while a waiter arrived with a tray of coffee. 'I think it really started when I tried to analyse what had happened already. Mr Martin had been sent from London on a mission of some kind. Our Foreign Office knew nothing about it. Our Ambassador here knew nothing about it. Why? If it was something routine like a treaty with all kinds of clauses and things, the diplomats would all have been involved. Nothing they like better than criticizing each other's drafts and correcting the Ambassador's spelling. But no. Therefore it probably wasn't a treaty. But what was it? And why had somebody been killed? Was it because of what they said or what they refused to say? Then there were the words you overheard the Tsar saying to his wife about how many dead members of their own family did she want to have before she followed the path of the dead Martin. If you think about it that means there is a way to keep the family alive, Martin's way, which must involve them not being in St Petersburg at all. When you mentioned to Mikhail about the Trans-Siberian Railway egg having disappeared, I didn't think very much of it at first. Gone to be cleaned perhaps, clockwork engine needs a service. But then you said that some other toys had gone and that Alexis was very devoted to the railway egg. I thought of the French Revolution and the whole royal party trying to escape from their semi-imprisonment in the Tuileries in 1791, only to be recaptured at Varennes the following day. The toys were sent ahead so the children, and especially the little boy, wouldn't feel so homesick when they were moved. A British frigate has been on patrol in the Gulf of Finland now for weeks waiting to take them all off. Surely in terrible times it would only be natural for any royal household to think of getting their women and children out before it may be too late. But that knowledge would be dynamite in today's Russia. The Tsar is sending his family away! He's deserting his people! It could have meant the beginning of the end of the Romanovs. Maybe those security agencies like Major Shatilov's suspected something of the sort was afoot, some plot to send Alexandra and the children away. It must, as you know better than I, Natasha, be very difficult to keep anything secret in that palace. That's why they were so keen to know what happened between the Tsar and Martin and between me and the Tsar. The information was so important they were prepared, quite literally to kill for it. Twice.'

Powerscourt paused and poured himself a cup of black coffee. The orchestra was tuning up, the first enthusiastic dancers beginning to form up on the floor.

'Why England?' asked Natasha. 'Why not Sweden or somewhere closer?'

'Well,' said Powerscourt, 'I think it could only be England in the end. You want to choose somewhere similar – I mean, if you're a great power you're only going to be happy going to another great power. Sweden or Norway would have been slumming it, and perhaps a bit too close so your enemies might pop over the water and blow you to pieces. Germany had the problem of the Kaiser nobody liked, France had a revolutionary tradition that might not welcome foreign royalty, but England was full of cousins and most members of the imperial family speak English. So they sent a secret message to King Edward and Mr Martin brought the answer. That confused me for a long time. At first sight when you hear about a man going from London to St Petersburg, you assume he's bringing a message from London to St Petersburg. It's only natural because you don't know about the first message that has gone from St Petersburg to London. But once you work it out, that Martin was bringing, not a question, but an answer, then everything begins to fall into place because there's really only one question the Tsar of Russia might want to send secret messages to the King of England about at this time of assassinations and explosions, and that's to see if he could send his family there.' Powerscourt drank some of his coffee. 'Clear?' he said.

'Perfectly clear,' said Natasha. 'But why haven't they gone?'

'Good question,' said Powerscourt. 'All I can say is what I said to the Tsar. Maybe the Empress didn't want to go. Maybe the children didn't want to go. Maybe they thought it would look defeatist, as if they thought they were beaten. I'm not sure.'

'Well, Lord Powerscourt, I'm now so well trained in telling you what's going on in Tsarskoe Selo, that I have to make one last report. And this might, just might, have something to do with why they're not going. This might be your answer.' Natasha glanced quickly over at the beginnings of the dance. 'Tomorrow, out there at Tsarskoe

Selo, they're expecting a visitor. Or, to be more precise, the Empress is expecting a visitor. I don't know if you're aware of it, but the Tsar and the Tsarina are deep into mystics and seers and tarot cards and psychics and all that rubbish. They had some crook of a Frenchman on board a couple of years ago. Now they think they've found another one, a man who calls himself Rasputin, Father Grigory Rasputin. They say he can heal the sick. Alexandra has ordered at least eight reports about him, from fellow mystics, from priests, even from people he's claimed to have healed. Maybe she thinks he can help with Alexis. Maybe she thinks he's the answer to all her prayers. Maybe this is why they haven't gone to England, why they've stayed here. Maybe she thinks he will cure the little boy. He's due to call on her at two o'clock tomorrow.'

Powerscourt wondered if this was another piece of gossip he could report back to the Prime Minister in London. Then suddenly Natasha was by his side and she was pulling him to his feet.

'You can't leave St Petersburg without dancing, Lord Powerscourt. It's not allowed. And you can't leave St Petersburg without dancing with me. That's not allowed either. Come along, please.'

Thirty seconds later they were floating round the floor to a waltz by Johann Strauss. Powerscourt thought Natasha was a perfect partner. She leaned forward to whisper in his ear.

'Will you come to our wedding, Lord Powerscourt? Me and Mikhail?'

'Congratulations,' said Powerscourt. 'This is all very sudden. I didn't know you were engaged. Mikhail didn't mention anything. Is the wedding soon?'

'Well,' said the girl defensively, swinging round happily in Powerscourt's arms, 'it hasn't really happened yet. I mean so far Mikhail hasn't actually asked me, but he will. He will do it very soon.'

Powerscourt thought of asking if she too had psychic powers but he thought better of it.

'It's my grandmother, Lord Powerscourt. She's always told me that the girls decide on the marriages, the young men merely ask the question.'

On reflection, Powerscourt thought there might be something in it. Perhaps he should check with Lucy when he got back home. But Natasha hadn't finished with him yet.

'Anyway, Lord Powerscourt,' said Natasha Bobrinsky, 'I wanted to ask your advice. You've travelled a lot. You've been nearly everywhere. Where is the most romantic place in the world to get married and have your wedding reception?'

Powerscourt hesitated for about five seconds before he gave his answer. Rome, Paris, London, Madrid, Vienna, Salzburg, all fell at the early hurdles.

'There's only one answer,' he said, smiling at Natasha and feeling at least seventy years old, 'Venice. You get married in the Basilica of St Mark, or if you can't manage that, San Giorgio Maggiore across the water. You have your reception in the Doge's Palace. If that's not possible, I'm sure you could rent a whole palazzo on the Grand Canal. It would be wonderful. Mikhail's father and yours might have to throw quite a lot of money about, but the Venetians have been taking bribes for centuries. Anyway, you should all feel at home there.'

'Should we?' asked Natasha.

'Of course you should,' said Powerscourt cheerfully, 'whole bloody city's built on the water. Just like here.'

Shortly before two o'clock the following day Rasputin was within sight of the Alexander Palace at Tsarskoe Selo. He had walked all the way from St Petersburg, believing that this would give a better impression than coming by train. Holy men don't need public transport. Up on the roof Alexandra had been watching the road for some time through her husband's binoculars. Was this new holy man going to be the answer to her prayers? Was he the greater figure Philippe had spoken of? Every single report she had received about him had been favourable.

In the first class section of the St Petersburg to Berlin express Powerscourt and Johnny Fitzgerald were settling into their seats. Their train was due to leave at five past two. Johnny had asked Powerscourt for a period of silence at the beginning of their journey. Never, he said, in a decade or two of drinking, had he come across somebody with such a capacity for alcohol as Ricky Crabbe. The young man had drunk him, not merely under the table, but under the floorboards as well. Only once before, Johnny confessed, had he been blessed with such a hangover, and that was the morning after the publication of his first book when he had been taken in hand by a couple of alcoholic publishers.

Now Alexandra could just about make Rasputin out as he approached the sentry post that led into the palace grounds. She could see the tattered green coat, the dishevelled beard, even the long fingernails. Yes, he must be a holy man, she promised herself as she rushed down the stairs to greet him, how I hope he is the answer to all my prayers, how I hope he can heal Alexis.

'Good afternoon,' said Rasputin in his thick Siberian accent to the sergeant on duty. 'I believe you are expecting me. My name is Father Grigory. I have come to save Russia.'

The Berlin express was pulling slowly out of the station. Powerscourt stared out of his window as the outer parts of St Petersburg slid past beyond the steam from the engine. He was going home to Lucy and the children. He was safe. He had not been killed in this, his first investigation since he had nearly died after the encounter in the Wallace Collection. Ricky Crabbe had sent a cable from him to Lucy, via William Burke, telling her he was safe and well and returning to London. He remembered that he had promised to take Lucy to Paris to celebrate his safe return. Maybe they could call on the elegant M. Olivier Brouzet of the French secret service and his Watteau in the Place des Vosges.

Haemos. Blood, the Greek word for blood. *Philos*, love of something, as in philosophy, love of wisdom, philology, love of words. Haemophilia, literally, love of blood. Powerscourt was thinking about blood and the Russians' love of it. He thought of the blood on the snow in the streets of St Petersburg as the workers tried to reach the Winter Palace to hand in their petition to the Tsar, mown down by the Imperial security services, their faces chopped into bloody pieces by the cavalry, their children shot as if they were criminals. He thought of the end of that terrible day when he and Mikhail and Rupert de Chassiron had tried to help the wounded outside the Stroganov Palace. Often all they could do was to wipe away the blood and send the dying off to meet their Orthodox God with clean hands and clean faces. Cleanliness next to Godliness. He thought of the blood being spilt in that ludicrous war between Russia and Japan, the disfigured and the maimed and the blind and the deaf returning to beg on the streets of their capital. He thought of the blood flowing in the basement cells of the Okhrana, of the terrible whips lacerating men's backs till their blood ran down in red puddles on to the floor, of Roderick Martin's lifeblood dripping into the dust as he was lashed to death in Major

360

Shatilov's squalid office. He thought of Grand Duke Serge, cousin of the Tsar, married to the Empress Alexandra's elder sister, his blood and guts blasted by the nitro-glycerine explosion all over the walls of the Nicholas Gate in the Kremlin.

He thought of the little boy called Alexis, the Tsarevich, growing up in the Alexander Palace, the blood flowing uncontrollably round his body.

Haemophiliac Son. Haemophiliac Nation.